Penny In

Penny Ingham has a degree in
archaeology; she is often to be fou
trench with a trowel in her hand. ...wspapers
and the BBC, Penny now lives with her family in rural Hampshire and writes full time.

You can find out more by visiting Penny's Facebook page, and by following her on Twitter @pennyingham

Praise for Penny's first novel, The King's Daughter

'A pacy, engaging, enlightening and hugely enjoyable novel.'
The Historical Novel Society

'An exciting best seller bringing history alive, featuring forbidden love, jealousy and betrayal and based, to a large extent on fact.'
The Basingstoke Gazette

'For history and archaeology buffs, this novel is a treat.'
Book Bag

Also by Penny Ingham

The King's Daughter

The Saxon Wolves

PENNY INGHAM

NERTHUS

First published in Great Britain in 2016 by Nerthus

A CIP catalogue record for this title is available from the British Library.

ISBN 978-0-9955034-0-3

Cover design by S. Hunt

Printed and bound by Marston Book Services Ltd

Published by Nerthus

For Steve, James and Louise

PICTS
Hadrian's Wall
BRIGANTES
Eboracum
(York)
CORITANI
CATUVELLAUNI
DOBUNNI
SILURES
(Wales)
Calleva Atrebatum
(Silchester)
Aquae Sulis
(Bath)
ATREBATES
DUMNONIA
(Cornwall)
Tintagel
Fort at Andereida
(Portchester)

'The wanderer rows upon the ice-cold sea, travelling the paths of exile, for Fate is inexorable…'

'The Wanderer', an anonymous poem written in Old English.

'The proud tyrant invited the Saxons into his kingdom, like wolves into the sheep-fold…'

'The History of Britain' by Gildas, sixth century AD.

PROLOGUE

Britannia, July 455AD

The gusting wind was stronger at the cliff-edge. It tugged their cloaks about them, the driving rain lashing against their faces. Through the gloom of the starless sky, the fire beacon atop Tintagel's fortified walls cast blotches of light across the coal-black sea.

They watched as the ship hit the rocks, creaking and moaning as if in physical pain. Wood shattered like breaking glass. And then, above the roar of the waves, they heard the screams, faint like the ghostly cries of the lost souls who wandered the earth on Samhain Eve. They climbed slowly down the cliff path, their boots slipping on the mud that cascaded in torrents down the track. There was no need for haste for it was unlikely anyone could survive such a storm.

Reaching the base of the cliff they began to spread out across the beach, and their torches, bobbing like fishing boats upon the blackness, hissed and crackled in the rain. Waves crashed on the shore line, throwing spray high into the air as the drowned bodies of raiders and captured slaves alike washed steadily upon the beach. They moved carefully along the wet sand, surf swirling around them as they crouched by each body, searching for signs of life. Suddenly one of the men called through the driving rain.

'Silvanus, over here! This one's alive!'

Further down the shore a man broke into a run, his cloak flapping behind him in the wind. He was tall and broad shouldered, his physique honed by the leanness of youth. Rain plastered his short, dark hair to his face and dripped steadily into intense, hazelnut-brown eyes.

Reaching the crouching man's side, Silvanus wiped the rain from his face then looked down at the motionless heap of rags lying upon the sand.

'Are you certain she's alive?'

Evric pressed two fingers to the girl's throat.

'Yes, Lord, but barely. She is the only one saved.'

Silvanus bent down and gently pushed the long, matted hair from the girl's face. Her complexion was as white as salt bleached driftwood apart from the faint smudge of freckles across the bridge of her nose. Her lips were slightly parted, as if she was about to talk in her sleep. She reminded him of a sea creature, a mermaid or perhaps a siren, with seaweed and the remnants of her tattered clothing coiled around her bare arms and legs.

As he looked at her features, Silvanus felt his breath catch in his throat. There was something strangely familiar about her, as if he had seen her before. And yet how could that be possible, for hers was the face of a stranger?

He stood up slowly, deep in thought, before finally speaking.

'See what can be done for her.'

ONE

Germania, two months earlier

Emma sat bolt upright on the bench, her hands neatly clasped in her lap. Her two long, red plaits fell over her shoulders, perfectly braided with not a hair out of place. At just thirteen years of age, her serious, young face rarely smiled and her skin was sallow from a life lived behind closed doors. Anya opened the door quietly so as not to startle her sister, but Emma's forehead still creased into a worried frown at the unexpected noise.

It was dark in Emma's chamber. The air was heavy with dust from the freshly laid rushes on the floor, and sweet from the lavender heads strewn amongst it. Her neatly made bed stood against the far wall. A rectangular table, polished with beeswax, occupied the centre of the room, framed by two simple wooden benches. Emma had placed the plate, bowl and glass beaker from her last meal in a perfectly straight line on the table in front of her. Anya closed the door and walked slowly towards her sister.

'Mind the plate, the bowl and the cup!' Emma's arm jerked forward, a statue brought abruptly to life.

'I won't touch them,' Anya promised. She sat down carefully on the bench, keeping her distance, but Emma still recoiled and shuffled anxiously away from her elder sister.

Emma was different from the other children born to Athelwald, high king of Saxony. She did not play with her siblings, nor look them in the eye. She sought out the solitary places where she could count the weft of a piece of cloth, or sort the fine bone sewing needles into perfect rows of ascending size. She had never been comfortable living in the women's quarters of the great hall. There was too much laughter and chatter, too many untidy heaps of pillows, blankets and furs, and too many baskets of oily sheep's wool piled haphazardly against the plastered walls.

Nor was she comfortable amongst the noise and bustle of the village. For as long as anyone could remember, Emma had sought order in the chaos of the world around her and when she could not achieve it, her frustration exploded into terrible tantrums. Athelwald, embarrassed by her uncontrollable outbursts, beat her viciously, publicly and repeatedly.

And although Anya had often tried to comfort her, there was no understanding in Emma's eyes, no return of her sisterly love. She simply removed Anya's arms from around her bruised body, and retreated within herself. And so it came to be generally accepted amongst Athelwald's kin that Emma was closer to the gods of the dark places and sacred groves than to the men who walked the earth. Athelwald had quickly decided that the best solution for everyone was to hide his youngest daughter away. She lived in her own private chamber and as the seasons turned, she rarely left the security of its four walls.

'Today is a very special day, Emma. It's Horsa and Elsbet's

betrothal feast.' Anya paused, and searched her sister's face. She had no idea if Emma understood, for there was no flicker of recognition in her eyes. But she lived in hope that one day, if the gods willed it, Emma might smile, or say her sister's name, or look her in the eye.

Anya's thoughts drifted to the fateful day Emma had entered the world. She had stood at her mother's bedside and watched her life blood seeping through the blankets and dripping steadily onto the floor rushes. She had looked into her mother's deep green eyes and even at just six summers old, she had understood. The woman she loved more than anyone else in the world was dying, just as the tiny scrap of life she held so tightly in her arms, was struggling to live. Anya had clambered onto the bed. 'I will look after her,' she had whispered in her mother's ear.

By the next morning, Eown was dead, and whilst Athelwald blamed Emma for taking his beloved wife from him, Anya never forgot her promise. She visited Emma every single day and she did not begrudge her these quiet moments. They were a time to remember the beautiful, unsmiling baby with the shock of hair as red as a fox's pelt. And a time to remember Eown and the look in her eyes as she lay dying on that cold winter's night - so much love and regret, and hope and loss.

Slowly, so as not to startle her, Anya stood up.

'I have to go now, Emma. The betrothal feast is about to begin. I will come and see you tomorrow.'

'Mind the plate, the bowl and the cup!' Emma said anxiously.

'I will be careful. I love you, Emma.'

But Emma did not reply.

TWO

The betrothal feast of Horsa, son of Athelwald, high king of Saxony to Elsbet, daughter of thane Carl, took place in Athelwald's great hall. Its vaulted roof was so high that trilling sparrows flew between the rafters, swooping through the drifting fire-smoke like sky-larks darting through summer clouds. Two parallel rows of broad, towering pillars held the roof aloft. Some were decorated with depictions of serpents, chasing their own tails in a tangle of knotted flesh. Others bore carvings of lush foliage, paying homage to the generous bounty Athelwald granted to all his guests.

It was an undisputed fact, acknowledged throughout Saxony, that the high king possessed a blessed and golden hall. Its walls were bedecked with rich Byzantine tapestries, its chairs with silks from the Orient, its table with plates of solid silver and bowls of solid gold. Its lintels were protected by charms and spells, cast by the high priest himself. Each deeply carved rune was enhanced by pure gold leaf and in the sunlight, the invocations to Odin, the father of all the gods, shone brightly towards the heavens.

On this day, Athelwald sat upon his gift-throne at the high table. Despite the lines that time had etched around his eyes and mouth, he was still a handsome man, tall and proud of bearing. As befitted a king, he was adorned with gold and precious stones, from his arm rings and the torque about his neck, to his richly enamelled cloak brooches and belt fittings.

Anya sat at Athelwald's left hand, taking the place of her late mother. From her vantage point on the raised dais, she looked down at the over-crowded hall and smiled wryly to herself. Her father's guests sat shoulder to shoulder at long trestle tables. They ate his rich food and drank his fine wine, but they were not here to wish Horsa and Elsbet a long and happy life together. The thanes of Saxony had come to see and be seen, just as it had always been. They had come to scheme and to make alliances, and to judge how his daughter's advantageous marriage would affect thane Carl's standing with the high king.

The summer afternoon was airless and the hall was disagreeably hot. The intricately carved oak doors were fastened open, but no welcome breeze drifted over Athelwald's raucous guests, nor sought to disturb the ancient, fraying war banners that hung limply from the rafters - fragile, dusty memorials to the victories of long dead ancestors.

Anya sensed her father's affectionate gaze and she turned to smile fondly at him. Despite her aching head and the overwhelming heat, she felt content. She did not mind that the air was acrid with the stench of rank sweat, nor that the smoke drifting from the fire in the central hearth was making her eyes sting for she had always been fascinated by the way it lingered like rain clouds until, little by little, it sneaked through the blackened thatch and escaped to the sky.

She did not mind that the hall was filled with the cloying aroma of rich food, or that the floor rushes were slimy with spilled wine. She scarcely noticed such things because this was her home, the place where she belonged. The bards said it was dangerous beyond the borders of Saxony. They told of hostile wastelands inhabited by fearsome monsters, but inside the great hall, she felt safe and protected. Its richly decorated walls and high rafters had swaddled her for as long as she could remember; the stifling heat as comforting as a warm embrace.

Anya had not eaten all day and the slices of meat on her plate smelled delicious. She took a bite of crunchy pork crackling and glanced at her brother, Horsa, seated at the far end of the high table. First born of Eown's three children, he, like Anya and Emma, had inherited her fire-red hair and deep green eyes. He was a handsome young man with a good-humoured, guileless face and today, like every other day, he had eyes only for his betrothed.

They sat side by side, giggling and whispering excitedly, reminding Anya of the pair of collared doves that billed and cooed on the high roof of the great hall. Horsa and Elsbet belonged to one another, as inseparable as the stars from the black night sky.

Anya's smile faded. She was uncomfortably aware that Hengist, her elder half-brother, was staring unblinkingly in her direction. His eyes were disconcertingly pale, an almost transparent blue, and there was a coldness about them that she always found deeply unsettling. Unable to meet his icy gaze, she dropped her eyes to her plate, her appetite suddenly gone.

'I need to piss,' Hengist announced.

He scraped his chair back and strode across the raised dais behind the seated guests. When he reached Anya's chair, he clasped her shoulder in a vice-like grip and leant towards her so she could feel his warm breath against her ear.

'Your mother was a whore,' he whispered. 'You have no

right to sit so brazenly at my father's side.'

Anya attempted to turn to face him, but his right hand held her fast.

'Let go,' she hissed under her breath. 'You're hurting me.'

'Good.'

Anya bit her lip anxiously. Today was supposed to be a day of joy and celebration and she prayed Hengist was not about to spoil it with unpleasantness.

Athelwald turned to face his daughter. 'Are you unwell?'

Anya shook her head.

Athelwald glanced curiously at Hengist. 'Do you wish to speak to me, my son?'

'No, father,' Hengist replied curtly.

He released Anya's shoulder, turned away and slammed hard into a slave carrying a tray laden with jugs of wine. The jugs wobbled and the tray crashed to the floor, splashing Hengist liberally with warm wine.

'You clumsy oaf!' Hengist roared, and lashed out with the back of his hand. His ring tore a deep gash across the young man's left cheek. The slave did not beg for forgiveness but gave Hengist a look of raw hatred. Hengist moved to strike the slave again but his fist froze in mid-air and recognition flickered across his face.

'I remember you,' he said quietly. 'I remember killing your father. He put up quite a fight. And I remember raping your wife. She put up quite a fight too. Ended up with her pretty face in the embers of the fire as I recall. And here you are. A spoil of war.'

Deafened by the din, the majority of Athelwald's guests in the crowded hall remained oblivious to Hengist's outburst, but those seated at the high table had heard every word. Anya no longer felt hot. Instead she felt deathly cold.

The slave stared at Hengist for a finite moment before he launched himself at the high king's son, his fists pounding wildly into Hengist's face. The howl that issued from the slave's mouth was full of agony, like a helpless, tortured animal.

Calmly, Hengist stepped back a pace, drew a dagger from his belt and thrust it into the man's chest. The slave sank to the floor, dead before he reached the soiled rushes. Anya glanced along at the table towards Horsa. He was clasping Elsbeth's hand tightly, his green eyes wide with shock.

Anya felt sick with revulsion. The omens for Horsa and Elsbet's marriage had once looked so promising. Beneath a full moon, the augury priests had slaughtered a pure white goat and pronounced the union to be blessed by the gods. But now, Hengist had shed blood in the great hall, and the omens had soured like curdled milk. The slave's body was hurriedly removed. Few in the great hall were aware of Hengist's momentary loss of control, but the mood at the high table was now blighted with unease.

'Leave us. I wish to speak with Hengist,' Athelwald commanded his three eldest sons, seated at his right hand. Born to his first wife, they each bore a striking resemblance to their father; tall, strong, and fair haired. They stood up obediently, bowed before Athelwald, and left the high table.

Hengist sat down with a swagger and glared at Anya.

'Father asked you to leave,' he said pointedly.

'No,' Athelwald shook his head. 'Anya can stay.'

Hengist frowned, his eyes full of fury. Tactfully, Anya turned away and listened to the young bard who was attempting to make his verses heard above the tumultuous noise. Under normal circumstances, she would have been entranced by his story of gods and monsters, but today she had one ear surreptitiously fixed upon her father and her half-brother's conversation.

'You have disappointed me again, Hengist,' Athelwald said quietly. 'I had hoped that as you grew into a man you would learn to control your temper.'

'It was a slave, father. Plenty more where he came from,' Hengist replied carelessly.

'You shed blood in my hall,' Athelwald went on. 'When will you learn to think before you act?'

'On the battlefield you praise my impulsiveness.'

'We are not on the battlefield! We are celebrating the betrothal of your brother! There is a time and a place for recklessness, but you do not appear to have learnt that simple truth.'

'Forgive me, father,' Hengist said woodenly.

Anya glanced at her half-brother. She knew him well enough to recognise the anger that was bubbling like spring water beneath his frozen exterior. His entire frame was as taut as the warp threads of her loom.

Athelwald stared thoughtfully at his son.

'I have mused long and hard about your future. I love you, as I love all my sons, so I say this with your best interests in my heart - I intend to accept Vortigern's offer. You will journey to Britannia to serve in his warband.'

Anya glanced at her father in astonishment, for Athelwald was effectively banishing Hengist to the life of a common mercenary.

'No father!' Hengist exploded. 'By all accounts, Vortigern is a barbarous thug. Surely you cannot expect me to serve such a man?'

'Vortigern is one of the island's most powerful kings. I am offering you a great opportunity,' Athelwald replied calmly.

'But father, you heard what our emissaries said - Britannia is in a state of civil war, tribe fighting tribe, the north over-run by the painted Picts. For all we know, Vortigern could be dead in a stinking mire by now! I beseech you, do not send me to that god-forsaken island!' Hengist's expression was one of utter disbelief.

Athelwald was silent for a long time. When he finally spoke, Anya saw regret in his deep blue eyes.

'I have five sons, and you are but the fourth. Much as I would wish it, I cannot offer you a gift throne in Saxony. But Britannia is in turmoil. It is yours for the taking.'

Hengist shook his head vehemently.

'I beg you -' he began again, but his father silenced him with a look.

'One more thing,' Athelwald said, picking up his wine cup. 'Horsa will accompany you to Britannia, and serve as your second in command.'

Anya gave up any pretence of listening to the bard and stared in horror at her father. She had long suspected her father saw Hengist as a liability, but Horsa was cut from very different cloth. Surely there was some mistake?

'Tell no-one of my decision,' Athelwald added quickly. 'Not even Horsa. I will announce it when the time is right. Swear to it.'

'I swear, father,' Hengist repeated dully.

Athelwald turned to Anya. 'I know you are listening. You must also swear an oath of silence on this matter.'

Her eyes widened. She wanted desperately to plead with her father, to go down on one knee and beg him to reconsider, but she could not defy the will of the high king.

'I swear, father' she replied dutifully. 'But I must ask - do you intend Horsa to marry Elsbet before he leaves?'

Athelwald shook his head. 'No. They can wait. They are betrothed, and that will suffice. They are both still very young.'

'So Elsbet cannot accompany Horsa to Britannia?'

'No! He is going to join a warband, not found a farmstead.'

'I understand.' Anya bowed her head respectfully, but cast a furtive glance towards Horsa, at the far end of the high table. He had his arm around Elsbeth's shoulders, no doubt trying to reassure her that Hengist had not cursed their union with his wanton slaughter. Anya was filled with sadness. Hengist's thoughtless actions had driven Athelwald to his far-reaching decision. In the thrust of a sword he had consigned Horsa and Elsbeth to an uncertain future. The spilling of blood at a betrothal feast had indeed proved to be the very worst of omens.

THREE

The following morning Anya went to break her fast with Emma. She found her sitting at the table in her room, immersed in her embroidery. Needles, thimbles, thread and linen were arrayed in neat groups; phalanxes on a battlefield of polished wood. Emma's serving girl was kneeling on the floor, a sewing basket at her side. She was patiently unravelling long strands of knotted thread.

Anya sat down at the table. More than a stride separated them, but Emma still flinched as if she had been struck.

'Good morning to you,' Anya said, glancing fondly at her sister. She had always found it comforting that they shared their mother's colouring, the same red hair, green eyes and skin as pale as sheep's wool.

'Good morning,' Emma replied tonelessly. She did not look up.

'My stomach has been rumbling from the moment I woke up. I can't remember the last time I felt so hungry,' Anya chatted amiably, breaking off a piece of warm, crunchy bread and holding it out towards her sister. 'Would you like some?'

Her sister did not reply. She hunched her shoulders, and concentrated on her work. Emma's embroidery was extraordinarily intricate, and Anya smiled proudly. The stitches were exquisitely small, and her designs were strikingly unique, geometric boxes within boxes, a maze of perfect symmetry.

'Your embroidery is beautiful,' Anya said, putting a piece of tangy cheese into her mouth and chewing it hungrily. 'I wish I could sew as well as you.'

Emma's fingers continued to weave back and forth. 'I like sewing,' she said absently.

Anya smiled contentedly. Emma seemed happy today, and it made her feel happy too.

'Horsa and Elsbeth were given some beautiful betrothal gifts,' Anya went on. 'Some of them are in the hall. I'll take you to see them if you wish.' She paused. She knew Emma wasn't listening, but she chattered on regardless. 'My favourite was a huge silver platter, embossed with nymphs and gods. I think it's probably Roman. It's quite beautiful.'

Horsa stuck his head around the door. 'My head feels as if someone is kicking it,' he said miserably.

Anya glanced at her brother. He looked tired and dishevelled, his long red hair held loosely at the nape of his neck by a frayed leather tie.

'Too much wine,' she replied. 'I have no sympathy for you.'

'It was my betrothal feast. Have some pity.'

Anya forced a grin for her brother, but her heart twisted as she remembered Athelwald's decision and the oath of secrecy she had sworn. It felt a heavy burden to carry. Horsa sat down beside her, and rubbed his aching temples. He glanced at Anya's plate, broke off a piece of cheese, and ate it.

'Do you mind?' she exclaimed indignantly.

'No, not at all.' Horsa reached next for Anya's bread, but she snatched the plate away from him.

'But I'm hungry!' he complained.

'So am I,' she replied. 'Go and find your own food.'

Horsa began to drum his fingers on the table but Emma's body tensed, and Horsa quickly withdrew his hand.

'How are you today, Emma?' he asked gently.

'I am sewing.'

'Your sewing is good - unlike Anya's pitiful attempts. She's all fingers and thumbs,' Horsa grinned.

Anya punched her brother lightly on the shoulder but it was a half-hearted rebuke. She could not bear the thought of losing Horsa to the warband of Vortigern of the Dobunni. She could not begin to imagine how much she would miss him, or how many sleepless nights she would endure worrying about him.

'Are you unwell, Anya?' Horsa asked. 'You seem…' his voice trailed away uncertainly.

'I am well. Just a little tired.'

Horsa nodded, seemingly satisfied with her answer. He watched Emma work on her embroidery for a moment and then he frowned.

'Why does Hengist behave like a savage? Elsbet is frightened he has brought ill fortune to our marriage.'

'I like sewing,' Emma said vaguely. 'Do not touch anything!' she added anxiously.

'I won't,' Horsa reassured her. He eyed Anya's food longingly, but she simply slid the plate further away from him. Horsa sniffed and folded his arms.

'Elsbet hates sewing,' he said fondly. 'She prefers to be outdoors -'

'Eown's brood – three peas from the same lowly pod!' Hengist's sneering voice cut across Horsa's words like a knife. 'I thought I would find you here.'

The needle came to abrupt stop in Emma's fingers and she froze like a frightened animal. Anya looked up. Hengist was standing in the doorway. She thought she saw a flash of envy in his pale eyes before it quickly vanished.

'Father is looking for you, Horsa,' he said coldly.

'I'm coming brother.' Horsa stood up. He glanced apprehensively at Emma, taking care not to scrape his chair noisily across the floor.

Anya glanced at Hengist again. He was glaring at her, and she felt his hatred as if a cold gust of wind had swept across her skin. She reached for her plate and forced herself to take a bite of bread. When she looked up again, Hengist and Horsa had gone.

Emma started sewing again.

'I have to go now,' Anya said quietly. 'I promised to meet Elsbet. But I will come and see you tomorrow and maybe we could look at Horsa and Elsbeth's betrothal gifts?'

Emma's gaze was fixed upon her embroidery. 'Do not knock the table,' she said fretfully.

'I won't. I promise.'

FOUR

The path that ran alongside the great river was quiet. A storm had arrived in the night. Its heavy rain had beaten against the thatch of the great hall and washed clean the world, rinsing it of its heavy air and foul deeds, until it smelled as fresh as newly laundered linen.

It was a perfect morning. Pale wisps of pink cloud trailed across a deep blue sky. The air was still; the only sound the buzz of insects and the songs of blackbirds in the trees. Walking side by side with Elsbet in the shade of the overhanging trees, Anya took a deep breath of the cool air and revelled in the tranquillity of the river after the raucous revelry of the previous day.

'Hengist shed blood in the hall. Has he offended the gods? Is my marriage cursed?' Elsbet asked fearfully.

Anya shook her head. 'The gods blessed your marriage, Elsbet. I watched the augury priests and I understood the signs. And last night, I stood on the very spot where the slave died. I purified the defiled earth with hyssop and vervain, and I listened.'

'And what did you hear?'

'The earth was as it should be,' Anya lied. She had heard nothing, but she had seen a great deal. As the vervain had fallen into the blood soaked rushes she had seen upheaval and death - a field of ripening wheat torn up by its roots and tossed aside, as if a giant had weeded the earth.

'All will be well,' she added reassuringly.

Elsbet nodded, relieved.

'Horsa brought me his dowry this morning,' she went on excitedly. 'Two huge oxen, two mares, a spear, a shield and a finely decorated sword. And then he recited the dowry oath. The words are so beautiful, aren't they - he asked me to share his toils and dangers, and to be his partner in all his sufferings and adventures, be it peace or war.'

Elsbet put her arms around Anya's waist and hugged her.

'I'm so blessed to be joining your family. I'm so thrilled we will not only be the best of friends, but sisters too.'

Anya smiled fondly and hugged her back. Elsbet was full of goodness, as sweet as a freshly picked strawberry.

'You are a dear friend, Elsbet. You and Horsa will make a perfect couple. You are both so kind and thoughtful and think the best of everyone. I fear your stewards and your slaves will rob you blind, and you won't even notice!'

Elsbet laughed, fiddling absently with her long blond hair. It fell in perfect waves to her waist and when the sun caught it, it shone like strands of filigree gold.

'Which flowers should I wear in my hair for the wedding, Anya? Will you help me choose the ones to bring me luck?'

'I would like that very much,' Anya replied, but her heart felt unbearably heavy. There would be no wedding for many months, perhaps even years. Elsbet's excitement was as shiny as a soap bubble and she pitied the person who would be given the terrible task of bursting it.

'Would you rather we didn't talk about the wedding?' Elsbet asked quietly. 'Does it upset you?'

'No, truly it doesn't. I joined the priesthood when I was eight years old. I've had ten years to come to terms with the fact that I can never marry, but I pray that you will have countless healthy children, Elsbet, and that as their aunt, you will allow me to spoil them mercilessly.'

Of course!' Elsbet laughed.

They walked on in companionable silence. Two swans glided past them, their brilliant white feathers barely disturbing the surface of the wide, slow-moving river. Everyone knew swans mated for life, separated only by death. It seemed too cruel that Horsa and Elsbet were soon to be separated by many miles of dangerous sea. Her father had sworn her to silence, and no one disobeyed the word of the high king, but Anya thought it was a terrible secret to keep.

The big meadow was bathed in sunlight and they wandered slowly through the wet grass, chatting idly. Anya did not need to show Elsbet which flowers to collect, for her friend had accompanied her many times before. Tiny flower heads of eyebright and potentilla were soon carefully packed into the wicker basket, alongside powdery yarrow and prickly thistle.

They heard the barge before they saw it, the boom of the oar-master's drum carrying on the still morning air. Elsbet and Anya looked at each other, their eyes alight with anticipation.

'Merchants!' Elsbet breathed. 'What do you think they're carrying? Silk? Garnets? Perfume? Oh Anya, I hope they have perfume! Come on! Quickly, or we'll miss them at the quayside!'

Anya carefully placed a handful of poppy seed heads into the basket and hurried after Elsbet.

They reached the path just as the barge sailed by. It was a long, wide, shallow bottomed vessel with a large cabin, and it was moving at great speed. The oarsmen were rowing as one, slicing through the water with perfect precision. The deck seemed curiously empty of goods.

Elsbet waved at them. 'Good morning! What are you bringing us?'

The oarsmen did not acknowledge her, nor did anyone on deck. Anya frowned. Merchants were renowned for their banter. They began their showmanship long before they reached a quayside, often strutting along the deck draped with samples of their most valuable furs. They were never silent. Something was wrong.

The two girls looked at one another. 'We should go back to the village,' Anya said quietly.

The barge was moved at such speed that it had already disappeared around a wide bend in the river. The girls broke into a run. Anya's mind raced with fear. Had the merchants found signs of the plague further up the river?

By the time Anya and Elsbet reached the quayside, the barge had already moored and a huge crowd had gathered. The arrival of a merchant ship usually resulted in much haranguing, jostling and pushing, as villagers fought to see what cargo they were carrying but today the atmosphere was subdued.

Merchants, villagers and a handful of Athelwald's retainers were helping a motley assortment of humanity disembark along the gangplank. They were not Saxons; their hair was black, their skins the colour of tanned leather. Many were too weak to stand and were being carried from the vessel. They looked filthy and frail, their clothes torn, and their bodies bloodied and bruised. Even from a distance, it was obvious that many were seriously injured.

Anya recognised one of the merchants, a huge, muscular

man with skin as black as Roman olives. She hurried to his side.

'Balhazar, what's happened?'

The merchant bowed low before Anya. 'The villages along the great river have been razed to the ground, their people slaughtered.' He swallowed hard, visibly distressed by what he had witnessed. 'Many of the corpses were without heads, perhaps taken away as trophies.'

'Who would do such a thing?' Anya asked, horrified.

'The survivors described their attackers as horsemen with dark skin and unnaturally elongated skulls, like demons. Their swords were curved and their garments were gaudily patterned.'

Anya had heard the merchants describe such men.

'Huns,' she said grimly.

Balhazar nodded. 'Yes, I fear it must be so.'

'My father will wish to hear of this.'

Balhazar bowed again. 'Yes, of course. I will go to him now.'

'Thank you for your kindness to these people,' Anya replied, then took a deep breath and stepped forward.

'Bring the wounded to the place of healing,' she said loudly. 'Follow me.'

FIVE

The place of healing was a long high vaulted building, a great hall in miniature. Inside, the plastered walls were painted a brilliant white, the floor rushes were sweetly fresh, the simple wooden furniture gleamed with beeswax polish, and the air was strongly scented with oil burners of juniper and fennel.

In the healing room, every bed was occupied, and the priests and priestesses were moving calmly and purposefully from bed to bed, like bees upon a row of lavender. Many of the refugees bore terrible wounds and five had died shortly after their arrival. Anya knelt beside the bed of a barely conscious man. His face was grey, his breathing fast and shallow.

She had applied a thick padded bandage steeped in a sage poultice over the gaping wound in his belly, but he was far beyond a cure. There was little to be done, other than ensure that he met his gods with as little suffering as possible. She lifted his head and tipped thick poppy syrup down his throat, then lowered him back onto the soft pillow. He did not stir. He was already far away.

She stood up slowly. She would have liked to stay with him until the end, but there were too many other patients who needed her attention. With a stab of regret, she said a silent prayer that he would find his ancestors in the world beyond, for she doubted he would be alive when she returned.

Anya put the vial of poppy syrup into her basket. The vial and the basket were almost empty. She frowned, and hurried back to the medicine room. Yesterday the wooden shelves had been stacked with bottles and jars of all shapes and sizes, but today they were almost empty. Her eyes widened with alarm. They were going to run out of medicine very soon.

In the preparation room, the central table had disappeared beneath piles of roots and rhizomes, fresh and dried flower heads and linen bags full of seeds. Two priests and three priestesses were working in studied silence, their faces sombre with concentration. They all wore the long white robe of the priesthood, with white linen aprons tied about their waists.

Gunther, an old man with a deeply lined face, saw her standing hesitantly in the doorway. He smiled, revealing a row of crooked teeth, stained black from a lifetime's fondness for elderberry juice.

'Don't look so worried. The shelves will be full again soon. The goddess is working through our fingers. See, the infusions are ready.' He pointed to the central hearth. Four large cooking pots were suspended from a fire dog over the flames. 'We have rosemary, chicory and cornflower. Their restorative powers are unequalled.'

The priestess at his side nodded in agreement. Clara's hair was shorn close to her scalp, as soft and grey as a sparrow's feathers.

'I've made three jars of a quince and flax poultice for their wounds.' Her voice was rough and grating, like the blade of a sword dragged across cobble stones.

Anya smiled, relieved. 'I'm sorry to have disturbed you,' she said politely. 'I will leave you to your work.'

As she entered the healing room once more, Anya wiped her hands with a cloth soaked in purifying juniper oil, picked up her basket and moved on to the next bed. The little boy was painfully thin and his expression was blank, as if he had withdrawn, like a snail into its shell, to shield himself from any further harm. She picked up the untouched bowl of soup on the table beside his bed.

'Shall we try and eat something?'

She knew he did not understand the Saxon tongue but she hoped her tone might reassure him. The soup smelled good, seasoned with healing rosemary, and she felt her stomach rumble. She had eaten nothing since her simple meal of bread and cheese with Emma earlier in the day. The little boy gave no sign that he was even aware of her. He continued to stare into the middle distance.

'You must eat,' Anya said softly. 'It will make you strong again.'

She glanced at the boy's thin wrists. A rope had cut distinctive welts into his flesh. It would need a salve of sage, before the wound festered. Very gently, she lifted his hand to take a closer look. Her fingers touched his skin, and the vision came upon her without warning. The white walls of the healing room faded, blurring to a dark windswept day. She saw a row of stakes, uprooted from a palisade, and re-planted throughout the village. Men, women and children were bound tightly to them, like beanstalks to a pole. Their wounds were terrible and she could feel their suffering as if it were her own.

Her world spun dizzily as the vision faded. The little boy was no longer staring into the middle distance. His gaze was now fixed upon her face and his eyes were full of tears. Anya put down the bowl and spoon and held the little boy close.

'You are safe,' she whispered into his wiry black hair. 'No-one will hurt you now.'

His sobs lasted for a long time, but gradually his breathing eased into soft snuffling and he fell asleep in her arms. She laid him down gently then stood up. Her head was throbbing and her hands were shaking. She needed some fresh air.

Outside, the earth was soaking up the sun's heat and the warm grass tickled her bare feet. The sacred grove stood in the centre of the priests' compound, the hub around which the priests' world turned. Clustered about it, and in no obvious order, stood the place of healing, the priests' school, living quarters, kitchens, workshops and animal enclosures.

The grove was ringed by a circle of ancient oak trees, bathed in dappled sunlight. It was unusually quiet because most of the priests and priestesses were occupied in the place of healing. Anya paused at the edge of the grove. Directly ahead stood the sacred shrine, a simple thatched structure to house an omnipotent goddess, shielded from unworthy eyes behind her thick, blood-red curtain. As always, Anya was filled with an overwhelming sense of awe and humility, for her goddess lived in the leaves of the ancient oaks, and she soared with the eagle. She was everywhere, and she was everything.

Anya knelt before the shrine. The sun's warmth filtered through the canopy of bright green leaves and wrapped her in momentary calm. In the distance, the sacred white horses whinnied to one another in the paddock. Insects hummed as they settled on the smooth surface of the ancient stone altar, drawn to its warmth, and to the faint traces of human blood the spring rains had failed to wash away. She closed her eyes and prayed for the patients in the healing room, especially the little boy with the nightmare in his eyes.

When she finally rose to her feet, Horsa was waiting patiently at the edge of the sacred grove.

'How long have you been here?' she called out, surprised.

'A while. I didn't want to disturb you.'

Taking the loosely knotted rope that hung from the bough of a sacred oak, Horsa bound it around his wrist and then stepped tentatively into the grove. He looked apprehensive and Anya smiled reassuringly at him.

'Nerthus means you no harm,' she said gently. As the son of the high king, he had every right to enter the sacred circle, and the rope showed the goddess that he was but a humble slave in her domain.

'Father wants to know if there is anything you need.' Horsa's eyes were darting nervously in the direction of the sacred shrine.

Anya laughed humourlessly. 'Every bed is full, and we are running out of medicine. Can he help me with such a problem?'

Horsa frowned. 'You look exhausted, Anya. Sit with me for a moment.'

'For a moment,' she agreed.

They sat side by side, in the cool shade of the oak trees. A soft breeze sprang up and caught the wind chimes high above their heads. Anya turned to her brother.

'What was decided at the council meeting?'

'Hengist wanted to send the refugees away, but Father said we are Saxons, not barbarians. He said they will stay, at least for the time being.'

'I don't understand how the Huns can slaughter innocents. Where is the honour or the glory in such an act?' Anya asked grimly.

'They come from far away, where the mountains rise up to

high barren steppes. They are barbarians. They do not think like civilised men,' Horsa replied.

'And will they come here?'

'No-one can say, but we will be ready for them if they do. Father's warriors have defeated every army that has dared to stand before him.'

'But the Huns sacked Rome itself! What chance do we have against them?'

'The people of Saxony can count the gods as their ancestors, Anya. We are blessed, first amongst men. The gods will not allow us to be over-run by barbarian hordes. Father is sending out riders to give warning to the outlying villages to look to their defences. And he is raising a muster.'

Anya looked out across the grove. The curtain of the sacred shrine was blowing in the breeze.

'Athelwald will turn to the priests for answers,' she said softly, her head full of vivid, gruesome memories of the last prisoner of war the priests had sacrificed to appease the gods. She turned to face her brother, and like so many times before, each knew the other's thoughts.

'There *will* be a sacrifice,' Horsa said grimly. 'The high priest announced it at the meeting of the council.'

Anya shook her head angrily. How could the high priest misunderstand the wishes of the gods? She had left the priests' school one summer since, and she bore just one initiation tattoo upon her forearm. She was lowly in the eyes of the priesthood, a skilled healer but nothing more. It would be many years before she was deemed worthy of divination, but she felt certain the goddess had no thirst for human blood. Pointless torture and death would not stop the barbarian tribes.

She turned away, trying hard not to think about glistening

entrails stretched upon the altar stone, and screams so terrible they seemed to rent the air in two. She shook her head, struggling to push the terrible images from her mind.

'How is Elsbet?' she asked. Her friend had looked shocked and distraught as the refugees were carried from the merchants' barge.

'Her mother is keeping her occupied, as usual,' Horsa said lightly. 'Our moments alone are few and far between, but all that will change as soon as Father grants me some land. I know it won't be much, but I'm not interested in power or great wealth. All I ask is that I have enough land to give Elsbet a comfortable life.'

Anya looked down at the grass, unable to meet his gaze.

'What's the matter?' Horsa asked, concerned.

She shook her head. 'Nothing. I have to go back. I've been away too long.'

She stood up wearily and embraced her brother, holding him for a fraction longer than usual.

'Take care, Horsa.'

Horsa ruffled her long hair affectionately.

'Always, sister.'

She watched him walk away and sadness settled on her heart. Soon Horsa would travel across the dangerous sea to Britannia. Soon he would be far away from Elsbet.

And far away from her.

SIX

The days that followed fell into an exhausting routine for Anya. She worked in the place of healing from dawn to moon rise, and each night she dropped onto her bed in the women's quarters of the great hall, and fell instantly asleep.

Daybreak always came much too soon. A slender shaft of sunlight from the window in the eaves edged her into wakefulness. She sat up wearily and pushed aside her bedding. The room was hot and the air was musty with sleep. Small children were beginning to stir, wriggling like puppies beneath dishevelled blankets. Nursing mothers, still half-asleep, lay with tiny babies feeding noisily at their breasts.

She dressed quickly. Her hair brush had disappeared from beside her bed, no doubt taken by an inquisitive child, so she hurriedly ran her fingers through her tangled hair as she crept along the narrow corridor that divided the great hall from the living quarters. Emma was still asleep. Her long red hair was un-braided and it spilled across the pillow like the ribs of a scallop shell. Her expression was calm and peaceful and Anya wondered if sleep freed Emma's mind of its fetters and chains, and blessed her with tranquil dreams.

Emma's serving girl came in, holding a bowl of water.

'Would you like me to wake your sister, my Lady?'

'No, let her sleep. When she awakes, tell her I will come again.'

In the great hall, slaves were laying fresh rushes, sweeping the ashes from the hearth and filling the log baskets. They moved hesitantly and cautiously because Hengist was sitting at the high table. He looked up disdainfully at Anya. 'Why do you insist on visiting that abomination? She should have been drowned at birth,' he shouted across the hall.

Anya froze. 'May the goddess forgive you for speaking ill of your own kin,' she said softly.

'What do you know of the goddess? You are but a lowly healer.'

Anya bit her lip and did not rise to his insult.

Emma is different from you and me,' she said quietly. 'But if you spent some time with her, you would see that the gods have blessed her with many gifts.'

'Hah!' Hengist snorted scornfully. 'She's no use to anybody! She will never marry. I'd wager she would sooner stick a man with a dagger than let him stick his cock in her.'

'Keep your voice down!' Anya whispered, glancing nervously about the great hall.

Hengist laughed. 'Why? Who is listening? Only slaves.'

Anya did not reply. As a small child, she had not understood why Hengist had drowned her kitten and threatened to hang her by her long plaits in a storage pit if she ever told anyone. But Eown had understood. No matter how vicious Hengist's cruelty, she had always been unfailingly kind to her young step-son.

'Forgive him, my sweet', she would say. 'He has lost his mother, and there is no greater sadness for a child.'

Her mother had never failed to see the good in everyone. Eown had been a slave, captured in Siluria, in the far western mountains of Britannia, and eventually bought by Athelwald at a slave market in Saxony. It was Eown's striking looks that had caught the high king's eye, but it was her compassion that had caught his heart. Hengist had been just eight years old and still in mourning for his mother's passing when his father had married Eown, and Athelwald loved her to her dying day.

But Hengist had never forgiven his step-mother, or her three red haired, green eyed children. Anya sighed. Eown would have been saddened to see such animosity. It was not easy to endure Hengist's brutishness but she would try harder to keep the peace, for her mother's sake.

'Enjoy your meal, brother,' she said and walked out into the early morning sunshine. Like all settlements in Saxony, Athelwald's stronghold had no formal plan. It was a haphazard collection of houses, barns and workshops, linked by tracks that over the years had become deeply rutted by the wheels of heavy carts. Athelwald's thanes were still abed but his bondsmen, his servants and his slaves were busily preparing for the day ahead, feeding livestock, drawing water, grinding corn, lighting ovens and sweeping hearths.

Anya looked about her curiously. An uneasy air of disquiet hung over the village. Colourful rumours of an impending barbarian attack were spreading like a forest fire, and Athelwald's people were afraid.

She paused as she passed beneath the lintel of the place of healing and took a deep breath to calm her beating heart. She ran her left hand along the blessing carved upon the door frame, felt the familiar shapes of the runes beneath her finger tips, and said a quiet prayer. 'May the goddess keep Saxony safe, on this day and all the days to come.'

She walked slowly along the rows of beds, making mental notes on the tasks for the day ahead. Many of the patients were still sleeping, but the little boy was wide awake. She sat down on the edge of his bed. He looked very frail, as if the slightest infection would send him to meet his gods.

Anya smiled gently. 'Did you manage to sleep, young man? Or have you sat there all night, listening to the mice in the thatch?'

He cocked his head to one side and looked at her. His brown eyes were huge. Despite all he had seen and all he had endured, they were still full of the heart wrenching innocence of childhood. Anya pointed above her head, then ran her fingers rapidly along the blanket, imitating a tiny mouse.

His eyes lit up with understanding. He gabbled something in his own language and Anya nodded, although she had not understood a single word.

'Lots of mice,' she said slowly.

'Mice,' he repeated, his tongue struggling with the alien sound.

'Yes!' she laughed. 'And now, you must eat.' She handed him the soup bowl. Tentatively, he took a spoonful then wrinkled his nose in disgust. He put down the spoon and there were tears in his eyes.

Her heart went out to him. He was alone in a foreign land, without family or friends. And then a sudden thought struck her - she hoped he didn't think she was trying to feed him mouse stew. She placed a comforting hand on his arm, and instantly her world swam dizzily.

The place of healing faded into a night sky alight with bright flames. The air was thick with smoke and the stench of burning thatch. She saw a man and a woman, screaming in terror. They were trying to reach the little boy, trying to grab his hand, but they were slipping away. She could feel the small boy's suffering and loss. His memories were dark and heavy and they hurt so much, like a wound that would not heal. Someone was screaming. The sound grew louder and louder, pushing its way relentlessly through the smoke and the darkness.

She opened her eyes, blinking wildly as the vision faded. The little boy had pulled his knees up to his chest and wrapped his arms about his spindly legs. His shrieks were deafening, pitiful howls of agony. Ignoring the upturned bowl and the soup soaking into the blanket, she pulled him into her arms and held him close. Taking a deep breath, she cleared her mind. She let her thoughts float idly, like a dandelion seed on a still day. She drifted until, little by little, she felt the tension leave the little boy's body. He slumped against her and closed his eyes.

'I need an assistant and you need a distraction,' she whispered as she laid him back down. 'We will work well together, you and I.'

The atmosphere in the healing room was calm and quiet and the little boy slept on undisturbed as Anya cleaned wounds, applied poultices and replaced bandages. It was well after midday when the boy awoke. There was a trace of colour in his cheeks now, but his huge brown eyes were still haunted.

She sat down on his bed. 'My name is Anya.' She tapped her chest. 'What's your name?'

Understanding dawned in his eyes. 'Abberlen,' he replied, pointing at his own painfully bony chest.

She held out her hand. 'Would you like to help me, Abberlen?'

The child clutched the blanket to his chin and looked at her warily.

'I won't hurt you,' she smiled reassuringly.

Slowly, he let go of the blanket. Anya took his hand and helped him down from the bed. His own filthy, blood-stained clothes had been taken away and burnt. Now he was wearing a plain, loose tunic that reached to his knees. His feet were bare and he looked so vulnerable, her heart lurched.

'You can carry my medicine basket, young man,' she said brightly. 'Come with me.'

Like a faithful hound, Abberlen trotted after her. He watched her intently as she worked, never flinching at the sight of blood, or soiled bandages or open wounds. Anya pointed at an earthenware pot in the basket and Abberlen opened the lid obediently. He sniffed its contents cautiously and his eyes sparkled. Without hesitation, he dipped his forefinger into the pot and licked the sticky sweetness from his finger tip.

'Honey drips from the branches of the world tree of Yggdrasil,' Anya said, laughing. 'And it's the only medicine that tastes like a gift from the gods. It's miraculous on the tongue and just as miraculous when applied to a festering wound.'

Abberlen dipped his finger into the pot again. There was the faintest trace of a smile playing at the edges of his sticky mouth, and Anya felt her spirits lift. She looked up suddenly. Someone had opened the doors. A hot afternoon breeze was surging across the place of healing and displacing its cool clean air.

The soldiers were armed for battle, with leather cuirasses over their summer tunics, shields at their elbows and swords at their belts. They swarmed into the place of healing with all the fury of a disturbed wasps' nest, but came to a faltering halt before the rows of sleeping refugees. Suddenly uncertain, they looked back in unison towards the door.

Anya stood up hurriedly. 'What is the meaning of this intrusion?' Her voice was calm and controlled, but her rage was palpable.

Hengist stood in the doorway, his sword drawn.

She hurried to his side. 'Put your weapon away! This is a place of healing, blessed by the goddess herself. You must not defile her sanctuary!'

Ignoring his half-sister, Hengist shouted over her head at his soldiers. 'Remove the prisoners!'

Her eyes widened in alarm. 'What are you doing?'

'By command of the high king, these people are to be taken to the holding pens.'

'What? No!' Anya cried, horrified. 'These people are innocent refugees, not prisoners!'

'Athelwald has received intelligence that they are spies in the pay of the barbarian army,' Hengist replied.

'And who gave him such outrageous information?'

'I could not say.' Hengist refused to meet her eye.

Anya turned away from her half-brother in disgust. His men were already taking the refugees from their beds. Some were being gentle in their own way, offering a supportive arm or shoulder. Others were simply dragging the half conscious patients across the rushes, their blankets trailing behind them.

'For the love of the goddess I command you to stop this now!' Anya shouted.

One of the soldiers caught her eye and stopped in his tracks but Hengist quickly rounded on him. 'The order came from the high king. Get it done, before I hang you for treason!'

Anya glanced helplessly towards Abberlen. He was standing stock still, his eyes full of fear once again. She silently willed him to hide by crawling beneath a bed. Instead, he ran to her, burying his face in her apron.

Hengist wrenched the child from her grasp, hoisting Abberlen onto his shoulders as if he were a sack of flour.

'Let him go!' Anya shouted. 'He's just a child. Leave him, I beg you!'

'Father's orders were most specific, Anya. I am to take them all. Men, women and children.'

Abberlen screamed in pure terror as Hengist carried him towards the doorway.

'Shut up!' Hengist clattered Abberlen with the back of his hand and the child's screams lessened to a whimper. At the doorway, Hengist turned back.

'The high priest has chosen the time for the sacrifice – sunset, tonight. Father has sent out riders to the surrounding villages.' He smiled thinly. 'Everyone is expected to attend.'

Anya stood motionless, her mind reeling with shock. Save for the beds occupied by three elderly priests who would end their days in the place of healing, the high vaulted hall was empty. Tables and chairs were overturned and blankets, rugs and drinking cups strewn across the floor. She wondered despairingly why Hengist had chosen to spread such a rumour about the refugees, and why Athelwald had chosen to believe it.

She put her head in her hands. The whole village was suffocating beneath a fog of fear and suspicion, and the innocent refugees were paying heavily for Saxony's paranoia. She had tried so hard to help the refugees. And yet it had all been in vain. She knew full well that many of them were too weak to endure the hardships of the prisoner holding pens. And what of Abberlen? He would not understand why he was being punished. He did not deserve this torment.

SEVEN

As the high priest had decreed, the sacrifice took place at sunset. The priests and priestesses formed a circle around the perimeter of the grove, their white robes dazzling in the evening sunlight. They stood motionless, like a ring of standing stones, staring fixedly at the sacred shrine. Behind them, Athelwald's kinsmen, his warriors, his thanes, his craftsmen, blacksmiths and the bondsmen who worked his fields were assembling, talking in subdued whispers.

Anya had no time to wash her face or comb her hair. Removing her apron, she heaved the long white robe of the priesthood over her blue linen gown and fastened her belt as she ran. She was late and the last to arrive for she had not wanted to leave the place of healing in such a state of desecration. She had worked tirelessly and now each bed bore fresh linen, the tables were gleaming with beeswax polish, and the air was purified with oil of sage and rosemary. In truth, she had not wanted to leave the place of healing at all, for she had no desire to enter the sacred grove on such a terrible night as this.

Clara frowned disapprovingly at Anya's late arrival but nevertheless made room for her in the circle. Anya glanced surreptitiously around the sacred grove. The atmosphere was fraught with suspense, as still and as silent as the grave. Her throat wobbled with emotion. She had no power here tonight. She could not prevent what was to come.

She looked across at the prisoner holding pens. Crudely built of wood, they resembled giant bird cages, offering no privacy or comfort for their unfortunate occupants. Some of the refugees were standing at the bars, straining to catch a glimpse of the sacrifice, but many more were simply lying huddled on the bare earth.

She could not see Abberlen. She looked harder, but there was no sign of the little boy. The sun sank lower in the sky, bathing the grove in an intense golden light. The leaves upon every tree were utterly still, as if frozen by a deep hoar-frost. Three rooks flew overhead, croaking their ugly cacophony. They settled in their roosts in the sycamore trees beyond the paddock and fell silent. The sacred mares lifted their heads from the pasture, but neither whinnied nor snorted. In the giant oaks, the blackbirds no longer sang. Around the sacred grove, the assembled crowd stood stock-still, as if collectively holding their breath. No-one fidgeted or whispered, no-one coughed or sneezed. It was as if a spell had fallen upon them, rendering each and every one of them to stone.

Anya had been so preoccupied at the place of healing, she had given little thought to the victim who was about to die. Athelwald was not renowned for his mercy to prisoners' of war. The poor wretch was probably seriously wounded, half-starved and fatally weakened. She felt her body tremble with terrible anticipation. She was a healer, and being forced to watch suffering, rather than alleviating it, was entirely alien to her nature.

Her eyes darted once again to the prisoner holding pens. Where was Abberlen? Why couldn't she see him with the other refugees? She was suddenly struck with a terrible thought. Abberlen was young, pure and innocent, a perfect offering to the gods. Was that why the refugees had been moved to the holding pens? So the high priest could quietly make his choice, away from prying eyes?

It all made sense now. The high priest had chosen Abberlen. Fear tightened about her lungs and she felt suddenly chilled to the bone. This was wrong. This was horrifically wrong. Nerthus had no wish to see the blood of an innocent child pouring across her altar. She could not begin to imagine Abberlen's terror. He would not understand, and there would be no-one at his side to comfort him.

Anya's heart was pounding ferociously. There was nothing she could do or say that would change the high priest's decision. She could only pray that the priests had given the little boy a generous cup of the milk of the poppy, mixed with mead to dull his senses.

The high priest entered the grove alone. His tiny, bird like form, shrouded in the white tunic of his office, seemed to barely make a mark upon the warm grass. His fine, grey hair fell to his waist, giving him the appearance of being draped in a shawl of woven cobwebs. In his right hand he held aloft the solid gold standard of the priesthood. Mounted on a long shaft crafted from the original sacred oak, it resembled a glinting wheel. From the sun's hub, the spokes radiated the power of the gods.

The priests and priestesses bowed their heads respectfully as he began to speak. 'Saxony is our land, bequeathed to us by the gods. It is our birth-right, and its sanctity is our responsibility. These are difficult times. The gods see the barbarian tribes from the distant steppes, and they are angry. The gods see our weakness and our folly, and they are angry.

We must offer them the greatest, most valuable, sacrifice. Only then will they be satisfied. Only then will there be peace.'

The atmosphere in the sacred grove was charged with tension now, like the air before a storm. Without any warning, a wind sprang up, whipping the trees as if the very air was angry. The wind chimes clashed together, their notes jarring and discordant.

Two priests were leading the sacrificial victim into the sacred grove. A slight figure, hooded, hands bound behind their back. The figure stumbled slightly, and the hood fell back to reveal the victim's face.

A shock of long, fire-red hair.

Unmistakeable green eyes, full of confusion and distress.

Anya stared at her sister in stunned disbelief. Her mouth fell open and time stopped.

This was a nightmare, and soon she would awaken. This was not happening. This could not be happening. Emma's eyes were darting wildly about the sacred grove as she writhed in the priests' grasp, like a fish caught on a hook. Quite suddenly, Emma's gaze settled on her sister, and Anya knew in that single terrible moment, that this was not a vision or a dream, but utterly real.

The two sisters looked at one another.

'Anya?' Emma asked plaintively. 'I don't like it here. I want to go back to my chamber.'

It broke the silence, and it broke Anya's heart. She had yearned for Emma to speak her name for such a long time, but not now, not like this. As if awoken from a trance, Anya broke away from the sacred circle of the priesthood and ran across the grass to her father. She put both hands on his shoulders, forcing him to face her.

'Tell them to stop this, I beg you!' she pleaded. 'How can you do this to your own flesh and blood?'

Tears brimmed in Athelwald's pale blue eyes, and his face was racked with pain and anguish.

'The gods demand it,' he whispered. 'There is no more potent gift to the gods than a virgin sacrifice, one life to spare many lives.'

'You knew about this? You knew what the priests were planning?'

'Yes, I knew, but I had no choice.'

Anya glanced wildly at Hengist and Horsa. Tears of shock and anguish were running unchecked down Horsa's cheeks. Hengist's expression was hard to read but she thought she saw a glint of satisfaction in his eyes.

As the rope was placed around her neck, Emma opened her mouth and began to scream. It was a terrible sound, like a tortured animal. The rope began to cut into her throat, pulled tighter and tighter by the two priests on either side of her, an obscene tug of war. Her face contorted with effort as she tried to scream again but no sound reached her lips.

'Stop! Stop this, now!' Anya screamed. 'The high priest is wrong. The gods do not want this!'

She tried to run to her sister's aid, but Athelwald held her fast, his eyes blinded with tears.

The rope was cutting tighter into Emma's flesh. Her small frame was bucking and twisting in her agony, every muscle straining beyond endurance. She was staring fixedly at her sister, her eyes full of raw and visceral terror as her brain screamed for air, for release. And Anya stared back, overwhelmed with horror.

She had promised her mother on that cold winter's night all those years ago that she would protect Emma, but today she was helpless. There was nothing she could do to save her sister.

The three augury priests paid no heed to Anya's screams. They watched Emma's death throes avidly, each jerk and spasm a message from the gods only they could decipher. Athelwald's kinsmen, thanes and churls cast nervous glances towards Anya but they dared not speak, for the dominion the Druid priests held over them all was terrifying indeed. They stood in awed silence and watched as the will of the gods was done.

Emma's death throes were weaker now, the fear and agony in her eyes beginning to dim, her expression fading to a chilling blankness. Quite suddenly, Emma's body went limp. Anya froze, no longer struggling in her father's strong grasp. Emma's soul was rising. Like smoke on a still day, it lingered, as if reluctant to say good-bye and then, suddenly, it was swept away towards the darkening sky.

Emma's lifeless body was now held upright only by the taut rope at her neck. Carefully, the two priests lowered her to the ground.

Anya wrenched herself from her father's grasp. 'You've murdered your own daughter! Your own kin! This is not what the gods demand!'

The high priest turned at last, his expression one of disbelief that Anya, one of his own priestesses, should dare to question the will of the gods. Overwhelmed with rage, Anya turned and ran, not back towards the village where she knew punishment would await her, but deeper into the forest. And when she could run no further, she collapsed to the forest floor, and sobbed until she had no more tears.

Night had fallen when she finally opened her eyes. The colour had drained from the world. All was black or white, like the pieces on a gaming board. A great swathe of woodland was enveloped by black shadows, whilst the rest was illuminated by a huge, full moon gliding silently through the trees. Luna, the virgin goddess, was lighting the skies for the predators of the night.

Anya stood up wearily, numb with grief. It was too early for sunrise but a faint, golden glow was dimly visible on the horizon. Anya frowned and looked harder. A small flame was bobbing up and down, appearing then disappearing between the trees. It was far away, but what else could it be but a torch? She could hear distant voices now, carrying on the wind.

Had the high priest sent out a search party? There were special deaths awaiting those who defied the gods. Some were hung from the sacred oaks. Others were drowned, pressed beneath wattle hurdles into the marshes. Gripped by fear, she looked about anxiously. What should she do? Where should she go?

She knew this forest like the back of her hand. It was her vast and bountiful medicine cupboard. She spent her life here, harvesting celandines in the spring, anemones and garlic in the summer, berries and sloes in the autumn and mushrooms in the winter.

Anya turned and hurried along the narrow deer-track that led through a swathe of foxgloves, their stalks stripped bare for their precious seeds. As she ran, brambles snagged at her heavy gown and she tugged it free, her breath coming in short, sharp bursts. She stopped and looked back the way she had come. The torches were lighting up the forest and her heart sank. Athelwald's kin knew how to hunt deer and wild boar, knew how to read the signs of a broken twig or a crushed toadstool. These men were following her trail.

The great oak lay across the track. It had fallen three winters since during a storm and the priests had taken it to be an ill omen, although Anya knew the tree had been rotten for a long time. She had been sad to see such a majestic tree fall but, as with all things, death had brought life, and all manner of fungi now grew from its grizzled trunk. The track forked at the oak and she took the left path, plunging deeper into the forest.

Rain began to fall and she pulled up the hood of her priestess's gown and peered into the blackness. She had been confident she would come to the charcoal burners' settlement if she followed this trail, but now she was not so certain. Had she taken the wrong turning? She glanced over her shoulder. The torches were closer now, bright as the sun. She had no choice but to keep going. Lifting the soaked hem of her gown, she ran blindly, brambles snagging her arms and whipping against her face.

Stumbling over a fallen branch, she came to an abrupt halt. Wiping the rain from her eyes, she stared desperately into the darkness. Faint traces of smoke were drifting from a collection of turf-covered mounds. She breathed a sigh of relief and went on, more cautiously now. There was no sign of firelight beneath the closed doors of the round houses; it appeared the charcoal burners were all abed.

Anya hesitated. These people of the forest lived an isolated life, never straying very far from this small clearing. The events and troubles of the world tended to pass them by and it seemed wrong to involve them in her troubles. But the voices behind her were louder now, clearly audible above the falling rain. She had no choice. She did not know where else to go.

The door of the wood store was slightly ajar and she

peered into its dark interior. Along one wall, a pile of neatly stacked logs reached the rafters. Against the opposite wall, a line of upended wheelbarrows rested like a row of sleeping sentries. Anya stepped inside. Closing the door quietly behind her, she crawled into the small space behind the nearest barrow and clasped her knees to her chest. In the pitch blackness she could hear her own breathing amplified like an echo in a cave. The air was filled with the scent of freshly hewn wood and deeper, musty undercurrents of earth, cobwebs, and mushrooms sprouting in the darkness.

Suddenly, the door of the hut opened. Anya froze. She could see very little behind the barrow but she was aware of torchlight illuminating the wood store, and footsteps across the earthen floor. The footsteps ceased and she caught a glimpse of the outline of a man's boots. He was standing just inches away from the barrow. Her heart began to pound so fiercely she felt sure the soldier must hear it.

The boots vanished. Shadows flickered across the wood store and the torch crackled as the soldier swung it into the dark recesses of the shed. She heard his footsteps crunching through the wood chippings strewn upon the floor; he was very close again now. Anya closed her eyes, not daring to breathe. A silence fell save for the hiss of the man's torch and the sound of rainwater dripping steadily from his cloak. She wondered what he was waiting for.

She said a silent prayer to Nerthus, begging for protection. But would Nerthus want to save her now? She knew the goddess did not ask for human sacrifice, but Anya had openly defied the high priest in the sacred grove. Perhaps the goddess was angry with her? She remained absolutely still, her arms wrapped tightly around her knees. Her legs were aching now and she began to think her lungs might burst. After what seemed like an eternity, she heard the soldier's footsteps retreating across the wood store. She heard the rush of the torch, the grating of the door across the earth and quite suddenly, the shed was once again plunged into darkness.

Anya took a deep breath and filled her aching lungs. She felt overwhelmed with relief. Perhaps Nerthus had not forsaken her after all. Her legs were numb but she remained motionless for a long time, not daring to move. What should she do now? Where should she go? She had been born in Athelwald's golden hall, and she had expected to live out her days serving her goddess in the sacred grove. She knew nothing of the world beyond the borders of Saxony. But now, in the blink of an eye, she had no kingdom, no hall and no kin.

Without warning, the door of the wood store opened again and torchlight flooded the darkness. She heard a man's voice shouting above the driving rain.

'Look harder!'

Anya jolted with shock. Involuntarily, her arms loosened their grip around her knees and her left foot skidded across the earthen floor, banging softly against the wooden wheel of the barrow. In the silence, the noise sounded like a thunder clap. In a heartbeat, the barrow was wrenched away. The torch was very close to her face and she squinted blindly, the distinctive stench of pitch filling her nostrils. The soldier lifted her to her feet and manhandled her out of the shed.

'I have her!'

Athelwald's men had rounded up the charcoal burners and their families. They were huddled together in the rain.

'They are innocent!' Anya pleaded, struggling desperately in the soldier's arms. 'They knew nothing about this. I beg you, leave them be!'

The soldier ignored her. He grabbed her hands and bound them tightly behind her back.

'Let go of me!' Anya shouted angrily. 'I am the daughter of your king!'

He paid no heed to her protestations, dragging her unceremoniously back towards the village. Some of Athelwald's men stared curiously at her, but most looked away, as if afraid of being tarnished by her ungodly ways.

'I demand to be taken to my father!' Anya insisted as they neared the village, but the men continued to ignore her as if she had not spoken. Instead she was taken to a small storage shed at the edge of the settlement. Her gown was soaked. Leaves were caught in her long, tangled hair, like fishes in a net. Her face was dirty and streaked with tears, but she was offered neither dry clothes, nor food, nor water. The soldier simply pushed her inside and bolted the door. She sank down onto the make-shift bed. Nerthus *was* angry. Her goddess *had* forsaken her. Anya's thoughts turned to Emma and she sobbed until she was utterly spent, until her chest ached and her eyes felt raw once again.

A long time later, she realised she was not alone. Horsa was looking down at her, his forehead furrowed with deep concern. She sat up slowly. Her body felt heavy, as if her limbs had turned to stone. She looked into his much loved, familiar face and a curious sound escaped her lips, half laugh and half sob.

'I thought I would never see you again,' she gulped. 'I'm so glad you're here.'

Horsa sat down beside her on the bed and picked a leaf from her tangled hair. 'Did they hurt you?' he asked anxiously.

Anya shook her head, struggling to hold her tears in check.

'Have they offered you any food or drink?'

Again, she shook her head.

Horsa shot to his feet. 'Unforgiveable!' he roared angrily. 'They are treating you like a common criminal! I will have them fetch you some food.' He glanced at her dirt streaked hands and face. 'And some soap and water,' he added more gently.

'No!' Anya grabbed his sleeve. 'Please don't go.' She did not want to be alone with only dark thoughts for company.

Horsa sat down again. 'I swear I didn't know what was going to happen to Emma,' he said softly. 'No-one did.'

'Father knew,' Anya replied dully. 'And he did nothing.'

'There was nothing he could do, Anya. Once the high priest has spoken, there is nothing anyone can do.'

'She said my name,' Anya whispered falteringly. 'She was thirteen summers old, just a child.'

Horsa nodded. 'When I saw her, when they brought her into the sacred grove… as long as I live, I will never forget the look on her face.' He took a deep, shuddering breath.

Anya's face crumpled with grief. She put her arms around him and held him tightly.

'The priests are wrong,' she sobbed into his shoulder. 'The gods do not want blood.'

When they finally drew apart, she wiped away her tears, smearing yet more dirt across her face. 'Father stood by and watched the murder of his own daughter. How could he do such a thing?'

'Father is suffering, Anya. His pain is terrible to behold.'

'Emma's suffering was far, far worse,' Anya said bluntly.

Horsa's jaw clenched and he closed his eyes.

Anya looked down at the thin copper band she wore on the forefinger of her left hand. It had once belonged to her mother. Despite the ring being of little value, the warband who had carried Eown into slavery had still tried to wrench it from her finger. But she had worn it since childhood, the band was tight, and they could not remove it. And so Eown had eventually given it to Anya, who cherished it more deeply than any gold, for it was her last link to the half remembered woman who had comforted her when she cried, all those years ago.

'I made a promise to our mother, and I haven't kept it,' she whispered, repeatedly twisting the ring round her finger until her skin began to itch.

'Yes, you have. No-one could have been a better or a more loving sister to Emma.'

Anya shook her head. 'I allowed her to die. I didn't stop it.'

'No-one could stop it.'

'Well, I will see them both again, very soon.'

She felt her brother tense. 'Anya, don't say that. I couldn't bear to lose you too.'

Anya shook her head. 'What's the point in pretending? We both know that I will be sentenced to death. No-one can defy both the high king and the high priest so publicly and hope to live.'

'I will talk to father,' Horsa said desperately. 'I will see what can be done.'

'We both know that nothing can be done,' Anya said dully.

Horsa squeezed her hand then stood up and walked slowly towards the door. He hesitated for a moment then turned back. 'There is always hope, Anya. Never forget it.'

Anya forced herself to smile. 'I won't.'

She waited until he had closed the door behind him then she fell back against the wall and shut her eyes. The wattle dug into her spine, but she barely noticed. She prayed to

Gevyon, the goddess who takes all those who die a virgin, and begged her to look kindly on her sister. Her fingers dug deep into the thin blanket.

She did not want to die.

Not yet.

She slept fitfully and her dreams were full of blood. It poured down her throat, choking her until she could no longer breathe. She awoke with a start. Clara was looking down at her.

'You must remove your robe of the priesthood and give it to me.'

'Where is Abberlen?' Anya asked, struggling to shake the dream from her mind. 'I didn't see him in the holding pens.'

'What do I care about an orphan boy?' Clara rasped. 'You have shamed us all, Anya.'

Anya's eyes widened. 'My sister is dead. Tortured to death by command of the high priest. I am not the one who is shamed.'

'How can you even think such a thing? Emma died a noble death.'

'The gods did not ask for her.'

'You are beyond our prayers. Will you give me your robe of the priesthood, or will I have to tear it from your back?'

Anya pulled the heavy white robe over her head. She held it out and Clara snatched it from her. The blue linen gown Anya wore beneath was full of creases, and her hands trembled as she tried to straighten them.

'You deserve to die, Anya. You are a disgrace to the priesthood,' Clara said bitterly.

'I only wanted to spare my sister's life,' Anya began, but Clara had already gone, slamming the door behind her. Anya sat down on the edge of the bed again and stared into space.

Her hands were trembling uncontrollably now. But there was some comfort in the thought that Eown and Emma would be waiting for her in the feasting halls of the gods. At least she would not be alone.

As dusk fell, Anya was brought before the council. The blue sky was deepening, like a bruise spreading across the heavens. The wind still blew viciously, just as it had the day Emma had been sent to her death. It seemed the gods were still angry. The council met in a smaller, wooden version of the amphitheatres that stood outside the walls of every Roman town. It was packed that evening, for Athelwald's people were curious to learn the punishment that Anya would face for so openly defying the high priest's decision.

Anya stood in the centre of the arena and looked around at the sea of faces staring down at her. She was surrounded by the men and women of Saxony, people she had known all her life but the arena's expanse of baked earth stood between them now, separating her from them as irrevocably as if a deep fissure had opened in the earth. Surrounded by a vast crowd, she had never felt more alone.

Athelwald stood up slowly. His voice sounded stilted, his throat constricted with grief. 'The council has reached a decision.'

The crowd was utterly silent, waiting. Cold terror enveloped Anya like a shroud. She didn't want to die. There was so much she had yet to learn, so much she had yet to do. She wanted to see Horsa and Elsbet wed and she wanted to watch their children grow. She wanted to see Abberlen smile again.

She knew she should be brave, but she didn't feel brave at all. Her heart was pounding so rapidly she could barely breathe, her entire body trembling violently. She wondered if the high priest would choose the slowest, most agonising punishment of all – slitting her open from groin to gullet so that he might study her death throes. It was highly unlikely he would choose to show mercy and simply hang her by the neck from a sacred oak.

Athelwald looked down at his daughter. 'The council was strongly divided on this matter, but the votes have been cast,' he said at last. 'Anya's punishment is exile.'

A gasp of surprise ran around the amphitheatre, for everyone had expected a sentence of death.

'Anya will accompany her brothers Hengist and Horsa and their warriors on their journey to Britannia where they are to serve Vortigern, high king of the Dobunni.'

Anya's mouth fell open in confusion and disbelief. She was not going to die. She stood, rooted to the spot, struggling to make sense of her father's words.

Exile? Britannia? Did he mean she was to leave Saxony forever?

She looked up at the stands, and searched for her brothers in the sea of faces. Hengist's eyes were hard and calculating but Horsa's expression was terrible to behold. She watched the colour drain from his face, watched the meaning of Athelwald's words take hold in his deep green eyes, and her heart went out to him.

'Horsa,' she whispered, although she knew he could not hear her above the tumult of the crowd. 'I am so sorry.'

The wind had dropped by the following day; the gods' anger had subsided. A wasp flew out from beneath the thatch of the great hall, then another and another. Anya watched them thoughtfully. A wasps' nest was a good omen and she surely needed some good fortune, after all that had come to pass.

She paused beneath the ornately carved lintel. Today, like every other day, she raised her fingertips to the ancient runes that promised blessings for those within. She could still remember being held aloft in her mother's arms, their fingers intertwined as they touched the runes together. The memory was suffused with the scent of camomile in Eown's hair, and the warmth of her embrace.

Anya struggled to control the strong emotions that were threatening to overwhelm her. The doors were fastened open, but it was still stiflingly warm in the great hall, the air rich with the aroma of venison stew bubbling in the huge copper bowl suspended over the fire. But there were also baser undercurrents. During the night many of Athelwald's men staggered from the great hall to relieve themselves against the outside walls, and the stench of their stale urine was seeping through the lathe and plaster. And further away, the warm weather was doing nothing to disguise the nauseating smell of the middens.

As her eyes became accustomed to the gloom of the hall she realised Athelwald was seated upon the gift throne, staring blankly into the middle distance. Anya remained motionless, her gaze fixed upon her father. She felt as if a bond had been severed between them on that terrible night in the sacred grove. Athelwald had done nothing to save Emma. He had simply stood by and watched her die. He had betrayed his own kin, and Anya doubted she would ever find it in her heart to forgive him.

She walked slowly towards the gift throne. Her father's gaze focussed upon her and she felt a tremor of shock, for Athelwald had aged in the passing of a day. His cheeks were sunken and his face haggard.

'My dearest child,' he began.

'I don't want to go to Britannia,' Anya said bluntly.

'Nor do I want you to go but I had no choice. The council demanded your life yesterday, but I have already given one daughter to the gods and I was not ready to lose another. Britannia was your mother's birthplace, so perhaps you will feel some affinity to its people.'

He put a hand lightly upon his daughter's arm, but she recoiled from his touch. Dismay spread across Athelwald's face and he quickly withdrew his hand.

'This is my home, father. I know nothing else. How can I leave it all behind?'

'If you remain here, you will die for dishonouring the gods.'

'But the gods do not want human sacrifice! If my mother had still been alive, she would never have permitted Emma's life to be thrown away!'

'Enough, Anya!' Athelwald closed his eyes tightly, as if he were gripped by pain. 'I must live with my guilt for the rest of my days, but I am a king first, and a father second. I cannot act against the will of the priests. You must believe me when I tell you there is no worse torment than to watch your own flesh and blood die, but there was no greater gift I could offer to my kingdom. There was no greater sacrifice.'

A shadow darkened the doorway.

'Father! I don't want to take Anya…' Hengist's voice trailed away as he realised his half-sister stood beside Athelwald.

Athelwald turned to his son. 'You will do as I command.'

'But the high priest demanded exile. She can go anywhere. She doesn't have to accompany me.' Hengist sounded like a petulant child.

'You would have her cast adrift, alone in the world, without kin or friendship?' Athelwald asked in astonishment.

Hengist fell silent.

Athelwald shook his head wearily. 'You will take your sister to Britannia. She will be under your protection. I entrust her to your safe keeping. She speaks with the gods. She will be a great asset for you. See -' Athelwald reached out to touch Anya's red hair but she flinched away again.

Athelwald lowered his hand and when he spoke, his voice sounded fractured and hollow. 'Her hair is the colour of blood, which means she is sacred to Andraste, goddess of war. She will keep *you* safe, my son.'

'As always, Father, I bow to your judgement,' Hengist said coldly. Then he turned and walked out into the bright sunshine, leaving Anya alone with her father.

Silence fell, so heavy it seemed to bow the air.

'I miss your mother… so much. And I will miss you too,' Athelwald said at last.

Anya did not reply, her mind in turmoil. She glanced at her father again. His powerful frame was slumped against the fine silk cushions of the gift throne. A sharp needle of guilt jabbed her heart. No matter what had come to pass, she loved her father, and she had not meant to add to his suffering.

'I will miss you too,' she said softly.

EIGHT

Aquae Sulis, kingdom of the Dobunni, Britannia

Rufus Aufidius Maximus, quaestor to Vortigern, high king of the Dobunni, was in a hurry. His rapid footfall echoed like the sound of rain drops upon the high, vaulted roof of the old Roman council chamber. He was an unimpressive man, slightly built with a thin, pointed nose and black, greasy shoulder-length hair. With his hunched shoulders and scuttling gait, he gave the appearance of a frightened rat. Rufus dropped the armful of scrolls onto the long table and tried to catch his breath.

Vortigern eyed him with a look of disdain. 'You wouldn't last a heartbeat on a battlefield! You're wheezing like an old woman.'

Rufus ignored him and began to sort the scrolls so their edges were exactly parallel to the edge of the table.

'Shall I call the barber, Lord?' he asked, when he was satisfied the scrolls were all perfectly aligned.

Vortigern ran a hand over his close-cropped stubbly head.

'What for? He will find no employment here.'

'To trim your beard perhaps, Lord?' Rufus suggested hopefully. Vortigern's coarse features and pock-marked skin were fast disappearing beneath a straggling brown beard flecked with grey.

'Trim my beard?' Vortigern mocked. 'Since when do I primp and preen? I'm a man, not a simpering eunuch!'

Rufus eyed Vortigern thoughtfully. The high king of the Dobunni was now more than forty years old. He was a big man, tall and broad. In his youth he had been an intimidating mass of pure muscle, but over the years his body had softened like a loaf of bread left out in the rain. His huge belly now hung over his breeches, as plump as a cushion beneath the fine purple linen of his tunic.

'Forgive me, but I thought perhaps, for your betrothed -' Rufus began.

'You think too much, Rufus. You always have.'

'I think for both of us,' Rufus mused, *'because you do not think at all.'*

He stared fixedly at the unfurled parchment on the table before him. He gave every appearance of reading the neat Latin script, but his mind was elsewhere, dwelling on life's injustices.

He had known Vortigern his entire life; they had grown up together in Aquae Sulis. Vortigern, and his father and grandfather before him, had held positions of high authority under Roman rule. Just as Rufus, and his father and grandfather before him, had held less influential positions. The words blurred on the parchment as he continued to seethe. His own family were renowned for their honesty and integrity and as such, remained as poor as a landless peasant.

Vortigern's family on the other hand, were a corrupt, bullying brood, growing rich from receiving payments for court judgements in a plaintiff's favour and farming out public offices to the highest bidder. As the last Roman tax-collector had withdrawn from the island, Vortigern had remained the elected Governor of Western Britannia. He was extraordinarily wealthy, owning vast tracts of rich agricultural land, and his authority was far reaching.

Rufus had hated Vortigern all his life. Hated him, and envied him and longed to be just like him. Even as a child, Vortigern's ambition had been plain for all to see. He would always play the king, always wear the hawthorn crown, whilst the other children would always play his men. Childhood led to adulthood and in a world of anarchy and chaos, a charismatic bully with a forceful personality would always make his mark.

Rufus forgot all about his pretext of reading the parchment and stared blankly into space, remembering the day Vortigern had been accepted as the unopposed leader of the Dobunni, simply because there was no-one else with the strength of arms to challenge him. He had stood on the steps of the basilica of Aquae Sulis, arms raised to the crowd as if he was a Christian priest blessing his congregation. They had clapped and cheered and shouted his name, but all Rufus could see was the hawthorn crown of their childhood. Yet again, it sat upon Vortigern's head.

'What's that noise?' Vortigern asked sharply.

Rufus realised he had been grinding his teeth together.

'Nothing, Lord,' he said hurriedly.

'So, she *is* beautiful?' Vortigern asked.

'Beauty is hard to define, my Lord. One man may see it, where another sees only weeds.'

Vortigern threw up his hands in exasperation. 'For the love of God, you promised me she was beautiful. I hope you've not lied to me. I hope I'm not disappointed.'

'She is well proportioned and fair,' Rufus lied. He had found Loisa, daughter of Pascent, high king of the Coritani, to be a plain girl with few redeeming features, but Vortigern badly needed this marriage alliance.

'Alliances are more trouble than they are worth,' Vortigern grumbled, as if he had read Rufus's mind. He pulled irritably at his unkempt beard. 'It would have been simpler to defeat Pascent in battle. He's a frail old man who rules over a rich kingdom.'

'And so one day soon, if you marry his daughter, and if God is just, you might inherit it all,' Rufus said mildly.

'Fair, you said?' Vortigern mused. 'Fair skinned, fair haired?'

'Coarse brown hair, like a mongrel bitch', Rufus thought to himself. 'Fair indeed,' he replied. 'And now, if you will give me leave, I must read the marriage contract. I wouldn't want you to stamp your seal on something you later regretted.'

Vortigern waved his hand dismissively. 'Read it later - just make sure you don't miss anything vital, or I'll have your inky fingers as treats for my hounds. Go and tell my son that we leave at noon.'

'But…' Rufus caught sight of Vortigern's expression. Snatching the scroll from the table, he stood up and hurried out of the chamber. Resentment was burning a hole in his gut. He ensured the smooth running of the potteries, the mines, the mills, the markets. He drew up grain-tax schedules and organised the supply routes to feed a vast army and an overcrowded city, and yet Vortigern treated him little better than a slave.

'Vortigern may be the loom, but I am the yarn,' he thought bitterly. *'If I were to ride away from him now and never look back, the many threads that bind Vortigern's kingdom would unravel like carelessly woven cloth. He needs me, and yet in all our years together, he has never thanked me. Not once.'*

Still seething, Rufus did not bother to knock on the door of Ronan's bedchamber. He stormed into the room but came to an abrupt halt, his furious expression twisting to one of undisguised revulsion. The youth was still asleep. The chamber was airless and stank of stale wine and unwashed clothes. Its walls were decorated with ancient, fading frescos of a bygone age; green foliage spilled from ornamental urns and delicate birds perched in the branches of fruit trees in blossom. Delicate Roman chairs and tables lined the walls, their garish paint now chipped and peeling. The floor looked as if a high spring tide had swept through the basilica and left behind a tangled strand line of Ronan's undergarments, tunics, breeches, sword belts, cloak clasps and hunting knives.

Ronan's bed was in disarray, the blankets half way to the floor. He was naked except for the whore draped across his belly. Rufus's hands clenched into fists, his mind swirling with conflicting emotions. He felt lust for the whore but also a confusing sense of disgust. He felt envy for Ronan's honed, warrior physique but also a strong sense of loathing, for Ronan was simply a younger, more finely honed version of his father.

'We leave at noon,' Rufus announced loudly.

'Go away.'

'Noon!' Rufus repeated vehemently.

Without opening his eyes, Ronan reached for a pillow and flung it in the direction of Rufus's voice. 'I heard you the first time.'

Rufus caught the pillow and threw it back. It hit the whore on her plump behind. She awoke with a start and wriggled, attempting to sit up, but Ronan held her fast. Rufus noticed there were finger-mark bruises the colour of ripe plums on her breasts and wrists.

'Why do I need to be there?' Ronan groaned 'Surely my father can seal a betrothal without me at his side? Pascent's stronghold is a good day's ride away. I have better things to do.'

Ronan's hand slid appreciatively over the whore's behind and Rufus saw a flash of fear in the young girl's eyes.

'You shouldn't keep your father waiting,' Rufus said sharply.

'Then get out,' Ronan snapped. 'I need to get dressed.'

Rufus's expression darkened. '*Like father, like son.*'

He turned on his heel, picking his way fastidiously through the detritus and dirty garments on the chamber floor. He found it deeply disturbing that anyone would choose to live in such chaos and filth. His own chamber was meticulously tidy and spotlessly clean. As he closed the door behind him he heard the whore yelp in alarm and then Ronan's voice.

'Father can wait. I'm sure there's time for a little more entertainment.'

A strong, warm wind was sweeping across the vast forum of Aquae Sulis. Vortigern and Rufus were already mounted up, surrounded by a warband of some fifty men. The doors of the basilica flew open and Ronan ran down the wide sweeping steps, hastily fastening his sword belt.

Vortigern narrowed his eyes. 'You're late!' He turned in his saddle and spat out a piece of dried beef he had been chewing for too long. The meat landed with a tiny splash in a nearby puddle.

'I had things to do,' Ronan replied airily.

'And did you 'do' her to your satisfaction?' Vortigern asked sarcastically.

Ronan did not reply. He wrenched the reins of his warhorse from the stable boy, and mounted in a flamboyant sweep of his fine woollen cloak. Vortigern shook his head. The boy was a wastrel. He often wondered if a sprite had snatched his true son from his crib and replaced him with a changeling child.

Kicking the flanks of his stallion with more force than necessary, Vortigern led his warband beneath the colossal arch and out into the city's narrow streets. They were crowded with refugees from the countryside, all seeking sanctuary from Irish raids and Pictish warbands. Some came on farm wagons pulled by plodding donkeys, but many more came on foot, their meagre belongings strapped to their backs.

Vortigern and his warband rode north on the old Roman road, beneath the banner of the black boar. Vortigern pulled another piece of dried beef from his saddle bag and began to chew it noisily. He noticed there were far more fallow fields than the last time he had ridden this road. The Dobunni were hiding behind hastily dug defences, like frightened children behind their mothers' skirts. But without a crop to harvest, they would more likely die of starvation than from a Pictish axe or an Irish sword.

He turned in his saddle and rounded on Rufus. 'You command my grain supply so tell me, why are these fields fallow? My army can't march on empty bellies!'

Without waiting for a reply, Vortigern turned to his right and took out his frustration on his son. 'I told you we were leaving at noon and yet you kept me waiting. You're not a child anymore and yet you still behave like one! Pray God this Coritani girl gives me sons, for I swear you'll not inherit an inch of my kingdom.'

From the corner of his eye, Vortigern saw Rufus smiling broadly.

'Something amusing you?' he asked sharply.

'No, Lord,' Rufus's smile disappeared in an instant. He quickly pointed down the valley. 'I see a new mill - there, where the river forks. It's not been declared. There'll be a fine due, and a higher tax to be levied.'

Vortigern had no interest in such trivia. He nodded vaguely and turned back to his son. Ronan had adopted his usual blank expression, as if a barrier had fallen behind his eyes to distance himself from his father's criticism. When Ronan was younger, Vortigern had regularly taken a stick and beaten the boy black and blue, drawing blood just so that he might see a flicker of response in those expressionless eyes.

'God's teeth! Listen to me!' Vortigern grabbed his son by the shoulder and shook him violently.

Ronan wrenched himself from his father's grasp, flushed with anger and humiliation. He refastened his cloak pin with exaggerated care and when he turned to face Vortigern again, his expression was carefully composed.

'I have an idea of what to do about the Picts,' he said calmly.

'Why should I listen to the ideas of an arrogant youth who spends his days drinking and whoring?'

'Because it's a good idea,' Ronan replied, glancing slyly at Rufus.

Vortigern eyed his son dubiously. 'Then I suppose I will hear it. I have little else to do. Rufus, move down the line. This is men's talk.'

By noon, there was a change in the weather. The sky darkened ominously and the wind swung round, no longer a soft southerly breeze, but a fierce gale from the north. Vortigern watched the rain sweeping across the bleak landscape. By the time it reached them, it was torrential. He hated the northern lands. They were bleak and unforgiving. His mind wandered to Pascent's daughter. He wondered if she *was* beautiful, or if Rufus was embellishing the truth, as usual.

Vortigern had not loved his first wife. It had been a political match and she had died in childbirth five winters since. The babe, a jaundiced girl-child, had died with her. He missed neither of them. In truth, he had no patience for another marriage but he badly needed another son, because he seriously doubted Ronan would ever be capable of leading the Dobunni.

It was dusk by the time they reached Pascent's stronghold, and Vortigern's bones had begun to creak like badly made furniture. He longed for a hot bath and a warm bed. The old Roman villa was surrounded by ancient walls, further shielded by a freshly cut bank and ditch. The villa commanded a fine view, a perfect vantage point to keep watch over the steep sided river valley to the north and the vast agricultural flat lands to the south. The gate-house was an impressive two storey building. A row of severed heads atop blood-stained spears adorned its dark stone battlements.

Within the villa complex, Pascent had created a small but bustling town of barracks, stables, workshops and granaries. Vortigern wiped the driving rain from his face and scanned the stronghold with a soldier's keen eye - five large barrack blocks, stabling for perhaps a hundred horses. Pascent had a sizeable army, and his stronghold was well defended.

They rode on through rapidly forming puddles. Pascent's soldiers, stable boys, farmhands and slaves stopped in their tracks, and eyed Vortigern's warband warily as they passed by. Directly ahead lay the main villa, flanked by long subsidiary wings. Its grand facade was marble clad and shaded by tall, graceful colonnades. Unruly hedges of box marked formal gardens long since overgrown with rampant nettles and thistles.

Pascent of the Coritani stood beside his wife and two children at the top of the worn marble steps. Vortigern scrutinised Pascent minutely as if he were about to face him on a battlefield, weighing odds and assessing risks. Should he view Pascent as ally or enemy? The high king of the Coritani was old now, but in his prime he had outfought and outwitted the bravest and wisest of men. And so, despite Pascent's advancing years, Vortigern instinctively notched up the old man as a potential threat.

Vortigern dismounted, handing the reins to a stable boy. He noticed that Pascent was dressed in the old Roman style of a finely woven, ankle length tunic, belted at the waist, which meant the old man was a traditionalist, trapped in a past that no longer existed. He also noticed the old king looked tired and ill, which meant there was a good chance the kingdom of the Coritani might fall into his lap sooner than he had expected.

'It has been too long, Vortigern,' Pascent said, smiling broadly. 'More than twenty years, if my memory serves me. We give you warm welcome to our home.' Pascent held out a hand to greet his future son in law, and winced as Vortigern's firm grasp tightened around his swollen finger joints.

'This is my son, Ronan,' Vortigern said gruffly.

Ronan stepped up beside his father, and stared wordlessly at his hosts. His manner was vaguely threatening.

'You have not met my wife, Amice,' Pascent continued.

Vortigern nodded curtly. He thought Amice was a sharp featured, plain woman, not worthy of note.

'And these are my children, Aquila and Loisa.'

Vortigern glanced briefly at Pascent's son. Aquila was still a child, but he had steady, intelligent eyes and he was the sole heir to the throne of the Coritani. He nodded at the boy and mentally notched him up as a potential future threat.

He turned next to Loisa and he looked at her for a long time. Rufus had lied. The girl was as dull as ditch water, an unattractive little thing with a round face and lumpish features. Her dull, brown hair was scraped back and without ornament. Disappointment flooded through him. How dare Rufus deceive him?

'Come,' Pascent said smoothly. 'No doubt you wish to rest. Tomorrow I hope you will join us for the betrothal feast.'

Vortigern glanced venomously at the high king of the Coritani. He felt so angry and so disappointed by the look of Pascent's daughter that he was sorely tempted to take his sword from his belt and plunge it into the old man's heart. A simple sword thrust would solve two problems instantaneously. It would free him from an undesirable betrothal, and the kingdom of the Coritani would literally fall at his feet. He turned slightly, sensing Ronan's gaze boring into the side of his head.

'Father?' Ronan prompted quietly. There was a subtle edge to his voice.

Vortigern took a deep breath and felt some of his anger dissipate. He was of a mind to mount up and ride straight back to Aquae Sulis, but it was a long ride home and his entire body ached with exhaustion. With ill grace, he pushed past his hosts into the grand atrium, dripping a stream of rain water onto the marble floor.

‘I want some food, some dry clothes and a warm bed,’ he demanded.

‘Of course,’ Pascent replied. ‘We have everything prepared for you.’

The bed smelled fresh and Vortigern fell asleep almost instantly. His rest was frequently disturbed by searing cramp after the long, difficult ride and his dreams were tortured nightmares of being trapped in dark dungeons with no hope of escape.

NINE

Pascent's villa was crumbling like over-ripe cheese. Tiles, unseated by years of storms, were slipping from the roof, smashing like thunder-claps as they hit the ground. In the decaying splendour of the dining room, a thousand footfalls had loosened the tiny *tesserae* of the geometric mosaic, and they rattled beneath Vortigern's boots as he took his place at the table for the betrothal feast. He had not slept well and the coming of dawn had not improved his mood.

Rufus moved to sit beside him, but Vortigern pointed at the far end of the table. Rufus could sit beside the lowliest of his warriors and be offered the poorest cuts of meat. Loisa was as plain as a sack of flour, and it was all Rufus's fault. The man was as spindly and ineffectual as a twig, good for nothing but collecting taxes. The time had come for Rufus to stop meddling in politics.

Pascent was a generous host, and many courses were brought to the table: eels, bream, mussels, oysters, roasted boar, venison and suckling pig. The food was excellent. Vortigern ate a great deal, but he barely tasted the rich and varied flavours. He felt so angry with Rufus he wanted to snap his neck.

'Perhaps now would be a good time to discuss possible dates for the wedding?' Pascent began, but Vortigern waved his hand dismissively.

'Loisa is still very young. Let a year pass. There's time enough.' *'Time enough for the plague to take her,'* he thought.

'As you wish,' Pascent replied. He shot a quick glance at his wife, and Vortigern saw the shared look of relief in their eyes.

The news that his daughter's wedding was not imminent appeared to put Pascent at ease, and he began to tell a lengthy story about a Celtic priest called Pelagius. Vortigern quickly grew bored as well as angry. He took a glass of wine, and then another. How else would he endure this frustrating, tedious day?

'Pelagius teaches that we do not need to be burdened by Adam's sin. He teaches that we have free will to find salvation through God,' Pascent went on fervently.

Vortigern filled his glass to the brim again. He wished the old man would shut up. Philosophy was for men too weak-livered to wield a sword.

More courses were brought to the table: fruit platters, pastries, cakes, and honey puddings topped with poppy seeds. Vortigern tried them all but their sweetness did nothing to alleviate his foul temper. He glanced again at Pascent's young daughter. She was such an unattractive little thing. Her only redeeming feature was her bosom. Her breasts were appealingly pert and he could see their outline clearly through the fine silk of her dress.

Each time Vortigern glanced at her, Loisa looked away, as terrified as a cornered mouse. Seething with frustration, Vortigern made no attempt to speak to his future wife. He signed the betrothal contract without a word, ramming his seal into the gleaming wax with such fury that the table shook. Rufus had trapped him, lied to him and betrayed him. Finding no discernible outlet for his rage, he continued to drink steadily. He reached for another jug of wine, but his vision blurred and his fingers struggled to grasp the handle. His belly ached and his head was pulsing as vigorously as a severed artery. He had eaten too much, and drunk too much.

'I'm tired. I'm going to bed,' he announced. His words were slurred and he could barely stand.

Pascent rose to his feet. 'I wish you good rest. Until tomorrow.'

Vortigern leant heavily on Rufus's arm as they left the dining chamber, for he was finding it hard to put one foot in front of the other.

Once in the bedchamber, he dismissed Rufus and drank another jug of wine. Then he lay on his back on the huge bed, staring blankly at the ornately plastered ceiling. He felt ill. And angry. So angry he wanted to kill something. Or fuck someone. He couldn't remember why he was so angry. Or why he was lying on this huge bed. Where was he, for the love of God? He needed to piss. He climbed down from the bed and the world swayed dizzily. He staggered aimlessly around the room, looking for a chamber pot. When he couldn't find one, he pissed against the wall.

His anger was burning a hole inside him. He badly needed a woman. There had been a girl at the feast. He couldn't remember who she was, or how he knew her, but she had huge breasts. He wanted *her*.

In the shadows of the central courtyard, behind a statue of a scantily clad nymph, Ronan watched his father's unsteady progress. He presumed Vortigern was simply searching for another jug of wine, and he shook his head in wry amusement. He turned his attention back to the naked slave girl, taking her with such force that her buttocks slid across the smooth, cold marble tiles and her head rammed hard against the base of the statue.

Ronan's release came quickly. He rolled off the girl, and she did not wait to be dismissed. She snatched her tunic from the floor and fled. He was fastening his breeches when the screaming began in Loisa's room. The noise was ear piercing. Ronan looked up, just in time to see Pascent's daughter running through the darkness, her clothes in disarray. His eyes narrowed; this was not good. He ran across the courtyard with a sinking heart. Vortigern lay collapsed in a pool of vomit on the floor of Loisa's chamber, his breeches around his ankles.

'Father?' Ronan shouted, shaking him by the shoulders. Vortigern did not stir. Ronan ran an exasperated hand through his mop of unruly curls.

Rufus appeared in the doorway and hurried to his side.

'He cannot be found here,' Rufus said urgently. 'We have to get him back to his room. Quickly!'

'I don't take orders from you,' Ronan snarled.

'There's no time!' Rufus replied desperately. He put his arms beneath Vortigern's shoulders and attempted, unsuccessfully, to heave him upright.

Ronan shook his head derisively. The taxman was as weak as a kitten. 'On the count of three,' Ronan commanded and between them, they dragged Vortigern across the courtyard. It was not easy because Vortigern was as heavy as an ox and barely conscious, but they succeeded in dumping him unceremoniously on his bed.

Rufus turned to Ronan urgently. 'Make sure your father stays in this room. Post guards - your strongest men. No-one must see Vortigern. No one must speak to him. Do you understand?'

'You are addressing the heir to the throne. You would do well to remember that!' Ronan snapped, affronted.

'For the love of God, Ronan, just do as I say! I need to speak to Pascent. I need to convince him this was all a terrible misunderstanding.'

Ronan hesitated. It was intolerable that he should be given orders from a pitiful scribe, but in truth, Vortigern had placed them all in an intolerable situation. And, much as he was loath to admit it, Rufus was right. If Pascent laid eyes on Vortigern in his present state, it was highly likely they would all die this night.

Ronan nodded curtly, and left the room. Vortigern's men were housed in the barracks, ten men to a room. He roused them as quietly as he could. They were well trained, dressed and armed within moments, shadow-like forms running silently through the dark villa.

The blockade they created across the threshold of Vortigern's chamber was a solid mass of menacing muscle and steel. As Pascent's soldiers drew near, they were confronted by an awesome sight. Upon their shields, Vortigern's warriors each bore the emblem of a black boar, incised from leather. Protruding shield bosses marked each boar's snout, their black eyes formed by two iron studs.

Pascent's centurion stepped forward. 'We are here for Vortigern, by command of the high king.'

Ronan eyed him mockingly. The centurion looked ridiculous, as if he had raided a long-forgotten, dusty store room. He wore the full regalia of his now obsolete rank. A helmet with a high crest of red horse hair, a short skirt of neatly bound strips of leather, and a corslet of mail armour studded with the gold oval discs of military decoration - family heirlooms marking ancient acts of heroism.

'Vortigern is ill. He cannot be disturbed,' Ronan said carelessly.

'I am ordered by the high king to bring Vortigern before him. If you do not stand aside, then you leave me no choice but to take Vortigern by force.'

The tension in the air was palpable. A smile twitched upon Ronan's thin lips, and in reply, the centurion drew his sword.

'I would like to fight you. There's nothing I would like more than to slaughter you all,' Ronan replied. 'But I would ask you to think on this. Did Pascent tell you to murder the son of the high king of the Dobunni? Did he ask you to spill the blood of his honoured guests beneath his own roof? Do you want to be responsible for starting a bloody vendetta between two powerful houses?'

The centurion lowered his sword to his side, a look of uncertainty in his eyes. He turned to his optio. 'Vortigern is heavily guarded. I need new instruction. Go.'

Ronan squared his shoulders, and the fingers of his right hand settled around the grip of his sword. He was not afraid. Four seasons at Vortigern's side in battle had taught him how to fight and how to kill. His skill with a blade was the one facet of his life that his father never criticised.

There was still no sign of Rufus, and Ronan began to wonder if the old king had simply run him through. He imagined the annoying little scribe dying slowly, his blood seeping around the tiny *tesserae* of an exquisite mosaic, and it was quite a pleasing thought.

He refocused his gaze on the centurion and smiled benignly. The man simply stared back, his expression impassive. In an attempt to rile him, Ronan drew his sword and began to swing it sharply from side to side, like a cat flicking its tail. But the centurion did not respond.

After what seemed an age, Ronan heard footsteps, and turned to see Rufus scurrying round the corner. The optio, who was not far behind him, marched up to the centurion. 'The high king commands you to stand down, Sir.'

The centurion nodded curtly, sheathed his sword and stood aside.

A brief, self-satisfied smirk flickered across Ronan's young face before he turned to face his men. 'Stand guard. No-one is to enter.'

Opening the chamber door, he manhandled Rufus inside. The room stank of vomit and piss. His father was sitting on the edge of the bed, his face as green as a stagnant pond. Ronan grabbed Rufus by the shoulder. He noticed the scribe's hands were shaking.

'Well, what happened?'

'Pascent was not in a forgiving mood,' Rufus said grimly. 'He believes Vortigern raped his daughter.'

Ronan exhaled deeply. He deemed Rufus and his father equally to blame for this disastrous turn of events. Rufus should have thought beyond his political machinations, and accepted Vortigern would never want a girl like Loisa for his wife. And his father should have fucked a slave, not the virgin daughter of the high king of the Coritani.

'Let go of me. I need to speak to your father,' Rufus said icily.

Ronan frowned at the man's disrespectful tone, but he released his grip on the scribe's shoulder and shoved him roughly towards Vortigern.

Rufus approached the bed tentatively. His hands were clasped together like those of a Christian priest.

'Pascent is old and sick. He does not want war, Lord,' he began in a soothing, placating tone.

Vortigern's eyes slowly focussed on Rufus. 'That's no surprise,' he grunted. 'Why would anyone choose to make war against me?'

'They would be fools indeed,' Rufus agreed smoothly. 'But, as recompense for his daughter's loss of honour, he demands you give him half your harvest, for the next ten years.'

'What? The old man has lost his mind. I'll never agree to that. I didn't touch the bitch.'

'If you do not agree to his terms, he swears he will have our heads mounted upon his gate house. And if you renege on his terms, he swears he will lead his army against you.'

Vortigern bent double and vomited onto the floor. Rufus recoiled as if he had been struck, a look of utter revulsion on his face.

Vortigern wiped his beard with his sleeve. 'This is all your fault, Rufus.'

'I fail to see how -' Rufus began, but Ronan interrupted him. 'It doesn't matter who is to blame,' he said urgently. 'We need to find a way out of this God forsaken mess. Pascent's garrison is huge. I'd wager we are outnumbered by at least five to one.'

'If you agree to his terms, I believe he will allow us to leave unharmed,' Rufus said quickly. 'Pascent is a man of honour.'

'I came to seal an alliance, and instead I find myself subservient to an old man, paying tribute like a defeated warlord. This will not stand!'

'If we choose to fight, we will die,' Ronan said firmly. He folded his arms across his chest and glared expectantly at his father. Vortigern glared back at him; a silent battle of wills.

'Loisa's an ugly bitch,' Vortigern said at last. 'She's not worth dying for.'

'So you will agree to his terms?' Rufus asked hopefully.

'It seems I have no choice,' Vortigern grunted. 'I want to get out of this shit-hole.'

Rufus's face lit up with relief. 'I will go to Pascent now, Lord.'

Vortigern belched loudly as he watched Rufus scuttle away.

'That man led me here under false pretences, Ronan. I swear I won't forgive him for this. And you are as much to blame.'

Ronan's mouth fell open in astonished indignation.

'Why? What did I do?'

But Vortigern did not reply. Collapsing sideways onto the bed, he began to snore loudly.

Afraid that Pascent might change his mind, Ronan awoke his father at daybreak. There was no-one waiting on the steps of the villa to offer them God's speed and farewell. Ronan helped his father mount up in silence; his eyes constantly scanning the empty alleyways for any signs of ambush, but at this early hour, Pascent's stronghold appeared deserted. Vortigern's guards were already assembled. They looked subdued and wary. The steady beat of their warhorses' hooves echoed ominously around the silent buildings as they rode towards the gatehouse.

Ronan looked up at the row of severed heads, their empty eye sockets staring out blankly across the distant flat lands. The skulls had proved to be an empty threat. Pascent, old and sick and without an adult heir, had chosen tribute rather than bloodshed as retribution for his daughter's shame.

Ronan knew his father would never have made such a choice, never have allowed himself to appear so weak. The show of strength was everything to Vortigern; it was the very air he breathed. Ronan's eyes narrowed as he remembered his first experience of battle. He had been just fifteen years of age. He had watched his father slaughter the king of the Catuvellauni. Vortigern had cleaved the old man's head clean from his neck. Vegetius had remained standing for what seemed an age, just as a chicken runs around the coop without its head.

Ronan had watched with a mixture of revulsion and awe as the old king had finally collapsed like a felled oak into the mud and Vegetius's warriors had fled the field like a flock of frightened sheep. He had envied his father at that moment. With one mighty flourish of his sword, Vortigern had changed his fortune forever. From that day onwards, his father had wielded great power. Ronan suspected that once you had a taste for it, nothing less would suffice.

He glanced at his father, whose face was still as green as bile.

'How do you feel this morning?' he asked quietly.

'How do you think I feel?' Vortigern snapped. 'I feel fucking angry! That girl was mine, to take as I pleased, and yet the ungrateful bitch had the audacity to cry rape. I tell you, blood will be shed on a thousand fields of battle before that old man sees a single grain of my precious wheat.'

TEN

Saxony, Germania

The land was steeped in blood. It stained the dark mountains and the fast-flowing rivers. She was running now, running for her life, but the blood was pouring from the steep mountain sides. Abberlen was running beside her, but when she turned, he was no longer there. The blood surged, warm and sticky, over her body, clinging to her skin, filling her nose and mouth…

Anya flung aside the bed-rug and sat up, eyes wide with fear. There was no blood, but sweat daubed her linen under-gown to the contours of her body. One moment she felt uncomfortably hot. The next, she was chilling rapidly in the cool air.

It was the same dream, night after night - the blood surging down her throat and filling her lungs. Her mind gingerly probed the receding images. She did not recognise the land. There were no high mountains in Germania, no bleak, isolated valleys.

She shivered, filled with a terrible sense of foreboding. Perhaps her dreams were foretelling *Ragnarok*, the end of the world, when Fenris the wolf breaks his chains and devours the sun and moon, and the earth sinks beneath the sea, engulfed in blood and fire.

Anya took a deep breath to calm her pounding heart. In the milky light before a summer dawn, the great hall was quiet, save for the gentle snores of those around her in the women's quarters, and the much louder snores of the men asleep on the wall benches beyond the partition. Today would be a day of farewells. She would say goodbye to her home, her family, her friends and her place within the priesthood, and she wondered if she had the strength to bear it.

The light was subtly altering. Dawn was breaking. She cast her bedding to one side, dressed quickly and swung her cloak around her shoulders. She took a small loaf of bread from a basket upon the high table and crept from the great hall, taking care not to step on any sleeping bodies. Closing the heavy oak doors behind her, she followed the track that led to the priests' compound.

The place of healing was full of patients again. Athelwald's parting gift to her had been to release the refugees from the prisoner holding pens. Those deemed fit enough had been put to work in the fields, but many were still so weak they had returned to their beds.

Abberlen was seated at the table in the preparation room, carefully placing thin slivers of angelica root onto a wooden drying tray. His legs did not reach the floor and he was swinging them vigorously back and forth. The little boy looked up as Anya approached. He dropped his knife onto the table with a clatter and struggled down from the chair. Flinging his arms around her, he buried his head in her gown.

'Anya!'

She held him close and ruffled his soft, brown hair. He was as warm as a puppy. Gunther laughed merrily but Anya felt overwhelmed with sadness.

'Will you will permit him to stay?' she asked.

Gunther nodded. 'For certain. Abberlen is one of us now. He is a bright boy. He is already learning our tongue.'

Anya smiled with relief. 'I have something for you, Abberlen.'

The little boy looked up at her excitedly. Reaching into her draw string purse, she pulled out a tiny, wooden owl. She unfurled Abberlen's sticky fingers and placed the wood-carving in his palm.

'It's an owl,' she explained. 'He is the wisest of all the birds.'

'Thank you,' Abberlen said fervently and he hugged her again.

Anya knelt down beside him. 'I have to go away for a long time, but Gunther will take care of you, and I know you will be happy here.'

The little boy was staring at her curiously and she realised he did not understand what she was trying to tell him.

'You should go back to work, Abberlen,' she said brightly.

Abberlen nodded. 'Owl,' he repeated, savouring the sound of the unfamiliar word.

'Owl,' Anya agreed.

She watched him return to the table and clamber onto his chair. He sat the owl carefully on the table beside him, picked up his knife and began to slice the angelica again.

Gunther put a hand lightly on her shoulder. 'Don't fret, my dear. The boy will thrive here. Come. Let's leave him to his work.'

Anya glanced back at Abberlen. He was content in the place of healing, and she found some comfort in that. He would soon forget her, which was as it should be, but she suspected she would not forget him so easily. She cast a last lingering look around the place of healing, sealing its tranquillity and soothing scents into her memory, like a potion into a bottle.

'You are stronger than you know,' Gunther said suddenly.

'I would give anything not to leave Saxony,' Anya replied sadly. 'I will be so far away from everyone and everything I have ever known, and so far away from the goddess.'

'The goddess breathes life into every living thing,' Gunther said softly. 'She will always be with you, wherever you go. Never forget that.'

Fathers, mothers, brothers, sisters, wives and children gathered to watch Hengist muster his two-hundred-strong warband before the gates of Athelwald's stronghold. Anya mounted up with difficulty. She had little skill in the saddle and the brown mare, sensing her uncertainty, jittered nervously. She shortened the reins and rubbed the horse's neck, attempting to steady the animal.

The lump in Anya's throat was growing steadily and she blinked back the tears welling in her eyes. She was surrounded by so many familiar faces, so many poignant scenes of farewell. She glanced at the bracelet of red twine she had bound around her wrist earlier that morning, each strand blessed by a journey charm. Perhaps, if the gods were kind, it would keep Hengist's army safe on the road ahead.

She glanced curiously at her half-brother. He sat straight-backed upon a black stallion, beneath his newly crafted banner of the white wolf. Dressed for battle, he displayed the wealth of Saxony. His sword pommel and shoulder brooch were of gold inlaid with garnets. Lapis lazuli adorned his sword belt fastenings, and exquisite carvings of intertwined animal figures ran along the strips of gold upon his scabbard.

In sharp contrast to those around him, his expression was one of cold determination. If he had been disappointed by his father's decision to send him to Britannia, he gave no sign of it now. He held his head high, proud and aloof, giving every appearance of relishing his first command.

Anya turned in her saddle and gazed anxiously at Elsbet. The young girl had collapsed in her mother's arms, sobbing inconsolably. Anya's heart went out to her friend. Distracted, her grip loosened on the reins, and the mare began to sidestep wildly.

'Look to the animal!' Hengist shouted.

Anya jumped, startled by his sharp rebuke. She shortened the reins again, struggling to bring the animal under control.

Hengist shook his head patronisingly.

'You would be better travelling in the supply wagons.'

'No!' she replied indignantly. 'I will learn.'

'By all the gods, I wish you weren't coming with us. You're like shit on my boots - an unwelcome hanger-on.'

Anya's eyes widened. 'I-' she began, but Hengist had reined around and raised his right hand above his head. It was the signal to depart.

His warband marched away from Athelwald's stronghold beneath the fluttering banner of the white wolf. It was an impressive sight; massed ranks of riders and foot-soldiers bristling with spears. The people of Saxony left their villages to stand in awe as the high king's son rode by, but Anya noticed that Hengist kept his eyes straight ahead, and made no attempt to acknowledge them.

The sun reached its zenith in a cloudless sky, and the air felt as hot as a hearth. They rode on through small roadside villages that straddled fields of wheat, barley, beans and cabbages. She was relieved when Hengist made no attempt to ride with her and Horsa. He kept his distance, ignoring them as if they were no longer worthy of his company.

The sound of an army on the move was deafening. The drum of hooves and the measured tread of two hundred marching men reverberated like the earth's beating heart. Its pulse was hypnotic and Anya's mind began to drift. She yearned for the comfort of the great hall, for the sound of Elsbet's laughter at the fire side. But most of all she missed Emma, and burned with anger at the utter futility of her wasted life.

As the days passed, Horsa withdrew into himself, replying in monosyllables or often not at all, and Anya had never felt more alone. At the great Rhine delta, they crossed the river Waal by the ancient Roman bridge at Noviomagus. The Rhine marked the edge of the Roman world. Behind her lay Germania; ahead lay Gaul, a province of a fallen empire.

The people of Gaul were on the move. The old Roman road was a ribbon of refugees, doggedly heading in the opposite direction to Hengist's warband. Men, women and children, some on foot, others on farm carts drawn by oxen, piled with their belongings. They eyed Hengist's supply wagons with hungry eyes, but he rode on, ignoring them as if they were invisible. Anya wondered who these people were fleeing from. Was it the same men who had sent Abberlen's parents to meet their gods?

They reached the town of Bavacum at dusk. There were no earthen banks or wooden palisades, but stone defences so tall they reminded Anya of the mighty wall the gods had built to protect the world of men from the frost giants. The gates of the town were torn from their hinges. A pall of smoke clung to the blackened roofs, unburied bodies lay on the streets, and the stench of burning and decay was overwhelming.

Anya moved to dismount, but Horsa grasped her reins and shook his head. 'There is nothing to be done here.'

'But -' she began.

Horsa held fast to her reins. 'Believe me, these people are far beyond your help.'

She looked around at the devastation. A strong westerly wind was stirring up the layer of grey ash that had settled upon the town. She had no doubt that this was the work of the same men who had filled Abberlen's eyes with nightmares. She closed her eyes and said a silent prayer for the souls of the dead.

They did not linger in Bavacum. By day, Hengist sent out advance scouts, for he had no desire to march blindly into the path of the barbarian army. By night, he made camp in open countryside, ringed by hastily dug defences and patrolling guards. Cold and uncomfortable, Anya lay on her back and watched Nerthus, the brightest planet in the sky, as she sank steadily into the east. Nerthus was going home - to Saxony, to her people, and Anya's heart felt full of envy.

She had not slept well since they had ridden away from Saxony. The bare earth was a hard, unyielding bed fellow and when sleep did find her, it was often disturbed with nightmares of high mountains and blood. The dream had subtly altered of late.

More often than not, she saw a man, barely visible against the red-black sea of blood. His back was turned; she could not see his face. He seemed unaware of the devastation around him. She followed him through the village, her boots sinking into the rivulets of blood.

She walked faster but the figure was further away; she caught a glimpse of a black cloak as he disappeared from view once again. The blood was deeper now. She could feel herself sinking, pulled deeper into its gory torrent. But the figure continued to walk away, unharmed, untouched. Where his footsteps fell, the blood shrank back, recoiling as if it was afraid.

She glanced at Horsa. He was staring blankly into the flames of their camp fire. There was a far-away expression on his face and she knew he was thinking of Elsbet.

Anya sat up again. Glancing at her mother's copper ring, she began to twist it round and round her finger. Eown had never talked about her homeland. And Anya had never thought it strange, until now.

'Do you think mother was homesick for Britannia? Do you think she missed her kin?' she asked.

Horsa glanced at his sister. 'I imagine she must have.'

Anya nodded. She thought it a curious twist of fate that Eown had been born in a kingdom made of high mountains, whilst she, born on the flat plains of Saxony, had never even seen a mountain. Except in her dreams.

Horsa took another draft of wine from his leather bottle. 'You look tired, sister.'

She shrugged. 'I don't sleep well.'

'You're having nightmares. I hear you call out in your sleep.'

Horsa picked up her blanket and draped it around her shoulders. 'Try to get some rest.'

'I worry about Abberlen,' she said suddenly.

'Who?'

'The little refugee boy in the place of healing.'

Horsa's eyes softened. 'The priests will take care of him. Here, drink this. It might help you sleep.' He held out the leather bottle.

She took a sip and shuddered at the wine's bitter taste.

Horsa laughed. 'It's foul, isn't it? I thought the Gauls were famous for their wine, but this is vinegar.'

She handed him back the leather bottle. 'Thank you, but one sip is enough.'

Horsa turned his head slightly. 'Can you smell it?'

Anya sniffed. She could smell the unwashed bodies of two hundred warriors. She could smell watery stew in blackened cooking pots, and fire smoke drifting in the wind.

'What?' she asked curiously.

'The sea. We're close now.'

Anya sniffed the air again. 'What does it smell of?'

'Salt, and fish on a strong westerly wind,' Horsa replied.

Anya had never seen the sea, although as a child she had enjoyed stories about Frey the adventurer-god. His ship sailed through both sea and air, and it was crafted with such skill that it could be folded up like cloth and placed in his pocket.

Anya sighed, homesickness creeping over her again. Each day they had travelled further from Germania, further from home, and the sea crossing would take them further still. Pulling up the blanket around her shoulders, she lay down and closed her eyes.

ELEVEN

They reached the coast the following day. Four ships were moored at the edge of the water, awaiting Hengist's men, and the turn of the tide. Single masted, square rigged and clinker built, their wide, flat hulls sat sturdily in the shallows like a row of sleeping ducks. Anya dismounted, and stared at the sea for a long time. She had heard stories that the sea could roar and foam like an angry beast, but today it appeared gentle and subdued. It lapped onto a wide, flat beach that stretched as far as the eye could see. It was a vast, desolate place, mile after mile of windswept dunes, wading birds and crying gulls.

A man was striding across the beach, waving his arms above his head.

'Greetings! Greetings! My name is Cato, ship's captain, at your service. A fine day for a crossing, and no mistake!' Cato hissed like a snake, because most of his front teeth were missing. 'I have four of the finest cogs this side of Bononia, all ready for you, and you'll not find a better, braver crew.'

Anya bit her lip nervously.

'Oh, now then, don't you be a-feared, my princess,' the captain hissed. 'I knows what I'm about. This is my son, Cato Junior, and together we'll see you safe to shore.'

Cato Junior stared sullenly at the Saxons. Anya noticed that his gaze dropped to the bags of coins that dangled from Hengist's belt.

'You would do well to be afraid,' the boy muttered. 'The northern sea is like a woman. You never know what she's going to do next.'

'Shut up, Junior,' Cato said under his breath then turned quickly to Anya. 'Smile, princess!' A spray of spittle flew between the gap in his teeth and landed on his salt-swollen lips.

Anya had to force herself not to step back a pace, for the man stank like five day old fish. Cato waded into the shallows and slapped the side of the nearest ship.

'Look at the height of her. I'd like to see any pirate try to ram us, or board us, or gut us from neck to navel. These ships keep us safe, and no mistake.'

Hengist's nose wrinkled with obvious distaste as he dropped a bag of coin into the captain's outstretched hand.

'Enough prattling!' Hengist said sharply. 'Start loading. I do not want to miss the tide.'

They put to sea in a westerly wind, the four ships holding a steady line over the gentle onshore waves. The sea was the colour of jade, and sunlight sparkled on the white caps. The wind was tugging Anya's hair from her face, whipping it around her cheeks, and she felt her fear slipping away, replaced by a sense of exhilaration. She raised a hand and waved at Horsa on the next ship. He waved back.

The air was full of noise; the wind tugging and snapping at the sail, Cato and his son bickering at the rudder, the surge of water across the bow. Anya took a deep breath and the sea-wind filled her lungs. It smelled of fish and salt, and freedom.

Quite suddenly, she understood why merchants' eyes shone when they talked of the sights they had seen, and the oceans they had sailed.

She looked up. Seagulls swooped above them, circling like the buzzards over the fields of Saxony. The cog approached the next wave. At the crest it seemed to hesitate for a brief speck of time, before it sailed towards the trough. Her stomach heaved along with the cog, and she gripped the clinker planking to steady herself.

The coast line of Gaul was rapidly receding, bobbing in and out of view as the ship rose and fell. Anya stared at the waves smacking the bow. She had heard stories of mermaids who lured men to their deaths with their beautiful, haunting siren songs. She didn't think she believed in mermaids, but then again, the sea looked very deep. The bards told of Loki's son, the great serpent, that lay on the sea bed coiled full round the earth, biting its own tail. Who was to say what sea monsters lurked beneath her feet in the dark murky depths beneath the keel?

Horsa's ship was further away now, and although she waved again, he did not see her. She took another deep breath of the sea air. It smelled fresh and clean, untainted by midden pits and dung heaps. Hengist's soldiers sat at mid-ship. Some were playing at dice, their laughter carrying above the gusting wind; others were sleeping, their heads lolling against the clinker planking.

Anya sat down on a cross timber and wrapped her cloak tightly about herself. It had taken a long time to reach the coast. Seventeen long days in the saddle, and seventeen long nights of broken sleep, tormented by unsettling dreams. She yawned loudly, and closed her eyes.

She awoke to the sound of Cato shouting. She stood up

unsteadily and shivered. The sun had been shining when she had fallen asleep, but a blanket of flat, grey cloud now covered the sky. The sea looked cold, grey and ominous without the sun upon it. The wind had picked up and there were black clouds on the horizon. They seemed to be erupting from the sea itself like a monstrous birth and as she watched, they grew taller and fatter, as if nurtured by the wind. Her eyes were watering now and her face felt numb. She tried in vain to hold her long hair in check, but it lashed wildly against her cheeks. A fierce gust knocked her back a step, and she stumbled into Hengist.

'Watch where you're going!' he snapped.

'Prepare to come about!' Cato shouted. 'Move yourself, my princess unless you want to lose your pretty head.'

Hengist manhandled her towards the stern. His soldiers moved aside to let them pass. They had been full of banter not an hour since but were quieter, more wary now. The ship crested another swell. It heaved then sank heavily into the trough. Anya slid awkwardly across the wet keel and Hengist caught her before she fell.

'Sit down, before you fall down,' he said roughly then looked up at the sky. 'This is going to get a lot worse.'

'Too close to the wind!' Cato shouted.

Anya followed Hengist's gaze. The black clouds were no longer on the horizon. They were just off the bow, and racing towards them as if propelled by the gods themselves. The sea had come to life, rough and choppy as if a giant ladle was stirring it from on high. A wave crashed over the bow and surged the length of the ship. It swirled and sloshed around her boots, frothing and foaming like a weir after rain. The ship rolled and listed, and her stomach heaved again.

'We should try to outrun it. See if we can find calmer

waters!' Cato Junior shouted above the roar of the wind.

'We'll do no such thing!' Cato yelled. Tiny droplets of salty water clung like snowflakes to his straggly beard and bristling nose hair. 'If we run with this wind we'll be back on the shores of Gaul before you can say 'coward'. I want his purse of gold, not a flogging until I bleed.'

'Then heave-to, for God's sake, father,' Cato Junior pleaded.

'Are you mad? All it takes is one breaker and we'd pitch-poll like a dolphin. Don't argue with me, boy. We will beat to the wind.'

Cato Junior's eyes widened with fear. 'But, father -'

'Don't 'but' me, boy. A storm can sense your fear, and by all the gods, I'm not afraid of this one.'

'I am,' Anya thought, *'I'm very afraid.'* She looked at Cato Junior, and she realised that he was too. Cato had called this gale 'a storm', and she had heard terrible tales of whole fleets of ships lost at sea to unforgiving storms.

The ship lifted and slewed with such force that she fell to her hands and knees. She tried to stand up but the boat pitched again, and she slid further towards the stern, choking as the salt water surged down her throat. For a brief moment, the wind calmed, but it was merely a prelude to the rain. It arrived suddenly and violently, huge droplets that pierced the waves like arrows. The rain turned to hail; huge, hard balls of ice that battered the ship's wet planks and stung her cheeks.

Thunder cracked, lightning flashed and the sea lit up, silhouetting the seething clouds, foaming silver against the black sky. Tor, the warrior-god of the storm, was riding his chariot across the heavens and she stared in awe. She had never seen anything quite so beautiful and terrifying in equal measure.

The soldiers were crouching at mid-ship now, hail bouncing fiercely from the shields they held above their heads. Cato and his son were struggling to reef the sail, their shouts carried away by the howling wind. Another wave hit the ship, and its timbers creaked and groaned. Water surged the length of the keel, stirring up the hail stones. It surged over the cross timber, lashing Anya's face with icy water. Her eyes stung and her throat burned from the bitter salt.

She gripped the side of the ship and hauled herself upright. She had not understood much of Cato and his son's argument, but she knew they were not running away from the storm. They were facing it head on, tacking a torturous and painfully slow route through the heaving sea. And the storm was fighting back with all its raw, angry power.

She felt her stomach heave again, and she turned just in time to vomit over the side. Her fingers gripped the shiny wet planks, and she stared blankly at the foaming, churning sea as it swirled and boiled beneath her. There was no sign of the other ships, and her heart lurched as violently as the waves.

Where was Horsa? Was he safe?

She looked up at the sky. The storm was all around them now, full of noise and fury, enveloping them in its strong arms. Compared to its overwhelming power, the ship was a tiny irrelevant speck upon the ocean. How could they hope to survive this? Confronting the storm was like fighting against the gods, and how could mere mortals hope to win such a battle? Had she escaped death in the sacred grove only to meet it on the northern sea?

'Bare poles!' Cato yelled.

Anya wiped the rain from her eyes, and watched the captain and his son take down the already tattered sail. Cato had sworn he was not afraid, but it seemed the storm had defeated him. Anya wondered if this was the end, if this was how she would die, but moments later, Cato bellowed:

'Out oars!'

Hengist's soldiers were sliding awkwardly to the sides of the ship to join Cato's crew at the oars. Many of the Saxons had never lifted an oar before, and Cato Junior was roaring orders at them. He had attached himself to one of the ship's mooring rings by a rope tied about his waist.

'What the hell do you think you're doing?' Cato shouted at his son. 'Do you want the fishes to feed on your pimply skin? If you go overboard you'll take us all down with you, you stupid arse!' Cato took his dagger from his belt and sawed through the rope about his son's waist. 'Now, get to an oar!'

'Me, father? I'm not a galley slave!'

'Neither are these soldiers, but they'll damn well row until their palms bleed, unless they fancy spending the rest of their days in a watery cave being buggered senseless by mer-men.'

Cato Junior picked up an oar.

Cato turned to Hengist's men. 'Just one thing to remember, boys. Keep the bow head-on to these swells. It only takes one breaker over the side, and we're all done for.'

Anya sank down onto the cross timber again. Her cloak was soaked and she was drenched to the skin. Her fingers and toes were numb, and her teeth were chattering. Lightning lit up the sky again and, moments later, thunder boomed overhead.

Cato stood at the bow, roaring encouragement to Hengist's men who rowed as one now, their faces masks of pain, their muscles burning with the agony of rowing against the storm.

Hengist staggered awkwardly to her side. 'Make yourself useful, and pray to the gods, Anya. Pray that they will deliver us safely from this tempest.'

Anya stared at him. In Saxony, there had been certainty in her life but she felt no such certainty today. Instead, she felt very alone, and very afraid. Hengist shook his head in disgust and walked away from her. Anya blew warm breath on her numb hands. She suspected Tor, the fierce and warlike god of the storm, thought Hengist's warband was too small and insignificant to save. But nevertheless, she closed her eyes and prayed to him. She told him there was nothing insignificant about the love Horsa and Elsbet shared, nor the devotion Hengist's warriors felt for their wives and children.

'I see land!' Cato Junior shouted.

Anya tugged her drenched, matted hair from her eyes and peered at the horizon. A faint sliver of grey bobbed in and out of sight on the horizon.

Britannia.

Had the god of the storm listened to her prayers?

She stood up unsteadily. The air was not so full of noise and anger now. The wind had dropped and the sea was calmer. The storm was no longer overhead; it was behind them, sweeping across the sea towards the coast of Gaul. Was it possible they were going to survive this? Was it possible she would live to see her mother's birthplace after all? She stared at the rapidly approaching coastline. She had expected to live and die in Germania, never imagining she would be forced to make a new life on a troubled, warring island. Had the gods sent her here for a reason, or had Nerthus abandoned her the moment she left Germania?

TWELVE

The south coast of Britannia

The rain lessened as the tug of the onshore waves jerked the ship unevenly to the shore. Anya half climbed, half fell onto the sand and she swayed, her body confused by the world's sudden lack of motion. Unlike the silent fields of Saxony, the beach was deafeningly loud. The sea roared, the wind howled like wolves and the seagulls shrieked like the evil banshees that dwelled in the dark forest. Anya's drenched gown and cloak weighed her down and her sodden leather boots sank into the water-logged sand. Her relief at surviving the sea crossing was quickly tempered by exhaustion, hunger and fear.

What was she doing here?

Still out at sea, beyond the breaking waves, she could see Cato's three other ships, and she prayed Horsa was safe. She looked about her. A fine rain fell from a leaden sky onto a dull, flat beach that stretched for miles. Britannia was colourless; grey sand lapped by a cold grey sea, merging into a grey horizon. Several small fishing boats had been dragged above the high tide line, and nets were draped on the rocks.

Beyond a low bank of dunes, dotted with tufts of dune

grasses, stood a huge, stone-built fort. She guessed it was one of the forts Athelwald had spoken of, constructed by the Romans to guard the southern coast of Britannia against the pirates of the German tribes. It dominated the sky, its high walls undamaged by the passing of the years. She stared nervously at its forbidding towers, but there was no sign of life.

Cato hurried by her. His dark curls were more bedraggled than ever.

'Thank you for saving our lives,' she said through her chattering teeth.

'I told you there was no cause to worry,' Cato replied brightly. 'She was a bitch of a storm, but here we are, safe and sound. But I won't be staying long on this God forsaken island. The barbarians of Britannia make the eastern tribes look like Christ's heavenly angels.'

Cato paused, and scratched his arm. 'Why have you come to Britannia, princess?'

'My brothers are to serve in Vortigern's warband.'

'Then God help you all,' Cato replied fervently. 'Vortigern's very name is feared on this island. They say he dreams of being king of all Britannia and will kill anyone who stands in his way -' Cato broke off. 'Talk of the devil.'

Three horsemen, bearing the distinctive mark of a black boar upon their shields and cuirasses, were riding along the track that ran parallel to the beach. They reined in and one of the soldiers dismounted. He began to clamber down the dunes, his boots sliding through the wet sand.

'Vortigern's men,' Cato said grimly. 'You see the emblem of the black boar upon their shields?'

Anya eyed the soldier curiously. She had never seen a Briton before. His face was beardless and his hair cropped short but in his manner of dress, he looked much like a Saxon.

The soldier bowed before Hengist. He was out of breath from his long ride.

'I am sent by Vortigern, high king of the Dobunni, to give word to Hengist, son of Athelwald, high king of Saxony. Are you that man?' He spoke in the Latin tongue but with a strange, clipped accent.

'I am Hengist, son of Athelwald.'

'We have been waiting for you. We were expecting you to land further down the coast. When the storm came, we feared the worst. God be praised for your safe deliverance. Allow me to give you this, Sir.' He handed Hengist a parchment map. 'Vortigern looks forward to welcoming you to Britannia. He awaits you in Calleva Atrebatum.'

Hengist unfurled the map. 'Calleva?' he repeated, staring blankly at the unfamiliar map.

'Yes, Sir. The roads are passable at this time of the year. It should be a three day ride, no more.'

The soldier made to leave but Hengist called after him. 'What do you know of the fort?' He nodded towards the imposing stone edifice.

'It's deserted, as far as I know, Sir.'

Hengist watched Vortigern's men ride away, then he stared at the old Roman fort for a long time, lost in thought.

A short time later, the three remaining ships reached the shore, and Anya ran across the sand to greet Horsa. Her head fell against his sodden leather cuirass. Despite the drenching from the sea, he still smelled familiar, of home.

'I thought we were all going to die,' Anya whispered.

Horsa nodded grimly. 'I was *certain* we were going to die. I know now why the gods did not give Germania a sea.'

Hengist's men used ropes to haul the ships up beyond the tide mark, lit fires from driftwood, and erected their tents. Anya heaved her cloak from her shoulders and slung it over a rock. She held out her ice-cold hands towards a spluttering driftwood fire, grateful for its meagre warmth.

With the ships safely above the tide line, Hengist addressed his men. 'Since the Romans departed this land, these people have looked to their own defences, so we must treat this land as hostile. Post guards -' he began but stopped in mid-sentence.

Five men were walking along the top of the dunes from the direction of the fort. Their dark hair was cut short in the Roman style and Anya saw that they wore the long, hooded, woollen cloaks Britannia had always been so famous for, exported across the breadth of the Empire. She watched Hengist's right hand settle on the hilt of his sword.

'They may come in peace,' she whispered. 'They have no show of arms.'

'But what do they hide beneath those cloaks?'

'Perhaps they wear cloaks because it's raining,' she persisted, under her breath.

But Hengist wasn't listening. He nodded to his chosen bodyguards and they hastened to his side.

The small group of Britons made their way through the dunes and stood before Hengist and Horsa. Despite their drenching from the sea, the Saxons were a fearsome sight; their sword belts ornate with lapis lazuli in gold filigree, their helmets intricately engraved by Athelwald's finest craftsmen, their shield bosses the glaring heads of monstrous beasts.

By contrast, the five Britons looked more like humble scribes than soldiers. One of them stepped forward. He carried himself with dignity and bearing but Anya could see the fear in his eyes. She thought these men were very brave to face an army of two hundred Saxon warriors.

'We are from the fort of Andereida. We have heard news of a host come to serve Vortigern. Are you that host?' He spoke in the same clipped Latin as the soldier, and Anya realised he must be speaking with the accent of Britannia.

'Serve?' Hengist repeated incredulously, in Latin. 'I am no slave!'

Anya felt certain Hengist had misunderstood what the Briton was trying to say. She stepped forward apprehensively.

'He means no offence. He has come to welcome -' she began but Hengist rounded on her.

'Be silent!'

He turned back to the Briton, his hand straying once again to his sword hilt. 'How many of you in the fort?'

The Briton's eyes flickered to his companions. 'We are not a military garrison. We are a small group of families who have chosen to live behind high walls for security in these troubled times. We have nothing of value. We are no threat to you, we are unarmed and I humbly beseech you to allow us to live in peace.'

Hengist took a step closer. 'I asked you a question. How many in the fort?'

The Briton took a step backwards, his hand fumbling inside his cloak. Hengist reacted instantly. He drew his sword and in the space of a heartbeat, he had thrust it, both hands hard on the hilt, through the Briton's heart. Hengist stared the man in the eye, their noses just inches apart.

'I am slave to no man.'

He pulled the sword from the Briton's chest, blood spraying out across the sand, and the man fell dead at

Hengist's feet, a look of terrible surprise on his face. The four remaining Britons turned and fled towards the dunes. Hengist waved a hand derisively in their direction and his bodyguards ran after them and cut their throats with military precision. Anya felt as if her blood had frozen in her veins. Hengist leant forward and whispered in her ear.

'Contradict me in front of my men again, sister, and my face will be the last thing you see.'

Their eyes locked in a silent battle, but it was Anya who looked away first and knelt down beside the dead man. She gently pulled aside his blood-soaked cloak. The Briton held neither a sword nor a dagger in his hand but a neatly rolled scroll. She untied the hemp string that bound it, unrolled the vellum and glanced at the neatly scribed Latin text. Then she stood up to face Hengist and thrust the scroll broadside against his chest.

'He was not armed. He was trying to show you this.'

'What is it?' Hengist asked irritably. He had never learnt the skill of reading and nor had any of his kin. It was a skill passed down to the priests alone, who fiercely guarded the power it gave them over the high kings.

Anya read the vellum quickly. Vortigern had permitted the men and their families to live within the fort on condition they acted as his eyes and ears on the sea, sending word of each and every passing merchant ship or pirate galley.

'It's a legal document bestowing upon the community the fort and the land surrounding it,' she replied.

'Well, we will have their fort and all within it.'

'But they are unarmed civilians!' Anya replied, shocked.

Hengist's hand came down on her shoulder like a vice.

'You have no authority here, Anya. You are a woman under my protection and you will keep your opinions to yourself. I hadn't realised you are so naïve. Kingship is all about war. Our father is not high king thanks to his bread making skills. He defeats any man who dares oppose him. There is no place for compassion or mercy.'

Hengist made to walk away but suddenly turned to face her again. 'I intend to make my mark on this god-forsaken island and no-one,' he jabbed her shoulder forcefully. '*No-one* will stand in my way. I tell you, the people of Britannia will live to regret the day Vortigern chose to invite Saxon wolves into the sheep pen.'

Anya watched her half-brother walk away to join his men. She did not need the gift of Sight to see the bloodshed that lay ahead. Hengist had called her naïve. Was he right? Did she owe her previous life of comfort and privilege to her father's skill on the battlefield, rather than his learning or compassion?

During her years at the priests' school, she had learnt to recite the ancient poems and songs of her people. She understood the movements of the constellations and she knew how to read their omens. She knew how to listen to the gods who inhabited the wind, the waves, the trees, the plants. They spoke of balance, of stability and of healing, but never once had she heard them demand war or death.

No, Hengist was wrong. A world with no compassion or mercy was a place of darkness and despair.

The sea had settled, now as flat and calm as a mill pond. Anya sat down beside Horsa and took a sip of watery soup. It was straight from the pot and it burned her tongue. Hurriedly, she put the wooden beaker down on the wet sand. Her skin was covered in a powdery sheen of dried sea salt and it itched mercilessly. She ran a tentative hand over her tangled hair. It felt as knotted and as dry as rope.

Horsa was watching his half-brother through narrowed eyes. 'He means to take the fort.'

Perhaps he will reconsider,' Anya said hopefully, although in her heart, she knew that he would not.

Horsa shook his head. 'My brother and I are very different. He wants his own gift throne. He wants to be a king.' Horsa prodded the struggling fire with a piece of driftwood, but only succeeded in making more smoke and fewer flames. 'I'll fight Vortigern's battles for him and I'll fight them well, just as father taught me. But I don't seek fame or glory. I just want enough land to build a fine hall for Elsbet and the children I hope the gods will grant us.' Horsa's eyes blazed with quiet determination.

Anya smiled. 'You fight for a fine cause, Horsa. I can think of none better.'

Horsa was watching his half-brother again. Anya followed his gaze. Hengist was mustering his men. Without another word, Horsa stood up and adjusted his sword belt.

'Horsa, there are women and children in there. Please don't do this.'

'I fight in Hengist's warband now. I obey his commands. He would sooner run me through than listen to my objections. Wait here with Cato. I fear this will not take long.'

Anya watched Horsa as he walked across the sand to join his half-brother. Her mind was churning with indecision. At length, she stood up and hurried to Hengist's side.

'I need to talk to you,' she began.

'Go away, sister. Tend the fire, or fetch more fresh water.'

Anya held her ground. 'It's important.'

Hengist manoeuvred her out of the earshot of his men.

'Well?'

'Leave them be,' she pleaded. 'You don't have to do this.'

'You still have so much to learn about life, Anya,' Hengist said coldly. 'I need this stronghold as a landing base for reinforcements and supplies. I don't intend to answer to Vortigern for any longer than is necessary.'

'There must be another way to resolve this without using force. I know you are impatient to make your mark, but there will be plenty of opportunities to prove yourself to your men.'

Hengist could barely contain his outrage. 'I will hear no more from you, Anya!' The back of his hand was raised as if to strike her but he hesitated, lowered his hand to his side and marched back to his men.

With frustration boiling in her veins, Anya went to join Cato and his fellow mariners. He moved aside to make a place for her beside the camp fire.

'I have heard old Tincommius got a knife in the gut in a backstreet brawl in Massilia. Not surprising. He was a tetchy old devil -' Cato looked up suddenly. Hengist was standing beside him.

'I need one of your masts,' Hengist said curtly.

Cato laughed and the other mariners joined in.

'Keep laughing and I'll rip out your tongue.'

Cato's laughter died in his throat. 'What do you want a mast for?'

'I need it to break down the gate of that fort over there.' Hengist pointed across the sand dunes.

'If you want a battering ram, look to the forest over yonder,' Cato replied.

Anya shifted uncomfortably. Cato was unwittingly digging his own grave.

'Listen to me,' Hengist said benignly. 'If you bring me your broadest mast, I will permit your hairy head to remain on top of your scrawny shoulders. Do we have an accord?'

Anya stood on top of the sand dunes and watched Hengist and his men march along the road towards the fort. Their close formation was creating a protective barrier around the soldiers carrying Cato's mast upon their shoulders. Horsa was marching at Hengist's side - she caught a glimpse of his distinctive red hair, and her throat dried with fear. The fort looked impregnable and ominously silent. Strong bastions, perhaps meant for heavy artillery, had been added to each corner of its towering grey walls. Was it manned by defenceless families, as the Briton had said, or were there soldiers waiting for Horsa on the other side of those heavy gates?

The Saxons were perhaps thirty paces from the gate-house before she heard Hengist's warning cry.

'Look out above!'

The first spear thrown from the battlements fell short.

'Keep going! Keep moving forward!' Hengist bellowed. 'And close up!'

A second spear thudded into a soldier's shield, knocking him into the path of the man behind him. He wrenched at the spear in vain, before giving up and casting his shield aside. As they approached the gate, the defenders began to hurl a furious stream of spears down upon the Saxons.

'Close up!' Hengist roared again. 'Raise shields!'

Another volley fell as Hengist's men began to unleash the mast against the heavy oak gate. Anya couldn't see Horsa now but she could imagine him, surrounded by soldiers, all crushed tightly together. She knew there was nothing for them to do but hold their ground and hope the gate fell quickly. Again and again, Hengist's men drew back the mast and smashed it into the oak gates with an ear shattering thud.

Put your backs into it!' Hengist shouted.

A large stone flew hard and fast and bounced off a Saxon shield. Anya realised the defenders had used up all their spears and were using sling shot now. There was a howl of pain as another stone found a gap and smashed a man's nose to a bloody pulp.

Above the shouts from the men on the battlements, and the deafening din of stones and rocks bouncing off raised shields, Anya heard the gate begin to splinter under the mighty toll of Cato's mast. Her heart sank. She knew Horsa didn't enjoy killing. She knew he took no pleasure in it. She suspected he hated the moments before a battle most of all, when there was still time to think about what was to come, before the world shrank to a split second choice between kill or be killed.

'Keep together and go in hard. I don't need prisoners!'

The oak gates tore from their rusting hinges, groaning as they fell. The Saxons charged forward, clambering over the shattered wood. The sounds of battle rose from the fort and Anya's blood ran cold. Men shouted in the chaos; frantic, barked instruction. Iron clashed with iron. She heard screams, the heart-wrenching sounds of men dying in agony. And then a different sound - the yelps of a terrified child, cut brutally, horrifically short. The sound tore through Anya's heart. Instinctively, and without any conscious thought, she began to run towards the fort.

'Now then, lassie. You stop where you are!' Cato called after her. 'You don't want to be going in there. I'll wager it's no place for a woman right now.'

Anya ignored him.

'Princess!' Cato yelled anxiously. 'It's too late! Stop!'

But Anya did not stop. Nearer the gate-house, the road was strewn with abandoned shields pierced by spears. Her heart was beating rapidly as she clambered over the fallen gate. Within the high walls, the courtyard was littered with bodies. Hengist's soldiers were walking amongst them, putting a sword to any who still breathed.

Anya came to an abrupt halt, dazed with shock. The air smelled like a butcher's block. Cato was right. She was too late. Horsa came to her side, his face grave. His long red hair was dark with sweat from the exertion of killing. There was blood on his leather cuirass, on his sleeves, his hands.

'Are you hurt?' she asked anxiously.

'It's not my blood. The Briton on the beach lied. This place was manned by a garrison of Vortigern's soldiers.' He paused. 'What are you doing here, Anya? I told you to stay on the beach.'

Anya glanced at her brother. She knew him well, every nuance and every expression. He looked guilty and ashamed.

'What happened here?' she asked.

Horsa laughed humourlessly. 'You need to ask?' He waved a hand carelessly around the courtyard. Hengist's men were piling bodies onto a wagon. Some bore the black boar upon their cuirasses, but there was a boy-child amongst the blood-soaked corpses.

'After we'd fought our way through Vortigern's men, we came face to face with a group of civilians - grandfathers, fathers and sons.' Horsa's voice was flat. 'Some were armed with swords and spears, but many had only pitchforks or staffs. They wore no armour, and held no shields. It was a massacre.'

'You killed children?' Anya asked, appalled.

Horsa shook his head. 'No, I didn't. I sheathed my sword. As far as I'm concerned, killing soldiers is an acceptable evil. Killing innocent civilians is most definitely not.'

'Are they all dead? Even the women and children?' Anya asked in stunned disbelief.

Horsa shook his head and pointed across the courtyard to a large, stone-built building. 'I think they are in there – that's the building the civilians died trying to protect. Hengist hasn't touched them yet - but by the time these soldiers have finished with them, they'll wish they had died along with their men folk.'

Anya looked up at her brother. 'I cannot let that happen.'

'No! Anya! No!' Horsa called after her, but she was already striding across the bloodied cobbles. The soldier guarding the door was a huge man. He towered over her, like an ancient standing stone.

'Stand aside,' Anya demanded.

'My orders are to allow no-one to enter unless the Lord Hengist commands it.'

'I am the daughter of Athelwald, high king of Saxony, and you would do well not to disobey me.'

The soldier bowed his head and stepped aside. Anya opened the door. The hall was sparsely furnished and smelled of damp. The glass had fallen from the windows long ago, and been replaced by roughly hewn shutters that made the room feel dark and cold. Wooden boxes lined the walls, filled with neat rows of upright vellum scrolls. Anya thought they looked sad; obsolete vestiges of the order that was once Roman authority, now quietly gathering dust.

At least thirty women and children were huddled together in the far corner. She noticed that their eyes were strangely blank, as if they had all known this day would come, all known it was only a matter of time. A young man was standing beside them. He was clean shaven, his hair was cut short, and he wore a simple, floor length tunic of rough wool.

There was a book in his hand and he held it in front of him like a talisman. 'So the pagan pirates send a woman to do their foul work,' he said, in Latin.

'I mean you no harm. I am here to help,' Anya replied.

'If you truly wish to help us, then get into your ships and sail away! You will never take this land from us. Your pagan gods will not harm us. They are mere figments of your barbaric, murderous imaginations. They are nothing compared to the healing, redemptive power that the love of our Lord Jesus Christ can bestow!'

'Anya!' It was Hengist. 'What are you doing?'

Anya turned to face her brother. His eyes were unnaturally bright. His blood lust was high, still pumping through his veins after the short, sharp slaughter in the courtyard.

'I accept these people are now your slaves, but you must not harm them.' Anya's voice was calm, but her heart was pounding fiercely against her ribs. 'And you will show the women respect – each and every one of them.'

'How dare you tell me what to do? My men have served me well today. These women will be their just rewards!'

Anya shook her head. 'These women will be necessary to harvest the fields for the garrison you intend to leave here. Treat them well, Hengist. I tell you, the goddess demands it.'

Hengist froze in his tracks. His face fell and she saw sudden, paralyzing uncertainty in his eyes.

'Hengist is afraid of the goddess – and so he is also afraid of me,' Anya thought. *'And he hates that he is afraid of me – for I am his base-born half-sister, not worthy of note.'*

A strong sense of foreboding was beginning to knot her stomach. She was placing her brother in an intolerable position and she knew it was a dangerous game to play.

Hengist rubbed his cheek. One of the soldiers of the black

boar had charged at him, slamming an old Roman shield hard into his jaw. He spat and a tooth covered with blood hit the floor tiles inches from Anya's feet.

She took a deep breath. 'We should settle this here, brother. You would not want your men to know you denied the wishes of the goddess. You would not want them to think you were cursed by her wrath.'

Hengist's eyes locked menacingly upon hers for what seemed an age. 'They will not be harmed,' he grunted at last.

'Do you swear, before the goddess?'

'I swear.' Hengist turned on his heel, slamming the door behind him.

Anya's hands were shaking. She knew her half-brother well enough to realise there would be a high price to pay for this small victory.

The Christian priest was staring at her incredulously. 'You are not what I expected.'

Anya turned to face him. 'What did you expect?'

'We were told to prepare ourselves for heathen priests driven insane from a diet of human blood.'

'I thought it was the Christians who drank blood? The blood of Christ?' Anya asked, confused.

The priest looked affronted. 'Christ is not a mortal man. He is the son of God.'

Anya was too exhausted to engage in a philosophical discussion. 'I apologise if I caused you offence, but I have met very few Christians. I must leave you now, but I wish you good fortune, Sir.'

'Thank you for saving the lives of these women and children,' the priest said quietly.

She sighed. 'I've done all I can. I hope it will be enough.'

THIRTEEN

They left the fort of Andereida two days later, leaving behind a small garrison to stake their claim, and the women and children to repair the gates, tend the fields and bury their dead. They followed the old Roman road, straight as an arrow across the countryside. Grass was beginning to sprout between the cobbles, and the frost of the previous winters had gouged it with pot holes. The thanes rode on horses taken from the stables of Andereida, the soldiers went on foot. The sun glinted off the massed ranks of their tall spears, as if a dazzling crop of iron had uprooted itself and now marched along the length of the old road.

Since leaving Germania, Anya had learnt that homesickness was a truly descriptive word. She missed her homeland so badly that she felt physically ill; listless, wretched and miserable, with a hollow ache in the pit of her stomach that refused to go away. She didn't want to be here. Everything about this country felt alien. The light was different, paler, less intense than Germania. Even the air felt wrong, with its salty tang of the sea and its fierce buffeting wind. She belonged in Germania, and she wanted to go home. But she couldn't go home. Not now. Not ever.

Southern Britannia baked under a cloudless sky as they

marched north. Sweet scented cow-parsley and bright yellow dandelions crowded the verges. Vast tracts of land were covered with dense forest, where the temperature dropped like a stone, the trees a shield against the sunlight. But when the road emerged from the forest, fallow fields of ragwort and poppies grew towards the sun.

They stopped in a small village that straddled both sides of the road. Anya took a few mouthfuls of water from her leather water bottle and watched Hengist's foot soldiers break ranks to chase the village chickens. They wrung their necks and slung them across their shields for the evening's cooking pot.

The village was eerily silent; no children played in the shade, no women gathered around the well, no men worked in the fields. They were hiding from Hengist and his warband. They were hiding from her. She attached her water bottle to her belt again with a heavy heart. She did not want to be a part of any of this. She was meant to heal, not slaughter.

They left the sea behind, climbing to sweeping uplands where the air smelled sweet with the drifting scent of yellow gorse. They passed many villas. Some were still inhabited, but water no longer trickled from lichen covered fountains and chickens scratched at the dandelions between the statues of forgotten emperors. Their once grand courtyards now housed goats and pigs, and piles of steaming manure. Finely carved wooden doors had been torn from their hinges to create a track-way over the mud.

Many more villas were deserted and falling into ruin. Weeds sprouted along their graceful colonnades and nettles clambered over tangled heaps of rusting farm implements. Anya decided she hated this island the Romans had called Britannia. There was too much decay, too much fear.

They reached Calleva on the evening of the third day. The town stood on a gentle rise in the land of the Atrebates, its high walls towering over the surrounding fields. An amphitheatre stood just beyond its walls and Anya glanced inside as they rode by. Over its long years of neglect, moss had crept along the stone benches and tall grasses filled the arena. She thought it looked a sad and desolate place, and she felt a sudden pang of melancholy. The amphitheatre reminded her of home, of standing before the council of Saxony, alone and afraid, waiting to learn her fate.

Anya tore herself from her memories and focussed on the man on horseback who was waiting to greet them. As they drew nearer the east gate, he trotted forward.

'I am here to escort you to Vortigern, high king of the Dobunni. My name is Rufus Aufidius, his second in command,' he said, in Latin.

Anya doubted the man was a soldier for he wore no armour over his tunic and breeches, and no sword hung at his plain leather belt. His black hair hung to his shoulders, hiding much of his pallid, clean shaven face. Thin and small of stature, he was unremarkable in appearance, but there was nothing unremarkable about his keen, intelligent eyes. He reminded her of a hawk; she sensed very little would escape his notice.

Rufus looked Hengist up and down coldly but his gaze lingered over Anya's slender frame, and she stared back at him, shocked and embarrassed. At home in Saxony, no man would have dared look at the daughter of the high king with such blatant appraisal.

'Your men are to be billeted in the fort,' Rufus said curtly. 'And you are to come with me.'

Anya kicked her mare forward, looking about in

fascination. Calleva was nothing like her father's stronghold. Soaring towers and high walls blocked out the sun. If she had not known better, it would have been easy to believe this city built of stone was the work of gods or giants.

The street ran alongside a temple precinct and continued uphill, lined with rows of decaying buildings. Roof tiles were falling, daub walls disintegrating to reveal the rotten wattle beneath, and piles of refuse spilled onto the cobbles. Anya experienced a growing sense of unease. She was surrounded by cold brick and tile. There was not enough earth or grass or timber. The town made her feel trapped, as if she was trying to breathe underwater.

At the end of the street, tents made of hide were crammed haphazardly between piles of demolition debris. Women with tired faces cooked over open fires whilst their children played on the rubble heaps. Elderly grandparents sat quietly in the tents, sadness etched upon their gaunt faces. It seemed to Anya that they had lived too long, for they surely would not have chosen to see their world come to this.

'Too many people,' she said, almost to herself.

'Calleva is over-run with refugees from the countryside, like every other town. They are all afraid,' Rufus glanced at Hengist. 'Strangely enough, they are all afraid of people like you.'

The road climbed steadily towards the highest point of the town and they passed the vast, deserted forum. Nettles grew between its flag stones. Anya thought it looked a sad, forgotten place, peopled only by ghosts.

'Vortigern is staying as a guest of Marcus Aurelius, the leader of the town council,' Rufus announced, turning west into a street where the houses of the rich hid behind high, ivy-clad walls. Dismounting, they handed their reins to the waiting stable boys. Their footsteps echoed on cold marble as Rufus led them through the high ceilinged entrance hall and passed the formal gardens of the inner courtyard. He came to a halt before a pair of ornate bronze doors, pushed them open and gestured curtly that Anya and her brothers should step inside.

Anya glanced nervously around Marcus's dining room. There was no high table, no smoky fire, no wolf hounds sprawled in the rushes and no sparrows in the rafters. Marcus's home was a shrine to old Roman taste, from its frescos of nymphs and satyrs to its fine mosaic floor depicting Bacchus, god of feasting. Tiny oil lamps bathed the room in a soft light and the air was sweet with the fragrance of roses and white lilac. The room felt so alien that homesickness swept over Anya once again.

Four couches bordered a rectangular table laden with small platters of food. Marcus was reclining on one of the couches, propped up by his elbow, taking titbits with his right hand. He was a handsome man, with a long aquiline nose and dark, intelligent eyes. His wife sat demurely on a small chair to his right, her green silk gown falling to the floor in gentle folds. She wore her hair up and intricately styled, emphasising her long, slender neck. Neither Marcus nor his wife rose to meet their guests. They simply ignored them as if they were invisible.

Anya noticed Rufus made straight for a slave bearing a bowl of water and a towel. He washed his hands with great care then dried them meticulously. Vortigern was on his feet and Anya stared at him incredulously. He was as huge and solid as a watch tower. His head was perfectly round and his features coarse. His black hair was shaved to bristles, and his scalp reminded her of a plucked chicken. He was one of the most powerful men in Britannia and yet he looked for all the world like a thug for hire. Vortigern's eyes settled on her, and she shifted uncomfortably.

'This is Hengist, son of Athelwald,' Rufus announced.

Vortigern continued to stare at Anya.

Rufus coughed loudly.

'Ah, yes.' Vortigern's gaze finally slid to her brothers.

Anya realised she had been holding her breath and she exhaled, grateful to be released from the intensity of his gaze. She glanced proudly at her brothers. No-one had thought to disarm them and they were still dressed for battle, resplendent with gold and garnets.

Hengist bowed before Vortigern, and Horsa followed suit.

'Hengist and Horsa, sons of Athelwald, who claims his descent from the great god Odin, come before you in peace. We swear to serve you and protect you, not flinching in our loyalty, even when faced with death.'

Hengist's Latin, learnt from the many treaties and trade agreements carried out across the northern borders of the Empire, was slow and imperfect, but it seemed Vortigern understood him.

'You speak of loyalty, but I wonder if you know the meaning of the word,' he replied mildly, walking across the mosaic floor until he stood just inches from Hengist's face. Suddenly, Vortigern's voice was a roar of fury. 'You slaughtered my fucking garrison! To the last man! Give me one good reason why I shouldn't have your heads?'

'Your garrison?' Hengist asked faintly.

'Yes, Andereida. My fort. My garrison. My men.'

'They ambushed us, Lord. We acted in self-defence.'

'Don't lie to me!' Vortigern snapped. 'By God, I should never have brought you here. But I *will* have use of you –

your heads can adorn my gate house and put dread into the hearts of my enemies.'

'I -' Hengist began but Vortigern held up a hand to silence him. He glared threateningly at Hengist for a very long time before his gaze shifted sharply to Anya.

She forced herself to match his stare, but her heart was thudding violently.

If only Hengist had been less eager to prove himself. If only he had not acted so rashly.

She wondered if losing your head was a quick, merciful way to die.

Finally, Vortigern looked back at Hengist.

'Listen to me, Saxon. I don't care if you're descended from Jesus Christ, you do not slaughter my troops! I brought you here because I need more fighting men. I didn't bring you here to kill the ones I already have. Do you understand?'

'Yes, Lord.'

'If we sign this treaty, you will do exactly what I tell you to do, when I tell you to do it. Do you understand?'

'Yes, Lord,' Hengist repeated woodenly.

'Good, good.' The tone of Vortigern's voice had flashed from menacing to convivial in a heartbeat. 'Shall we seal the treaty now, so we can eat Marcus's food?'

Anya glanced at Vortigern in amazement. Had he been playing with them all along, like a cat tormenting a mouse?

'My scribe has the treaty prepared,' Vortigern said amiably, gesturing to a side table bearing a large pile of vellum scrolls.

Anya noticed that Rufus bridled at being called a scribe. He looked pained and tight lipped as he walked to the table and selected a scroll. It was bound with a red ribbon. Rufus slowly untied the ribbon, folded it neatly then placed it in his pocket. Then he set about making minute adjustments to the remaining scrolls until their edges were exactly parallel to the edge of the table. Vortigern let out a strange harrumphing sound and swore loudly but Rufus did not appear to notice. Only when he was satisfied the remaining scrolls were all perfectly aligned, did he hand Hengist the vellum.

Hengist unrolled it and stared blankly at it for a few seconds.

'Brother,' Horsa said softly.

Hengist looked up. 'Anya!' he said curtly, 'Come here.'

He thrust the vellum into his sister's outstretched hand and an awkward silence descended. She quickly scanned the Latin text. It was as Vortigern's emissaries had originally promised them: land in exchange for military service. She looked up at her brother and nodded.

Hengist took the scroll from her without a word and turned to Vortigern.

'This land. Who did it belong to? Will they give us trouble?'

Vortigern shook his head. 'They are peasants. I assure you there will be no trouble. They will work for you.'

Anya looked away. She could imagine Rufus waving vellum at farmers who had never learnt to read, and pushing them off land they had owned for centuries, instantly reducing them to the status of slaves.

'I will seal it,' Hengist said. 'Give me the wax.'

An image, sudden and unexpected, seared across Anya's mind.

The chariots of the Valkyries blazing like fire across a blood-soaked battlefield as they garnered their fallen warriors.

She shuddered and pushed the image way.

'Good, good. So, it's done. Let's eat.'

Vortigern ignored Marcus's curt offer of a reclining couch. Instead he dragged a wicker chair from the corner of the room. Hengist, Horsa and Anya sat down awkwardly on the couch opposite.

Vortigern waved his hand towards Marcus. 'This is Marcus Aurelius, and his wife Lavinia.'

Marcus did not acknowledge the Saxons. He continued eating, his manner blatantly hostile, and Anya wondered if he resented Vortigern requisitioning his home to greet a band of foreign mercenaries.

Vortigern gestured towards Rufus. 'And you have already met Rufus. He nags like a wife.'

Anya watched Rufus's expression harden. He had not been invited to sit at the table, but left to stand in the shadows. It seemed the high king of the Dobunni cared little for his alleged second in command.

'So Marcus,' Vortigern said genially. 'Our fathers were once great friends, if I remember correctly.'

Marcus finally looked up. 'Yes, they hunted together, in the days when we had time for such frivolities.'

Vortigern downed the contents of his cup and held it out to the serving girl again. She refilled it quickly and he just as quickly emptied it. He stabbed a piece of venison with his knife and its rich, dark sauce dripped across the table. Pushing the huge lump of meat into his mouth, he continued to talk with his mouth full.

'I notice you've dug a deep earthwork around your town.'

Vortigern wiped his mouth with the back of his hand and Anya thought it curious that a man of such influence should have such coarse table manners.

'But ditches will not save you, Marcus,' Vortigern went on. 'What you need is an army - *my* army. Each time the Irish come, I rout them. Each time the Picts cross the wall, I'm ready for them. Each time the Saxon pirates dare to drag their boats up our shingle, I turn the waves red with their blood.'

'Your achievements are well known to us. We are honoured that you chose to spend this evening with us,' Marcus said smoothly.

Vortigern laughed. 'You and I both know I'm not here for the pleasure of your company. I'm here to offer Calleva the same protection I provide for the rest of the towns under my care. My army is undefeated in battle.'

Marcus's expression hardened. 'You believe these heathen barbarians,' he nodded towards Hengist and Horsa, 'will fight to keep their own kin at bay? I find it inconceivable that you would welcome Saxons into Britannia, when others like them pillage and loot the southern coast.'

Anya saw Hengist tense at her side and she glanced apprehensively at her half-brother, praying he would not rise to the insult.

Vortigern shook his head, clearly exasperated. 'The Roman army employed auxiliaries from all over the known world. There's nothing new or radical about my policy.'

'But will they be loyal to you?' Marcus persisted.

'The Germanic tribes have no loyalty to each other but if I pay them enough, they will be loyal to me,' Vortigern said sharply. 'So, what do you say to my offer?'

'The council of Calleva will not -' Marcus began, but Vortigern cut him off.

'Out of deference for the friendship our fathers enjoyed, I chose not to march my army to the gates of Calleva.' Vortigern paused to take another draft of wine before continuing. 'I assume you've heard the town of Venta has recently accepted me as their overlord? Which means Calleva is the only town in the territory of the Atrebates not yet under my protection.'

No one spoke. The atmosphere in the room was as sour as curdled milk.

'So, it's settled,' Vortigern said triumphantly. 'Rufus will meet with your council tomorrow to draw up the treaty.'

Marcus stood up, his face a mask of impotent fury. 'Nothing has been settled, Vortigern. Nothing whatsoever!' Marcus turned to his wife. 'Come!'

And they left the room without another word.

Anya sat in stunned silence. To her horror, she realised Vortigern was staring at her again. She glared back at him, her eyes wide and intensely hostile and it was Vortigern who looked away first. He stabbed another piece of meat and chewed it noisily. The sauce ran down his chin in greasy rivulets and splattered onto the white table cloth.

'And so, to the problem of the Picts,' he went on, as if nothing untoward had occurred. 'And believe me, they *are* a problem. I can't rely on the Brigantes to keep them at bay – they're brainless oafs, very slow of speech and too intent on fucking sheep to look to their own defences. I want you to man the wall. I'll ride north with you, show you the lay of the land…' His voice trailed away and his eyes slid to Anya once again. 'I must ask you, who is this?'

'Her name is Anya,' Hengist replied. 'She is my half-sister.'

Vortigern looked at Anya for such a long time that she felt her cheeks begin to flush. She stared fixedly at her hands in her lap, twisting her mother's copper ring round and round her finger.

'And does she have a husband?' Vortigern asked, very slowly.

Anya looked up, gripped with a sudden sense of unease. She wondered why he would ask such a question.

'No, she doesn't,' Hengist replied.

Vortigern continued to stare unblinkingly at her and she felt her flesh begin to creep.

'That's convenient,' he said at last, 'for I am in need of a wife and what better way to ensure your loyalty, Hengist, than to give me your sister in marriage?'

Anya shot to her feet. The glass of wine fell from her hand and shattered, the wine running like blood across the mosaic floor. She stared at Vortigern incredulously. He had not spoken a single word to her and yet he was proposing a marriage betrothal. Was the man drunk? Had he lost his mind?

'Sit down, Anya,' Hengist said calmly.

She remained standing.

'Will you give her to me?' Vortigern asked Hengist, ignoring Anya completely.

Hengist appeared to consider Vortigern's request for a moment. 'Yes, I will,' he replied. 'As a seal upon our treaty.'

'No!' Anya rounded on her brother in utter disbelief. 'Are you insane? I will not be Vortigern's hostage!'

Hengist turned to his sister. His voice had changed. It sounded ugly and full of spite. 'You were entrusted to me by our father. You will do as you are told.'

Horsa leapt from the couch and clasped Anya's hand in a gesture of unity. 'This will not stand, brother!' he said firmly. 'This is not what Father intended!'

'Sit down!' Hengist replied harshly. 'You have no authority here!'

Horsa glared at his half-brother and remained firmly at Anya's side.

'Sit down or I will run you through,' Hengist said under his breath.

Surreptitiously, Anya tugged Horsa's sleeve, silently

pleading with him. Horsa sat down again and Anya followed suit. Her legs felt as wobbly as marrow jelly.

Rufus took a few steps towards Vortigern. 'Is this wise, Lord? She is a Saxon! Should such an important decision be made so rashly?'

Anya nodded vehemently. 'Yes, this is rash! And foolish!'

'Be silent, Anya,' Hengist warned.

'I will not -' Anya began but Vortigern over-rode her, as if she had not spoken. 'Since when do I need your permission to take a wife, Rufus? In fact, when do I need your permission to do anything?'

Rufus backed away, but Anya could see the resentment in his eyes; it was hard and cold, like stone.

Vortigern turned to Hengist again. 'So, do we have an agreement?'

'Yes.' Hengist replied.

Anya felt as if she was falling from a great height, but she turned to Vortigern, forcing herself to remain calm. 'I cannot marry you because you are a Christian and I am a pagan priestess.'

'A pagan priestess?' Vortigern looked shocked but he recovered quickly. 'It's of no consequence. You can convert to the true faith before our marriage.'

'I will never do that!' Anya exclaimed in bewilderment.

Vortigern waved a hand dismissively. 'Mere details.'

Anya stood up. 'This is madness and I will hear no more of it. I need some air.' She turned to Hengist. 'You too should take a breath, brother, and then perhaps you will see some sense.'

Hengist merely shrugged and smiled.

Anya walked out of the dining chamber with her head held high, but her legs were trembling and her head was pounding.

She wandered aimlessly through Marcus's town house, but she did not notice the exquisite mosaics or the delicately painted frescoes. She was so angry she could hardly catch her breath. How dare Hengist try to barter her away like a box of hack-silver? When she could walk no further, she sat down in one of Marcus's echoing reception rooms and put her head in her hands.

After a while, she heard footsteps and looked up. Her brothers were approaching.

'What were you thinking, Hengist? You must know I will never marry that man!'

'Yes, you will,' Hengist said smugly. 'His ugly little scribe, Rufus I think he's called, took a quill and added your marriage contract to the treaty. You will marry Vortigern in Aquae Sulis when he returns from the north.'

'I don't believe you,' Anya began faintly. 'We are kin. You wouldn't do such a thing.'

'I had no choice, Anya. I killed his entire garrison. I had to give him something. Besides, you should be grateful to me,' Hengist said briskly. 'Vortigern is a powerful man and I have made you an excellent marriage. When all is said and done, you can't go home because you have been banished. You have nowhere else to go.'

Anya prayed Hengist was simply tormenting her, and this was merely one of his cruel jokes. She glanced beseechingly at Horsa but found no reassurance. His eyes were full of guilt and shame.

'But I'm a pagan priestess,' she said shakily. 'What would a Christian want with me?'

'I'm sure he can think of quite a few things,' Hengist sniggered. 'He wants you to share his bed, Anya, each and every night, for the rest of your worthless life.'

Anya's eyes widened, shocked by her brother's harsh words.

'Enough, Hengist, for pity's sake!' Horsa began but Hengist rounded on him.

'I am your warlord. You cannot tell me what to do!'

Horsa fell silent, but his eyes blazed with unspoken fury. Appeased, Hengist yawned loudly. 'It's late. I'm going to bed.'

'I will stay with Anya a while,' Horsa said softly.

'As you wish.' Hengist turned on his heel and strode from the room.

Horsa sat down next to Anya, and the spindly, brightly painted chair creaked beneath his weight. 'I swear before the goddess, I tried to change his mind, Anya, but he wouldn't listen. How will you ever forgive me?'

Anya shivered. She felt nauseous and bitterly cold.

'I don't blame you, Horsa. I know there was nothing you could do.' Her voice was flat, devoid of all emotion.

Horsa looked around him, absently fingering the grip of his sword. It had been a leaving gift from his father.

'I hate this place,' he said at last. 'There's too much cold stone. We shall build our homes in Britannia of wood and thatch. And one day, I swear, when I'm as rich as a treasure-guarding dragon, I *will* return to Saxony, where I belong. And I'll take you with me, Anya.'

Anya gripped the edges of her cloak to stop her hands trembling. 'I can never go home, Horsa. I never imagined my life would lead this way. But what was I supposed to do? Watch my sister murdered and be silent? Was that the price to keep my life, my kin, my homeland?' She glanced at her brother. 'And nor did I ever imagine Hengist would betray me.'

'He's always been jealous of you, Anya, and afraid of your

powers. He's an ambitious man, unlike me. How does the old song go - the bear belongs on the heath, the boar belongs in the forest, and a good man belongs in his native land, forging his reputation.' Horsa sighed heavily. 'All I ever wanted was to marry Elsbet. Instead I'm forced to leave my homeland to fight for a tyrant in a country I despise. They say it's always winter in the north. They say the Picts beyond the wall paint themselves blue with dye from the woad plant and it gives them immortality. They say they slaughter without fear of death, and drink the blood of innocent children.'

Anya put a hand on his shoulder.

'The Roman scribes write such tales about us, Horsa, but we know they're not true. The Picts are mortal men, just like you. And it will be summer in the northern lands, I'm sure of it.'

Horsa smiled sadly. 'I will miss you, sister. Hengist is a fool to want to be rid of you. This is not what father wanted. He intended you to stay at our side.'

Anya nodded wearily. She had accepted long ago that her body belonged to the goddess alone. But now Hengist had given her to Vortigern, and she could not begin to contemplate married life at his side.

'What am I doing here?' she said plaintively

'The gods have sent you here for a reason, I'm certain of it.' Horsa put his arms around his sister, and she rested her head on his shoulder. There was still a trace of the scent of home about him, but it was beginning to fade. They sat together for a long time and when they finally drew apart, Anya looked into his gentle, green eyes and wondered if the world would ever seem right again.

FOURTEEN

In the dappled shade of the courtyard of Marcus's town house, Calleva Atrebatum surrendered its independence to Vortigern. In exchange for a permanent garrison of Vortigern's soldiers to protect their town, the council signed a treaty accepting Vortigern as their overlord. They were also obliged to provide a large contingent of fighting men to serve in Vortigern's ever expanding army, and to send fifty percent of their harvest each year to feed it. As Anya watched Marcus press his seal into the wax, she wondered grimly how he was supposed to give away half his harvest, and still feed his horrendously overcrowded town.

She had only known Vortigern for a short time but she already suspected he was far more dangerous than the Picts and the Irish and the Saxon pirates combined. Over the last few days, Anya had said little, but learnt a great deal. She had learnt that Vortigern was undisputed warlord of the vast kingdom of the Dobunni. He appeared to hold on to power through sheer force of character, the unfailing ability to muster a larger army than his enemies, and unrivalled skill on the battlefield.

Recently, he had added the people of the Catuvellauni to his list of conquests. And as of today, he now controlled the rich, grain producing territory of the Atrebates, which encompassed much of southern Britannia.

Vortigern drew Anya to one side. 'I have chosen a beautiful wife. I look forward to our wedding night.'

The smirk on his face turned Anya's stomach. She stepped backwards, but he grabbed her shoulder.

'Don't back away from me. You belong to me now.'

'Let go of me! I didn't agree to this marriage and I warn you now, you should release me from it. We will bring each other no happiness.'

Vortigern's hand flashed to her throat and his fingers tightened their grip. 'You *will* make me happy, you pagan bitch, or I'll slit your throat.'

Anya could not breathe. She tried frantically to prize his fingers from his throat, but his grip was too strong.

'Anya!' Horsa began in alarm. He took a step towards his sister, but Hengist held him back, shaking his head in a silent warning not to interfere.

Vortigern let go of Anya abruptly, and nodded over her head to Rufus.

'Take her to Aquae Sulis, and wait for me there.'

From the high stone ramparts of Calleva Atrebatum, Anya watched Vortigern and her two brothers ride away. She touched the bruises at her throat gingerly, and it crossed her mind that a Pictish spear might end Vortigern's life in the far northern lands.

Hengist did not look back. Horsa, however, turned in his saddle and raised an arm in a gesture of farewell. Anya waved back, forcing a smile for him. She prayed that the goddess might keep her kind, gentle brother safe from harm. Horsa had been her last link with home and now she was alone in an alien land. She wondered if the goddess had forsaken her, for what possible purpose could she serve married to a man she despised, in this cowering, miserable country. In the waxing and waning of a moon, she had fallen from grace. One moment the daughter of a king and a priestess of the sacred grove, the next a mere possession of a tyrant warlord.

Anya looked out over the gently rolling countryside of the Atrebates, absently turning her mother's ring round and round her finger. Marcus had told her that further west, beyond the dense forests, lay the mountainous land of the Silures, her mother's people. It was from them that she had inherited her flame-coloured hair and skin as pale as sheep's wool. Staring at the western horizon, she wondered if her mother's kin still lived in the far mountains.

She closed her eyes. The gusting wind died away and the noise of the city faded. The vision came upon her suddenly, at first blurred, then sharply in focus. The dark mountains dominated the bleak, wild valley and the stream stained brown by peat. And then she saw the village, the huddle of stone and slate, and she heard the bleating of sheep as dusk fell.

It was the village she had seen so many times in her dreams. Her mother's home.

But there was no blood, no terror, just an overwhelming sense of peace.

'Are you ready to depart for Aquae Sulis?' Rufus eyed Anya curiously.

Anya jolted. She felt nauseous, and her head throbbed angrily.

'Are you unwell?' Rufus asked.

'I am quite well,' she replied, and walked quickly down the rampart steps.

Hengist had no right to promise her to Vortigern. She could never marry such a man. Her mind was made up. She would travel to Aquae Sulis with Rufus, and from there she would find her way to Siluria, to the village in the lonely valley, in the shadow of the high mountains.

The home of her ancestors.

The commander of Vortigern's warband was a young man with the body of a warrior but the eyes of a philosopher. He bowed before Anya, with one hand on the grip of his sword and the other across his heart.

'Vortigern has requested that I guard you with my life, and I shall be honoured to do so, Lady Anya.'

'Let's hope that won't be necessary,' Anya replied lightly.

He straightened up and smiled gently at her. 'My name is Gaius.'

Anya returned his smile. She thought he had kind eyes. She sensed Rufus's gaze upon her and turned to face him. He looked furious, and her smile faded. She wondered what had made him so angry.

'I am ready to depart,' she said formally.

'As you wish, Lady Anya,' Gaius replied.

They travelled west, along the old Roman road that ran straight as an arrow across the gentle, rolling countryside of the Atrebates. After the foul odours of Calleva, the air smelled clean and sweet. Cow parsley crowded the road side and delicate dog roses and honeysuckle clambered through the hedgerows. Small, rectangular fields of young wheat and barley made a patchwork of green across the hills, leeching to blue on the far horizon, but the further they travelled from Calleva, the more fallow fields they saw. Many were overgrown with thistles, their seed heads swaying gently in the wind.

They passed several villages, each surrounded by a freshly cut bank and ditch. Concealed behind their defences, they were ominously quiet, save for the occasional clang of hammer against anvil, or the mournful bellowing of a cow.

There were very few people on the road. A caravan of merchants with their gaudily painted wagons took one look at Vortigern's heavily armed men and made no attempt to sell their wares. A farmer pulling a hay-cart kept his head down and avoided making eye contact.

Shortly after noon they came to a burnt out village. Only the charred frames of the houses survived, black and skeletal against the blue sky. All was silence but for a skylark trilling high above their heads.

'The trademark of the Irish,' Gaius said in a sombre voice. 'Or it could be the work of pirates from across the northern sea.'

'Not all the Germanic tribes are pirates,' Anya said quietly.

'You are right, of course,' Gaius said hurriedly. 'Forgive me.'

'I forgive you,' Anya replied, smiling. She hesitated for a moment. 'I would ask you something, Gaius.'

Gaius nodded. 'Of course.'

'Why did Vortigern choose me? Surely he could have secured a more profitable marriage alliance?'

Gaius frowned and began to look deeply uncomfortable.

'I'm sorry – I shouldn't have asked,' Anya said hurriedly.

Rufus kicked the flanks of his horse and trotted to her side.

'I will answer your question. Vortigern is desperate to marry again because Ronan, his only surviving son, is a drunken wastrel. Vortigern craves another heir - he fears

Ronan will never be capable of ruling the Dobunni. And after what happened with Pascent of the Coritani…'

'What happened with Pascent of the Coritani?' Anya asked, intrigued.

Gaius was shaking his head at Rufus, but the scribe was warming to his theme.

'Not two months since, I arranged for Vortigern's betrothal to Pascent's daughter, Loisa. It would have been a good match, the political binding of two powerful kingdoms. But after the betrothal feast -'

'Rufus!' Gaius cut in. 'Enough!'

But Rufus rounded on Gaius. 'She is to be Vortigern's wife, for Christ's sake! Doesn't she have a right to know?' He turned to Anya again. 'We rode to Pascent's stronghold to seal the betrothal papers. But Vortigern got blind drunk and that night, after the feast, he raped Loisa. He claims he was so inebriated he thought she was a slave girl but still, we were lucky to escape with our lives.' Rufus stared grimly ahead, remembering. 'Pascent is old and sick. He did not want to fight and so he demanded tribute in reparation but Vortigern refuses to send him even a single grain of wheat. In retaliation, Pascent has called for war against the Dobunni. My spies tell me he is mustering an army.'

Anya swallowed hard, shock rendering her speechless. Why had Hengist arranged her betrothal to Vortigern? And why had she not found a way to stop him?

'That unfortunate incident is not common knowledge,' Gaius said sombrely.

Rufus laughed humourlessly and shook his head. 'Half Britannia knows of it. It's impossible to sweep stories like that into corners. And you know the worst of it? Vortigern blames me for the fiasco.'

Rufus sank into a morose silence. Anya could sense his frustration and his rage; it hung over him like a swarm of persistent midges. She glanced at Gaius. His mouth was set in a thin, hard line. He was angry too, but Anya suspected his rage was aimed at Rufus's spectacular lack of tact.

The road began to climb steadily towards the sweeping uplands. Over the years, its metalled surface had washed away, leaving behind a deeply rutted track of white chalk. A vast forest stretched across the far horizon, an undulating wall of green. Anya's grip tightened on the reins. She did not fear the forest at home for it was as familiar to her as the back of her hand. But she did not know this forest and everyone knew the dangers - bears, wolves, sinking swamps, outlaws.

As they drew nearer, the jovial banter of Vortigern's men ceased and they looked about with wary eyes. The forest quickly closed around them. Towering pines blocked out the sunlight and the temperature plummeted like a stone. The track was narrow and covered in last year's dead leaves which muffled the sound of the warhorses' hooves. The forest was so still and silent that the men spoke in whispers, as if not daring to disturb its peace.

A sudden snapping sound reverberated through the undergrowth, as sharp as the pulling of a wishbone. To a man, Vortigern's warriors reached for their swords, their eyes scanning the tall bracken and dense clusters of saplings. Another branch snapped underfoot, followed by an eerie, heavy silence.

Anya stared anxiously into the undergrowth.

Something was moving. The silver birch saplings were swaying and jostling although there was not a breath of wind. Her lungs constricted with fear. She had seen many caged bears, pitiful in defeat, but she had never faced one in the wild. The bracken rustled and crackled, deafeningly loud in the still air.

Anya's hand went to the dagger she wore at her belt, although in truth, she knew it would be useless against such a huge and dangerous beast. She closed her fingers around the grip, her heart pounding furiously.

The deer darted out from the bracken, no more than a yard ahead. It stopped and turned to look at them, its huge eyes wide with alarm and then it was gone, bounding lightly across their path.

Anya's heart leapt into her mouth. She gripped the reins of her mare to steady both herself and the startled animal. All around her, men were sheathing their swords and laughing with relief.

'Are you alright?' Gaius asked. He sounded concerned.

'Yes, thank you,' she smiled, patting the mare's neck. 'No harm done.'

They rode on and the soldiers visibly relaxed. Some took bread and meat from their saddle bags, eating one handed as they rode. They began to banter again. Anya took a deep breath of the cold forest air. It was rich with familiar scents - earth and leaf mould, mushrooms, bluebells, honeysuckle and pine. It reminded her of the forest in Saxony and homesickness settled on her heart. She turned in her saddle, suddenly curious. There was another scent now, one she did not recognise.

The warband descended like a flock of crows. They were short, stocky men with black, ragged hair, their coarsely woven cloaks streaming behind them like wings to give them flight. Anya froze, open mouthed with shock, as the mounted warband charged down the wooded hillside.

Gaius turned to her urgently.

'Go! They are Irish! They come for slaves. You must go! Now, Anya!'

Anya nodded, terror rendering her speechless. She wrenched the reins of her mare, attempting to turn in the crush of Vortigern's warriors, but Gaius shook his head.

'No! On foot. The forest is too dense for horseback.'

Anya felt strangely numb, as if she were no longer a part of the world. Out of the corner of her eye she watched Rufus slide from his horse and hurl himself into the undergrowth, flattening himself into the long bracken. She saw him lift his head slightly and peer at her through a gap in the prickly undergrowth.

'Go! Before it's too late!' Gaius shouted desperately.

Anya turned back to face Gaius. Vortigern's soldiers had drawn their swords and were closing ranks around her.

'But I -' she began.

Shock was forcing all rational thought from her mind. Gaius leant forward, prized her fingers from the reins and hauled her from the horse. Anya stumbled as she hit the ground. As if awoken from a deep sleep, she looked about her in bewilderment. She was surrounded by terrified warhorses and in grave danger of being crushed beneath their rearing hooves. Through the melee of jostling horse flesh, she could see the Irish, bearing down upon them.

An axe flew through the air, somersaulting like a jester, whistling as it fell. Time slowed as she watched it spin. Without warning, the world speeded up again. Brutally fast, the axe dived like a hawk after its prey. The soldier shuddered and slipped from his saddle, the axe embedded in his chest.

'Go!' Gaius yelled again. 'Unless you want to die here!'

The Irish were upon them now. Their ponies looked shaggy and unkempt, as if fit only for hauling ore from the mines but they were surprisingly fast and agile, turning on a dagger point. To her left, a horse screamed and buckled, its throat slit by an Irish blade. Vortigern's soldier fell with his warhorse, one foot still trapped in its stirrup.

Anya glanced about her helplessly. East, west, north or south? Which way should she go?

Another Irish spear flew and found its mark. The soldier grunted and slumped in his saddle, pierced clean through. His bloodied fingers grappled weakly and hopelessly at the shaft, before the life went out of his eyes and he slipped from his warhorse.

Gaius's patience appeared to run out. He slapped the flat of his blade against Anya's back and shoved her hard.

'Just run!'

Anya raised her hands to shield her face and began to push her way through the crush of Vortigern's warriors. A warhorse skittered sideways. It crushed her against a saddle, knocking the air from her lungs. Dazed, she reached blindly for a hold. She felt a soldier's hand take hers, felt the rough calluses on his palm.

'That way,' he gestured, and then his firm grasp was gone. Vortigern's soldiers were edging their warhorses apart for her, creating a gap. Ahead, lay the dark forest. She took a deep breath, and then she ran, faster than she had ever run before.

The forest hugged the hillside, shutting out the sunlight and the air felt cold against her cheeks. Between tall trees of oak, birch and sycamore, slender saplings were struggling towards the light.

Half way up the steep hillside, she stopped to catch her breath, looking behind her anxiously. She could hear nothing but her own breathing. The forest was eerily quiet. She glanced at her long, un-braided hair. It stood out like a fire beacon amidst the vivid greens of early summer. Hurriedly, she pulled up the hood of her cloak.

She began to run again, zigzagging her way through the dense trees, stumbling over brambles and ferns. Just as she thought she had reached the summit, the ground levelled slightly and then continued to rise again. Her lungs were screaming but she forced herself to keep going. She would be out of sight once she had rounded the brow of the hill.

Suddenly, she heard men's voices carrying on the still air. They were not speaking Latin. She threw herself down into the undergrowth. Her cheek landed hard on a fallen branch, hidden in last year's dead leaves. A cry of pain formed in her throat but she bit her lip, and lay still. After a moment, she propped herself up on her elbows and peered through the tangled thicket. Two men were walking up the hillside, their swords drawn, their gaze steadily moving from left to right, scanning the forest.

Her mind raced. She could not stay here. She was far too exposed. She had no choice but to try and reach the top of the hill. Slowly, she began to crawl through the undergrowth. Her cloak snagged on thorny brambles, ripping her gown and cutting her hands and elbows until they bled.

One of the men shouted something to the other. She looked over her shoulder. They had split up. One was a hundred yards to her right, the other was much closer, and moving a good deal quicker than she was.

'Nerthus,' she whispered. 'Goddess of the living earth, tell me what to do.'

The answer came to her without lightning bolts or visions. She lifted herself to her knees, took a deep breath, and ran.

They spotted her instantly. She heard their shouts, and the sound of twigs breaking underfoot as they pursued her up the hillside. She forced herself on. Her blood was pounding in her ears now, deafening her to all other sounds. She came to the brow of the hill at last and stopped for a moment, resting her hands on her knees, trying to catch her breath. Which way should she go now?

She looked about desperately. She was standing on a drovers' way; hoof prints of cattle were sealed in the sun-baked mud. In a clearing nearby stood an ancient burial chamber, its massive earth mound covered with ferns. A treasure hunter had dug a deep shaft into its bank and the bare earth looked like an open wound. Ahead, the hillside fell away steeply again, the forest as dense and impenetrable as before.

The men's voices were closer now. At any moment they would reach the brow of the hill. She had to make a decision. Anya turned east, towards the sun. She ran along the drovers' way for as long as she dared, then hurled herself into the forest again. Her boots skidded through a sea of bluebells as she hurtled down the slope. She glanced behind her but she could not see the men.

Momentarily off balance, her feet went from under her and she fell heavily, a sharp pain shooting through her left ankle. She slid for several yards before coming to a stop, her cloak entangled in brambles. Wrenching herself free, she stood up gingerly, but the pain in her ankle was so severe it made her wince.

She stood absolutely still and listened. The Irish were on the ridge-way. They had turned east, just as she had done. Her heart sank. She wondered if they were skilled trackers, or was it pure luck they were still on her trail? She tried to run again but faltered to a halt, her face contorted with pain. She had to find somewhere to hide. She listened again, turning her head this way, then that, and sniffed the air. There was a river close by. She caught the scent of muddy water, wild iris, bulrushes.

Biting her lip against the pain in her ankle, she set off down the hill once again. The river meandered along a narrow valley. Trees guarded its calm waters, their roots burrowing into its banks. She looked back the way she had come. She could see two short, stocky figures picking their way down the hillside. They had found her trail.

Anya looked back at the river, her mind racing. The water looked fairly shallow. She could see the riverbed, gently swaying weeds and trout lurking between glossy stones. The river bank hung over the water, like a fat man's belly spilling over his belt. She knelt between the long gnarly fingers of exposed tree roots and dipped her hand into the river. The water felt like ice, but the Irish were half way down the hill.

She gritted her teeth and quickly lowered herself into the river. It was so cold, she gasped with shock. The water was much deeper than it had appeared and she felt a sudden surge of panic. By the time her boots had stopped sinking into the soft silt of the riverbed, the water had reached her waist. Her sodden cloak weighed her down as she struggled to press her body close against the overhanging bank.

The Irishmen were very close now. She could hear their footsteps in the undergrowth; hear every broken twig, every rustle of leaves. They were following the river, just as she had done. Suddenly, there was silence. She held her breath, not daring to move.

'So? Where is she?'

'I don't know. I was following a trail, and now it's gone.'

'Christ's blood, Connor! We'll be in trouble with Angus if we've lost her.'

'Don't fret. We already have a full cart. One more won't make much difference.'

Gritting her teeth to stop them chattering, Anya listened to their conversation, but she could not understand a single word. She was so cold, her arms and legs were starting to go numb but at least she could no longer feel the pain in her ankle. She shivered then froze in horror as the ripples she had created spread across the calm water. She wished she knew what the men were saying.

'She looked high-born. And young, so she's worth at least three times as much as one of Vortigern's men. So, we keep looking.'

Anya heard a loud, weary sigh.

'Connor?'

'Aye?'

'The trail you followed. Are you certain it was the girl?'

'Aye, I'm certain. In all my days I've never seen a deer walk on two legs.'

'So, we follow the river. You go north, I'll go south. She can't have gone far.'

Anya heard footsteps again but the sounds were coming from two different directions. The men had split up. She listened hard; the footsteps were fainter now, further away. A surge of relief flooded through her. Miraculously, they had not discovered her hiding place. She closed her eyes and said a silent prayer of thanks.

Her fingers and her toes were numb and the cold was beginning to seep into her bones. She could not stay in the water for very much longer. She wondered how long she should wait before she dared to move. And where should she go? Images of the Irish warband flying out from the silent forest flashed across her mind and she shuddered. What horrors awaited her on the old Roman road? Had Gaius and his men all died trying to save her?

Anya remained absolutely still, but she could not hear the Irishmen. No footsteps, no shouting. Perhaps she was safe now?

Connor knelt down and dipped his leather bottle into the water. As he waited for his bottle to fill, something caught his eye. There was a black shape in the river. Connor's eyes narrowed. He looked again.

'God's teeth! Fergus! Over here!' He scrabbled towards Anya on his hands and knees, flailing awkwardly over tree roots in his shock and surprise.

Just as Connor skidded to a halt at the edge of the bank, Anya pushed herself away from her hiding place, her mind racing with fear. She knew she would never outrun the Irishman now. But she couldn't just give up. She turned and grabbed the only part of the man she could reach, the heavy shoulder buckle of his leather cuirass. Her fingers were numb and they struggled to gain a hold, but she wrenched as hard as she could and Connor fell head first into the water with a loud splash.

Drenched by the spray of water, Anya struggled to find a hand-hold to heave herself from the river. Her fingers scrabbled on slippery tree roots, and loose pebbles and earth tumbled into her face. Connor surfaced like an enraged sea monster, roaring curses. He lunged at her and she felt his strong hands on her shoulders, forcing her down. Her knees buckled beneath his weight and she clamped her mouth shut as the water surged over her head.

She kicked out, trying to gain a foothold to right herself but her boots slid uselessly through the churning silt. Anya opened her eyes. She could just make out the Irishman's blurred form standing over her in the murky water. She twisted in his grasp, desperately trying to kick him in the groin, but he held her fast, pressing her further into the water. Terror and panic surged through her. Her lungs were burning for air and she fought an almost overwhelming urge to open her mouth and take a breath.

Straining against his weight, she tried desperately to reach for her dagger. Suddenly, the pressure of Connor's grip increased. She felt the weight of his boot-clad foot on her chest, pushing her deeper, until her nostrils began to fill with the fine silt of the river bed. Every inch of her being was crying out for air now and she wondered if this was how Emma felt, on that terrible day in the sacred grove.

'Connor? What the devil are you doing?' Fergus shouted from the riverbank.

'I've found her!'

'I can see that. And now you're drowning her?'

'I'm teaching the bitch a lesson!'

'For Christ's sake, let her up! We'll get nothing for her corpse. Angus won't thank you for this!'

Connor grunted something unintelligible. Reluctantly, he removed his boot from Anya's chest, reached into the water and heaved her upright. Anya took a deep breath. Air surged into her lungs and she began to cough and retch.

'Don't leave her there. Get her out!'

Connor turned back to Anya, grabbed her cloak and began to drag her towards the river bank. Fergus helped him pull her from the water.

'Well, well,' Fergus said mildly. 'You're a feisty one.'

Anya was shivering violently, overwhelmed by waves of nausea. She felt so light headed she could barely focus on the Irishman's face, as if she was still beneath the water, still drowning. She sank to her knees and retched into the grass.

Fergus squatted beside her and stared at her thoughtfully.

'The gentlemen of Rome prefer their British slaves blond and angelic. I wonder what they will think of you. Come on. Let's take you to Angus.'

Fergus hauled her upright and slung her over his shoulder as easily as if she were a sack of grain. Anya had no strength to resist, her world revolving sickeningly as he carried her unceremoniously back to the clearing.

Like the rest of his kin, Angus was short and stocky, with pale skin and black hair. 'What have you been doing?' he asked angrily. 'We need to move on.'

Fergus lowered Anya to the ground, where she swayed unsteadily. 'I'd wager she's high born. She has a fine torque about her neck,' he said, by way of appeasement.

Angus grabbed her by the chin and looked at her appraisingly. She jerked her head out of his grasp, struggling to focus. She wondered what had become of Rufus and Gaius. Had the Irish slaughtered Vortigern's entire warband?

'Let go of me!' Her ice-cold fingers were fumbling for her dagger. These men had come for slaves but, as long as she still breathed, she would never be a slave.

Angus grabbed her wrist and held it tightly.

'Feisty one, eh? Well, I've no time for histrionics. I want a quiet journey back to Ireland.' He spun her around, drew his sword and smashed its pommel into the back of her skull. Anya's world went black, her knees buckled and Angus caught her as she fell.

The Irish rode hard for the coast with their fresh catch of slaves. Slumped in the back of the covered wagon, Anya drifted in and out of consciousness. Her wakeful moments were painfully uncomfortable as the wagon pitched and rolled over the pot holes, but her dreams were far worse. She was being pursued but the faster she ran, the slower her progress became. She was surrounded by blood. It clung to her cloak, dragging her down. It was deeper now and she sank beneath it, unable to breathe, smothered by its thick, metallic gore.

Anya opened her eyes. She could smell the sea. Someone was carrying her in their arms. The beach was wide and empty save for a small ship moored in the shallows. The sun was rising, a ball of fire on the horizon, lighting up the sky in a swathe of vibrant pinks and oranges. Her world swam sickeningly and faded into blackness once again.

The Irish put to sea in the clear light of a still dawn. The wind came unexpectedly, surging across the calm sea, gusting and squalling. The storm was not far behind it and no matter how hard the Irish rowed, the wind drove them relentlessly further down the coast. Barely conscious, Anya lay huddled beneath her cloak on the floor of the small cabin. The ship heaved and she was flung forwards violently, coming to rest against the rough planking of the cabin wall. She let out a cry of pain. Gingerly, she touched the wound at the base of her skull and her fingers came away covered in fresh blood.

Ice cold sea water was surging across the floor, swirling around the prostrate bodies of Vortigern's men. Close by, Gaius lay motionless, his eyes closed, his hair matted with blood. The ship pitched violently, throwing her against the wall again. Disorientated in the gloomy darkness, Anya crawled on her hands and knees through the icy water towards Gaius. Much to her relief, there was a pulse at his throat. He was still alive, but there was no sign of Rufus. She remembered he had taken refuge in the undergrowth and she wondered if he had managed to escape.

Her head felt clearer now, shocked into wakefulness by the bitterly cold water. She became aware that the air was filled with noise. She had heard that sound before, on Cato's ship. It was the almighty roar of a storm. The ship lifted and slewed again and her stomach churned with fear. She had survived one terrible storm at sea. She had appealed to Tor, god of the storm, and he had listened to her prayers but she doubted he would do so again. The gods were notoriously fickle. Standing up unsteadily, she waded through the swirling water and opened the cabin door. The wind was so strong it wrenched the door from her hands and slammed it back against the cabin wall.

Anya held fast to the door frame and stared, horror-struck, into the storm. The sky was as black as night and the sea was a churning cauldron of towering waves. The wind howled about the ship like a malevolent spirit, lashing ice-cold rain against its lurching timbers. Above the fierce roar of the storm, she could hear the frantic prayers of the Irish as the looming cliffs grew ever closer.

Anya tugged her drenched hair from her face and stared curiously at the struggling sparks of the fire beacon, high above them, dimly visible through the driving rain. Was this the coast of Ireland, or had the storm driven them back to Britannia? Was Tor watching this tiny ship as it fought against the awesome power of the storm? Did he care whether the helpless souls aboard lived or died?

The ship rolled again, the gust of wind so vicious it took her breath away. Anya closed her eyes, and sought the goddess. 'If you brought me to Britannia for a purpose, then I ask you to spare me from this storm,' she prayed. 'Give me the chance to do your bidding, whatever it may be.'

Anya opened her eyes. The wave was as tall as a mountain,

blocking out the horizon, towering over the ship like a giant sea creature. It hovered, building its strength, a living, foaming wall, before it surged over the deck. The ship juddered, suddenly as fragile as a tiny insect, and the wooden hull shattered like glass against the hidden rocks beneath its keel. The wall of water tore her fingers from the door frame and swept her across the deck, carrying her along as easily as if she were a piece of driftwood. And suddenly, she was falling, tumbling, and then there was nothing but the overpowering strength of the sea, the choking pulse of water to her lungs, followed by blinding white, then blackness.

Then silence.

FIFTEEN

Tintagel, Dumnonia

Anya sat up slowly. As the last wave had carried her over the side of the ship, she had been certain that death had found her, and yet it appeared she was still alive. She looked curiously around the tiny watch-tower room. A dull light was seeping between the shutters across the high window and the air was bitterly cold. There was no fire, but a thick cloak lay beside her and she pulled it around her shoulders as she stepped from the bed. Her boots were nowhere to be seen and the cold flag stones stung her bare feet. Cautiously, she felt the wound at the nape of her neck where the Irish sword pommel had sent her world into darkness. It was tender to the touch but some-one had applied a sticky poultice with the pungent odour of sage.

Anya opened the door and looked along the narrow passageway. It was lit by a flickering torch and the bright light made her blink. A spiral staircase descended into darkness. A distant hum of conversation drifted up the stairwell but she could not hear what language was being spoken. She hesitated, her body tense with fear. Where was she? Ireland?

The stairwell was not lit, and she ran her fingers against the stone walls for guidance, her bare feet feeling for the edge of each ice-cold, stone step. The voices grew louder the further she descended and then, without warning, the stairs came to an abrupt end. The great hall was stiflingly warm, the air sweet with wood smoke. Fine tapestries of hunting scenes hung from the walls and intricate carvings of horse races spiralled up the wooden aisle posts towards the blackened thatch. Three hunting dogs sprawled, fast asleep, beside the huge fire that burned in the central hearth.

Twelve men sat around a long, rectangular table that was strewn untidily with parchments, wine glasses and platters of food. Their conversation ceased and each man turned to look at her. Anya's heart began to pound. Were these the same men who had slaughtered her guards on the road to Aquae Sulis?

One man rose to his feet, and the rest quickly followed suit.

'Welcome to Tintagel, fortress of Etar, king of Dumnonia. I am Silvanus, his son.'

He spoke in the language of the Dumnonii and Anya did not understand him. She looked blankly at him, so he tried again, repeating his greeting in Latin.

This time, Anya understood, but she had never heard of Tintagel. 'Are you Irish?' she asked, in Latin.

Silvanus took a step towards her, but Anya retreated a pace. He stopped in his tracks, holding his hands out in a gesture of surrender.

'There's no need to be afraid. We are not Irish. Dumnonia lies in the far west of Britannia. You were shipwrecked on our shore, and you were the only survivor. You are safe now.'

'The only survivor?' Anya repeated faintly.

So Gaius, the warrior with the eyes of a philosopher, had

drowned with the rest. Anya stared at Silvanus. She had no idea if she should believe this man, no idea if she truly was safe. She tugged the edges of her cloak together defensively and shivered, despite the fierce heat in the hall. She had never heard of Dumnonia, and she was far from everything and everyone she had ever known. This man presumably realised she had been destined for the slave markets of Ireland. Did he now consider her his property?

'I am not a slave,' she said firmly. 'And never will be.'

'There are no slaves in Dumnonia,' Silvanus replied solemnly. 'We do not sell men for profit. We are not barbarians.'

Anya's eyes widened in disbelief, for there were many slaves in Germania.

'So, if you are not a slave, then who are you?' Silvanus asked gently.

Anya did not reply, torn with indecision. Could she trust this man? He did not appear to be much older than her. He dressed as a Saxon might, but he looked very different to the men of Germania, with his short, brown hair and eyes the colour of ripe hazelnuts. He was strikingly handsome, with a long straight nose, and a strong, angular jaw-line. Over six feet tall, he had a warrior's build; broad shoulders tapered to narrow hips and strong muscular legs. She frowned slightly. There was something familiar about this man, as if she had met him before, a long, long time ago.

Silvanus was watching her closely, one dark eyebrow raised, as if awaiting her answer.

'I am -' Anya began, but then hesitated.

If she revealed her high-born status, she offered herself as a perfect hostage. 'My name is Anya, and I am a free-born Saxon of Germania,' she replied.

Silvanus's eyes widened with astonishment. For a moment he appeared at a loss for words.

'The Irish do not usually raid the shores of Germania,' he said at last, and there was an edge and a question in his voice.

'I was… it's a long story…' her voice trailed away. It was stiflingly hot in the hall and the wound at the base of her skull from Angus's sword pommel was beginning to throb angrily.

Silvanus visibly softened at her obvious distress.

'No doubt you are anxious to return to your homeland and your kin. We will see you safely home, I swear it.'

His kindness and concern was so unexpected that Anya felt her body tremble and her world begin to spin. She could never go home. Exile was such a harsh word. It sounded like a blow from a sharp sword. She realised Silvanus was still waiting for her to reply.

'Thank you for your kindness,' she said stiffly. 'And thank you, also, for saving my life.'

'The gods saved your life, not me,' Silvanus replied. 'I can see that you are unwell. You should sit a while. Will you eat with us?'

'Thank you, but no. I am tired and would like to rest.'

'As you wish. I will have some food sent up to you.'

The men around the table bowed their heads respectfully as Anya climbed the narrow spiral staircase back to her chamber. And they remained standing for several minutes, as a heavy silence descended.

Silvanus was deep in thought. The heap of lifeless rags they had found on the beach two nights since, had literally risen from the dead and was virtually unrecognisable now. He would never have guessed from the girl's appearance that she was a Saxon. For many years now, her kind had raided the shores of Britannia, looting and pillaging. The Saxons brought death and suffering. They were, without doubt, the enemy.

And yet, she had not acted like the enemy. The girl was a curious mix of both brave and vulnerable, for although she had held her head high, her feet were bare, and her hair uncombed.

Evric spoke first, his face alight with excitement. 'It's her!'

Silvanus turned to face his oldest friend. Together they had faced the boredom of the school-room, mastered the skills of the sword and bow, and learnt to ride across the bleak moors of Dumnonia. Silvanus loved Evric like a brother but his boyish enthusiasm could at times border on the naive.

'Don't be foolish, Evric,' he said dismissively.

'But I saw the way you were looking at her! I know what you were thinking. And she sensed it too. You could see it in her eyes.'

'There was nothing in her eyes but fear and confusion,' Silvanus said grimly.

'But the prophecy!' Evric promptly broke into song. 'There will be chaos and destruction at the world end, but a second earth shall arise. Epona shall come, from the depths of the green sea, and she will bring hope and life to this new, golden earth.'

'I know the song, Evric,' Silvanus said patiently.

'It's more than a song! It is a prophecy!' Evric turned to the men seated around the table. 'Boult? Gorran? Jago? Who will speak for me?'

Jago raised his hand. Like so many of the men of Dumnonia, he was noticeably good looking, black haired and dark eyed. 'Perhaps Evric is right. The girl came from the sea, just as the prophecy foretold. Would it be such a hardship to marry such a beautiful girl? She would give you fine sons. New life for a new golden earth.'

Silvanus shook his head. 'The prophecy can be interpreted in many ways. And I must point out that the world is not ending, and that girl is not an earth goddess called Epona. She was bound for the slave markets of Ireland.'

'She's not a slave,' Evric persisted.

'So she says,' Silvanus replied. 'But even if she isn't a slave, she *is* a Saxon. She is our enemy.'

'But Taliesin has seen Epona in his dream paths,' Evric continued doggedly.

Silvanus held up his hand, and Evric was silenced.

'I respect our priest, but throughout his long years on this earth, he has foretold many things, most of which have not come to pass. Enough. I will hear no more of this.'

Silvanus sat down on the edge of his father's bed, taking care not to awaken him and watched him as he slept. Etar, high king of Dumnonia had been bed-ridden these last few months. His room was in darkness save for the fire that burned constantly to warm his tired bones, and thick tapestries adorned the walls to keep out the drafts. The air smelled of wood smoke and old age, intermingled with the pungent odour of medicinal potions.

Etar's strong face was ravaged by sickness, his sallow skin stretched thinly across his cheekbones. He had once been such a strong, virile man. As a child Silvanus had watched his father ride away from Tintagel to rout the Irish, and he had seemed god-like, immortal and invincible. It was heart-rending to watch Etar growing frailer with each passing day.

Etar opened his eyes, and smiled at his elder son.

'I am sorry I must leave you at such a time.' His voice was

little more than a whisper, his breathing shallow and uneven.

'Do not talk of leaving,' Silvanus began but his father raised a thin hand, his finger joints swollen with age.

'We must talk of it. It is the way of things. When I was a child I used to believe Dumnonia wore a cloak of invisibility, and that the troubles of the world would never find us, but I fear our days of peace may be numbered.'

Silvanus looked into his father's pale, watery eyes. He did not wish his father to live out his final days in fear, and so he chose to lie.

'All will be well, father. The Irish tribes fight amongst themselves. They have no unity to create an army large enough to seriously threaten us.'

'I am not thinking of the Irish. I may be dying but I still know what is happening beyond these four walls. The tribes of Britannia are at war. The merchants bring news and they speak of Vortigern of the Dobunni, of his greed and ambition. And what of the men of Germania who raid the southern shores?'

'You must not trouble yourself, father. You know that our kingdom is my first priority, my only priority. I would give my life for it.'

'I know this,' Etar nodded. 'I am proud of you, Silvanus. You are everything a father could wish for in a son. That is why I die with an easy heart.'

Silvanus looked uncomfortable. 'No more talk of death, father, please.'

Etar shifted slightly, trying to relieve the pressure on the terrible sores that now afflicted him. Silvanus rose to help but Etar gestured his son away. Silvanus sat down again, his heart heavy. Etar had been a strong, wise ruler of Dumnonia. He had dedicated his life to his kingdom and served its people with great integrity but now he was dying and it was tearing a hole in Silvanus's heart. Nor was he ready for the burden of kingship that would soon fall upon his shoulders.

Silvanus knew his own strengths. In the heat of battle with a sword in his hand, he gained a kind of terrible clarity of vision and his men followed him unquestioningly. But in matters of state, on the other hand, he felt woefully inadequate compared to his father. Etar ruled with such wisdom that everyone thought Dumnonia was blessed by the gods. How could he ever hope to emulate his father's success? How could he ever hope to keep Dumnonia safe?

He commanded a warband of just fifty warriors, men who would gladly fight to the death to protect their kingdom, but Dumnonia had no army. Etar had always sworn that his kingdom's isolation was its shield, but of late he had begun to wonder if the deep forest of Selwood and the wild moors of Dumnonia would hold an enemy at bay.

'So Silvanus, tell me about this girl saved from an Irish shipwreck. They tell me she is beautiful.' Etar paused, but his son did not reply, so he went on. 'Taliesin says she is Epona.'

Silvanus looked at his father.

'Since when have you taken notice of earth goddesses and ancient legends?'

'But she *is* beautiful?' Etar smiled, a glimmer of his wicked humour still remaining.

Silvanus shrugged and did not reply.

Etar's smile faded. 'Taliesin has seen Epona in his dream paths. He truly believes this girl could be the one.'

Silvanus shook his head in disbelief. 'But she is a Saxon! You know I have always had the utmost respect for our priest, but he is not in the fullness of youth, and there are times when he seems confused.'

'But you must agree it is curious that she came from the sea? New life for a new golden age. Isn't that how the prophecy goes?'

'It might not even be a prophecy. The song is so old, no-one knows where it came from, or even what it means.'

Etar looked hard at his son. 'There is war in Britannia. How long before our borders are threatened?'

'Are you seriously suggesting I should marry a Saxon, our known enemy, to fulfil an ancient, ambiguous prophecy? It can be interpreted in many ways. It does not necessarily mean marriage and children.'

'I know, I know. I may be old, but I am not yet a fool. I have always known that the gods walk amongst us, but who can say what Taliesin sees in the cave of fires? He has been mistaken many times before. You are my son and heir. Your wife will bear the future king of Dumnonia. It would be madness to bind you to a girl who was destined for the slave markets of Ireland, on the strength of an ancient prophecy and an old man's mumblings.'

Silvanus nodded, relieved his father was seeing sense at last.

'Yes, father, it would indeed.'

'I would need proof. A good deal more proof,' Etar added.

Silvanus raised his eyebrows incredulously.

'Proof?' he spluttered. 'There can be no proof!'

Etar's eyes were closing.

'Go now, I am weary and must rest.'

Silvanus stood up. 'Of course, father. Sleep well.'

He closed the door of his father's chamber and then walked quickly through the great hall of Tintagel. He felt angry with the world. He did not want his father to die. And he certainly did not want to marry a Saxon girl simply because

Taliesin claimed to have spoken with the gods in the cave of fires.

Had Etar conveniently forgotten the tribes of Germania were pirates, thieves and murderers? It was as good as opening the gates of Tintagel and welcoming the enemy with open arms.

Had his father finally lost his mind?

SIXTEEN

Anya stared out to sea. The ever present wind whipped her hair across her face and its fierce blasts rocked her backwards. After the silence of her watch-tower room, the fortress was deafening – the gulls caught in the wind as they circled overhead, reeling and wailing; the regular chime of the blacksmith's hammer; the carpenters' saws; the plaintive bleats of the corralled sheep; the laughter of playing children.

Etar's seat of power sat upon a craggy mound of splintered grey rock, endlessly pounded by the waves of the Atlantic sea. Only a narrow neck of land connected it to the mainland of Dumnonia, guarded by a wide ditch more than fifteen feet deep. Etar's ancestors had terraced the sloping cliff top of Tintagel and the huge fortress was now densely packed with buildings. Some were built of stone but many more were timber framed with roofs of turf or thatch, like those of her homeland. Anya smiled to herself. She liked this place. So much of Britannia seemed forlorn and bereft, like a fallow field awaiting a new crop but Tintagel bustled with a sense of community and purpose. It reminded her of home.

Homesickness tugged at her heart and then she thought of Vortigern, and her stomach lurched with fear. She had learnt enough about him during her time in Calleva to know that if he set his mind upon something, he would not cease until he possessed it. He would not stop looking for her. She could not remain in Dumnonia.

She began to twist her mother's copper ring round and round her finger. She closed her eyes and her mind wandered to the village in the shadow of the black mountains. She could hear the stream as it hurried over its rocky bed, she could smell the air, cold and crisp and clean, and she could hear the bleating of sheep as dusk fell.

Perhaps in Siluria, shielded by towering mountains, she would be safe from Vortigern's reach. Anya opened her eyes again. Much as she yearned to seek sanctuary with her mother's kin, how long would it be before Vortigern found her there? And then what terrible price would the villagers in the shadow of the mountains have to pay?

Anya walked closer to the cliff edge, where a dry stone wall guarded the vertical drop. Far beneath her in the harbour, a merchant ship had moored, and pack-mules, laden with cargo from the far corners of the world, were making the slow, agonising climb up the winding cliff path to the fortress. As they reached the cliff top, she approached the man who appeared to be in charge. His face was tanned like leather, and he had worn the same set of clothes for so many months that they had almost become a second skin. He smelled appalling.

'Who is your captain?' she asked, in Latin.

'I am. The name's Lucius. Who are you?'

'I am Anya.'

'And you're a Saxon,' the man said accusingly. 'I know that accent.' He glanced nervously behind him, out to sea, as if expecting to see Saxon ships rounding the headland.

'I'm alone,' Anya assured him. 'I want to ask a favour.'

'I'm not in the habit of doing favours for Saxons – even if they do look as good as you.'

'I can understand your reluctance,' Anya said politely.

'Oh, you can, can you?' Lucius mocked. 'Your kind are pirates. They would slit our throats and tip us overboard as soon as look at us. We haven't traded on the south coast of Britannia for years because of your kind. It's too dangerous, so we go the extra distance and come in here. It's safe, and Etar makes us welcome. We often stay for weeks at a time. Etar likes us to tell him what we've seen on our travels. He says we are his ears and eyes on the world. And he's a good customer too - he buys our wine, figs, dates, olive oil, pottery from Gaul, gold from Constantinople, glass from Alexandria, silk from the east. They like to live well, these Dumnonii. And in exchange, we buy his copper, his tin, his fleeces.'

Lucius eyed Anya, his voice softening a little. 'So, what was this favour?'

'I need to leave Britannia. Will you take me with you?'

'What have you done? I will not have some mad, murdering bitch on my ship even if she does look like an angel.'

'I am no murderer.' She hesitated. 'I am to be married.'

'And you don't like the bastard?'

'Something like that,' Anya nodded. 'I have this.' She tugged her cloak aside and pointed to the thick torque about her neck. 'It's solid gold and it's yours if you take me with you, but you must swear to tell no-one of our conversation.'

Lucius looked at the torque. 'When I leave Tintagel, I will make sail for the coast of southern Gaul. Would that suit you?'

'Yes. That would suit as well as anywhere,' Anya replied.

She held out her hand, and Lucius shook it. His palm felt

hard and rough against her skin, but his smile seemed genuine enough.

'Lucius!'

Startled, Anya glanced over her shoulder. Silvanus was striding towards them, followed by a man she recognised from the great hall. Silvanus was glaring at their hands, clasped in accord. Unnerved, she quickly released the merchant's hand and stepped away from him.

'Welcome to Tintagel, old friend,' Silvanus went on, suddenly amicable once more. 'It's been too long. Evric will escort you to your quarters. I look forward to hearing your news this evening.'

Lucius nodded deferentially. 'We thank you for your hospitality, as always, Lord.'

Evric led Lucius and his crew towards the great hall. Anya waited for Silvanus to say something but he looked intensely hostile and an awkward silence fell.

'I will leave you,' Anya said at last.

'You have business with Lucius?' Silvanus asked abruptly.

'No,' Anya lied.

Silvanus's eyes narrowed slightly. 'I trust you are recovered,' he said curtly.

Anya touched the wound at the nape of her neck.

'Yes, thank you. I am well.'

She cast a glance at Silvanus. His smouldering anger hung around him like a heavy cloak, and she wondered what was the cause of it.

'I would like to see this kingdom of yours,' she said softly.

She saw his shoulders tense and he did not reply for a long time. Finally, he said: 'I have to inspect the horses. You could ride with me, if you wish'.

'Yes, thank you. I would like that,' Anya replied.

The village in the shadow of the fortress stood high on the cliffs, cowering against the wind behind deep ditches. As they rode nearer Anya could smell the stench of fish and hear the seagulls. They swirled around the village reeling and shrieking like mourners at a funeral. The village was alive with activity. Pigs, sheep and goats were crammed in wicker pens between squat huts, thickly thatched against the elements. Women stood at long tables, up to their elbows in fish guts. They chattered, laughed and scolded the barefoot children who played at their feet.

The villagers gathered around Silvanus and Anya, excited by this unexpected visit from their future king. Anya did not understand their language but their kindness did not need translation. They showered her with gifts, even though they had very little to give - hurriedly picked flowers, a freshly baked loaf of bread, a shiny, sparkling stone. And some reached out to touch her, as if she were a goddess, and said just one word: 'Epona'.

Anya watched the anger return to Silvanus's face. He turned away, his good humour evaporating in an instant. They rode on across bleak moors, along narrow tracks between a sea of purple heather. The wind swirled and swooped around them and she savoured its flavours on her tongue - salt and fish and seaweed, fading to the flowery sweetness of yellow gorse bushes.

Silvanus was a fine horseman and she had to dig in her heels to keep up with him. When at last Silvanus reined in and leapt from his horse, she was exhilarated and breathless. Before her, vast horse-pounds stretched far down the valley. She had never seen so many horses gathered together in one place.

Silvanus leant against the top railing of the wooden fence,

his eyes scanning methodically as he counted the herd. The wind tugged Anya's cloak about her as she waited for him to finish.

'Who is Epona?' she asked at last.

'There are not enough hours in the day for me to teach you the language of the Dumnonii,' Silvanus snapped. He stared out over the horse pounds, his eyes narrowed against the fierce blasts of wind that raced down the valley.

Anya refused to be intimidated by his cold hostility. 'Do your horses ever run free?'

He turned to face her, his mouth pressed into a hard line.

'They are free for most of the time, but they have been rounded up for our annual horse fair. The Irish tribes swap their swords for their purses and come to trade with us.' Without warning, his expression softened. 'They drink too much of our beer, but they will leave behind their gold. It's a fair exchange.'

Anya's face broke into a smile. She glanced back at the horse pounds. 'Your cavalry must be a sight to behold.'

'Why do you say that?' Silvanus asked sharply, his manner guarded once again.

'No reason,' she replied quickly. She wondered what had caused his sudden, renewed hostility. Silvanus's moods were as changeable as the weather and she was struggling to keep up with them.

Another awkward silence descended. Finally, Silvanus spoke. 'The Dumnonii are renowned horsemen. Long ago, my family bred horses for the Roman army. Nowadays our customers are the Irish, the Gauls, and our neighbours, the Durotriges. And Vortigern of the Dobunni, of course, for his cavalry.'

Anya gasped involuntarily. She felt as if she had been

punched in the gut. She had not expected to hear Vortigern's name and quite suddenly, she felt afraid and off balance, as if she was no longer standing on solid ground.

'What's the matter?' Silvanus asked, watching her intently.

Anya's eyes met his, but she was not seeing him. She was back in Calleva, watching Hengist dispose of her as casually as if she were a broken bucket, in order to bolster a treaty few thought was wise.

'What's the matter?' Silvanus repeated.

'Nothing,' Anya replied dully.

Silvanus sighed and ran a hand through his short hair. He looked frustrated. Silence descended once again. Anya stared blankly at the vast herd as it grazed peacefully in the afternoon sunshine. She was thinking about Vortigern and the naked lust in his eyes.

'Is Saxony very different to Dumnonia?'

Anya jolted, startled from her thoughts. The tone of Silvanus's voice had changed yet again. It was much gentler now.

She nodded. Saxony was entirely different to Dumnonia. Here on the moors, the cold wind was a physical force, exploding with a raw, vibrant energy. But at this time of the year, Saxony was lethargic with summer heat. The wheat and barley were ripening in the fields and at harvest time you could taste their sweetness in the warm, sleepy air.

She sensed Silvanus was waiting for an answer, but it hurt too much to think of home. She lowered her gaze and stared at the ground.

Silvanus raised an eyebrow and began to toy with the signet ring he wore on his right hand, repeatedly twisting it round his middle finger. Anya smiled to herself for she shared the same habit. She wondered if he was angry again, or merely deep in thought. The heir to the throne of Dumnonia was a difficult man to read. She glanced at his ring. She recognised the cartwheel shape cut into the sun-stone, glinting each time the ring turned full circle.

'The cartwheel?' she asked. 'It represents Lugh, the sun god?'

'Yes, the spokes of the wheel are the rays of the sun reaching out over the earth,' he replied absently.

'We also have such a god, at home.' Anya touched her cartwheel brooch that held her cloak together.

'But you are far from your home. And I am sorry for that.'

Anya was surprised by the sincerity in his voice. 'Have you travelled far beyond Britannia?' she asked.

'I've never been beyond the borders of Dumnonia. My father sends emissaries to make treaties and trade.'

'Then you are indeed fortunate. There is no greater happiness than home, the hearth and loved ones.'

'And we will not keep you from them,' Silvanus said quietly. 'We will see you safely home, just as I promised.'

Tears pricked her eyes. She turned away from him, angry with herself for her weakness. She swallowed hard and forced herself to face him again. 'Thank you.'

'You are most welcome,' Silvanus replied formally, but the compassion in his eyes was unmistakeable and it took her breath away. She stared at him, bewildered and confused. The heir to the throne of Dumnonia was a baffling, contradictory man, as volatile and unpredictable as the vast northern sea.

SEVENTEEN

Anya was sitting on the low stone wall at the cliff edge, staring at the ocean again. There was something mesmerising about the never ending waves, their foaming spray crashing angrily against the black cliffs far below. She thought she could look at the sea forever and never grow bored.

'You must be the girl who survived the shipwreck.'

Startled, Anya stood up and spun around.

'I am Lucan, Silvanus's brother.'

He clasped her hand and the vision knocked the air from her lungs as if she had run headlong into a wall. A gusting wind was squalling against high cliffs, and a small figure was falling through the air, arms and legs flailing wildly. A terrible scream was cut short and Anya jolted as the figure hit the beach, the broken body splayed like a starfish on a strand line.

Who was falling? Was it Abberlen? And yet there were no cliffs in Saxony.

Lucan quickly released her hand, as if afraid her Saxon blood might be contagious.

'What's the matter with you?' he asked curtly.

Anya took a deep breath, leaning back against the wall to steady herself. 'Nothing is the matter. I'm still a little weak from my injury.'

Lucan was neither as tall, nor as handsome as his older brother. Unruly black hair flopped into a pair of cold, slate-grey eyes. There were unsightly pimples on his cheeks and a thin line of dark downy hair on his upper lip.

'Why were you staring at the sea?'

'Because it fascinates me. I'm a Saxon. We have no sea,' Anya explained, still struggling to make sense of the image that had seared across her mind.

'How can the Saxons be pirates without a sea?'

'Some of the Germanic tribes may be pirates, but many more are not,' Anya replied calmly.

'It's hard to believe you were the only one saved. The gods of the ocean must love you,' Lucan went on slyly.

'I don't think so.' Anya shuddered as memories flooded back. 'I would be happy never to endure another sea crossing.'

'So why were you talking to Lucius?'

Anya's heart began to thud in alarm. 'Lucius?'

'The merchant.'

'Ah, yes.' Anya thought fast. 'I asked him what merchandise he was carrying. In Germania, there is always great excitement when a merchant barge arrives at our village.'

'You shook hands. You made an accord.'

'You are mistaken. Why would I make an accord with a merchant? I have no coin, and nothing to barter with.'

Lucan was staring at her, his eyes full of mistrust and suspicion.

'I may be a Saxon, but I am not your enemy,' she added honestly.

'Then why are you here?' His tone was cold and accusing.

'I'm not here by choice, as you well know.'

Lucan laughed humourlessly. 'So you say. I should warn

you, the people of Tintagel do not want a Saxon in their midst. And you should bear in mind that my father metes out harsh punishment to spies discovered in our kingdom. More often than not, he throws them from the cliffs.'

Anya's eyes widened. 'I am no spy!'

'Can you prove your innocence?'

'Can you prove my guilt?' Anya retorted.

Lucan snorted. 'You have a sharp tongue but, be warned, it will not save you.'

He turned abruptly and walked away, leaving Anya to stare in alarm at his retreating back. She wondered anxiously how long Lucius intended to remain in Tintagel. She prayed he would make sail soon, for Lucan had made it painfully clear she would find no sanctuary here.

Anya tugged the edges of her cloak together as she walked back towards Etar's stronghold. Summers in Saxony were hot, the earth baked hard beneath a benevolent sun. But in Tintagel, even at the height of summer, the strong and constant wind was sharp and full of bite.

An old man was walking towards her along the cliff path. He had a deeply lined face like the bark of an old vine. He was painfully thin and a filthy robe hung from his bony shoulders. The robe had once been white but now was stained and crudely patched. His long, grey hair hung lifelessly over his shoulders and as he drew closer she could smell the grease and dirt that bound it into cotters. He raised his right hand in greeting and his wide sleeve fell back to his elbow to reveal fading tattoos that adorned every inch of his loose skin, one for each anniversary of his initiation, many years ago.

Anya stopped in her tracks. The old man was a member of the priesthood. Images of the sacred grove flooded her mind: Emma's final terrible moments and the high priest's indifference to her suffering as he studied her death throes. Anya turned away and began to hurry back the way she had come. She did not want to talk to this man.

'Wait!' the old man shouted. 'Wait! I would speak with you!'

She slowed her pace, torn with indecision, her distaste battling with her innate sense of good manners. She was a guest in Tintagel and it would be a gross insult to ignore Etar's priest. She turned to face the old man.

'I have been eager to meet you,' the priest said, in Latin. He clasped her hands and his grasp was surprisingly strong. He looked her firmly in the eye and it was more than a greeting - it was a reckoning. After several moments he let go of her hands and nodded, as if satisfied.

'Welcome to Tintagel, Anya.'

She nodded wordlessly.

'I would like to invite you into my home, such as it is.'

'I -' she began, desperately searching for a feasible excuse.

'I will hear no excuses,' Taliesin said gently, as if he had read her mind.

Taliesin, high priest of Etar, king of Dumnonia, lived alone. His turf walled and thatch roofed hut was just large enough for one simple, sparsely furnished room. It stood within the walls of Tintagel, surrounded by a low, wattle fence that enclosed a haphazard garden of herbs and medicinal plants. The narrow path to Taliesin's door was made up of broken shards of pots and amphorae, and straggling rosemary and lavender plants threatened to engulf it.

Anya stepped inside and hoped her face would not betray her dismay. It was obvious Taliesin had no slave to tidy or clean for him. The hut smelled fetid; of unwashed flesh and dirty, flea infested bed rugs. The wooden rafters were festooned with cobwebs, and the floor rushes were slimy and rotting. There was little in the way of furniture apart from a table that was covered with chipped glass ink pots and piles of scrolls. Every available inch of wall was filled with wooden shelves, haphazardly crammed with baskets of drying herbs, medicine bottles and wax-sealed jars.

Anya stepped closer, ducking her head to avoid the bunches of dried yarrow and thyme that hung from the roof joists. She made her way slowly along the shelves. Horseradish roots were useful in a poultice for wounds that refused to heal. Cowslip roots and flowers made a good linctus for a persistent cough. Rosemary leaves and burnet saxifrage were both powerful remedies for lung and stomach afflictions, rheumatism and memory loss. She wondered if these were for Etar, the high king of Dumnonia, who now kept to his room and was dying, if the rumours were true.

'You know something of the healing arts, I think?' Taliesin asked.

Anya physically jumped. 'Forgive me, I was lost for a moment.'

'No matter,' Taliesin smiled. 'But my medicines, they interest you?'

She did not answer. They interested her greatly, reminding her poignantly of home. She glanced at the two huge amphorae in the corner, their pointed bases dug into the earth floor. 'You do business with Lucius?'

Taliesin nodded. 'I'm partial to his fine wine. Our barley-beer lacks its refinement.' He stared hard at her. 'I'm glad Etar suggested I should meet you.'

Anya looked at him in amazement.

'I had no idea King Etar took an interest in a girl who was

destined for the slave markets of the Irish.'

'You are no slave and you cannot hide from me.' Taliesin stepped forward, and pulled up her sleeve. Her tattoo was shaped like a cartwheel. Lugh's rays extended from the hub, the source of his strength, to the rim of the world.

'It's new,' Taliesin said. 'You have not long been a priestess.'

Anya snatched her hand away. 'What do you want?'

'Nothing,' Taliesin said quietly. 'I am not your enemy.'

Anya's heart was racing. The high priest of the sacred grove had sent Emma to a terrible death, and she hated him for slaughtering her innocent, defenceless sister. As she stared at the high priest of Dumnonia she wondered if he too was capable of murder.

Taliesin led her to the fireside and handed her a cup of Lucius's wine. 'Talk with me a while. There is no need for secrecy here.'

She sat down, on edge and on her guard. 'So, Christianity has not found Dumnonia?'

'No, the ancient gods are still strong here. The Romans tried hard to extinguish our kind in Britannia. They were afraid of our powers, our knowledge. In the early days they followed our priests to Anglesey, one of our most sacred islands, and slaughtered them with terrible bloodshed. But some survived and the people of Britannia never abandoned their ancient gods.' He paused. 'Tell me, Anya, why did you leave Saxony?'

Anya stared at the old priest. Her secrets were burning a hole in her heart, but she did not want to confide in this man.

'Can I ask you something?' she said softly.

Taliesin nodded.

'War has come to Germania, and the priests are afraid.

They offer men, women and children as sacrifice. Do you think they are right to do so?'

Taliesin frowned. 'In Dumnonia, we decided long ago that human sacrifice is not the way to please the gods.'

'Then you are more enlightened than the priests of Saxony,' Anya said grimly.

Taliesin looked intently at her. 'I believe you have more to tell me?'

She lowered her gaze and shook her head. 'There is nothing else to tell.'

'As you wish.' Taliesin hesitated for a moment. 'You are a healer, I think?'

Anya looked up curiously. 'Yes.'

'A healer's skills are rare. You would be most welcome in Dumnonia.'

Anya did not reply. She knew she could not remain in Dumnonia, as tempting as it seemed. Vortigern's arm was long and he would find her here, sooner or later. She had no choice but to sail far away with Lucius to the southern coast of Gaul, where men said the sea was as warm as a cooking pot.

Taliesin was staring into the fire, his eyes far away.

'Epona,' he said, so softly that she wondered if she had imagined it.

EIGHTEEN

Anya paused in the doorway of the great hall. The air was warm, scented with wood smoke, fresh rushes and the mouth-watering aroma of a rich venison stew. It reminded her painfully of home, although she thought it curious that the raised dais stood empty and no high table separated the king from his people. Tonight, like every other night, Silvanus was seated amongst his kin, eating the same cuts of meat, drinking the same wine, and sharing the same gossip. Taliesin sat at his right hand. Their heads were close together and they were deep in conversation.

Wolfhounds wandered freely about the hall but Anya noticed that they lingered at Silvanus's side. He stroked their long, shaggy coats with one hand whilst he ate and drank with the other, and every now and then, he fed them titbits from his plate.

A feeling more powerful than homesickness tugged at Anya's heart. In the Saxon tongue it was called '*hiraeth*', a longing for days passed, for loved ones lost.

A yearning only a wanderer, an exile, could truly understand.

'Anya!' Lucan shouted. 'Come and sit with us. You have not met my wife.'

His words jolted Anya from her thoughts and she turned to Lucan in surprise. Tonight his manner was warm and amiable, yet earlier in the day he had been cold and hostile and accused her of being a spy. She walked towards the table uneasily.

Lucan's wife smiled serenely.

'I am Mairi. Welcome, Anya.'

'Thank you,' Anya replied and sat down. Mairi was very young, perhaps no more than sixteen years old. She was also very beautiful, with clear, dusky skin and artfully tousled, chestnut coloured hair but Anya noticed that her smile did not reach her deep brown eyes.

'So,' Mairi said brightly. 'I hear you are a slave.'

'I am not a slave,' Anya replied politely.

'Oh! I thought Lucan said you were the only survivor from the slave ship that broke up on the rocks?'

Anya frowned, irritated by the girl's brittle tone. Across the table, Lucius, the merchant, smiled sympathetically. He no longer reeked of the sea. On dry land, Lucius dressed like a king. His tunic of deep purple was finely embroidered with crescent moons, foliage and scrollwork, his shoulder clasps were gold inlaid with garnets, and thick hoops hung from his distended earlobes. Lucius raised his glass.

'I have not forgotten our deal,' he mouthed, glancing at the torque about her neck.

'Thank you,' she whispered back.

Anya took a sip of wine to steady her pounding heart. If Lucius came to learn she was running away from Vortigern, high king of the Dobunni, would his love of gold outweigh his promise to take her to the southern seas? She glanced nervously along the table. Silvanus and Taliesin had been staring at her for some time now and she had a horrible feeling that she had become the subject of their conversation.

'Lucan tells me Silvanus has promised to send you home again,' Mairi said sweetly. 'But I fear that may be impossible. Whilst it's true your kin visit the southern shores of Britannia, how can Silvanus ask a pirate for a favour when he's busy slaughtering our men, and raping our women?'

Anya turned back to Mairi, her eyes wide in astonishment.

'Mairi!' Lucan said sharply and the young girl physically jumped. 'Anya is our guest!' His words were a chastisement, but his eyes sparkled with amusement.

'Forgive me,' Mairi said daintily. 'I am with child, and even the smallest matter makes me cry. And it's hard not to weep when the Saxon pirates are causing such devastation and misery.'

'Yes, do forgive my wife,' Lucan said sarcastically. 'She had little wit before she carried a child in her belly. Now, sadly, she has even less.'

Anya opened her mouth then closed it again, lost for words. The great hall of Tintagel no longer felt so warm or welcoming.

Lucan turned away, seemingly losing interest in the conversation and Anya watched the hurt bloom in Mairi's beautiful eyes. The young girl's expression faltered for a moment then she gathered herself and began talking loudly to the young woman seated on her right.

'Taliesin says the prophecy refers to my unborn son.' She clasped her hands about her swollen belly. 'Taliesin says he is the new life for a new golden age.'

The woman at her side frowned. 'The prophecy could mean many things.'

'Do you doubt the word of our high priest?' Mairi said sharply.

Lucan rolled his eyes. 'Be quiet, Mairi.'

Lucius caught Anya's eye and winked. He banged his cup down on the table with such force that Mairi jumped.

'I believe it's time I told you all a story,' he said loudly. 'What tale would you like to hear tonight?'

'The tale of Circe,' Lucan said, without hesitation, his gaze fixed upon Anya.

'Circe?' Lucius said hesitantly. 'Surely not. Perhaps something a little more humorous?'

Lucan shook his head. 'Let it be Circe,' he said firmly.

Lucius glanced down the noisy table towards Silvanus, but the heir to the throne was still deep in conversation with Taliesin.

'As you wish.' Lucius cleared his throat. 'Circe was the most beguiling of all the immortal goddesses who ever lived in the lands of the Aegean. Her beauty was unsurpassed -'

'Don't forget that she was also a temptress, who used potions and witchcraft to achieve her every wanton desire,' Lucan interrupted. There was an unmistakeably self-satisfied smirk on his face. 'And she was the daughter of Helios, the god of the sun.'

Anya glanced uneasily at the gold sun brooch upon her gown. She had not heard this story. She wondered apprehensively why Lucius had seemed so reluctant to tell the tale and why Lucan was so keen to hear it.

'Yes, indeed, thank you for reminding me,' Lucius said graciously.

The merchant was a skilled story-teller. He told how Odysseus and his warriors, weary after ten long years battling before the walls of Troy, rested a while in the palace of beautiful and bewitching Circe. Overwhelmed by her witchcraft, one by one, Odysseus's crew were transformed into pigs. Only Odysseus, protected by his great grandfather, the god Hermes, slept on in human form, oblivious to the tragedy unfolding around him. Circe ordered a fire to be lit in the hearth, and a spit to be made ready.

'Then, she took four of the squealing pigs and slit their throats, revelling in the sensation of their warm blood running down her naked breasts,' Lucius went on.

A murmur of shock and excitement ran around his enraptured audience.

Lucius paused to take a draught of wine and Anya shifted uncomfortably in her chair. Lucan was watching her intently, his mouth curled into a small smile. She had no doubt why he had wanted Silvanus's kin to hear this lurid tale. Anya squared her shoulders and forced herself to return his gaze unflinchingly.

'Next Circe knelt beside the sleeping Odysseus, caressing him with hands still stained from the blood of his slaughtered warriors, and all the while, her palace was filled with the mouth-watering aroma of roasting pork.'

The great hall gasped in collective distaste. To Anya's dismay, she saw that many heads had turned questioningly in her direction. She took a deep breath, struggling to retain her composure. Angry and humiliated, she was sorely tempted to stand up and run from the hall, but she forced herself to remain seated until Lucius finished his lurid tale.

At last, Lucius raised his glass to the hall. 'Lords, ladies and gentlemen, the moral to my story is this: Beware beautiful women bearing cups of enchanted wine, unless you wish to be spit-roasted over an open fire!'

Lucius's audience broke into applause but Anya sat motionless, as if Circe the enchantress had turned her to stone. Despite the heat in the hall, she felt suddenly cold to her bones. Would she soon find herself on trial for witchcraft in this kingdom at the edge of the world? She remembered the curious vision that had come to her on the cliff top. The small figure falling towards the beach. She shuddered. Had she foreseen her own death? She glanced tentatively around the crowded table again. A hundred pairs of suspicious eyes were now staring fixedly in her direction. She stood up, suddenly unable to bear their scrutiny a moment longer.

'I will take my leave,' she said unsteadily. 'The hour is late and I am weary.'

Lucius put down his wine cup. 'It would be my honour to escort you to your chambers.'

She shot him a grateful glance. 'Thank you, Lucius. You are most kind.'

Silvanus leant back in his chair and watched Anya leave the hall. He noticed that Lucius was holding her firmly by the elbow, as if she needed support. He had watched her closely all evening but her expression had given nothing away. Taliesin could read people, as if their thoughts were words on parchment, but the harder Silvanus had stared at the Saxon girl, the more uncertain he had become.

He ran a hand through his hair and let out an exasperated sigh. Lucan was rarely subtle. It was obvious why he had chosen the story of the temptress Circe with her magic potions and seductive charms. Until this night, the majority of Tintagel's gossip mongers had claimed Anya to be Epona, the saviour of the kingdom. But following Lucius's dramatic rendition, Silvanus suspected opinion would shift sharply against her, and who could blame the people of Dumnonia for being mistrustful of a stranger in their midst?

'Circe is not flesh and blood, and nor has she ever been,'

Taliesin said reassuringly. 'She plays a small role in an ancient myth, no more, no less. It would be foolish to compare her to Anya.'

'Perhaps,' Silvanus replied, unconvinced. He glanced at Taliesin and his brow furrowed with concern. The old priest looked tired and frail and he felt a sudden stab of melancholy. The two men he admired and respected most in the world had both grown old and poignantly vulnerable.

As the days passed, Silvanus had come to realise that his father would not recover from this malady. Soon he would lie in the dark chamber beneath the burial mound of his ancestors with its odour of rich, warm earth, of dampness and of death. And he knew he would be utterly lost without him.

A wolf hound sidled up and rested its head on his knee. He stroked its coarse coat absently, his thoughts far away. As Etar's health continued to deteriorate, he had begun to shoulder more and more of the burdens of kingship. Yet again, the shire courts had failed to resolve their cases and so yet again, he had spent a morning listening to disputes involving cattle rustling, robbery and assault. And then a messenger had arrived with the news of an accident at the Tamar mine. A huge collapse had left twenty men trapped deep underground.

On days like this, he felt as if he was drowning in other men's troubles.

'Will you ride south to Tamar?' Taliesin asked, reading Silvanus's thoughts again.

Silvanus turned the sun stone ring round and round his finger, torn with indecision. Would the close-knit mining community welcome him, or think he was interfering?

'What would my father do?' he asked at last.

'He would ride south, to show his support.'

Silvanus nodded slowly. 'Then I will leave at daybreak.'

Silence fell again.

It was Taliesin who broke it. 'Anya is a priestess.'

'The Saxon girl? Are you sure?' Silvanus leant forward, astonished.

'Oh yes, I am sure. She has the mark of the priesthood, and she is a healer.'

Silvanus took a moment to digest this information. 'So how did she come to be on board an Irish slave-ship?'

'I do not know. She would not say.'

'We rode out together,' Silvanus said, remembering the afternoon he had spent in her company. He frowned, deep in thought. Until now, until this girl had come from the sea, the Saxons had never truly been flesh and blood. They were simply the enemy; they raided, raped and slaughtered. In truth, Anya was not what he had expected. She had behaved impeccably. She was refined, dignified and self-assured.

But she was also evasive beyond measure. Throughout their entire conversation, she had spoken in riddles, as if the words she had left unspoken were infinitely more interesting than those she had uttered. He shook his head in frustration. It was entirely possible that Anya *was* a spy, for she had remained infuriatingly tight lipped about all aspects of her life.

'That girl is full of secrets. I don't trust her. She's a Saxon. She's the enemy,' he said firmly.

Taliesin shook his head so vigorously that a long strand of dirty hair splashed into his venison stew. 'She is not your enemy.'

'Why do you say that?'

'Because she is Epona.'

Silvanus took a deep breath, struggling to control his

temper. 'It's a song, Taliesin. Just a song,' he said gently.

'I beg to differ. It is a prophecy, and I for one, believe it speaks to us. There is chaos and destruction beyond the borders of Dumnonia. Anya has seen it -'

'Does she claim to be Epona?' Silvanus interrupted sharply.

'No, no,' Taliesin said hurriedly.

Silvanus sat back in his chair wearily. 'One moment, you would have me believe that Anya is a goddess raised from the sea to fulfil an ancient prophecy. The next, that the tale of Circe is just myth and nonsense. Tell me, Taliesin, why should I believe one, and not the other?'

NINETEEN

The next morning, Anya awoke at dawn. Even at first light, Tintagel was alive with bustle and activity. She ducked her head to avoid the cord hung across the laundry courtyard and the linen sheets flapping in the wind. Fishermen's wives were hauling carts brimming with the catch of the day towards the kitchens, laughing and gossiping as they struggled over the uneven cobbles.

They came to a halt and bowed their heads respectfully as Silvanus and two of his warriors rode by on fine warhorses. The heir to the throne raised his right hand in greeting to the women and then he and his men were gone, galloping through the open gate in a storm of clattering hooves.

Anya watched them turn south. In the corridors of Tintagel, everyone was speaking of the accident at the Tamar mine. She gripped the edge of her cloak against the biting wind and said a silent prayer for the miners trapped so far beneath the unforgiving earth, and for Silvanus and his men, riding to their aid.

A small market lay in the lee of the westerly wall and even at this early hour, Lucius was already plying his trade. He looked resplendent in a cloak of imperial purple, hemmed with gold. Upon his head he wore an exotic turban of dark blue silk that barely contained his lustrous curls. In his hands he bore a large cushion, bedecked with necklaces, bracelets and ear-rings of jet, amber and gold. His progress around the courtyard was slow for he was surrounded by a crowd of entranced serving girls, buying his wares and hanging on his every word.

'I have seen sights and wonders beyond your imagining. Mountains that touch the sky, waterfalls of immense power, animals patterned like rainbows, and men so outlandish, with such customs so alien and bizarre, that they can only be gods come down to earth.'

One of his men was trailing along behind, yawning loudly and carrying a leather purse heavy with coin. He looked bored, as if he had heard it all before.

The high wall offered the stall holders little protection against the fierce, gusting wind. An empty wicker basket took to the air and flew high above Anya's head, before coming to land on a roof top. She smiled to herself. Tintagel thrummed with life and purpose, untouched by the chaos and fear beyond its borders.

Her smile faded. How long before news reached Vortigern, high king of the Dobunni, that a Saxon girl with red hair was a guest of Etar of Dumnonia? Vortigern would not want to listen to Etar's protestations of innocence. He would lead his army to the walls Tintagel, and slaughter the Dumnonii for daring to take what was his. She was putting these people in grave danger. She needed to leave, and it must be soon. She took a deep breath and approached Lucius.

'May I speak with you alone?' she asked.

Lucius waved his hand dismissively at the serving girls. They wandered away, eyeing Anya with barely disguised expressions of jealousy and suspicion.

Lucius turned to face her, spinning flamboyantly in his silk slippers.

'It would be my pleasure. He thrust the cushion at his assistant. 'Take this. Don't drop it!'

The merchant led her to a quiet corner of the courtyard.

'I fear I offended you with my storytelling yesterday evening, and for that, I offer you a thousand more apologies.'

'You are mistaken if you thought such a fanciful tale would cause me distress,' Anya replied calmly.

'Anya, I saw your tattoo the very first time I met you on the cliff top. You are of the priesthood, but you are also a Saxon. Many will believe you are blessed by the gods, but many others will believe you capable of curdling their cow's milk or cursing unborn babes to die in their mother's womb.'

A shiver of fear ran over Anya's skin. 'I am no witch!'

'I know,' Lucius said gently.

She stared at him uncertainly. 'When do you intend to make sail?'

'Not before the full moon. There is still much trade to be done and old acquaintances to be renewed.'

'Oh!' Anya failed to hide her disappointment.

'Don't worry,' Lucius said reassuringly. 'You may have enemies in Tintagel but you have allies too. I count myself in the latter camp, and I know Taliesin has faith in you, and trusts you.'

Anya could not bring herself to speak. In Saxony, she had felt loved and protected, yet in Dumnonia her only allies were an outlandish merchant and an old priest who stank like a piss pot. How had her life come to this?

'Come, come,' Lucius cajoled. 'You are too beautiful to be so sad. All may yet end well, for there are many here who believe you are Epona.'

'I have heard people speak of Epona. Who is she?' Anya asked curiously.

Lucius smiled. 'You should ask Taliesin that question, not me.'

Anya stood outside Taliesin's door for a long time. Torn with indecision, she watched the bees moving quietly amongst the flower heads of his straggling lavender bushes. She did not believe the high priest of Dumnonia could ever be her ally. Not only had his kind murdered her sister but the old priest also had the ear of Etar's son and heir. And yet despite all her reservations, she was strangely drawn to Taliesin, reassured by his gentle demeanour and his shelves crammed with familiar, healing herbs. She took a deep breath and knocked loudly.

Taliesin took a long time to open the door. He was still wearing the same filthy robe and he stank of rank, dirty hair and stale sweat. His complexion was pallid and he looked drawn and tired. Anya glanced over his shoulder. His round house was packed with men, women and children, all talking at once. An unhappy baby was wailing persistently and the noise was deafening.

'Today, I heal,' Taliesin shouted above the din. He looked her firmly in the eye. 'You could stay and help, if you wish.'

Anya glanced uncertainly around the crowded round-house. She had found great comfort caring for the sick in the place of healing but Taliesin's home was a very different kind of sanctuary. It was not scented with juniper, instead it reeked of the sour stench of rotting floor rushes and the musty aroma of unwashed linen. It was not calm or quiet, but thrumming with noise and chatter. She hesitated, full of doubt. Taliesin's round house felt overwhelming and alien but none the less, it *was* a place of healing.

'The people of Tintagel believe I'm a witch. I don't think they will want me to help them.'

Taliesin shook his head. 'They trust me, and therefore they will trust you.'

Anya frowned. Surely his optimism was bordering on the naïve?

'Come. Let me prove it to you.' Taliesin put a hand in the small of her back and propelled her over the threshold. She stood awkwardly at Taliesin's side, painfully aware that every man, woman and child had turned to stare at her.

'Anya is a priestess and a healer,' Taliesin said loudly and defiantly. 'She will be assisting me today.'

Many eyes continued to appraise her suspiciously, but no-one dared to challenge the word of the high priest of Dumnonia.

'You see?' Taliesin said encouragingly. 'I trust you will find everything you need on my medicine shelves.'

Without waiting for her reply, Taliesin pushed her towards the waiting throng. Anya looked nervously at the sea of distrustful faces then she forced herself to smile. She had trained for many long years to be a healer. She had no reason to be afraid.

The small boy was no more than six summers old. He had huge brown eyes and soft brown hair, and he held fast to his mother's hand as if afraid he might lose her in the melee. Anya noticed he wore a man's ring on a leather thong about his neck, a ruby set amidst creamy gold.

The boy's mother caught her looking at it. 'It belonged to his father. It's the only thing of value we possess. He never takes it off.'

'It's beautiful,' Anya said, then turned back to the small boy. 'What can I do for you, young man?' She smiled encouragingly at the child for he reminded her poignantly of Abberlen. The little boy looked anxiously at his mother.

'Tristan hasn't learnt the Latin tongue yet,' his mother explained apologetically. Her hair was the same colour as her son's, scraped away from her tired, drawn face and held at the nape of her neck with a leather tie. Anya noticed that although the woman's hands were rough and raw, her finger nails were immaculately clean.

'He has a new puppy,' his mother went on, carefully removing a makeshift bandage from her son's right hand. 'He adores the animal but it has sharp teeth.'

Anya leant forward for a closer look but the little boy twisted away from her, clutching his hand to his chest.

'I won't hurt you,' Anya said gently. Slowly, so as not to startle him, she unfurled his tiny fingers. The dog's teeth had punctured his palm and the wounds were infected and inflamed.

'He works beside me in the kitchens, but he's no use if he can't fetch water or chop the vegetables.' Tristan's mother ruffled his soft brown hair affectionately.

Tristan eyed Anya suspiciously as she carefully cleaned his palm with juniper oil then applied a poultice of thyme blended with olive oil.

'Your hand will begin to heal now,' Anya told him, quickly applying a fresh bandage.

'I don't believe what they say about you. I don't believe you are a witch,' his mother said suddenly. 'You have kindness in your eyes.'

Anya looked up in surprise. 'I am a healer. I cure people. I don't curse them.' She patted the little boy's arm reassuringly. 'All finished, Tristan.'

His mother stood up. 'Thank you, Anya,' she said softly.

She turned to her son. 'Say 'thank you' to Anya, Tristan.'

The little boy looked up shyly and slowly repeated the unfamiliar Latin words.

'You are welcome,' Anya replied.

She watched Tristan and his mother walk out into the sunshine, hand in hand. The little boy's puppy was tied to the gate post by a piece of string. Tristan crouched down and the animal began to yap loudly, plastering the boy's face with slathering licks. Anya felt a rush of melancholy as she thought of Abberlen so far away. She prayed that he was thriving and learning to smile again.

Anya worked steadily, at her usual calm, unhurried pace. Taliesin's medicine shelves were indeed well stocked. She found an infusion of burnet saxifrage and hyssop for a young girl's persistent cough, chamomile syrup for the colicky baby, and celandine and hawthorn tea for his exhausted mother. It was late in the day when the last patients took their leave.

'Will you sit and talk with me a while?' Taliesin asked, bending down to put another log on the fire. As he straightened up he winced, unable to hide his discomfort. Pulling up a chair beside the fire, he sat down heavily and Anya felt a sudden stab of pity for the old priest.

He was old, weary and all alone, struggling to carry out the many onerous tasks of the priesthood. It seemed ill-mannered to refuse the offer of a place beside his fire, so she pulled up another chair and sat down next to him.

'I am glad you came to my door today, for tomorrow I journey to see my sister. She is dying.'

'I'm so sorry -' Anya began, but Taliesin held up a hand to silence her.

'She is old. It is her time.' But his expression was wistful. 'So, Silvanus tells me he has sworn to see you safely home?'

Anya could not meet his eye. 'Yes, he has. Tell me about Dumnonia,' she said quickly, eager to change the subject.

'Ah yes,' Taliesin said thoughtfully. 'The legions worked our mines but we escaped the worst of the Empire's excesses. They built their ugly cities of stone elsewhere. Dumnonia is blessed by the gods. The precious metals beneath our moors have given us great wealth, and lasting peace.'

In her mind's eye Anya saw Vortigern's army riding across the moors towards Tintagel.

'If Dumnonia was threatened, could you protect it?' she asked fearfully.

Taliesin pursed his lips. 'Dumnonia has no army. Etar has trusted the gods to keep us safe this far.'

She looked at him in surprise. Much as she revered the gods, she wondered if Etar was naive to believe they would hold back an advancing army.

'Etar may keep to his room, but he knows the dangers Dumnonia faces,' Taliesin replied, answering her thoughts.

'And yet he does nothing?'

Taliesin sighed. 'I break no bonds of fealty when I say that the world is changing, but Etar is too tired and too sick to change with it.'

'So it's true that his health is failing?'

Taliesin nodded sadly. 'I have sprinkled valerian into the flames in the cave of fires and begged the gods to heal our king, but they have not yet answered my prayers.' He hesitated for a moment, as if trying to make up his mind before continuing. 'As I grow older, my dream paths become ever more unclear, but I am plagued by a terrible fear that it is not the shade of death that hovers over Etar, but a malignant, living foe.'

'I don't understand. Are you suggesting…?'

'In truth, I do not know,' Taliesin sighed and fell silent.

A log fell in the hearth, sparks flew into the air and Anya leant back in her chair, lulled by the fire's warmth. A companionable silence descended and she wondered idly if Taliesin would allow her to lay fresh floor rushes, and how she might persuade him to take a bath.

'Who is Epona?' she asked at last.

But Taliesin did not reply. His head dropped back, his mouth fell open and a succession of loud snores began to shake his wasted frame.

TWENTY

It was early evening when Silvanus, Evric and Boult returned to Tintagel. The accident at the Tamar mine was weighing heavily upon Silvanus and his expression was shrouded in anger and frustration. Each rescue team had brought him the same, grim story. There had been a massive collapse. The gallery was still blocked. There was no sound at all from the other side of the rock fall, nothing to suggest the trapped miners were still alive. The mood in the village of Tamar had become ever more sombre and subdued as the chances of finding anyone alive grew slimmer with every passing hour.

The first body was brought to the surface on the third day. In the days that followed, the bodies of the remaining twenty seven miners were hauled up the narrow shaft and laid out in neat lines on the black, dusty earth. Silvanus had watched the grieving families gather around the broken bodies and felt as if his heart would cleave in two. He was the king's son. They had believed he would find a way to rescue the trapped miners, but he had failed them all.

He handed the reins to a stable boy and turned to Evric and Boult. 'I'd wager the evening meal is being served. Will you join me?'

Evric shook his head and excused himself to take a bath,

but Boult stood in the fading evening light, lost in his thoughts. Silvanus clasped him on the shoulder. 'Come and drink with me.' Boult had lost his father in a mining accident long ago, and Silvanus suspected the accident had reopened old wounds.

'Thank you, but I am sore in need of some solitude.'

'I understand,' Silvanus said sympathetically. 'Until tomorrow, my friend.'

'Until tomorrow,' Boult repeated then bowed and walked away.

Silvanus stood alone for a moment, staring into the middle distance. His thoughts returned to the miners' broken bodies, and the terrible agony of their families. How could he ever hope to successfully inherit his father's throne when he had found no way to save his people from such appalling suffering?

Anya sat at the long table in the great hall, toying with her food, and thinking of her kin. She wondered how Horsa was faring in the far north of Britannia, and she wondered how Elsbet was passing her days. She missed them both so much. Perhaps one day, if the gods were kind, she would find a place to belong again. She took a deep breath and willed away her melancholy. If Hengist had not bound her to the most powerful man in Britannia, then she would have liked to remain in Etar's stronghold, perched like an eagle's nest on the soaring cliffs.

She glanced down at her mother's ring, and began to twist it round and round her finger. The village in the black mountains was often in her thoughts of late. And its pull was growing stronger with every passing day. In her nightmares, the village was bloodied and defiled, as tormented as

'*Ragnarok*', the end of all things. Yet in her waking moments, the round houses snuggled together behind a high earthen bank, as squat as duck eggs in a nest, tranquil and untouched.

Anya's gaze focussed. Silvanus had entered the hall and he was scanning the benches, looking for a place to sit down. The hall was crowded, but there was a space next to Anya. Scowling, and with an air of great reluctance, Silvanus sat down beside her. A cloud of black dust rose from his cloak and hair. He did not acknowledge her. He turned his shoulder and drank his wine, and ate his meat. She stole a glance at him. He looked exhausted, his face a mask of intense misery.

'Were there any survivors?' she asked quietly.

His jaw tensed. 'No.'

'I am so sorry,' she replied. 'It's unbearable to feel so helpless.'

Silvanus turned to face her. 'What gives you the right to presume to know how I feel?' he asked sharply.

'Because I have watched someone die. Someone I loved very much. And I didn't find a way to stop it.'

Silvanus looked down at his plate again and his shoulders slumped. 'You were not at the mine. You didn't see the suffering, the grieving families.'

'No, I didn't. But I saw my sister suffer as she was offered to the goddess of the sacred grove. I couldn't save her, and I have to live with my guilt and my regret, each and every day.'

Silvanus blinked, dumbfounded.

'Human sacrifice! So the stories are true. Saxons are little better than savages.' He turned away from her again, his manner hostile and dismissive.

'Not all Saxons believe the gods demand human blood,' Anya said softly. 'I for one believe the high priest was mistaken.'

Silvanus did not reply. His entire body was rigid with frustration and grief and Anya's heart went out to him. She knew he saw her as the enemy, but he was wrong. At that moment she wanted nothing more than to take away his suffering. She closed her eyes and let her body relax. She cleared her mind and drifted, as weightless as a dandelion seed caught on a breeze. They sat together in silence for a long time.

'I have failed my people,' Silvanus said at last. 'The foreman should never have sent them down there. They were lighting fires to fracture the rock, with no means of escape if anything went wrong.'

'He allowed profit to come before safety?' Anya asked.

Silvanus nodded grimly. 'The mines have too much autonomy and too few controls. I should have been aware of this, but I wasn't. I let them all down.'

'What's done, is done,' Anya said gently. 'The priests taught us to learn from the past, live in the present, and hope for the future.'

Silvanus raised an eyebrow in surprise. 'So your priests are not entirely without wisdom.'

Anya smiled faintly.

'An accident like this will not happen again,' Silvanus said forcefully. 'I will make sure of it.'

Taking a long draft of wine, he visibly relaxed. He yawned, leant back in his chair and stretched out his legs beneath the table. 'I had no idea what my father had to contend with, day after day,' he said slowly. 'Sometimes I feel overwhelmed by it all. I had no idea kingship would be so hard.'

'You knew what your future held,' Anya replied, her voice almost a whisper. 'And that is why you have been so angry, and so afraid.'

'How dare you speak to me in such a -' Silvanus began incredulously but Anya interrupted him, ignoring his outburst.

'Would you like some more wine?' she asked calmly.

Silvanus opened his mouth then closed it again. He looked utterly bewildered. Anya filled his glass and pushed it towards him. He drank its entire contents, banged it heavily back onto the table and then walked away without another word.

TWENTY ONE

As the evening meal was being served in the great hall, Mairi collected Etar's supper tray from the kitchens. She stopped in a quiet alcove, away from prying eyes, and removed a small glass vial from the purse at her belt. She stared at it for a long time. In her mind's eye she could see the wise woman, her face as wrinkled as an old apple. She lived alone on the high moor, far away from Tintagel, the boundary of her land marked by hanging chimes of jangling bones. Her cave was sheltered by a row of windblown trees, bent double like tired old men.

Inside, it was dark and musty and smelled of the earth. The cave's walls were lined with ancient, stinking animal pelts and every niche was crammed with human skulls. Many were fashioned into crude lanterns, and the warm glow of candlelight shone through a hundred empty eye sockets. The place reminded Mairi of the womb of a fiendish monster. A place of warmth and fecundity but at the same time, foul and malignant.

Mairi and Lucan had not visited the wise woman empty handed. It was known that her magic called on the darker powers of the earth, so they had taken generous offerings of food and coin as a sign of their goodwill. Mairi had stood beside Lucan, transfixed with awe, as the old woman sprinkled herbs onto her crackling fire. She had murmured incoherently, fallen to her knees, and scuttled across the floor like a startled crab. Suddenly, she had pointed at Mairi's belly with a long thin finger and said, quite clearly:

'Your son will be king. Many will bow down before him, just as many will remember him, through the turning years.'

The doubt faded from Mairi's eyes. She removed the wax stopper from the glass vial and tipped its contents into Etar's cup of blackberry juice.

Etar's bedchamber was dark, airless and stiflingly hot. A fire burned fiercely in the hearth and the air was thick with the fetid stench of old age. She fixed a smile to her face and walked towards the bed.

Etar turned his head slightly and opened his eyes. 'Mairi, you do not have to bring me my supper each and every night. You should be at Lucan's side.'

'Lucan is happy that I visit you, just as it is my pleasure to do so.'

She sat down on the edge of the bed, struggling not to show her distaste. The old king smelled of sickness and decay, as foul as a midden pit at the height of summer. 'How do you fare today?' she asked lightly.

Etar struggled to sit up. 'I am an old man, and I am dying, so let us not waste time talking about my health. Let us talk about you instead. Are you well? Is the child in your belly strong?'

'He is strong,' she replied.

'I pray that I may live long enough to see my first grand-child.' Tears welled in Etar's cloudy eyes.

Mairi pretended not to notice. She found it embarrassing how little control old people had over their emotions. They wept like tired children. She handed Etar the cup of blackberry juice, and he took it from her with trembling hands. He took a sip and shuddered.

'Why does Taliesin insist I drink this? It is too bitter.'

'He swears it will make you better,' she smiled encouragingly.

Reluctantly, Etar took another sip. His frail body shuddered again. A trickle of black drool ran down his chin and she quickly wiped it away.

Etar sank back onto the cushions. His eyes were closing.

'Thank you, Mairi, you are so kind. You go now. Lucan will be waiting for you.'

Etar fell asleep almost instantly. His head slipped sideways and he began to snore loudly. Mairi stood up and tiptoed to the door. The serving girl looked up from her sewing. 'He hasn't eaten anything, my Lady.'

'Then feed him if you must,' Mairi snapped.

Lucan was waiting for her in the corridor.

'He took two sips,' she whispered.

'Not here. Wait!' Lucan placed his hand on the small of her back and propelled her across the great hall and along the kitchen corridor. The narrow space was oppressively hot, the air heavy with the aromas of roasting meat, fermenting barley and over-cooked vegetables. Servants pressed themselves against the walls as Lucan swept by but he did not acknowledge them. At the far end of the corridor a flight of stone steps led down into gloomy darkness.

'Follow me,' he said curtly.

'I can't see,' Mairi said, staring warily into the blackness.

'Take my arm, then,' Lucan snapped.

At the bottom of the stairs, Mairi looked around nervously. The tunnel was hewn from solid rock. In the gloom she could just make out a series of chambers, their roughly hewn entrances like gaping mouths in the darkness.

Lucan snatched her hand impatiently and let her into the nearest cellar. It felt damp, musty and bitterly cold. Against the far wall, ancient amphorae were gathering mould and cobwebs. Six plump barrels, their parchment labels attached by blobs of sealing wax, squatted in the middle of the solid rock floor.

'Is it safe to talk now?' Mairi asked, shivering.

Lucan nodded. 'This place is out of bounds to all the servants. It's where my father keeps his most precious wine. Only his steward is permitted down here and even then, only on special feast days. Well? How fares my father?' he asked urgently.

'He's very weak.'

Lucan frowned irritably. 'He should be dead. Why is it taking so long?'

'Surely it's better if he dies slowly? If he sank too quickly, it would arouse suspicion.' Mairi hesitated, staring wide-eyed at Lucan. 'Will the gods be angry with us?' she asked falteringly. 'Will they curse us?'

'Why would you say such a thing? Etar is dying, with or without our help. We are being merciful, bringing a speedy end to his suffering. And besides, it's too late for an attack of conscience.'

'I know,' Mairi whispered. 'But I'm afraid…' her voice trailed away. She was overwhelmed by the thought of a royal child growing in her belly. There were days when she was giddy with excitement, and other days when she sobbed into her pillow from dawn to dusk for no apparent reason. Her serving girls said it was a sign that her child was strong, but she feared she might be losing her mind.

'You heard what the wise woman told us. We are doing the gods bidding,' Lucan said curtly.

Mairi shivered again. 'I remember what the old woman said,' she said slowly. 'How could I forget?'

The love she felt for her unborn son was overpowering. He was growing stronger day by day, flesh of her flesh, feeding on her, consuming her, his will and her will intertwining as one.

'Etar has already named Silvanus his heir,' she whispered anxiously.

'You don't need to concern yourself with politicking. You carry my son and that is enough.' Lucan slipped his hands around her waist and kissed her full, pouting lips. Mairi had spent much of the day feeling tired and nauseous but nevertheless she returned his kisses dutifully. Lucan's lips were trailing along her jaw, across her throat, skimming her collar bone.

'I can't help but worry, Lucan,' she whispered.

'I assure you, there is nothing for you to worry about. Soon I will have an army to oust Silvanus.'

'Dumnonia has no army,' she said, puzzled.

'No, but Vortigern does.'

Mairi's eyes widened with alarm. She placed her hands on his chest and pushed him away from her. 'No, Lucan!'

Lucan glared at his wife. 'I told you - matters of state do not concern you.'

'But they concern our son,' she hissed. She saw her husband's furious expression and added quickly, 'I'm only thinking of his safety.' She slid a hand behind Lucan's head, soothingly caressing the nape of his neck and was relieved to see the anger fade from his eyes.

'Don't worry. I'll keep you both safe,' Lucan said, mollified. 'I will seek an alliance with Vortigern. He will remove my brother, and place me on the throne.'

'But why would he do that? Wouldn't it be simpler for him if he just killed you as well?'

Lucan stroked her cheek reassuringly. 'That is not Vortigern's way.'

Mairi's stomach lurched with fear. Lucan had never even met Vortigern. How could he hope to know the workings of a tyrant warlord's mind?

'But you would have no real power. You would be a puppet king,' she whispered.

Lucan's expression hardened. 'I don't like that word. Don't use it again, do you understand?'

'I understand,' Mairi said meekly. But she didn't understand at all. Why, for the love of the gods, would Lucan choose to ask for Vortigern's help? If poison was working for Etar, surely it would work for Silvanus too?

'Good. Now come here.' Lucan unfastened the ties at her shoulders, and buried his face in her breasts. His teeth closed around a nipple and Mairi winced. Her breasts had felt very tender of late. She was weary to her bones and she did not want to do this. Not here. Not now. Lucan pushed his wife against the cold, damp cellar wall, grunting loudly as he took her. Mairi gritted her teeth, closed her eyes and dreamed of sitting next to Lucan on the raised dais of Tintagel with their beautiful boy at their side.

The sneeze was faint but unmistakeable. Mairi tensed in surprise, but Lucan did not notice, too lost in his lust for her.

'Husband!' she hissed. 'Someone is here.'

'What?' Lucan's breathing was ragged.

'Behind the barrels,' she whispered. She pushed Lucan away and hurriedly refastened the ties of her gown.

Lucan strode across the damp cellar.

'By all the gods, who are you?' he demanded, hauling a small boy from behind the wine caskets.

'I'm Tristan. I work in the kitchens with my mother,' the little boy stammered.

'And what are you doing here?'

Tristan's eyes were brimming with tears. 'I was looking for my puppy. I was certain he was here.'

'And have you been listening to our conversation?'

'No, my Lord!' Tristan stammered. 'No, I swear. It's not my place!'

Lucan turned his back on the boy and looked at his wife. The expression in his eyes was as cold and as hard as the granite rocks on the moors.

'We cannot take the chance,' he mouthed.

Mairi stared in horror at her husband. It was an act of mercy to end an old man's life, but Tristan was just a child.

Lucan turned back to the boy. He held out his hand and helped Tristan to his feet. 'There's no harm done. Let's go and find your puppy,' he said gently.

Tristan wiped the tears from his face.

'Thank you, my Lord. Thank you. Please don't tell my mother. She'll be so angry if she knew I'd come down here. And she'll be really angry if I can't find Finn.'

Lucan put a hand on the boy's shoulder. 'This can be our secret. Your mother will never know.'

'Thank you,' Tristan stammered again.

Mairi watched Lucan lead Tristan up the dark stairway. She took two faltering steps, fighting against an almost overwhelming urge to wrench the boy from Lucan's grasp and carry him back to the safety of his mother's arms.

Not so long ago, she had assumed marrying Etar's youngest son would be the answer to everyone's prayers. By becoming a member of the most exalted family in the land, she had elevated her parents' standing in Dumnonia and brought them riches beyond imagining. She had naively believed her marriage would bring her a life of privilege, her days filled with beautiful gowns, sumptuous feasts and delicious gossip. When she realised she was to bear Lucan a son, she had thought her happiness was complete.

Instead, the child in her belly was like a tick embedded in her flesh. He was greedy, feeding on her blood, leaving her with only tiredness and tears. She wanted desperately to be strong for him, but life as Lucan's wife was far more complicated than she had ever imagined. Her husband was foul-tempered, thoughtless and selfish. It was only when she lay in his arms in the marriage bed that he showed her any hint of compassion. He lusted for her flesh, but he did not love her, and nor did she love him.

She took a deep breath, her small, delicate fists clenched at her side. She had left the sanctuary of her parents' home as an innocent child but she had quickly learnt what it meant to be a woman. Now, a child of her own grew in her belly. A child the gods had decreed would one day sit on the throne of Dumnonia. So, no matter how weak or feeble she might feel, she must learn to be as strong as her husband, and as strong as her unborn child.

She put a hand lightly over her stomach.

Her boy. Her precious, golden boy.

TWENTY TWO

In Anya's dream, Abberlen was screaming as he fell. He hit the beach, and the dream shifted. The towering waves of a stormy sea solidified into high mountains. Rain was falling, huge droplets of blood that splashed against her face. The village was deserted and reeked of death but there was a man, walking away from her, untouched by the falling blood. He turned slightly, and she caught a glimpse of his face, half in shadow. He looked familiar, as if she had seen him before. The shadow lifted and she realised that the face staring back at her belonged to Silvanus, heir to the throne of Dumnonia.

Anya opened her eyes. Her head was throbbing fiercely and she rubbed her temples to ease the pain. Why was Abberlen falling from the cliffs? And why was Silvanus in the village of her mother's kin? She had no answers. Frustrated, she closed her eyes, emptied her mind and sought her goddess. She drifted on the edge of sleep. She could smell the scent of harvest on the drowsy air, hear the crystal clear wind chimes in the sacred oaks and see the simple shrine of Nerthus warmed by the heat of the sun.

'Please help me understand,' Anya whispered.

A gentle breeze tugged the scarlet curtain but the goddess did not reply. There was only silence, infinite, empty and cold.

The knocking was loud and persistent, wrenching Anya back into the bare watchtower room. She climbed out of bed, tugged her cloak about her shoulders and opened the door.

The young man reeked of the stables. He was spindly, pale and pock-marked, and his brown hair fell lankly about his face. 'My name is Brendan. Forgive me, but it's Renni, my wife, she's having a baby, I mean, she's not having a baby, I mean, she is, but…' he gabbled.

'Take a breath. Is the baby coming now?'

'Yes, but it's not. She's suffering, really suffering. I can't bear to watch, it's terrible to see her.' He hesitated, biting his lip. 'Taliesin's been gone for days. We hoped he would have returned by now…' His voice trailed away.

'I can help, if you will let me,' Anya said gently.

There was agonising uncertainty in Brendan's eyes.

'I've made a mistake. I shouldn't have come,' he said and turned away.

'I've brought many babies into the world. Your wife would be in good hands.'

Brendan turned back. He looked utterly exhausted.

'Taliesin trusts me,' Anya said simply.

Brendan ran a hand through his lank hair and exhaled loudly. 'It will have to be you.' His voice was flat, devoid of emotion. 'Because there's no-one else.'

'Very well,' Anya said calmly. 'I just need a moment to gather some things.'

Brendan led Anya across the stable courtyard, steering a path between steaming piles of horse manure. Brendan and Renni lived in a single room at the end of the main stable block. It was simply furnished and spotlessly clean, with newly white-washed walls and freshly laid floor rushes. A vase of purple lilac sat on the small, polished table.

Anya noticed that Brendan's gaze lingered over the tiny crib in the corner of the room and her heart went out to him. She guessed he had hammered, planed and polished the crib for the last nine months and now he yearned for a healthy baby to lie swaddled within it.

She squeezed his arm. 'Don't worry. All will be well.'

But for her massively swollen belly, Renni was small boned and slightly built, a tiny figure amidst a disarrayed heap of rugs. The straw mattress was sagging in the middle, as if the bed was attempting to devour her whole. Sweat had plastered her dark hair to her skull, and her brown eyes were red rimmed and bloodshot.

Anya put her basket on the table beside the bed. 'Hello Renni. My name is Anya.'

'Everyone knows who you are,' Renni replied coldly. 'You are the Saxon.'

'Yes, I'm a Saxon,' Anya agreed equably. 'I need to find out why your baby isn't coming. Will you let me do that?'

Renni glared at her husband. 'Why did you bring her here?'

Brendan squeezed his wife's hand. 'Because Taliesin trusts her.'

'Her kin are murdering pirates,' Renni hissed, her eyes wide with panic.

'You don't know that, my love. And besides, there's no-one else.' There was an edge to Brendan's voice now.

Renni screamed as another spasm of pain engulfed her, then she sank back into the rugs and closed her eyes.

'Renni?' Brendan said urgently. 'Please let Anya help you.'

Renni opened her eyes and nodded wearily at her husband.

It was as Anya had feared.

She wiped her hands on a juniper-soaked cloth and then sat down beside Renni again.

'Your baby is healthy but we're going to have to help him out.'

Renni turned frightened eyes in Anya's direction. 'What do you mean?' she gasped, tensing against another pain.

'Your baby's shoulder is stuck. I'm going to have to make a small cut.'

'You want to cut me?' Renni breathed frantically.

'Renni, listen to me,' Brendan urged. 'Let Anya do this. Please. For my sake. For our baby's sake.'

Renni's eyes shot back and forth between her husband and Anya.

'I don't know,' she gasped. 'I don't know. She's a Saxon.'

'Taliesin trusts her,' Brendan repeated desperately.

Another pain tore through Renni's abdomen. 'Yes! Alright! Do it! Just do it!'

Anya turned to Brendan. 'I need clean linen, and lots of freshly boiled water. And then you might want to wait outside.'

'I'm going to stay,' he said firmly.

'Good. Then you can hold her hand, and make sure you hold it very tightly.'

A fine drizzle was falling as Anya walked out of Brendan and Renni's home. She felt elated and exhausted in equal measure. Tears were tumbling down her cheeks, for no matter how many babies she delivered, the miracle of new life always made her cry. Closing her eyes, she sought the three Fates, the virgin goddesses present at the birth of every child. She prayed that they would choose a long and happy life for the perfect boy child now nursing at Renni's breast.

Anya opened her eyes again, suddenly aware of the sound of rapidly approaching footsteps. A moment later, Silvanus rounded the corner of the stables at speed. He came to an abrupt halt, narrowly avoiding crashing into her.

'By all the gods! What happened to you?' His eyes were wide with alarm.

'I -' Anya began hesitantly.

'Did you murder someone?'

Anya looked down at her blood-stained hands and clothes. She had been so elated by the safe delivery of Renni's baby she had forgotten how she must look, smeared with the gore of childbirth.

'I was -' she began again, hurriedly wiping away a stray tear with her sleeve. She glanced awkwardly at Silvanus. His expression was bemused, one eyebrow raised, awaiting an explanation.

Wiping her hands on her apron, she took a deep breath to compose herself.

'Brendan and Renni are the proud parents of a fine son.'

'Ah! So that explains…' Silvanus nodded towards her blood smeared clothes.

But Anya was no longer looking at Silvanus. Her gaze was fixed on a small group of people, slowly making their way up the hill. In their midst, a man was carrying the body of a small boy.

'Oh no,' Anya breathed. 'Oh, please, no.'

Silvanus frowned and followed her gaze. And then he sprinted away from her down the hill. With a mounting sense of dread, Anya hitched up the hem of her gown and ran after him.

Evric was carrying Tristan, and Jago was supporting Tristan's mother. Her long dark hair was coming loose from the leather tie at the nape of her neck and the wind was lashing stray strands against her tear streaked cheeks. She was so distraught she could barely walk, leaning heavily upon Jago.

'What happened here?' Silvanus asked, staring in horror at Tristan's small, broken body.

Anya came to an abrupt halt, her mind churning with confusion and guilt. She had foreseen this in the jumbled chaos of her dreams. And yet she had done nothing to stop it. Was it her fault the little boy was dead?

'He was found on the beach,' Evric said grimly. 'We think he may have been on the cliff path, and lost his footing in the darkness.'

'He must have gone out looking for Finn, his puppy,' his mother sobbed.

'This is Adain, Tristan's mother,' Evric began gently.

'I know,' Silvanus replied. 'I am so very sorry, Adain.'

'Thank you, Lord.' A sob caught in Adain's throat. Her fingers fluttered ineffectually over Tristan's bruised and swollen face before coming to rest on his torn tunic. With great tenderness, she carefully straightened a tiny bone toggle.

'He's all I have,' she said plaintively. 'He is such a good boy.'

Suddenly, she let out an agonised howl and collapsed against Jago's chest once again, overwhelmed by grief.

'I'll take her home,' Jago said quietly.

Anya stood respectfully to one side as the sad little procession continued to climb the hill. Silvanus led the way, his eyes downcast and full of pain. Anya's expression softened. She thought it extraordinary that in Saxony, slaves were murdered without a second thought, whilst in Dumnonia, kitchen boys fell to their deaths and the heir to the throne mourned their passing.

TWENTY THREE

Anya slept badly that night. She tossed and turned, her thoughts returning again and again to the broken body of little Tristan, and Adain's heart wrenching grief. When she awoke the following morning, a wave of guilt swept over her again. She had seen Tristan's death, and yet she had done nothing to prevent it. She had not understood what her visions were trying to tell her and now he was dead, and it was all her fault. Anya climbed out of bed. She dressed slowly, for her body ached with tiredness and remorse.

In the great hall, Mairi was sitting at the long table, chattering and laughing with three young women. At the sight of Anya approaching, their conversation came to an abrupt halt, their expressions instantly cold and guarded. Faced with such blatant hostility, Anya faltered. She had belonged in the great hall of Saxony, surrounded by kin. There, she had felt loved and wanted and needed. But here, she felt painfully, brutally alone.

Suddenly, unexpectedly, she remembered her mother's words: 'If people try to hurt you, it's often because they're hurting too.' Anya had heard Mairi's parents lived far away, on the border with the kingdom of the Durotriges. So although the young girl made an outward show of revelling in her position as Lucan's wife, Anya wondered if perhaps Mairi too felt lost and alone, struggling to cope with a selfish, immature husband and the trials of her first pregnancy.

Mairi cocked her head on one side. 'A tinker came to the great hall yesterday. Lucan sent him on his way because he had nothing worthy of trade. But he claimed to have heard rumours that Vortigern of the Dobunni has made a treaty with a Saxon warband. It seems hard to believe, does it not? What kind of fool makes an alliance with their enemy?'

Mairi was looking expectantly at Anya, as if awaiting a response, but Anya's heart was thudding violently against her ribs. By all the gods, what else had the tinker said?

'Come now, you are a Saxon. Surely you can shed some light on this? Is it true?'

Anya's mind was racing with fear. 'I have no idea,' she said lamely.

Mairi looked disappointed. 'You are something of a mystery, aren't you, Anya. You never did tell me how you came to be aboard an Irish slave ship.'

'I was captured,' Anya replied truthfully, remembering the moment the Irish had charged down the hillside, the noise and clamour of the slaughter, the feel of the Irishman's strong hands as he held her down in the river, her feet sliding through the churning silt. She had been convinced she would die there.

'Anya? Are you daydreaming?' Mairi asked sharply.

'What? No,' Anya said hurriedly.

Mairi shook her head in frustration and changed the subject. 'So, has Taliesin returned to us yet?'

'No, not yet.'

'Well, I pray it is soon. I have need of his remedies.'

'Would you permit me to help you? I can…' Anya began

but Mairi shot her a glance of such utter derision that her voice trailed off in mid-sentence.

'I will wait for Taliesin. You must be aware, Anya, that there are many in Tintagel who believe you to be a witch. I cannot in all conscience risk the life of my unborn son.'

Imperiously, Mairi turned back to her friends. They whispered behind their hands together and Anya sensed malice in their stifled giggles and delighted squeals.

'*Mairi is as lost as you are. Don't allow her to upset you*', she told herself.

Swallowing hard, she turned and walked away, her thoughts veering from hurt at being so cruelly excluded, to alarm at the tinker's news. So word had spread of Vortigern's alliance with a Saxon warband. How long before rumours also circulated of Vortigern's betrothal to Hengist's sister?

Anya's mind began to race. She suspected Vortigern's pride had been badly dented by her kidnap on the road to Aquae Sulis. Surely he would not want to publicly announce his betrothal to a missing girl, until she was safely in his grasp once again? She could only pray that very few people knew about her intended marriage to Vortigern.

Outside in the courtyard, the fierce wind tugged her hair about her face and whipped her cloak about her body. It tasted of salt and fish and seaweed. She drew it into her lungs, one deep breath after another and, little by little, she no longer felt so afraid.

She had promised Brendan she would look in on Renni and her babe. But first, she wanted to try and find the place where Tristan had fallen to his death. She wanted to pick some flowers in remembrance, and say a prayer for his departed soul.

The trackway hugged the coast and the view was breath-taking with tall cliffs as far as the eye could see, swathes of wild flowers, waves pounding endlessly onto the rocks below. She walked briskly, relishing the warmth of the sun against her cheeks. After a while, she slowed her pace and looked about. She sensed she was near the place where Tristan had fallen.

She turned off the track, wending her way through a maze of sweet scented yellow gorse. She found Tristan's puppy, close by a rocky outcrop, its body carelessly hidden beneath a handful of fern leaves, wrenched up by their roots. Someone had cut the dog's throat, and flies were settling.

Anya's hands shot to her mouth and she backed away, light headed with shock. She put her hands on her knees and tried to catch her breath. Straightening up, she looked about. There was a trail of flattened grass leading to the cliff edge. She walked closer and crouched down. Sea pinks were crushed, as if broken by heavy boots. It looked as if someone had been dragged, as if there had been a struggle.

A wave of nausea rose in her throat. Tristan had not fallen to his death accidently. Someone had pushed him over the cliff. Silvanus's kingdom had seemed so pure, so untouched by the evils of the world, but a child had been murdered on this wind swept cliff top.

What should she do about it? Who should she tell? Who could she trust? She closed her eyes and sought her goddess. The grass felt prickly against her palms, but the earth was silent and gave no reply. Frustrated, she stood up unsteadily.

She picked some sea pinks and bound them into a posy, using grass as twine. Placing them at the cliff edge, she said a silent prayer that Tristan might find his ancestors in the world beyond the veil. Then she walked slowly back to Tintagel. But she did not notice the sunlight dancing on the white caps out to sea, or the fleet of brightly painted fishing boats casting their nets, or the black seal swimming close by the shore.

Her mind was racing with questions.

Who would go to the trouble of murdering a kitchen boy?

When Evric had carried Tristan up from the beach, she had noticed his father's ring was no longer about his neck. Was his death a robbery gone awry?

And then another terrible thought struck her. She had heard it said that some men abused young boys for their own pleasure. Goddess forbid, was Tristan murdered to keep a sordid secret?

TWENTY FOUR

Anya was on her hands and knees in Taliesin's herb garden. Weeds were waging all-out war, threatening to overpower the rows of medicinal plants. Stealthy mares' tails had burrowed their long, pale roots across the entire garden, like siege tunnels beneath a fortified city, and vicious nettles resisted as she tugged them from the sandy soil. She worked methodically but her mind was elsewhere.

Who had murdered Tristan?

The tragedy of the boy's death was burning a hole in her heart.

'Come. Let's eat.' Taliesin's voice cut sharply across her thoughts. She looked up, and her frown deepened. Since his return, the old priest had looked tired and drawn. He had not wanted to talk about his sister's death but Anya suspected it had affected him deeply.

Wiping the sandy soil from her hands, she followed Taliesin inside. During his absence, she had laid fresh rushes on the floor, and scrubbed every surface with oil of juniper. Taliesin had made no complaint, even submitting to her gentle hints about taking a bath. His hair was now clean, as white and fluffy as a dandelion clock. He was wearing a freshly laundered robe, and he no longer reeked like a piss pot.

After a simple meal of bread and tangy goat's cheese, they sat side by side at the small table, binding bunches of cut lavender with twine.

'I don't think Tristan's death was accidental,' Anya blurted suddenly. 'I found his dog on the cliff top. Its throat had been cut. And there were signs of a struggle at the cliff edge.'

Taliesin's hands trembled and he looked deeply shocked.

'Does Adain know about this?'

'No-one knows. I wanted to talk to you first.'

Anya frowned, startled by her decision to confide in the old priest. When had she decided Taliesin was worthy of her trust?

'King Etar holds the lives of all his subjects, whether high born or low, in equal esteem,' the priest said soberly. 'You have my word he will hear of this, and justice will be done.'

Anya felt a lump growing in her throat as she remembered the look of desolation on Adain's face and the way her hands had trembled as she straightened the tiny toggles on Tristan's tunic, such a pitiful, heart-wrenching gesture. She closed her eyes and said a silent prayer to her goddess. She prayed that Tristan's killer would be found, so that there might be some comfort, however small, for Adain.

Opening her eyes again, she took a length of twine and another handful of lavender, its sweet scent both soothing and familiar.

'I must ask you, Taliesin – who, or what, is Epona?' she asked. 'I have heard the name mentioned several times.'

'You are Epona, my dear.'

'What do you mean? I don't understand.'

'Let me show you.' The small statue of Epona was no more than hand-high and carved from stone in a simple, naive style. Her right hand was draped possessively across the mane of the horse she sat astride, and her face smiled benignly. She wore the plain dress of the Dumnonii and her long hair fell in stylized curls to her waist.

'She is our earth goddess, the protector of our people, our sea, our land, our herds. An ancient prophesy tells us that Epona shall come from the sea to bring hope and new life to a new golden earth.'

'But I'm not Epona!' Anya said, astonished. She thought back to her first encounter with Mairi, all those weeks ago. 'I heard Mairi say that you believe the prophecy refers to her baby.'

Taliesin snorted derisively. 'That young girl's head is filled with nonsense. She and Lucan have visited the wise woman who lives on the high moor. She is a dangerous old crone, who practices dark magic. She told them their son will be king. They think no one knows, but I know everything that goes on in Dumnonia.'

Anya frowned. For Mairi's unborn babe to become king, Silvanus would need to die childless. It was a sad thought.

'If Epona is to bring new life, surely she must bear children,' she said thoughtfully.

'That is one interpretation,' Taliesin nodded.

'So who is she supposed to marry?' Anya asked, but Taliesin was struggling to his feet.

'Welcome, welcome, Lord,' he said breathlessly. 'To what do I owe this honour?'

Silvanus ducked beneath the low door beam, and stepped into the gloom of Taliesin's home.

'My father is in great pain…' His gaze fell upon Anya and he broke off, staring coldly at her.

His hostility was a physical presence and she shivered despite the warmth of the fire. Nevertheless, she stood up respectfully, and bunches of lavender spilled from her lap and to the floor.

Taliesin hobbled towards Silvanus and then he bowed low, white faced and clearly in pain.

Silvanus tore his gaze from Anya and placed a hand on the old man's elbow. 'There's no need for that,' he said quietly.

The old priest straightened up. 'Thank you, Lord,' he said gratefully. 'I will come straight away.'

He hurried to the shelves, quickly gathering medicines into a basket, muttering to himself. Anya selected a small box and then followed him to the door.

'Not you. Just Taliesin,' Silvanus said abruptly.

Anya stopped in her tracks. 'As you wish. But please take this.' She held out the box. 'It's crushed willow bark. It will relieve the king's pain.'

Silvanus's jaw tensed. He glared angrily at her for what seemed an eternity and then, to her immense surprise, the hardness went from his face. He stepped forward, took the box and looked her firmly in the eye. 'Thank you,' he said.

'You're welcome.'

A memory sprang unbidden into her head and her world span dizzily.

A battlefield at dawn, massed ranks of spears, the beating of a battle drum, as fast as a racing heartbeat. Silvanus, standing at her side…

She had recognised Silvanus from the first moment she had seen him in the great hall of Tintagel. At the time, she had not understood but now, standing so close to him, breathing in the scent of him - horses, polished leather and sandalwood - fragments of memory were stirring. They were hazy and indistinct, but she had no doubt she had known Silvanus many life-times ago.

TWENTY FIVE

Venta, kingdom of the Atrebates

'The executions have subdued the town, Lord,' Quintus announced. 'The streets are quiet and there are no further signs of rebellion.'

Ronan nodded absently at his second in command. Quintus was a military man. His bearing, manners and soul were born from the blood of the legions. He stood to attention, shoulders back, head held high. His hair and beard were neatly cropped, his cuirass and boots were spotless, his ornate belt buckle highly polished.

Ronan let his gaze wander around the vast council chamber. The room was cold and empty; the town council was dismissed, its members either executed or cowering in their homes. Ronan had not asked to be left in charge of the town of Venta. He had no idea how to impose martial law, or draw up a treaty, or levy tribute, or keep the peace. He had not wanted to find out either, but his father had given him no choice, snarling something about 'making a man of you yet'.

He ran a hand over his short cropped hair and sighed irritably. He had learnt a great deal these last few months, not least that hungry civilians would sullenly accept a new overlord but not the requisitioning of their precious grain supplies. The rebels had managed to kill two of his men before they had been cornered and cut down.

As punishment for the rebellion, Ronan had chosen to carry out decimation, the execution of ten townsmen chosen at random. It was a punishment his Roman ancestors had used, and he hoped it would make his father proud, because there was nothing worse than seeing the disappointment in Vortigern's eyes. And so he had stood on the steps of the basilica and watched his soldiers as they dragged the ten men into the forum. Watched them kneel on the cracked flagstones, bound and gagged, as helpless and terrified as sacrificial lambs.

A large crowd had gathered and then more flooded through the monumental arch. He had sensed their hostility, so venomous it seemed to curdle the warm summer air. Mothers, wives, daughters were crying out to him for mercy. And that was when the overpowering feeling of guilt had squeezed his gut and he had turned away and vomited behind one of the white marble pillars.

'The Lord Vortigern approaches!' Quintus clicked his heels and stood to attention, jolting Ronan from his reverie.

Vortigern was striding across the mosaic floor. The tiny, square tiles were loose and his heavy footfall sent them flying in all directions. Rufus, head down, brow furrowed, scurried rapidly along in his wake. He always reminded Ronan of an angry weasel.

At the sight of his father, Ronan felt a surge of conflicting emotions. On the one hand, he felt relieved, for now Vortigern was here, he would no longer be expected to make difficult decisions. He would be able to go hunting again, find a whore-house, get blind drunk. On the other hand,

Vortigern always made him feel uneasy and on edge. Nothing he did was ever good enough for his father.

'We were not expecting you. What are you doing here?' Ronan asked sheepishly, completely ignoring Rufus.

'Is that any way to greet your father?' Vortigern asked.

Ronan stood up reluctantly. 'Greetings, father,' he said dully. 'I am glad you are safely returned from your visit to the north. So, you have left Hengist and his men to hold the wall? Do you trust them?'

'I trust no-one,' Vortigern replied curtly. 'But they're like hungry dogs. If I feed them enough land, and enough silver, they'll be loyal – for now.' He noticed that Ronan would not meet his eye; his entire body was drooping like a melting candle. 'So, tell me, what have you been doing in my absence?'

'Keeping order, father, as you commanded.'

'The gate house needed decoration, did it?' Vortigern asked dryly. 'I saw freshly severed heads atop it.'

'There has been some civil unrest. The locals killed two of my men.' Ronan was staring at the floor.

'Look at me, Ronan!' Vortigern commanded.

Cautiously, his son looked up. He appeared embarrassed and uncomfortable, and Vortigern grimaced. There was no doubting Ronan had the makings of a fine warrior, for he showed no fear on the battlefield. But in all other aspects of his life, Ronan was worse than useless. For Vortigern, looking at his son was like looking into a mirror and being confronted by an image of his younger self, riddled with all the glaring flaws he had fought so hard to conquer. Looking at Ronan reminded him that he too had once been weak, lazy and naive. He had hoped this baptism of fire was what the boy needed to shake him from his lethargy, but it seemed he had been mistaken.

'I presume you've spent your time in Venta drinking and whoring. God help me, but it's hard to believe you are of my blood. The task I gave you wasn't onerous. I merely asked you to keep control of Venta.'

'The city is calm. Order is restored,' Ronan said defensively.

Vortigern grimaced. 'I wanted the council's seal on the treaty, not their heads on stakes! And decimation means one in every ten men. You couldn't even get that right.'

'How did you hear about -' Ronan began nervously.

'I know everything. It's how I survive. But you - you are a fool, Ronan. A dangerous fool.'

Ronan was now staring blankly into the middle distance. The familiar barrier had fallen behind his eyes again. Vortigern picked at his beard and stared menacingly at his son. If truth be told, he did not believe Ronan had acted rashly. Even the smallest spark of defiance could quickly lead to all-out, blazing rebellion but thanks to his son's brutal suppression, there would be no more trouble in Venta. It would not take long for word to spread amongst the people of the Atrebates that the high king of the Dobunni was in no mood for futile acts of defiance.

But Vortigern had no intention of meting out compliments or encouragement to his son. Ronan was an immature puppy who needed to be slapped down, not spoilt by praise.

'Look at me, damn you! I want you back in Aquae Sulis. Rufus will stay in Venta, although judging by the ugly mood I sensed on the streets, he'll need an armed guard whenever he sets foot outside the basilica.'

'But Rufus will lose control of the city in a heartbeat!' Ronan said angrily.

'Rufus will stay to carry out a full survey of the town's inhabitants for tax purposes, not to stick their severed heads over the gate house.'

'Father, I -' Ronan began, but Vortigern held up his hand. 'That's enough. I will hear no more.'

Quintus was still standing to attention, staring fixedly ahead. Vortigern shook his head wryly.

'At ease, for the love of God. We're not on the parade ground.'

'Lord!' Quintus barked. He squared his shoulders, clicked his heels and remained as stiff as a statue.

'Go away,' Vortigern said irritably.

'Yes, Lord!' Quintus jabbed his chest with his fist, turned and marched away, his rapid footsteps echoing around the marble walls.

'Where did you find him?' Vortigern asked sarcastically.

Ronan shrugged. 'If I gave him the order, he would march my entire garrison off a cliff.'

Vortigern raised his eyebrows. 'Blind obedience, eh? The quality a man should look for in a wife.'

'Tell me, would your Saxon girl have been an obedient wife?' Ronan asked pointedly.

Vortigern glared at his son. The girl had been full of spirit and defiance. He doubted she knew the meaning of the word 'obedience', but he would have certainly enjoyed explaining it to her. In truth, she still haunted his thoughts. He had found her utterly distracting with that barbaric red hair and those extraordinary green eyes. As a rule, there was only one way to deal with such a woman and that was to take her to his bed. Unfortunately, she was not a slave or a whore but the daughter of a high king and he needed her brothers to fight *for* him, not against him in some endless vendetta. And so he had chosen to marry her.

Vortigern experienced a sudden surge of violent emotions. Lust as he remembered her softly curved body, anger at the thought she had slipped through his fingers and jealousy that another man might now possess her.

'Do you think you will ever see her again?' Ronan asked.

'I know I will. She's mine and I won't stop looking until I have her.'

'But you've sent riders to Ireland and the trail is cold.'

'I will send men to the far corners of Britannia, to Gaul, to Iberia, to Constantinople if necessary. And I *will* find her,' Vortigern repeated menacingly. He glanced over his shoulder at Rufus. 'It's entirely your fault that she was taken.'

'We were ambushed. There was nothing I could have done,' Rufus said hurriedly.

'You hid like a frightened girl child,' Ronan sneered. 'How else did you survive, when all the rest perished?'

'I did not hide! I -' Rufus began but Vortigern silenced him. 'I will hear no more of your pathetic excuses. She was under your protection. And when Hengist and Horsa return from the north, I shall expect *you* to explain to them why their sister most likely warms some stinking Irishman's bed.'

Rufus turned pale.

'In the meantime, you will stay in Venta, and tax these people until they bleed,' Vortigern went on coldly.

'And you -' he jabbed Ronan's shoulder, 'you will come back with me to Aquae Sulis. My scouts tell me Pascent of the Coritani is preparing to march against us. It seems we are at war once again.'

TWENTY SIX

Tintagel, Dumnonia

The door of Taliesin's round house was propped open with a large stone and warm sunshine was slanting across the freshly laid floor rushes. Anya was seated beside Taliesin at the small table, surrounded by heaps of chamomile. She was cutting the flower heads from the stalks with a pair of tiny scissors and Taliesin was placing them in neat rows on the drying trays.

'I have informed the king that you believe Tristan was murdered,' Taliesin said. 'He was gravely distressed. Murder is not commonplace in Tintagel. He has appointed Jago, Silvanus's brother at arms, to investigate the matter.'

Anya nodded wordlessly. Tristan's murder plagued her dreams night after night, jolting her into wakefulness as the small, flailing body hit the sand. And with wakefulness came the guilt – guilt that she had foreseen his death and done nothing to prevent it.

Taliesin's stomach rumbled loudly and Anya glanced at the empty shelves.

'There's nothing to eat. The mice have taken the last of your cheese.'

'I care not. I have no appetite these days.'

'But you have to eat,' Anya said gently.

Taliesin stood up and walked slowly to his sleeping quarters behind the wicker partition. He returned with a leather purse and dropped it onto the table.

'If you insist I should eat, will you spare an old man's aching legs? Will you go to the market for me?'

Anya put down her scissors, tugged at the drawstrings of the purse and tipped a handful of tiny Roman coins into her palm. 'Will anyone accept these?' she asked dubiously.

'Not beyond the borders of Dumnonia, but within Tintagel's walls, five of those coins will buy you a loaf of bread.'

Anya picked up a tiny coin. There was the head of an emperor on one side and on the other, a horseman spearing a barbarian. Around the edge, an inscription in Latin read: 'For the restoration of happy times.'

Anya looked up curiously. 'Were their 'happy times' restored?'

'No. The annals tell us they were dark, violent days. The empire was crumbling and here in the west a succession of usurpers came and went without holding on to power for more than a year at a time.'

Anya tipped the coins back into the purse. She stared at Taliesin, but she was not seeing him. Long forgotten images of a distant past were flashing across her mind: an island in turmoil, so many promises made and broken, so many battlefields, and so many deaths.

'I have been here before,' she began falteringly.

'Of course you have,' Taliesin said mildly.

'But so little has changed,' she said urgently. 'How can we hope for a better future if we continue to make the same mistakes, again and again?'

Taliesin smiled sadly and did not reply. Anya looked down at the purse. She had no idea how to buy food. In Germania she had been the daughter of a king. Each day, the table in the great hall had been laden with food and wine but she had given little thought to how it came to be there. She had paid no heed to the slaves who had risen before dawn to toil in the kitchens or battle through winter's snow and ice to draw water from the well. It was hard to believe but in the passing of a single summer, her life had changed beyond measure, and yet she found herself strangely content.

'If you would prefer, I will find some-one else to go to the market,' Taliesin said.

'No, no. I will go.'

The market was loud and busy. Stall holders were shouting out, encouraging passers-by to sample their wares, dogs were barking, and women were laughing, gossiping and bartering. Anya went up to the baker's stall. The baker was a big man, enveloped in wobbling rolls of pale flesh as if he had been crafted from the dough he kneaded each morning. Covered in a light dusting of flour, he had a curiously spectral air.

Anya pointed at a large loaf of barley bread. 'How much is that?' she asked.

'For you! No charge!' He held up a huge, soft hand and waved away Taliesin's coins. 'You remember me, yes? I came to you the other day about my cough. My wife says it's all the flour in the air. She says my insides must be choked with it, but what can I do? I make bread. But you gave me a linctus that soothed my throat. So, no charge for the bread.'

It was the same at the butcher's stall. The butcher's wife handed Anya a bunch of freshly cut pink sorrel.

'These are for you,' she said shyly. 'The ulcer on my

father's leg is much better, thanks to your poultice. He asked me to find you and thank you, but you have saved me the task.'

Silvanus strode out into the main courtyard of Tintagel. He did not notice the clouds that had swept in from the west, nor the persistent drizzle that now clung to the air. He was in a foul mood, frustrated and overwhelmed, as taut as a strung bow. He badly needed to saddle up and ride hard across the moors. Perhaps the fierce wind might blow away his anger and clear his aching head.

His father was failing. Each day Etar's body grew weaker, although his mind was still as sharp as a sword blade. Silvanus could not begin to imagine life without him. Etar *was* Dumnonia; its voice, its heart, its conscience. There were times when he wondered if Tintagel would simply crumble into the sea at his father's passing.

Silvanus ran a hand through his hair, lost in thought. Word had reached Tintagel that Vortigern had made an alliance with a warband of Saxon mercenaries. It seemed a foolish decision, but Silvanus knew it would be naïve to dismiss Vortigern as a foolish man. Every scout, every emissary, every merchant brought the same warning -Vortigern's power and influence were growing. He was like a dark cloud building on the horizon, sweeping ever closer on the cold northerly winds of war.

Silvanus came to an abrupt halt, his gaze drawn to Anya, slowly making her way along the market stalls. His days had been busy of late. He had been so preoccupied with the burdens of kingship that he had lost track of how many days had passed since they had found Anya on the beach, half drowned, her skin as pale as bleached driftwood.

He twisted the sun stone signet ring round his finger, lost in his thoughts. Lucan and Mairi swore the Saxon girl was a witch, sent to curse the kingdom of Dumnonia. Perhaps they were right, for why else had he opened his heart to her on his return from the Tamar mine? Surely only witchcraft could have possessed him to spill his deepest anxieties to a stranger? He shook his head in frustration. Anya was as perplexing as a riddle.

Silvanus watched curiously as the butcher's wife handed Anya a bunch of flowers. He noticed that many of the stall holders were smiling at her and greeting her warmly. When had the people of Tintagel decided she was not the enemy sent to destroy them all? When had they decided to trust her? He began to twist the sun stone ring round his finger again. It had been a gift from Etar on his eighteenth birthday. And one day, if it pleased the gods, he would give it to his own son.

Silvanus looked up at Anya again. He remembered the kindness and compassion in her eyes as she handed him the box of crushed willow bark. The remedy had eased Etar's pain, just as Anya had promised it would.

He felt suddenly ashamed. Was he such a poor judge of character? Had he been wrong about her after all?

TWENTY SEVEN

Dumnonia basked in the heat of late summer. The wheat, barley, rye and grapes ripened in the fields, and in the hedgerows, blackberries and sloes turned towards the sun. In Dumnonia, just as in Saxony, every able-bodied man, woman and child toiled in the fields to gather in the harvest. The communal effort united the entire kingdom, binding them together like the tightly twined straw bales that dotted the stubble fields.

Anya, not used to such extreme manual labour, applied a poultice of mallow and chamomile to the bleeding blisters on her palms each night, and awoke so stiff each morning she could barely clamber from her bed. Yawning and fumbling for her clothes, she suddenly remembered Taliesin had insisted he needed assistance in the cool of his round house today.

With a profound sense of gratitude and relief, Anya made her way down the corridor towards the great hall to break her fast. The door of Etar's bedchamber opened and Mairi stepped out, carrying a bowl of soup and a small drinking cup on a tray. Anya, passing by at the exact same moment, felt a surge of hot, stale air mingled with the distinctive smell of old age, before Mairi quickly closed the door with her foot.

'What are you doing here?' Mairi asked sharply.

'I'm on my way to Taliesin's. How fares king Etar?' Anya replied. She had never laid eyes on the high king of Dumnonia and she was beginning to think she never would.

'I take him his meal, and stay with him whilst he eats it. He enjoys my company,' Mairi replied defensively.

Anya raised an eyebrow. Mairi had not answered her question. She noticed the soup on the tray was untouched.

'He has little appetite?'

'The high king's appetite is no concern of yours,' Mairi said curtly.

Anya gritted her teeth. She had grown accustomed to Mairi's hostility; its bite no longer felt as sharp.

'His appetite *does* concern me,' she replied. 'I work beside Taliesin, and he is the king's physician.'

'Not for much longer! You're a Saxon – and Etar's councillors want you gone.'

Anya suspected Lucan was campaigning vigorously for her removal from Tintagel. 'Then the council will be delighted to learn I have no intention of making Tintagel my permanent home,' she said, then eyed Mairi thoughtfully. The young girl looked tired, pale and drawn.

'And how do *you* fare?' she asked gently. 'I have a raspberry cordial which can ease the pains of childbirth, if taken early enough. How long have you carried the child? Six months?'

Mairi glanced up and down the corridor, as if checking she would not be overheard then replied in a whisper: 'I would sooner drink my own piss than swallow your potions, witch.'

As Anya watched Mairi hurry away, a sense of apprehension crept over her like a mist rolling in from the sea. It felt cold and clammy and she shivered as if someone had walked over her grave. She glanced at Etar's closed chamber door and then at Mairi's retreating back. Was she sensing the old king's frailty, or was she sensing Mairi's unborn child? Was the babe malformed? Or was there no child at all? Sometimes, a woman might carry a malignant growth in their womb. It mimicked the outward signs of pregnancy, a terrible, tragic cuckoo in the nest.

Anya shook her head and pushed her morbid thoughts aside. She walked quickly through the great hall. Serving girls were polishing the long oak table, and the smell of lavender scented beeswax polish reminded her poignantly of home. In the courtyard, the air was full of noise. Fishwives, laughing, gossiping and bartering, were selling the morning's catch of shiny mackerel, and seagulls cried and wheeled speculatively overhead.

Anya crunched up Taliesin's path, and into the cool shade of the round house. From behind the wicker partition, she could hear the old priest snoring loudly. Smiling to herself, and grateful for a brief respite from the hard labour of the fields, she settled down to less strenuous work.

Silvanus walked slowly through Etar's stronghold, enjoying the warmth of the sun on his back and relishing a rare moment of peace and tranquillity. He came to a halt at Taliesin's round house, hesitating, his hand resting on the gate. There was barely a sound to be heard, save for the bees buzzing on the lavender in the garden.

Through the open door, he could see Anya sitting at the small table, carefully slitting open unripe poppy seed-heads and squeezing the thick, milky liquid into a glass vial. She was alone and he thought how peaceful she looked. Her hair was neatly woven into a long plait that fell down her back, and her expression was one of calm concentration.

He opened the gate latch. At the sound of his footsteps on the path, Anya stood up and bowed her head respectfully. She glanced at the knife she was holding and put it down hurriedly.

'Can I help you?' she asked.

'Is Taliesin here?'

At that moment, a snore rumbled from behind the wicker partition. Anya smiled apologetically.

'He is still asleep. Would you like me to wake him?'

'No, let him sleep. I will come back later.'

At the door, Silvanus hesitated and turned back. This girl was a Saxon and her eyes were full of secrets. And yet, Taliesin trusted her, and it appeared the people of Tintagel did too. Torn with indecision, he stared at Anya for such a long time that she began to shift uncomfortably.

'Perhaps *you* can help me,' he said at last.

'If you wish.'

Silvanus rolled up his left sleeve and held out his forearm.

'We were hunting, some five days since. In the heat of the chase, it was I who was skewered, not the boar. I washed the wound and I hoped it would heal, but it hasn't.'

Anya stood up and walked over to him. 'A spear did this?'

'Yes,' Silvanus said grimly. 'Sadly, Gorran's aim is truly appalling. We didn't catch the boar, but I swear its days are numbered. Next time, we will have the beast.'

The gash was deep and oozing putrid, yellow liquid and the skin surrounding it was puckered and inflamed. 'Come and sit down,' Anya said quietly.

Silvanus winced as Anya re-opened the wound and carefully cleaned it with juniper oil. He watched her as she worked. She was concentrating intently, her lips pursed, her brows furrowed, and he could see no evil purpose in her eyes.

She was lost in her work, focussed solely on a desire to help and to heal. He felt a sudden pang of guilt. He had been wrong to doubt her.

Perhaps sensing his gaze fixed upon her, she glanced at him. Embarrassed he quickly looked away.

'Has Jago made any progress with the investigation into Tristan's murder?' Anya asked.

He turned to look at her again. 'Not yet, but Jago is a good man. He will leave no stone unturned.' He shook his head incredulously. 'It's hard to believe someone would kill a child. And it's equally hard to believe the murderer is living amongst us - one of my own people.'

'Not necessarily. Perhaps a stranger - a passing merchant, or a vagrant,' Anya suggested.

Silvanus looked into her eyes. He wondered if she meant it, or was just being kind.

'Wait a moment.' Anya stood up and hurried to the shelves, returning with a wicker basket and an earthenware pot.

Silvanus raised his eyebrows. The basket was full of cobwebs. 'Is there a spider in there?' he asked in astonishment.

Anya shook her head, a hint of a smile on her lips.

'By all the gods, what are you doing?' he asked incredulously as she began to carefully pack layer upon layer of cobwebs into the wound.

'I'm trying to save your arm,' she replied calmly.

Silvanus had never been this close to Anya before and he found himself staring at her in fascination. She was unlike any girl he had ever seen. The Dumnonii had dark eyes and hair as black as jet, but Anya's hair was a blend of many different colours, gold, copper, bronze, all intertwined like a pattern welded blade. Beneath thick, dark lashes, her eyes were an astonishing shade of green, like the sea after a storm. The summer sunshine had sprinkled her nose with tiny freckles and brought a touch of colour to her cheeks. He had looked at her many times but, until this moment, he had not truly seen her.

Anya was beautiful. How had he not noticed before?

'The wound should begin to heal now. Hold still a moment longer. This is a poultice of madder root and thyme and it will help to reduce the inflammation.'

She removed the lid on the earthenware pot and gently smeared some salve onto the skin surrounding the wound.

'Let it soak in for a moment,' she said, wiping her sticky fingers on a cloth.

'Very well,' Silvanus replied unsteadily.

An uneasy silence descended. Anya busied herself replacing lids on pots. Silvanus examined his wound. A loud snore erupted from behind the wicker partition and Silvanus's face broke into a smile.

'By the gods, is there a storm coming?'

'Nothing wakes him. If the earth quaked, he would sleep undisturbed,' Anya replied, smiling back at him.

'My father snores, just as loudly. Perhaps it comes to all who grow old.'

'How is your father?' Anya asked.

'He's old and he's sick. But the willow bark you gave me eased his pain.'

'I'm glad it helped.'

Another awkward silence fell. Silvanus looked about the round house. Taliesin's home, once a stinking hovel of rotting rushes and stale sweat, was now scented with lavender and beeswax polish. He presumed the old priest had Anya to thank for the startling transformation. He glanced back at the Saxon girl, his eyes softening.

'You must miss your kin,' he said quietly.

'More than I can say.'

Her eyes met his and he thought they looked immeasurably sad.

'I've not forgotten my promise to see you safely home.'

Anya looked away and did not reply.

'What is it? What's the matter?'

Anya would not meet his eye. 'I will dress your arm now.'

Silvanus sighed deeply. The girl was a mystery. He doubted he would ever understand the strong emotions that flitted behind her sea-green eyes.

He waited patiently as she bound a strip of linen tightly around his wound, tying the ends in a neat bow. He could not help but notice her long, tapered fingers, and how soft they felt against his skin.

'I look like a gift,' he said, attempting to lighten the mood.

'That may be, but your arm is badly infected. The wound needs to be dressed every day,' she replied soberly.

'Then I shall come back, every day,' Silvanus said. It was a pleasing thought.

He stood up, tugging his sleeve down over the bandage. At the doorway he hesitated and turned back. Anya was still seated at the table. She looked preoccupied, her expression unfathomable, and he wished he knew what she was thinking about.

'Thank you,' he said.

Anya looked up absently. 'You are welcome,' she replied.

TWENTY EIGHT

As soon as their harvest was gathered, the Irish chieftains turned their thoughts once more to plundering the riches of Etar's kingdom. When the beacon bell sounded, Silvanus was sitting beside Evric in the great hall, their heads bent over a parchment.

'May the gods curse the Irish!' Evric said angrily.

Silvanus let go of the parchment and it skittered across the table, curling itself into a tight scroll. The bell tolled again. As one, Silvanus and Evric stood up and sprinted across the great hall. They took the watchtower's spiral steps three at a time. The view from the top of the tower was breath-taking. Dumnonia basked beneath a deep blue sky; a panorama of heather-tinged moors, swathes of yellow stubble fields and beyond, the boundless ocean, sunlight dancing on its white-capped waves.

Silvanus and Evric paid no attention to the view. Their gaze was fixed on the line of beacon fires blazing across the hilltops, warning of Irish ships on the horizon.

Evric rapidly counted the beacons. 'By my reckoning, they're coming ashore near Clun. They will be far inland by the time we catch up with them.'

Silvanus did not reply. He simply turned and hurtled down

the watchtower steps again, bouncing off the walls in his haste. In his chamber, he pulled on a leather cuirass and a short tunic of overlapping mail, grimacing at its heavy weight. Then he grabbed his sword, shouting commands to his men as he strode through the great hall.

The stable courtyard was crowded with flustered stable boys, jittery horses and Silvanus's warriors, hurrying from all directions; fastening sword belts as they ran. Silvanus mounted up and reined around to face his men.

'The Irish are coming ashore at Clun. There's no time to lose. We ride now and we ride hard.'

Clun mine sat atop a high, bleak moor with wide, sweeping views that stretched to the distant sea. The mine itself lay beneath a permanent cloud of thick grey fumes, a sprawling stain upon a sea of purple heather and yellow gorse. The mine's sturdy gates had been torn from their hinges and were swinging in the wind. Silvanus dismounted and his men followed suit. Five miners lay dead. Three more were badly wounded. One tried to stand, pressing a hand against a deep gash in his thigh.

'They took everything,' the miner began, gritting his teeth against the pain. 'They loaded the ore onto carts. We tried to stop them, but they fought like demons. I killed one of the bastards.' He pointed to a corpse some distance away. 'Put my pick axe straight through his skull. I only wish I could have killed more of them. Our families are in the next village. They're finishing the harvest. I fear the Irish savages will take them as well as our grain. Please help them, Lord…'

'We will. Rest easy now. We will return once we know your families are safe.' Silvanus turned around to face his men.

'Mount up!'

They rode west across the moor to the wide plateau of farm land above the cliffs. The small, rectangular fields were resting now, sleepy after the exertion of harvest. A flock of crows had descended to scavenge the sprinkling of wheat grains left behind amidst the sun-bleached stubble. At the sound of Silvanus's warband approaching, they rose into the air, shrieking ugly warning cries.

The village was a cluster of stone walled, turf roofed round-houses, squatting on the westerly slope of a wide, flat-bottomed valley. For many centuries, the villagers had worked the fields and buried their dead on the hilltop above, so their ancient ancestors might keep watch over their countryside and their kin. But the spirits of their ancestors had been unable to protect them against the Irish warband. The village was silent. Corpses lay on the baked earth, cut down as they attempted to flee.

'Do the Irish have no conscience?' Jago asked, his eyes burning with fury.

Silvanus dismounted. The women of the village had been working at the threshing floors and the air was sweet with drifting chaff. The body of a small boy lay sprawled in the earth beside the village well. His throat was cut and flies were settling on the gaping wound. A thin, scabby dog lay protectively beside him. As Silvanus approached, the hound stood up and growled, his hackles rising.

'Not here to hurt you,' Silvanus said quietly. The dog lay down again, sad-eyed, and rested his chin in the dust.

The village storage pits were empty, their clay seals smashed. A thin trail of grain from a leaking sack marked the route the Irish had taken out of the village.

'We will come back and bury the dead,' Silvanus said. 'But first, we find these Irish bastards.'

As he had expected, the Irish had left an easy trail for him to follow. A pall of smoke was rising over the next village, storage pits were empty and bloodied corpses lay where they had fallen. At the edge of the settlement, he reined in, bent low in his saddle and examined the dusty track. Despite the lack of rain, the wheels of the heavily laden Irish carts had left tell-tale grooves in the earth. They were making for the coast.

He felt certain, from bitter experience, that the Irish had taken not only grain but also men, women and children for the slave markets of Ireland. If he was too late, if the Irish had already set sail, his failure would condemn the villagers to a life of unimaginable horrors. He thought fast. Which cove had the Irish chosen to moor their ship? Which offered the best shelter and easiest access to the beach? If he made the wrong decision, it would be too late.

'We ride for Bryanic Cove!' he shouted to his men.

The land began to dip sharply as it neared the coast and the road narrowed, its high banks lined with gnarled and twisted trees. Over the years the wind had bent them almost horizontal, their overhanging branches forming a steeply sloping, verdant tunnel that swayed in the wind.

Silvanus dug his heels into his stallion's flank, encouraging it to keep a fast pace despite the slippery, uneven stones. The road forked and he veered to his right. Round-houses lined the steep track that led down towards the cove, each one surrounded by vegetable patches and a jumble of fishing nets, gutting tables and lobster pots. Strewn amongst the clutter lay pieces of driftwood, all brightly painted to resemble fishes, sea monsters and mermaids. The village was deserted; the only sound was the jangling of shell wind chimes.

The small cove was sheltered by high cliffs. Fishing boats were pulled up beyond the high tide mark but the Irish ship, a wide flat bottomed cog, was moored in the shallows. The raiders had dismounted and were leading their horses across the beach towards their waiting vessel. Each horse was pulling a sled piled with sacks of ore and grain. The sight of Silvanus's warband galloping down the track threw the Irish into confusion, but their chieftain brought them sharply to order with a barked command. Hurriedly, the Irish abandoned their sleds of precious cargo and drew their weapons.

Silvanus counted twenty raiders, all on foot. He had forty mounted warriors; the odds were in his favour. He turned in his saddle and addressed his men. 'Protect your horses! They will try to bring them down! And stay together!'

The Irish chieftain responded with another command. No longer a loose rabble, the Irish closed up, raised their swords, and charged towards the warband of the Dumnonii, screaming at the top of their voices in their native tongue. Silvanus reeled his stallion around, narrowly avoiding an Irish blade swinging towards the animal's exposed neck.

He shortened his reins and drove his horse forward again. The Irishman stood his ground. Leaning low in his saddle, Silvanus thrust his sword deep into the man's ribcage. As he wrenched it free, he felt the blade grate over splintering bone. The Irishman's eyes widened with shock. His sword slipped from his grasp and he collapsed onto the sand.

Silvanus looked around. An Irishman was weaving through the melee of jostling horseflesh, holding his shield above his head to fend off a stream of blows from the mounted warriors of the Dumnonii. He was moving at great speed, dodging with great agility between the warhorses. Silvanus gripped the reins, jabbed his heels into his horse's flanks and galloped forward, keeping his eyes fixed on the rapidly approaching Irishman. The raider raised his sword, double handed. At the last moment, Silvanus changed direction, veering sharply to his left. As he crossed the path of the Irishman, he swung his sword, slicing a deep gash across the man's throat. The man froze for an instant then his knees gave way and he slumped to the ground.

Silvanus steadied his horse, and glanced around. His warband were dispatching the raiders with their usual brutal efficiency. Most of the Irish lay dead, but a few were trying to reach their ship. Boult had dismounted. Knee deep in sea water, he was dispatching an Irishman to his gods. Silvanus's gaze turned to the Irish ship. If they *had* taken captives, they must already be on board.

Evric followed his gaze and appeared to read his mind.

'I'll find them!' he yelled. He leapt from his horse, and ran up the gangplank. A man appeared from the cabin and hurled an ancient spear in Evric's direction. Evric swerved to his right, and the spear whistled past his left ear and embedded itself in the side of the ship.

The man disappeared into the cabin, and Evric ran after him, blinking as his eyes grew accustomed to the gloom. The Irishman's back was turned, reaching into a wooden chest for another spear. Evric grabbed him by the hair, wrenched his head back, and slit his throat. The Irishman convulsed, staggered backwards and crashed to the floor. Evric glanced quickly around the dark cabin. A huddle of women and children were cowering in the shadows.

'No one's going to hurt you. You're safe now,' he said firmly then ran out onto the deck again. 'They are unharmed,' he shouted to Silvanus.

'Thanks be to Epona,' Silvanus shouted in acknowledgement. He glanced about the beach. His men were loading the bodies of the Irish onto their own carts. He dismounted and walked to the sea. Crouching down in the shallows, he washed the blood from his hands.

Many Dumnonii had died today, innocent men, women and children. Yet again, he had let his people down. Yet again, he had failed. Silvanus sighed deeply, remembering the body of the little boy by the well, his dog sitting patiently at his side. There were times when he felt as if kingship was burning a hole in his heart.

Two days later, Silvanus and his warband rode back to Tintagel. In the great hall that evening they paid solemn tribute to the Dumnonii who had lost their lives at the hands of the Irish, but as the night wore on, the wake grew ever more raucous. Anya sat beside Taliesin, and watched Silvanus and his warriors drinking themselves into rowdy oblivion.

She thought it curious that Silvanus should choose to surround himself with such a varied group of men. Jago was impossibly handsome, quiet and deep thinking. Boult was solid, strong, slow but utterly dependable. Gorran was wiry, fast in both body and mind. He was never still, bursting with nervous energy, and when he spoke, his words tumbled over themselves in their haste to be aired. And then there was Evric, Silvanus's brother at arms. The savagery of slaughter had not yet dimmed Evric's boyish charm and enthusiasm for life, and his face was rarely without an impish grin.

Gorran was ruffling Jago's dark hair playfully. 'So beautiful,' he teased. 'So beautiful. I suppose it's not surprising you get more sex than all of us put together, you lucky bastard.'

In reply, Jago attempted to punch Gorran's left shoulder but Evric leaned forward at exactly the same moment, and

Jago's fist connected with the back of Evric's head instead.

Evric let out a howl of pain. 'What the fu...' he began, but Jago put his hands up in a gesture of surrender. 'Accident, accident,' he said quickly.

'Of course you get more sex than the rest of us,' Boult said with a mouth full of chicken leg. 'You're married.'

Jago smiled conspiratorially but said nothing.

'Why is Jago the only one of us to be married?' Evric asked, rubbing the back of his head.

'Because no female in their right mind would want you, Evric. I mean, just look at you!' Gorran laughed.

Silvanus put down his glass. 'Evric's right. Why aren't we married?'

'Are you looking at me?' Gorran asked innocently. 'Because, to be honest, Silvanus, you're not my type.'

Boult laughed so hard that he spat a huge half chewed lump of chicken into his lap.

'I wasn't asking why we aren't married to each other, you idiot!' Silvanus grinned.

'I would strongly recommend marriage.' Jago's expression had softened.

'Regular sex,' Evric said dreamily.

'Not necessarily,' Gorran grimaced. 'Not from what men tell me. Not after they've been married for a few years.'

Boult took another bite of chicken and belched loudly. 'Tell me, Silvanus, why isn't there a single whore house in Tintagel?'

'Because, my friend, my father expects us to marry and become decent, honourable husbands, and produce decent and honourable children.'

Boult's face paled to a strange shade of green. 'I would like a wife,' he said sadly, then vomited into the rushes.

'By all the gods!' Evric complained, pushing away the hound that was attempting to lap up the pile of puke. 'I thought you would've learnt to hold your drink by now, Boult.'

'I *can* hold my drink. It's the fifteen chicken legs I'm having trouble with,' Boult groaned.

Anya turned away, smiling to herself. Their good humoured banter hid something much deeper, something they would never put into words. She glanced at Silvanus again and wondered if he realised how fortunate he was? One day soon he would inherit a rich, untainted kingdom, supported by comrades who loved and respected him, and who would be willing to die for him. She felt a stab of envy. Silvanus belonged in Dumnonia. His future was laid out before him, full of promise, whereas her future was unknown. The cold, dangerous sea paths of the exile.

The noise in the hall was deafening now and her head was beginning to ache. She put her hand lightly on Taliesin's arm.

'I'm going to take some air.'

Taliesin began to struggle to his feet, but she shook her head. 'Stay where you are. I won't be long.'

The night air was deliciously cool and fresh after the stifling heat of the hall. Anya stood at the cliff edge, and rested her hot hands on the cold surface of the dry stone wall. Lucius's ship was still moored in the harbour far below her. She stared at it, filled with sudden anxiety. She had grown to love Tintagel and feel at home here, but she was being utterly selfish hiding in this beautiful place.

Vortigern would not believe Etar when he swore to have no knowledge of Anya's real identity. Instead, he would have vengeance for the old king's supposed treachery. In her mind's eye she could see Vortigern's warband riding across

Dumnonia, she could hear the screams and smell the burning timbers of the great hall of Tintagel.

'What are you doing here?'

She turned around, startled. She had thought herself to be alone. Silvanus was walking towards her through the darkness.

'Taking some air,' she said quickly. 'What are *you* doing here?'

'I was going to -' Silvanus stopped in mid-sentence. He glanced firstly at the cliff edge and then at Anya and a look of utter confusion slid across his face.

Anya tried to hide a smile. She suspected he had intended to relieve himself over the cliff.

'Same as you. Taking some air,' he finished lamely. His words were noticeably slurred.

There was a look of intense concentration upon his face as he walked unsteadily towards her, as if each time he put his foot down, the ground was not where he expected it to be.

Anya turned her face to the sea, so he would not see her smirk of amusement. She had never seen him this drunk before.

Silvanus reached the wall and swayed slightly.

'You look so beautiful tonight,' he murmured incoherently.

'Pardon? I didn't hear what -' she began, but Silvanus interrupted her, his eyes widening with alarm.

'I didn't say anything,' he said quickly.

'Oh!' Anya frowned, perplexed. 'How is your arm?' she asked politely.

'Healed,' he replied. 'I thought you were insane, wrapping me up in spider's web, but…' He appeared to lose his train of thought. 'Thank you,' he added vaguely.

'You're welcome,' she grinned, turning to stare at the

ocean again. 'Do you ever wonder what lies beyond this sea?'

'The end of the world, I suppose,' Silvanus replied faintly.

His complexion had turned an unhealthy shade of grey, and Anya wondered if he was about to vomit at her feet.

'The world isn't flat, it's a sphere,' she said quickly, attempting to distract him.

'Like a ball?' Silvanus asked, sounding puzzled. 'Now why would you say that?'

'Because we studied astronomy at the priests' school. None of it makes any sense if we are standing on a flat disc.'

'And what did the priests think of your idea?'

'It's not my idea. It's been mooted for a long time. Some believe it to be true, others say it's blasphemy.'

'I envy you,' Silvanus said suddenly.

'Why?' she asked, surprised.

'Because you went to a school to learn how to be a priestess. No-one has taught me how to be a king.'

'I'm sure Etar has taught you many things.'

'Oh, I know all about my duty to my people, but when you get down to the details, to the nitty-gritty, I'm useless. Utterly useless.' Silvanus stared morosely out to sea.

'I don't believe that,' Anya said gently. 'Your men follow you into battle without hesitation. They would die for you.'

'Oh yes, I know all about killing. I know how to look a man in the eye and thrust my sword into his gut. And I know exactly how to twist it out again, and bring the bastard's entrails along with it.'

Her face betrayed her distaste.

'Shocking you, am I?' he asked harshly. 'Killing isn't honourable, or pretty. But it's the only thing I'm good at.'

'From what I've seen since coming to these shores, it's all you need to succeed,' Anya said sadly. 'The details, the nitty-gritty as you call them, will follow. Just give it time.'

'I don't have time,' Silvanus snapped. 'How, for the love of Epona, am I supposed to pass legal judgements on cases the shire courts have failed to resolve? Why am I any better placed? I look at these men, the accused, and I can't see inside their souls. I can't see their guilt or their innocence. It's not written upon their foreheads.'

Silvanus put his head in his hands.

Anya stared at him for a moment, and then she took a deep breath. 'It's true. You are no better placed than anyone else to judge these men, but nor are you any worse placed. Have faith in yourself. You are a good man.'

Silvanus looked up, and smiled weakly.

'I am a maudlin drunkard.'

Anya returned his smile. 'Yes,' she agreed. 'You are.'

TWENTY NINE

Etar was propped up against an assortment of soft pillows. He was fast asleep and snoring loudly. Silvanus sat down on the edge of the bed but Anya remained respectfully in the doorway. The chamber was warm and airless. It shielded Etar from the outside world, a luxurious tomb of tapestries, blankets and cushions in the rich colours of the Byzantine world.

Etar opened his eyes. 'Silvanus? How do you fare?'

'I fare well, father.'

'Good, good.' Etar turned his head. 'Is this the girl?'

'Yes, father.' Silvanus gestured for Anya to come closer.

'I have heard much about you, Anya. I asked Silvanus to bring you here, because I wanted to see you for myself.' Etar's voice sounded as brittle and fragile as dead leaves.

Anya stared fixedly at the floor for fear of causing offence. 'I am honoured to meet you, King Etar.'

'Let me see your face, child.'

Anya lifted her gaze. Etar was old and frail but she could see wisdom and compassion in his pale, watery eyes. She stared in awe at the man who had ruled Dumnonia with such integrity for so many years. Until this moment, she had not truly understood the formidable legacy Silvanus would soon inherit, or quite how heavy a burden rested on his shoulders. She wondered what ailed the high king of the Dumnonii. His symptoms did not fit any disease she had treated in Germania. Taliesin said there were days when Etar rallied and others when he was weak as a kitten. Days when he had a great appetite, and others when he could keep nothing down.

Despite the intense heat in Etar's chamber, a cold shiver ran across Anya's skin, and she glanced fearfully into the dark corners of the room. She sensed a shadow, a threat. The high king was old. It was only to be expected that death was watching over him, but this shadow did not feel like death. It felt malignant, evil.

Anya bit her lip anxiously. 'If you would allow it, I have something that might alleviate your symptoms.'

Etar shrugged. 'I am dying, child, so I do not suppose one more potion could do me harm.'

'I have an infusion of hawthorn and agrimony to build your strength.' She reached into her basket and handed the vial to Silvanus. 'And I have foxglove, to steady your heart.'

Silvanus raised his eyebrows. 'I thought foxglove was a poison.'

She nodded. 'It can be, if it's not administered correctly.'

'So, you offer me poison?' Etar asked dryly. 'Taliesin warned me you were a most unusual girl. He also told me that you are Epona?'

Anya shifted uncomfortably from one foot to the other.

'Taliesin is concerned about your erratic heartbeat. We both think the leaves of the foxglove would help you.'

'Poison me, if you will, but answer my question first,' Etar persisted.

Anya hesitated. The temptation to lie was almost overwhelming. If Etar believed she truly was Epona, he would encourage her to stay in Dumnonia. The image of Vortigern's vast army marching over the moors towards Tintagel flashed across her mind. Etar had no army; he was utterly defenceless. In one wholly selfish gesture, she would singlehandedly destroy the kingdom of Dumnonia.

'I am not Epona,' she replied.

'Why do you say that?' Etar asked curiously.

'Because I do not belong here.'

'Ah yes, you are a Saxon,' Etar said mildly. 'I remember Silvanus telling me a long time ago that you were the enemy, sent to slaughter us in our beds.'

Anya glanced at Silvanus in surprise. He looked away, clearly embarrassed.

'Taliesin sings your praises,' Etar went on. 'He tells me you are a skilled healer.'

'I am flattered he thinks so,' she replied carefully.

'So, tell me child, what do you see in your dream paths?'

Her eyes widened. She wondered what the old king knew of such things.

'My dream paths are tangled and hard to follow,' she replied honestly. 'They show me things that have not yet come to pass. Sometimes they show me places I have never visited where high mountains block out the sun.'

She glanced at Silvanus again. Night after night he walked through the village of her mother's kin, and the blood retreated, as if it was afraid. She looked back at Etar. 'My dream paths show me many things, but they do not show me Dumnonia. I am not Epona.'

Etar stared at her for such a long time that a tear trickled from his watery eyes. He dabbed at it with his swollen knuckles. 'There is truth in your eyes. Thank you for your honesty. It seems Taliesin is mistaken on this matter. He would be the first to admit his dream paths are uncertain of late.' Etar was still watching her intently. 'It was you who brought the boy's murder to our attention,' he said suddenly.

Anya's heart jolted. Goddess forbid, was he accusing her of it?

'Yes,' she replied nervously.

'Jago has worked tirelessly, but the boy's killer has not yet been brought to justice, and I am sorry for it…' Etar's eyes were beginning to close.

'Will you take the potion of foxglove?' Anya asked urgently. 'I believe it would help you.'

Etar's eyes flickered open then closed again.

'I need to rest, but come back later, and I will drink your poison. Taliesin trusts you, and that is good enough for me.'

Moments later, Etar began to snore loudly. Silvanus stood up, gesturing for Anya to follow him. He opened the door but stopped abruptly, confronted by Mairi carrying a tray of food. Her expression hardened at the sight of Anya. Pointedly, she turned to Silvanus.

'How fares our father today?' she asked, fixing him with a truly dazzling smile.

'*My* father is brighter today,' Silvanus replied dryly. 'He is sleeping. Do not disturb him.'

'But -' Mairi attempted to push past him.

'Let him sleep,' Silvanus said firmly.

Mairi opened her mouth to protest but Silvanus held his ground. Their eyes locked in a silent battle, but it was Mairi who looked away first.

'As you wish,' she replied sweetly.

Anya watched Mairi as she hurried away down the corridor, and a shiver ran down her spine. She had sensed death many times in the place of healing. It had parted the air with its pure and unyielding force but in Etar's chamber she had sensed something much darker and more treacherous.

'Are you cold?' Silvanus asked, concerned.

Anya shook her head uneasily. 'I'm afraid,' she whispered.

Silvanus stared into her eyes. 'Why?'

'I don't know,' Anya replied honestly. 'I swear I don't know.'

THIRTY

The fort of Vercovicium, northern Britannia

Horsa stood on the parapet of the wall of Hadrian and marvelled at the ingenuity of the Roman engineers who had built such a mighty frontier against the northern barbarian tribes. His own kin built in wood and thatch, but this wall stood fifteen feet high, made of great square stones, undulating like a serpent over the craggy spine of Britannia. He had heard the bards speak of wonders such as this, and he could well understand why some men believed them to be the work of the gods. Since riding north, Horsa had inspected a great many of the forts along the wall, but he thought Vercovicium was by far the most spectacular. It clung to the edge of a soaring escarpment with far reaching views across the bleak land of the painted Picts.

Horsa stared north, across the deep defensive ditch, and beyond to the high hills and empty moors. If there was one thing he had learnt these last few weeks, it was that nothing was ever as simple as you expected. Beyond the wall, there were many tribes, not only the Picts but also the Caledonians, the Attacotti, the Scotti and the Votadini. They fought each other for land, and they stole each other's cattle as if it were mere sport. But when the mood took them, they would also happily unite and pour over the wall as one, and burn and steal and kill.

He turned away and walked slowly down the steps that hugged the wall. Vercovicium was much the same as all the other forts he had visited, the same stern walls, the same neat, regular pattern of barrack blocks, workshops, granaries and baths. Sometimes, when he walked past an empty barrack block, he imagined he could still hear the soldiers' laughter as they cooked their evening meal on the narrow veranda. Although the Picts had long since looted anything of value, there were poignant reminders of the Roman legionaries' daily lives. In the dark, damp shrine to Mithras, small earthenware cups still held traces of libation to the soldiers' god. In the latrines, accidently dropped coins glinted in the stinking slime of the clogged water course.

The fort was eerily quiet. The majority of Hengist's warriors were scattered thinly along the length of the wall, lighting fires in ancient hearths and staring out at the vast northern moors with wary, apprehensive eyes. Forty men remained in Vercovicium. Surrounded by oppressive stone and the ghosts of long-dead men, Hengist's warriors were ill at ease in such a place. Unlike Saxony, Vercovicium was perched at the very top of the world, buffeted by icy wind and rain that swept from the north like a malevolent spirit. They were far from home indeed and there was a surly, resigned expression in their eyes as Horsa walked by.

The garrison headquarters occupied the middle ground of the fort. Hengist was sitting on the raised dais, issuing orders like a king. He looked an impressive sight, bedecked with arm rings of gold and garnets and Horsa gave a wry smile. It seemed power was sitting easily on his brother's shoulders.

'Where have you been?' Hengist snapped.

'*Avoiding you*,' Horsa thought. 'The watch reported hearing something during the night. I was on the wall, taking a look for myself,' he replied.

'And?' Hengist asked curtly.

'I could see nothing out of the ordinary.'

Hengist grimaced. 'So, tell me, brother, what did Vortigern hope we would achieve in this arse-hole of the world? How can he expect me to patrol seventy miles of wall with just two hundred and fifty men? How can I be expected to effectively garrison twenty forts, scores of mile castles, and countless watchtowers? It's impossible!'

Horsa sat down on the bottom step of the dais and rubbed his eyes wearily. Hengist was right. The Romans had garrisoned the wall of Hadrian with thousands of men. It was utterly futile to attempt such a feat with a warband as small as theirs. He badly wanted to suggest that they should head south and never look back. He missed Elsbet so much he felt as if a heavy weight was crushing his heart.

The soldier was running so fast he careered off the door post and slid to a dramatic halt in front of the dais.

'Lord, the barbarians over-ran the wall during the night, some ten miles to the east. Reports say they have stolen a great many cattle,' he announced breathlessly.

Hengist raised his arms to the heavens in exasperation. 'This has gone on long enough! Dispatch a rider to the fort of Andereida. Command the garrison there to send word to the men of Saxony. Tell them there is gold waiting for any man who will fight for me.'

"Yes, Lord." The soldier made to leave, but Horsa grabbed his arm. 'Wait!'

He turned back to his half-brother. 'The treaty you sealed with Vortigern laid down the exact number of troops we could bring into Britannia, and we have already exceeded it.'

'I don't give a fuck about that strip of parchment!' Hengist said irritably. 'I can't achieve anything in this god-forsaken place without more men.'

'Perhaps the folk on this side of the wall might be persuaded to look to their own defences?' Horsa suggested.

'Don't be foolish,' Hengist snapped. 'They are a miserable bunch of flour-dusted bakers and ageing whores.'

'Anyone can be taught to dig a ditch and wield a spear,' Horsa said reasonably.

Hengist exhaled loudly and turned to the soldier. 'I repeat, send word to the garrison at Andereida. I want as many men as will cross the northern sea.' He paused. 'And I will ride out today. I want to see the damage these painted savages have wreaked. Look to it.'

'Yes, Lord.' The soldier bowed and hurried from the room.

The moment the soldier was out of ear shot, Hengist rounded on his brother. 'I will not have you contradicting me in front of my men, do you understand? And why are you sprawled at my feet? Stand up! You're a warrior, not a love struck bard.'

Horsa gritted his teeth and got to his feet.

Hengist walked down the steps and stood beside him. 'My father will come to understand he was wrong to dismiss me as a common mercenary,' he said fiercely. 'I will have my reinforcements, and I will sit upon a gift throne, Lord of a kingdom greater than any man has ever seen.

'I don't doubt it, brother,' Horsa replied soberly. 'I don't doubt it at all.'

Later that day, they rode out from Vercovicium beneath the banner of the white wolf. They turned east, along the old road that ran behind the wall. Although protected from the worst of the northerly winds by the steep escarpment, Horsa still shivered beneath his thick cloak. Summer in Saxony was an idyll of ripening wheat and warm, gentle breezes. Summer in northern Britannia was bleak, the air cold, the trees tugged horizontal by relentless gales.

The civilian settlement was surrounded by a rotting, wooden palisade. Wrenched from its post holes by the vicious wind, it was beginning to slide into the water-logged ditch. The inhabitants looked wary and apprehensive as Hengist's warband rode through their streets. Their homes were substantial two storey structures, at right angles to the muddy road, but the harsh northern climate was beginning to take its toll. Mushrooms sprouted from sodden turf roofs and green mould clung to crumbling lathe and plaster walls. The town had a forlorn, forsaken air and Horsa wondered why anyone would choose to live in such a place. The wall was virtually unmanned; these people were defenceless against the northern tribes.

Horsa frowned. Perhaps these people stayed in this sad little town at the end of the world because this was their home and they had nowhere else to go. There was no worse fate than being forced to abandon your homeland, your gods, and your kin. His mind flashed to Anya. There had been no word from Aquae Sulis since Vortigern had returned south. Was Anya now married to the king of the Dobunni? He shuddered at the thought.

Hengist dismounted and Horsa followed suit. The leader of the town was a man of middle years, with a gaunt face and hostile eyes.

'Vortigern pays you to protect us,' he began accusingly. 'But time and again, you arrive too late, only to watch us bury our dead. We have lost our entire herd of cattle to the painted men, but you have not sent a single soldier over the wall to bring them back to us.'

Hengist turned to his translator. 'Bradoc!'

Bradoc was a pale faced, hungry looking youth, shifting nervously in his saddle. 'Martia wonders if you might send soldiers over the wall to bring back the cattle the painted men stole?' he said tactfully.

Hengist's eyes narrowed suspiciously. 'Is that all he said?'

'Yes, Lord.'

'Tell him I might bring back his cattle, if he does something for me in return. I need his kin to man the wall. I will teach them how to fight, and in return they can live in the fort at Vercovicium. Their families will be safe there.'

Horsa glanced at his brother in surprise. It wasn't the first time Hengist had adopted his strategies and claimed them for his own.

Bradoc translated Martia's vehement opposition to the idea. 'Vercovicium has been over-run many times. The Picts climb its walls like spiders in the night.'

'Those days are gone,' Hengist retorted. 'Today the army of the white wolf guards its defences.'

Martia's eyes glittered. 'You can tell the bejewelled Saxon bum-boy that if we fight for him we will have no-one to harvest our crops.'

Bradoc bit his lip.

'He says no?' Hengist asked.

The boy nodded silently.

Hengist grabbed Martia by the scruff of his tunic. 'You are no use to me if you won't fight. You are just another mouth to feed.' Removing his dagger from his belt, he drew it sharply across the man's throat. Martia collapsed, blood bubbling from the wound.

Hengist stepped over him and walked back to Bradoc. 'Tell these miserable wretches that I expect them at the fort by the full moon. And if I am to go over the wall, I will need a guide. Find me one.'

He turned to his brother. 'A good idea to make use of the locals,' he said casually. 'I'm glad I thought of it.'

Horsa wondered if his brother was making a joke but there was no hint of a smile in his pale blue eyes. His glanced at Martia's woman, kneeling in the mud. Tears were pouring down her cheeks as she cradled her husband's body in her arms. A knot of anger tightened in Horsa's chest. Yet again, his brother had acted rashly. It was highly unlikely these people would fight for him now, for he had won neither their loyalty nor their respect.

'Wait!' someone called in the language of the Britons.

Horsa turned. A young girl stood between her parents. Her eyes were demurely downcast, her face partly hidden by her long brown hair.

'I would speak with you,' her father called out. He was simply dressed but there was dignity in his bearing and Horsa wondered if he had once enjoyed a more comfortable life.

Horsa gestured for Bradoc to join him. 'They are offering you their daughter, Domitia,' he explained. 'They say you would do them a great honour if you accepted her hand in marriage.'

Domitia looked up at him and Horsa raised his eyebrows in surprise. She was pretty and her blue eyes reminded him painfully of Elsbet. For a brief moment, he imagined holding the girl in his arms, the feel of her warm body against his. He looked again at Domitia. Her eyes were full of innocence but they were also full of fear. The girl did not want him. She was not Elsbet. Elsbet was far away.

'Tell them I cannot accept their proposal. Their daughter is beautiful and she would make me a fine wife, but I am promised to another.'

Bradoc listened to the father's reply. 'He understands, but he offers you his daughter nonetheless - to be your woman for as long as you remain here.'

'Why?' Horsa asked, shocked.

The guide grimaced. 'Our lives were good in the days of the legions but now, we have nothing. Look about you. There are very few young men left. The Picts have taken them for slaves, or slaughtered them in battle. You are a warrior. They believe you would give their daughter a better life. And if you give her your seed, this family's line will continue.'

'But I would dishonour her, and her family!'

Bradoc's eyes hardened. 'The painted barbarians have taken everything from us. We are mere Pict-fodder now. Honour is a luxury we can no longer afford.'

Horsa shook his head. 'A man's honour is something that can never be taken from him, no matter how far he may fall. Tell them I am sorry, but I will not dishonour either their daughter, or the vow I made to my betrothed.'

Bradoc shrugged wearily. 'As you wish.'

Horsa mounted up, swung his horse around and trotted to his brother's side.

'I'm glad you saw sense,' Hengist said curtly. 'Our bloodline is pure. It would be madness to rut with these peasants.' He reined his stallion around. 'So, brother, we ride north. It's time these painted savages learnt to stay on their side of the wall.'

Horsa nodded wordlessly. On the long journey across Germania and Gaul, his grief had threatened to overwhelm him. In order to preserve his sanity, he had sealed his love for Elsbet and buried it deep within himself. But the look of innocence in Domitia's eyes had ripped open the seal and bittersweet memories were flooding back.

He wanted to be in Saxony. He wanted to be with Elsbet. He did not relish crossing the frontier of the old Roman Empire. The bleak moors beyond the wall led to soaring mountain ranges and isolated glens where it was said an entire legion of Roman soldiers had been slaughtered by a confederacy of barbarian tribes. If this land and its people had beaten the might of Rome, what chance did Hengist's warband of forty men have against the terrifying painted Picts?

'Are you with me, brother?' Hengist asked coldly.

'I am with you,' Horsa said quietly, remembering his very last conversation with Anya in Marcus's town house in Calleva. He had spoken of the northern lands where men said it was always winter, where the Picts slaughtered without fear of death. Anya had assured him it would be summer in the north and that the Picts were mortal men, just like any other. It seemed he would soon discover if she had spoken the truth.

Horsa's shield was slung over his left shoulder and the strap was digging into his skin. He shifted in his saddle to adjust its weight and stared grimly ahead. Every now and then a shaft of sunlight pierced the grey clouds that scudded overhead, illuminating the bleak moorland and isolated dales. It was a landscape at once both empty and yet full of menace and threat. A place where evil wraiths hovered in the windswept trees and foul spirits lurked in the black marshes. Horsa pulled his cloak about himself and wondered what kind of men inhabited such a hostile and untamed land.

He glanced curiously at the guide. He was undoubtedly a Pict, for the parts of his body that were not enveloped in his cloak, were dyed with blue tattoos of circles within circles, but he did not have the look of a warrior who would drink the blood of children. He looked as scrawny and fragile as a fledgling knocked from a nest.

Horsa frowned. He wondered why Hengist had chosen to trust the guide. There was a good chance he was leading them into an ambush and in such unfamiliar landscape they would be at a fatal disadvantage. He looked up at the darkening sky. The weather had taken a dramatic turn for the worse. Storm clouds were surging from the north, blotting out the sun. Overhead, curlews cried mournfully, a winged siren song leading them deeper into the black foothills.

The clouds were lower now, and the first spots of rain splashed against his cloak. It was as dark as twilight. The foothills rose up before them, the track winding through a narrow, wooded valley. There was no birdsong, only the sound of rain spattering angrily against leaves. Hengist's warband looked about them warily, scanning the dense trees for the first sign of attack. Horsa could feel his heart beating as fast as a battle drum. He had the strangest feeling that they were being watched. A crow flew across their path, splitting the air with its ugly, jarring cry and Horsa jumped in his saddle.

The guide slowed his pace, falling in beside Hengist and Horsa. Wordlessly, he pointed along the track. The village sat in a small clearing. To Horsa's eyes, it was a pitiful place fashioned of mud and turf, as if the round houses had risen from the earth without any design by man. It stank of damp and rot, overlaid with peat smoke and animal dung. No banks or ditches protected the villagers, but they had taken great care to corral the stolen cattle within a sturdy palisade of upright posts.

The guide made to turn back the way he had come, but Hengist grabbed his reins. 'You stay with me.'

Horsa wondered if eyes had indeed been watching them from the dark forest, because the Saxons' arrival in the valley had not gone unnoticed. Like a nest of disturbed ants, the Picts were scurrying to defend their village and their stolen cattle. Within a matter of moments they had formed a barrier across the narrow track, a solid wall of men bristling with spears and axes. Horsa stared at the northmen curiously. They looked as savage as he had feared, with wild, unkempt hair and heavy fur cloaks worn over coarsely hewn breeches. Blue tattoos adorned every inch of their exposed flesh.

Hengist raised a hand and his men came to a halt. 'No prisoners,' he ordered. 'It is the only lesson these barbarians will understand.'

'But there must be women and children in there -' Horsa began.

'Be silent!' Hengist snarled.

Horsa's eyes narrowed. 'Father would not make this choice.'

Hengist grabbed his brother by his shoulder, almost wrenching him from the saddle. 'Athelwald abandoned me. I don't give a fuck what he would have done because I am no longer answerable to him. But I swear by Taranis that if you contradict me again, I will run you through.'

Hengist released his brother and turned to face his men.

'No prisoners,' he repeated. 'Kill every man, woman and child. Burn this village to the ground.'

Hengist kicked his horse forward. His warband dug in their heels and followed him, raising their drawn swords as they galloped towards the village.

Horsa remained on the track. He pushed his soaked hair away from his forehead and slowly drew his sword. It had been a leaving gift from his father and the thought of home made him think of Elsbet. He pushed her quickly from his thoughts. This was no place for her; this place was surely cursed. He sensed the guide was watching him, and he turned to face him.

'I am sorry,' Horsa said in his own tongue then he kicked his horse's flanks and galloped down the track. The Pictish war cries were bloodcurdling. They loosed their short throwing spears, hurling them with force and fury at the advancing Saxons. As Hengist's warriors thundered ever closer, the Picts closed ranks. They fought bravely, screaming curses in their ancient tongue but they were no match for a mounted warband and they fell quickly, bloodied and cleaved, into the churned mud.

'Search the houses!' Hengist shouted above the melee.

A handful of his warriors dismounted, swords drawn. They ducked their heads beneath the low door frames and disappeared into the darkness of the round houses. Moments later, Horsa saw a young girl dart from a house and race towards the log store. Her fingers were closing around the handle of the axe when a soldier caught her by the hair and slit her throat.

Horsa closed his eyes, guilt and shame surging through his heart. He said a silent prayer, asking Nerthus to guide the souls of the slaughtered villagers to their ancestors. He had heard men say the Christian god was willing to forgive any sin, but surely this crime was too great for even a merciful god to absolve. He opened his eyes. The dead - men, women and children - were being dragged into the centre of the village and heaped onto a bloody pyre. The guide had dismounted and was slumped on his knees in the mud. His head was bowed and his lips were moving in frantic prayer.

The rain had stopped but Hengist's soldiers struggled to light the pyre. The villagers' clothes steamed like suet puddings over a kitchen fire before more kindling was brought, and the slaughtered northmen finally began to burn. The round houses took even longer to ignite. Their turf roofs were saturated with the rains of a cold, wet summer and they belched black smoke before an inferno of fire finally engulfed the village. Sensing the intense heat in the air, the cattle in the pound began to bellow fearfully.

Hengist rode to Horsa's side. 'There's no blood on your sword, brother,' he said coldly. 'Where were you?'

'Your soldiers carried out your orders. You had no need of me.'

'The men in my warband do not choose the battles they wish to fight. If you disobey me again, I *will* have you put to death.'

'You would be cursed by the gods if you shed the blood of your kin,' Horsa said softly.

'You would see me cursed?' Hengist asked. 'Is that truly what you wish for?'

Horsa shook his head wearily. 'You misunderstand me, brother. I wish you no harm.' He glanced towards the animal pound. 'The cattle are afraid of the fire. We need to move them before they stampede.'

Hengist dismounted and kicked the guide. 'You! I know you understand my tongue. Get the animals out of that pound before we have more roast beef than even Taranis could devour in one feast!'

The guide stood up. There was raw hatred in the man's eyes and Horsa wondered if the Pict was about to strangle his brother with his bare hands.

Hengist put his sword tip to the guide's throat and the man backed away, towards the panicking animals. The village was ablaze and the air was as hot as a smithy.

'I hate this fucking place,' Hengist said angrily.

'Then we agree on something at last,' Horsa replied drily.

It was a long and troublesome journey back to the wall, herding the long haired cattle across the moor. It began to rain again, and the track quickly turned to a quagmire. Hengist paid no heed to his men's difficulties. He rode at the head of the column, silent and aloof, leaving Horsa to oversee the recalcitrant cattle.

Horsa glanced warily at his half-brother through the driving rain. How long would it be before Vortigern heard of the Saxon reinforcements flooding into the fort of Andereida? It was highly likely Anya would bear the brunt of her husband's fury. He couldn't bear to think of her suffering at Vortigern's hands.

Hengist's burning need to prove himself to their father was making him reckless, foolhardy and dangerous. His ambition was like a foul canker beneath his flesh, devouring all humanity and compassion and in truth, Horsa feared it would lead to the death of them all.

THIRTY ONE

Tintagel, Dumnonia

Lucan sat down beside his brother in the great hall. He was whistling loudly, and Silvanus put his hands to his ears. 'For the love of the gods, Lucan, be quiet.'

'It's not my fault you drink too much,' Lucan replied smugly. He glanced at Silvanus. 'You've been spending a lot of time with the Saxon slave girl recently.'

'Her name is Anya, and she's not a slave,' Silvanus said wearily.

'But she *is* a Saxon, and a witch. They say she is the reason father is dying.'

'Who are 'they'?' Silvanus asked sharply.

Lucan shrugged. 'People talk.'

Silvanus gritted his teeth. 'Anya is not a witch. She's a healer.'

'What's the difference?'

'You know very well they are not the same thing.'

Lucan shrugged again. 'I should warn you – I've raised a petition to have Anya tried as a witch. I have nineteen seals. I need one more and then I take it to the council.'

Silvanus felt his heart begin to hammer against his ribs. No witches had been burnt in Dumnonia for many, many years, but Etar's people were steeped in folk lore and superstition. They might easily be swayed by Lucan's rhetoric, and their own prejudices, to return a guilty verdict.

'Are you mad?' he demanded, his throat dry with fear. 'What has Anya ever done to you, that you would see her condemned?'

'She's dangerous, Silvanus. There's no doubt she has bewitched *you*. I've seen the way you look at her. Admit it, brother, you're under her spell.'

Silvanus shook his head angrily.

'How many times have you taken her to your bed?' Lucan asked, under his breath.

'You are mistaken. We are not lovers.'

But Lucan wasn't listening. 'Bastard sons are dangerous. Full of thwarted ambition,' he went on gleefully.

'She is not with child,' Silvanus insisted furiously.

'If you value her life, you should cast her out, before my petition reaches the council. Send her back to Saxony where she belongs. She has her claws into you already. You would be a fool to allow her to worm any deeper into your life.'

Silvanus stood up. 'I seem to have lost my appetite,' he said bluntly. 'I'm going to take some air.'

For the first time in many months, Anya drifted gently into wakefulness, accompanied by neither dreams nor nightmares. Instead, she lay beneath the warm rugs, enveloped by an unexpected sense of happiness. Like a butterfly on a buddleia tree, her thoughts skipped from the tiny, perfect fingers and toes of Renni's new-born son, to the kindness in Taliesin's eyes. From the sweet scent of wood smoke in the great hall of Tintagel, to Silvanus, who spent his days racked by self-doubt but who, nevertheless, continued to surprise her.

She looked up at the small window. The tiny patch of sky was a deep cornflower blue. She dressed quickly and hurried down the narrow spiral staircase. In the great hall, Lucan was devouring a bowl of porridge. He made a point of ignoring her as she walked by. In the courtyard she paused before a stall selling trinkets. A bracelet of tiny fishes, carved from wood, caught her eye. She was tempted to buy it, but apart from her cloak brooch and her torque, which she had promised as payment to Lucius, she had no coin and no means of barter.

The stall holder was a young girl. Her face was covered in freckles, as if a baker had dusted her with cinnamon. She picked up the bracelet and slipped it onto Anya's wrist.

'Do you like it?'

'I like it very much, but I have no coin. I'm sorry.' Anya removed the bracelet and handed it back.

'No, I want you to have it. My sister says you saved her life.'

Anya frowned in confusion.

'My sister, Renni – she's married to Brendan who works at the stables. You brought her baby into the light. He's a fine baby and no mistake. I've never seen my sister so happy.'

'I am glad,' Anya smiled.

'I want you to keep the bracelet,' the young girl said firmly.

'Thank you,' Anya replied. 'I will treasure it.'

Anya slipped the bracelet around her wrist once again. She had a sudden desire to see the ocean and feel the sand beneath her feet. She walked slowly down the cliff path, for the track was steep and littered with loose rocks and pebbles. The air was full of the sea; salt and seaweed, and the sound of crying gulls. She jumped the last few feet to the beach. The tide was out, but it had left behind a line of tangled fishing nets, pieces of broken amphorae, shells and salt bleached driftwood.

The retreating waves had created long ripples in the sand, as if sea snakes were slithering beneath the vast and empty beach. She removed her boots and wandered barefoot through warm, shallow pools of stranded sea. The sheen of water glittered with reflected light, a shimmering mirror of cliffs and sky. She sat down on a rock. The sun felt warm against her cheeks and she closed her eyes, lulled by the steady crash of the waves upon the shore. It was easy to forget her troubles in such a place. They seemed as insignificant as a speck of sand.

'That's my rock.'

Anya opened her eyes, her heart pounding with shock.

'I'm sorry. I startled you,' Silvanus said, more gently.

'What are you doing here?' Anya stammered, squinting up at him. There was no denying that the heir to the throne of Dumnonia was a startlingly handsome man. The sun had bronzed his skin and his eyes were alight with good humour. The gusting wind had dishevelled his short brown hair. It tugged at the loose shirt he wore beneath his leather cuirass, revealing the contours of his strong warrior physique.

'I came for some air,' Silvanus replied, sitting down beside her. 'I have a pounding head.'

Anya breathed in his familiar scent - horses, polished leather and sandalwood, and an unexpected tremor flickered beneath her skin. A memory was hovering, tantalisingly out of reach. The images were blurred, like reflections in a fast flowing stream, but she could see his face and feel the warmth of an embrace. Dawn was breaking, all too soon. Next, a battlefield; blood, pain and loss.

Confused, she pushed the images away.

'What do you mean 'my rock'?' she asked, focussing her gaze on him again and once begun, found it difficult to look away.

'I claimed it when I was ten years old. It has my initials carved in it. If you move, I'll show you.'

Anya stood up.

'There.'

Anya peered at the intertwined letters, barely visible beneath encrusted barnacles and shiny black mussels. 'That must have taken a while,' she said.

'Yes, but we didn't mind. We were hiding.'

Anya sat down again. 'From whom?'

'From my tutor. Evric and I were terrible students.'

'And are you hiding now?'

'Yes, I think perhaps I am.' A fleeting, troubled look crossed his face.

'Is something the matter?' Anya asked.

'I have a lot on my mind,' Silvanus replied dourly.

Anya waved a hand at the vast expanse of beach. 'I don't know why, but dark imaginings seem easier to bear in such a place as this.'

'I suppose.' Silvanus sounded dubious.

'It's hard to believe, but until a few months ago, I had never even seen an ocean,' Anya said, gazing at the waves.

'That is hard to believe,' Silvanus agreed. 'Dumnonia *is* the sea. It defines us.'

'I'm in awe of the sea,' Anya said softly. 'It's beautiful and yet utterly terrifying. I nearly died -'

Silvanus nodded sympathetically. 'Yes. The shipwreck, on those rocks out there.'

'And on the journey to Britannia, with my brothers -' Anya

began then broke off, but it was too late.

'Your brothers?' Silvanus asked sharply. 'Were they captured too? Were they on the Irish ship?'

'No. They are -' Anya hesitated. 'They are alive,' she ended lamely.

She stared at her bare feet. She could feel her happiness soaking away as rapidly as sea water into sand. She had no idea if Hengist and Horsa were still alive. For all she knew, they could have been slaughtered by wild tribesmen, left unburied for the wolves on some northern hillside.

'Where are they, Anya?' Silvanus asked.

'I don't know,' she replied honestly, and sank into silence. She wished she could tell Silvanus about Horsa, who was betrothed to Elsbet, her best friend. She missed them both so much. She wished she could tell him about Hengist, who had thrown her towards Vortigern, like a bone towards a dog. But she could not; she dare not. She let out a deep, sad sigh.

Silvanus ran a hand through his hair. He looked exasperated. The silence grew but it was Silvanus who finally broke it. 'I've not seen you wearing that before,' he said gently, glancing at the bracelet of fishes.

She ran her fingers across the shoal of tiny fishes swimming around her wrist. 'Renni's sister wanted me to have it. It's pretty isn't it?'

'Yes, it is.'

Anya glanced at him. He had such a tortured and brooding air; a man beset by self-doubt and uncertainties. He could also be irritable at times, full of bluster and complaint, but he was a good man. She wondered who had taught him to be so kind.

'Has your mother passed on?' she asked suddenly.

Silvanus's body tensed.

'I'm sorry,' Anya began. 'It was wrong of me to ask such a personal question.'

Without thinking, she put a hand lightly on his arm.

Silvanus jolted as if he had been stung. He shot a glance at her hand and she hurriedly removed it, thrown into confusion.

'My mother died when I was five summers old,' Silvanus said in a hollow voice. 'It was a difficult time. Branwen, my father's new bride, had no interest in rearing a step-son.' He paused, remembering. 'After a year or so, my father's warrior, Penhallon and his wife took pity on me and took me under their wing. They were good people.'

'Evric's parents?'

Silvanus nodded.

'I too lost my mother when I was very young,' Anya said, staring at the sand. 'I can remember the night she died as if it were yesterday. They say that time heals all wounds but it doesn't. I still miss her.' Anya fought the lump that was growing in her throat. 'She was from this island. She was Silurian by birth.'

'Which explains the colour of your hair,' Silvanus said quietly.

'I am a mongrel,' Anya replied, burrowing her feet deep into the wet sand and watching water ebb and flow between her toes.

'You are like no mongrel I've ever seen.'

Anya glanced at him. Was that a compliment? Feeling strangely unnerved, she blurted: 'Are you sure you have never been to Siluria?'

'No. I've never been beyond the borders of Dumnonia. Why do you ask?'

'No reason,' Anya lied. She had spent many futile hours

wondering why she saw Silvanus walking through the blood soaked village of her dreams. Her nightmares were glimpses into the future but the longer she spent in Tintagel her waking moments were haunted by memories of things past. And it was Silvanus's face she saw, time and time again.

'Your brother still believes I'm a Saxon spy,' she said quietly.

'Lucan is a man of many prejudices although most are not of his making,' Silvanus replied bluntly.

'Is he your half-brother?'

Silvanus nodded. 'He was born to Branwen. There was a time when we were very close. I used to take him on adventures, exploring the caves, climbing the cliffs, but as soon as Branwen found out, she demanded we were given separate nurses, and she kept us apart. It didn't take long before Lucan learnt to share his mother's hostility towards me, towards everyone.'

'I am so sorry.'

'Yes, I believe you are.' A shadow passed behind Silvanus's eyes.

'What is it?' Anya asked curiously.

You hold your secrets very close,' he said softly.

Anya stiffened, suddenly on her guard. She forced herself to remain calm. 'Why do you suppose I have secrets?'

To her immense surprise, Silvanus laughed, shook his head and changed the subject. 'Taliesin enjoys your company. I assume I have you to thank for the fact that he no longer smells like a homeless beggar.'

Anya smiled. 'I enjoy his company too, perhaps even more so now he bathes.'

Silvanus returned her smile then looked up at the sun. It was fast approaching noon. He stood up with an air of reluctance. 'My council will be sending out a search party if I hide any longer. I should go back.'

'I'll go with you,' Anya replied. 'Taliesin will also be wondering where I am.'

They walked side by side across the wet sand. Silvanus looked up at the towering cliffs whilst Anya pulled on her boots.

'My brother tests my patience but despite everything, he is my kin, my blood.' He sounded as if he was trying to convince himself.

She followed his gaze but she did not see the winding path, edged with clusters of sea pinks tugged by the wind. Instead she saw Tristan falling, faster and faster, his screams blending with the cries of the reeling gulls.

'Anya? What's wrong?'

She put a hand to her forehead, willing the terrible image away. 'I -' she began. 'You should -' She swallowed hard, and mustered a smile. 'I looked up too quickly. It made me dizzy.'

He returned her smile. 'As you wish.'

Anya stopped in her tracks. She had the strangest feeling that Silvanus knew she was lying to him.

'You must find me very strange,' she said quietly.

'I do,' he agreed. 'But I've grown quite fond of your peculiar ways.'

'I can't decide if that's an insult or a compliment,' she said, laughing.

Her feet skidded on the steep path and Silvanus put a hand beneath her elbow to steady her. His unexpected touch sent a shiver of tiny goose-bumps along her skin.

'Thank you,' she said unevenly.

'You are welcome,' he replied and they continued to climb the winding track. 'I hope you will stay with us to celebrate our harvest festival. We run horse races along the beach. All my men take part, and we are fiercely competitive. Especially Lucan and me.'

Anya nodded vaguely. The image of Tristan falling to his death flashed across her mind again. As they continued to climb she wondered if she should warn Silvanus that even though the same blood flowed through their veins, he was nothing like his half-brother. But she had no proof, nothing she could put into words - only a burgeoning sense of uneasiness and foreboding.

Anya was one of the first to arrive in the great hall that evening. The sea air had given her an appetite and the aroma of spit-roast pork was making her stomach rumble. She paused in the doorway, searching for Silvanus. He was crouched beside the hearth, tickling the chin of his favourite hound but he looked up suddenly, as if he had sensed her presence.

She walked towards him, keenly aware that he was watching her intently. When Vortigern had stared at her, it had made her flesh creep with revulsion but to be held captive by Silvanus's steady gaze was a strangely pleasurable and heady experience. He stood up as she approached, frantically twisting his signet ring round his finger. He seemed nervous, and came straight to the point.

'Will you sit beside me tonight?'

Anya smiled into his eyes. 'Yes, thank you. I would like that.'

She knelt beside Silvanus's hound and stroked his long, shaggy coat.

'And who are you?' she asked.

'This is Breg, and he's a mangy, smelly old brute.'

‘Pay no attention to your master, Breg. I think you are most handsome.’

‘Don’t encourage him! Look, he’s drooling over you now.’

‘Yuck!’ Anya laughed. The dog’s saliva was dripping through her fingers.

Silvanus was on his feet again. ‘Wait a moment. I’ll fetch you a cloth.’

‘No need -’ Anya began, but Silvanus was already striding away from her across the crowded hall.

‘By Taranis, he runs after you like a serving girl,’ Lucan said dryly.

Anya jumped; she had not heard him approach. Ignoring his jibe, she stood up. ‘How is Mairi? If she’s still suffering from sickness, I have a linctus that might help her.’

Lucan took a step towards her and whispered in her ear. ‘You will not go near my wife, do you understand, witch? And stay away from my father too.’

Shocked by the hatred in his eyes, Anya instinctively stepped back a pace, and crashed into Silvanus. She felt his hands clasp her shoulders, setting her back on her feet. Red faced and flustered, she spun around to face him.

‘I’m sorry. I had no idea you were behind me,’ she gasped.

Silvanus smiled, and handed her a linen cloth. ‘No, the fault is mine. I seem to make a habit of creeping up on you.’

‘I will leave you two alone,’ Lucan said pointedly.

Silvanus stared at Lucan’s retreating back. ‘My brother seems angrier than usual.’

‘Why did he tell me to stay away from your father?’ Anya asked.

Silvanus frowned. ‘Let’s not talk about my brother. Let’s eat.’

Anya sat down beside Silvanus, uncomfortably aware that

many pairs of eyes were furtively turning in her direction.

'It's a shame it's roast pork tonight,' she said under her breath.

Silvanus's face creased with concern.

'You don't like pork? I will ask them to bring something else.'

'No, no. I like pork but I was remembering the story Lucius told, of Circe turning Odysseus's men to swine.'

Silvanus smiled grimly. 'Lucan swears half the people in this hall take you for a witch, but I think it's more likely they believe you are Epona.'

Anya's cup stopped half way to her lips.

'I'm not sure which is worse,' she whispered.

Silvanus tipped his head back and laughed loudly. Anya glanced at him in surprise, for she had rarely heard him sound so carefree. She smiled contentedly and took a sip of Lucius's red wine. She did not mind that Lucan and Mairi were glaring at her as if she was a demon of the underworld supping at their table. She liked sitting next to Silvanus. She felt happy and safe beside him, and she had not felt happy or safe for a long time. She glanced at his handsome face and felt a sudden flare of longing.

For a brief, exquisite moment she allowed herself a perfect daydream. She would stay in Dumnonia. She would work beside Taliesin. She would hold babies up to the light, heal the sick and sing the dying to sleep. She would walk on the beach every day. She would eat her meals at Silvanus's side. She would fall asleep in his arms.

Her daydream shattered like breaking glass. Vortigern's face was staring back at her; an ugly, fractured image in each jagged shard. Dumnonia could not afford to go to war because it had no army. Etar would never choose to save her, over and above his kingdom, no matter how many prophecies Taliesin uttered.

'Will Lucius leave soon?' she asked unsteadily.

'He'll stay for the horse races. He likes a wager. But he will make sail before the winter storms,' Silvanus replied.

'Good,' Anya replied.

Silvanus frowned. 'Why do you say that? Has he done something to offend you?'

'No, I assure you, he hasn't.' Anya stood up. 'Please, excuse me.'

'Are you unwell? Shall I come with you?' Silvanus asked anxiously.

Anya shook her head. 'I'm quite well, but I need a moment alone.'

Silvanus stood up politely as Anya hurried from the hall. And then he sat down again, his mind racing with a thousand questions. He wondered how it was possible that a girl who could frustrate and confuse him beyond measure could also make him feel so happy. He had promised to see Anya safely home to Saxony but in truth, he did not want her to leave. He looked forward to the time they spent together. When he was with her, his life did not seem so overwhelming.

Evric took Anya's place beside Silvanus and looked thoughtfully at his closest friend.

'What's the matter?' Silvanus asked, more sharply than he had intended.

'I don't often say this, but I think your brother is correct.'

'About what?'

'About Anya.'

'I will not hear another word about Anya and her alleged sorcery,' Silvanus growled irritably.

'I'll grant you this much - Anya isn't a witch, but she *is* intelligent and well educated. You only have to look at her bearing and her manner to see that she's high born, which means that some-one, somewhere, is searching for her. Sooner or later, she will return to her homeland, no matter how much you want her to stay in Dumnonia.'

Silvanus glared at Evric. 'You're overstepping the mark.'

'I just don't want to see you hurt,' Evric replied simply.

The revelation hit Silvanus as suddenly and as violently as a lightning bolt. He had been so caught up in the tribulations of kingship he had failed miserably to see the glaring truth. It was too late to avoid getting hurt because he had already fallen irrevocably in love with Anya, the girl he had mistrusted, scorned and insulted. The girl who came from the sea.

'What is it?' Evric asked curiously.

'This conversation is over,' Silvanus said abruptly. He shoved a large piece of pork crackling into his mouth and proceeded to chew it loudly.

'Good, because it's ill-mannered to talk with your mouth full,' Evric said dryly. He raised his hands in a gesture of surrender. 'I apologise for my flippancy, Lord.'

Silvanus washed down the pork crackling with a large draft of wine then he took a deep breath and gathered his wits.

'You'll have your comeuppance at the horse races, you cocky bastard,' he said amiably. 'Just you wait and see.'

Evric raised his glass, and smiled at his oldest friend.

'I look forward to it, as always.'

THIRTY TWO

Anya stood in the ante room of the great hall, her heart hammering against her ribs. Her daydream had been as sweet as the honeysuckle that clambered up the hedgerows in Saxony but Vortigern had wormed his way into her imaginings, as bitter and deadly as black belladonna. She felt overwhelmed with conflicting emotions, as if a storm was raging inside her head.

How could the gods be so cruel? How could they allow her to fall in love with Silvanus? Were they punishing her for defying the high priest, or had they truly forsaken her the moment she set sail on the northern sea?

She had watched Horsa and Elsbet fall in love, seen the exhilaration in their eyes and it had all seemed as natural as breathing. She had often secretly wondered how it might feel to experience such joy, but she had never imagined she would fall in love with the heir to the throne of a beautiful, isolated kingdom at the very edge of the world. Her heart yearned to stay in Dumnonia and grow old by Silvanus's side but her head knew it was a futile, dangerous dream. She could not wait until after the horse races. If Lucius was not prepared to leave immediately, then she would have to find another way. There could be no more delays.

It was not difficult to find Lucius's chamber. She stopped a passing serving girl who smiled sheepishly and directed her to a room on the first floor of the watch tower. Anya knocked loudly on the door. There was a muffled, indistinct reply, which she assumed was an invitation to enter.

Lucius's bed was small and narrow but embellished with an artful array of exquisitely decorated rugs and cushions and a plump, naked serving girl. She straddled Lucius's swarthy flesh, riding him enthusiastically, as if she were just yards from the finish line of the Tintagel horse races.

Anya froze in her tracks. 'I apologise!' she gasped. 'I thought you said…'

She turned away, her cheeks burning with embarrassment, and crashed into the open door. The serving girl was so preoccupied she did not hear Anya's cry of pain. She continued to bounce up and down vigorously, her dainty gasps in a perfect, matching rhythm.

Lucius was not so delicate. He was panting like a wolf-hound, his hairy chest rising and falling like a set of bellows and his face was as red as a ripe pomegranate.

'Anya?' Lucius shouted, but she had already fled, climbing the spiral stairs to her room two at a time. It was only when she had closed the door that she allowed herself to laugh out loud.

A little while later, Lucius knocked on her door. His cheeks were flushed and his dark curls in disarray. He was wearing a long silk robe embroidered with fire breathing dragons in a clashing cacophony of colour.

'Please let me apologise,' he began, shamefaced. 'Most unfortunate incident, most unfortunate indeed.'

Anya shook her head.

'It is I who should be apologising for barging into your

room unannounced. I thought I heard you say -'

'No, no. I am to blame. I should have locked the door. It was unforgiveable.'

'Shall we forget it happened and never speak of it again?' Anya asked.

Lucius brightened. 'I think that's an excellent idea.'

'So, would you like to come in?'

'Am I intruding?' Lucius peered over Anya's shoulder.

'No, not at all. Please, sit down.'

Anya gestured for Lucius to take the chair whilst she perched on the end of the bed. Lucius's robe was a garish splash of colour against the bare, white walls of her room. He reminded her of the exotic birds the merchants carried on their barges. Their proud plumage was a rainbow of colours but she had always thought they looked sad and forlorn, trapped in their tiny cages.

Lucius ran his large hands over his silk-clad knees and looked about her room. There were no silk gowns, jewellery, mirrors, combs or perfume.

'You keep a simple chamber,' he observed.

'I came to Britannia with nothing, and I will leave with even less, for my torque will be yours,' Anya replied.

Lucius stared at her for a moment. 'What did you want to see me about?' he asked quietly.

Anya took a deep breath. 'I have been in Dumnonia for far too long. I have to leave, and I have to leave now.'

'I don't understand. I thought you were happy here. You work beside Taliesin, and you eat beside Silvanus.'

'I *am* happy here.'

'So stay. What could be simpler?'

'I fear it's not simple at all.'

'But they say you are Epona, come from the sea.'

'I am not Epona,' Anya replied dully.

Lucius leant forward in his chair and ran a hand over his perfumed hair. 'I can't help you if I don't know what ails you.'

'Do you remember when I first met you on the cliff path and I told you about my betrothal?'

'I remember.' Lucius tensed suddenly. 'Has the bastard found you?'

'No, not yet.'

Lucius's huge shoulders relaxed slightly. 'So, what's the matter?'

'He has not found me *yet,* but sooner or later, he will.'

Lucius's eyes narrowed. 'Who is he, Anya?'

'You will not have heard of him,' she lied, unable to meet his gaze. She was finding it hard to breathe as if creeping bindweed was smothering her lungs. 'Do you have to stay for the horse races? Couldn't you leave now?' she asked plaintively.

'You must not fret,' Lucius said gently. 'Whoever he is, he will not find you in Dumnonia. This place is as secret and safe as Atlantis itself.'

Anya shook her head. 'I disagree. Tintagel welcomes a steady stream of merchants and there are supply wagons to and from the mines. They gossip, and they bring news.'

'There will be no more merchants so late in the year. You must not worry. I will be gone from Tintagel before the first winter storms, and you can come with me, just as we agreed.' He looked sceptically at Anya. 'But are you sure that's what you want?'

'Yes,' Anya replied firmly.

Lucius eyed her curiously. 'Forgive me if I am speaking out of turn, but it cannot have escaped your notice that Silvanus has eyes only for you?'

Anya looked at the bare floorboards and did not reply.

'I believe he would marry you, Anya.'

'I have no desire to marry Silvanus,' Anya lied.

'Truly?' he asked sceptically.

'Truly,' Anya said firmly. 'I must sail with you, Lucius, and I beg you, let it be soon.'

The merchant stared at her for a long time. 'There's something I have been meaning to ask you.'

'Yes?' Anya asked politely.

Lucius took a deep breath. 'I am no longer a young man. The call of the sea is no longer a roar, but more of a whimper. I have enough gold to live out my days in comfort, and enough stories to fill the long dark nights of a thousand winters.' He glanced nervously at Anya.

'I have a house in Hispania,' he continued. 'It stands high on a hill surrounded by olive trees and vineyards. On summer evenings, you can sit on the veranda and watch the sun set, and hear nothing but the sound of crickets. It's a beautiful home, but I am sore in need of someone to share it with me.'

Anya stared at him in confusion.

'I am thinking about settling down,' he explained. 'I am a wealthy man, Anya. If you were to honour me by becoming my wife, you would want for nothing. I could give you everything your heart desired.'

Anya's eyes widened with alarm. Lucius had taken her completely by surprise. She had not intended to mislead him, or give him false hope.

'I want to thank you for your generous offer,' she began apprehensively, 'but I cannot -'

'We don't have to live in Hispania, Anya,' Lucius interrupted. 'We can live wherever you choose - Achaea, Constantinople, Syria - I care not, as long as you are happy.'

Anya shook her head. 'You are a good man, Lucius, a kind man, but I cannot marry you.'

His face fell.

'I cannot marry anyone,' Anya went on hurriedly. 'I am a priestess of the sacred grove. I swore an oath to my goddess and my body belongs to her alone.'

'Then why did you agree to the betrothal?'

'I didn't agree to the betrothal, but he is a Christian and he paid no heed to my wishes or my religion,' Anya replied.

'I see,' Lucius replied dully, struggling to hide his bitter disappointment.

'I am sorry, Lucius. Please forgive me,' she went on, overcome by a sudden pang of guilt. She would worship her goddess to the end of her days, but she was no longer bound by the laws of the priesthood. She had lied to Lucius to spare his feelings but if Silvanus were to make her the same offer, she knew her heart would ache to give a very different reply.

'There is nothing to forgive,' Lucius said stiffly. 'I should not have asked. It was wrong of me. I have insulted you.'

'I assure you, you have not insulted me in any way. I was flattered by your proposal.'

Lucius stood up and smiled sadly. 'I will take my leave. And I am so sorry Anya, about the other matter, earlier, in my room… you are a priestess, after all.' He stammered to a halt.

'We promised we would not mention that again,' she reminded him gently.

'Yes, yes, quite so.'

Anya opened the door. 'But our agreement still stands?'

'I am a man of honour, Anya. I swear to you that I will leave Tintagel before the first winter storms.'

THIRTY THREE

When the harvest was gathered in, the people of Dumnonia travelled great distances to attend the festival of Lugh the sun god at Tintagel and enjoy the famous horse races on the beach. It was a perfect, late summer's day. The air was warm, the sky cloudless, and the sun danced on the white caps far out to sea. A brisk onshore wind was mustering spectacularly high waves and driving them onto the beach in endless ranks of white-foamed shield walls.

Anya held her breath as the horses thundered past in a cloud of spraying sand and thundering hooves. The vast crowds were screaming encouragement, urging on their chosen horse and rider. She had no coin to place a wager, but she knew who she wanted to win and at the half way point, he was way out in front. She glanced at Taliesin, her eyes alight with excitement.

'Does he always win?' she shouted.

Taliesin shook his head. 'No, not always. Evric has been known to take the laurel crown.'

She turned back to the race. The noise was deafening; the roar of the sea inaudible above the pounding of hooves and the screams of the crowd. The gap between the riders was narrowing.

'Come on!' she yelled, jumping up and down. 'You can do it! Come on!'

The horses charged across the finish line. Silvanus raised a hand in triumph, turning in his saddle to acknowledge the roar of the crowds.

'Hooray!' Anya yelled, flinging her arms about Taliesin's thin frame and hugging him tightly.

Taliesin swayed unsteadily as Anya released him. 'How much gold did you wager?' he laughed.

'I have none to wager. But I'm delighted he's won!'

Her gaze returned to Silvanus. Their eyes met over the heads of the milling crowds and she watched his face light up in a broad grin. She raised a hand in a victory salute and he waved back. Anya felt a bubble of happiness burst against her heart. She had never imagined falling in love could be so utterly overwhelming. The world seemed brighter today, as if the sky was full of suns.

Silvanus was making his way towards her through the teeming crowds. His progress was slow for it seemed everyone wished to congratulate him. He had almost reached her side when Boult came thundering across the beach like a stampeding bull. Silvanus stopped in his tracks, smiled apologetically at Anya then braced himself for his friend's assault. Boult, a man of few words, slapped him hard on the back.

Evric was not far behind. He enveloped Silvanus in a huge bear-hug. 'I'll beat you next time, you bastard!'

Handsome, kind-eyed Jago shook Silvanus's hand. 'Well done. A good race.'

But Anya noticed Lucan made no attempt to congratulate Silvanus. He slipped from his saddle, his face shrouded with frustration and disappointment and stalked away. He did not speak to his wife, ignoring her as if she was invisible. And Anya noticed Mairi made no attempt to salve Lucan's battered pride. The look she gave him was one of undisguised loathing and contempt.

Later that day, twenty of Dumnonia's finest bulls were sacrificed to the gods, in grateful thanks for a safely gathered harvest. Their black blood was collected in sacred, gold cauldrons, and as the sun set over the sea, Anya and Taliesin poured the rich life-blood into deep pits dug into the earth, as libation to the thirsty gods.

That night, the moonlit beach was crowded with revellers, and the mouth-watering aroma of the bulls' roasting flesh filled the air. The huge bonfires cast sparks to the stars, and the laughter and singing grew steadily more raucous as the evening progressed. Silvanus was, as always, surrounded by his warriors. They sprawled upon the sand, and their laughter carried on the warm evening air. Jago lay with his arms wrapped possessively around his young wife. Evric was roaring with laughter at Gorran's latest obscene joke.

Jago raised a hand from his wife's waist in protest. 'Ladies are present, Gorran,' he said mildly.

'Oh, I'm sorry, Elouise. Did you miss the punch line? Would you like me to repeat it for you?' Gorran grinned.

'There's no need,' Elouise replied, struggling not to laugh.

Jago changed the subject. 'Our scouts returned with some interesting news from the Dobunni,' he said dourly.

'Yes, indeed,' Silvanus replied grimly.

Anya froze. Her entire body felt chilled as if she had been plunged into icy water.

'What news?' she blurted, too distressed to notice Silvanus glance at her curiously.

'Apparently, Vortigern's treaty with the Saxons laid down the exact number of men permitted to march under their banner, but they have exceeded that number a hundred fold,' Jago replied. 'By all accounts, they are encouraging men to join them from Germania. They hold the fort of Andereida on the south coast and more ships beach there with every tide. They are pillaging grain, silver and gold from Christian churches, taking men, women and children into slavery.'

Anya's hands began to tremble.

'Vortigern has control of the northern wall. He has conquered the Catuvellauni and the Atrebates, and they say he will soon have dominion over the Coritani. There can be no doubt he seeks to be overlord of all Britannia,' Jago went on grimly. 'It has never been more vital that our treaty with the Durotriges holds. They are our only buffer against him.'

Jago's words had soured the atmosphere. Silvanus sank into a moody silence, and Anya tried to calm her hammering heart. How could Hengist have been so rash, so foolish? She doubted Vortigern was a man to take betrayal lightly. Surely both her brothers' lives were now in grave danger.

Her life in Dumnonia had become painfully bittersweet. Up until this moment, today had been a good day, full of sunshine and joy, but the reality of her situation was just a scratch beneath the surface, as black and hopeless as Nifheim, the cold underworld of eternal mist and ice.

Silvanus stood up abruptly. 'I'm going to ride out. I need to clear my head. Anya, will you come with me?'

She looked up at him in surprise. 'If you wish.'

Silvanus held out a hand to help her up, and from the corner of her eye, she saw Taliesin smile to himself.

Dawn broke as Anya and Silvanus rode across moors tinted purple with flowering heather. After the stillness of the night, a wind arose. Dark clouds scudded across the pale pink sky and the shadows they cast raced along the valley sides, as if trying to keep up with them.

Grazing sheep raised their heads as they dismounted at the circle of huge standing stones. It stood at the highest point in Dumnonia and the view was breath-taking. Endless rolling moors fell away towards the distant sea.

'This is my favourite place in the whole kingdom,' Silvanus said. 'My father used to bring me here when I was a child.'

'How fares your father today?' Anya asked.

'He is sad not to be with us. The festival of Lugh is his favourite time of the year.'

'He must be proud of your victory this morning,' she said softly.

'He is,' Silvanus replied. 'I used to watch the horse races when I was a child. My father invariably won the laurel crown. I can remember watching him thundering across the finish line and praying I could be just like him when I grew up. I was in awe of him. I am *still* in awe of him.' He sighed. 'It's not easy to have such a father as mine. My greatest fear is that he will take his place in the feasting halls of the afterlife and look down on me with disappointment and regret.'

'You and your father are very much alike.'

'No, we're not. Winning a horse race means nothing. It doesn't entitle me to compare myself to Etar, the high king of Dumnonia.'

'I'm not talking about the horse race,' Anya said softly. 'I see much of Etar in you.'

Silvanus shook his head in disbelief and changed the subject. 'I was wary of the leaf of the foxglove, but I think it might be helping. He seems a little stronger today.'

'I'm glad,' Anya replied. 'Although I should warn you, it's

not something he should continue to take indefinitely. Too much, and it *will* poison him.' She hesitated, remembering the sense of menace she had felt in the dark recesses of Etar's chamber. 'More than anything, we need to find out what ails him,' she added.

'Old age,' Silvanus said curtly.

'Perhaps,' Anya replied, unconvinced.

'Come,' Silvanus said, gesturing for her to follow him inside the ring of stones. 'This is Epona's circle, and it's our most sacred place. A legend says that a group of witches, jealous of Epona's powers, met here one night. They planned to trap her, and take her powers for themselves. But Epona was too clever for them. She crept up on them as they plotted, and turned them all to stone. And here they remain, to this day.'

Anya looked up at the stones. They towered over her, a powerful, oppressive presence. 'I am not Epona,' she said firmly.

'I know.'

'I cannot be what Taliesin asks of me.'

'I know,' Silvanus repeated then he took a deep breath. 'When I first met you, I behaved like a fool. Can you forgive me?'

'There's nothing to forgive,' Anya replied. 'You were angry with your father because he's dying. You were angry with Taliesin because he talks of ancient prophecies and goddesses rising from the sea, when what Dumnonia really needs is a strong army. And you were angry with me, because I was the enemy that everyone was welcoming with open arms.'

Silvanus laughed. 'How is it that you know me so much better than I know you?'

'You know me well enough,' Anya replied. 'Because we have met before.'

We have?' Silvanus looked confused. 'When?'

Anya did not reply. The priests accepted reincarnation and rebirth as part of the natural cycle of the world, although she knew that not everyone shared their beliefs. She suspected Silvanus was too troubled by his immediate problems to be open to the idea of looking into a distant past. Many people lived their lives only dimly aware they had walked upon the earth many times before. For others, their ancient memories were a vivid gift. As the days passed, she had come to realise that she had known Silvanus in not just one, but many life-times.

As the blurred images had begun to focus into solid memory, one constant had held fast. Through the turning years, through all the ages of men, there had been bloodshed, suffering and loss. Empires rose and fell but men continued to make war, as naturally as they breathed the air. She stared into Silvanus's eyes. Their paths had crossed a thousand times but in all their lifetimes together, there had been no happy ending.

Without warning, Silvanus took her hand in his, and his unexpected touch sent shivers across her skin. He pressed her fingers flat against the granite, and held them there. Her palm burned hot as the power of the stones flooded through her veins, a pulse from the depths of the earth. The heart-beat of Dumnonia.

'Can you feel it?' he asked. 'It feels like…' He searched for the right words. 'It feels like a connection to something.'

She nodded. 'This is a very special place, a very powerful place.'

She was intensely aware of Silvanus's body so close to hers. His lips were brushing against her hair and she could feel his warm breath against her neck. Her skin tingled deliciously and a rush of conflicting, overwhelming emotions flooded her mind. She wanted to stay in Dumnonia. She wanted to stay with Silvanus, more than she had ever wanted anything in her life. She wanted to turn around, pull him into her arms, and taste his lips against hers. But soon she would sail away with Lucius, and it was unlikely she would ever see him again.

'I love you,' Silvanus whispered.

'And I love you,' she replied. The stab of regret as she tore her hand from his, felt like a knife thrust into her heart. She turned away, and walked quickly from the stone circle.

'Anya? What's wrong?'

'I'm sorry, but I have to go.'

'Why are you sorry? Anya, wait!'

But she did not wait. She mounted her horse and rode back to Tintagel at a fierce gallop. And as she rode, she watched the blood-red sunrise smother the eastern sky. There was no worse omen than a red sky at daybreak.

THIRTY FOUR

The clouds were low over Tintagel, as if the sky had fallen. A light drizzle clung to the air, enveloping the cliff top in muffled silence. Anya walked slowly, lost in her thoughts, her footsteps muted by the mist. The earth was turning. The days were shorter now and the sun no longer burned her cheeks. But life went on in Tintagel much as it had ever done. Etar kept to his room, and Silvanus continued to bear the burden of his responsibilities. Lucan and Mairi had departed some three weeks since to visit Mairi's parents. Anya did not miss them.

Homesickness settled on her heart. In Saxony, the great hall shielded Athelwald's kin from the worst of winter's hardships. The storms raged outside but inside there was warmth and companionship, roaring fires, roasting meat and stories of gods and warriors to bring light to the long dark nights.

She thought of the refugees on Balhazar's barge and she prayed Saxony was safe from the barbarian tribes surging across the eastern steppes. She prayed the harvest had been good. She wondered if Elsbet, preferring to feel the sun on her cheeks, was still grumbling about her needlework, and she wondered if Abberlen's terrible nightmares had eased. Her thoughts turned to Horsa, far away in the north of Britannia, and she prayed that Nerthus was keeping him safe from harm. She missed him so much.

Anya's boots crunched over Taliesin's path. The lavender bushes were neatly pruned and festooned with spider webs. Rain drops clung to their delicate threads, as if pearl necklaces were draped across the branches. She opened the door and went inside. A fire was burning in the hearth but the round house still felt damp and cold. Peeping around the wicker partition, she saw that Taliesin's eyes were closed. He looked old, the contours of his skull sharply visible beneath his sagging flesh.

Anya sat down beside the hearth. The kindling was damp and the fire was smoking. She picked up a long twig and prodded it half-heartedly, sending sparks into the cold air. She felt maudlin today, exile weighing heavily on her shoulders.

'Why did you bring me here?' she asked her goddess. 'Why did you show me such a beautiful place, when you know I cannot stay here?'

She closed her eyes and searched for answers but she heard only the hissing of the struggling fire and Taliesin's loud snores.

The fire caught at last, and it began to warm her cold fingers. She drifted on the edge of sleep and her dreams were of high mountains stained with blood, swaying fields of Saxon wheat, the army of the black boar marching across the moors of Dumnonia, and Silvanus. Always Silvanus.

'Anya?'

Taliesin was standing over her, holding a cup. 'Drink?' he asked.

She rubbed her eyes, struggling into wakefulness. 'Thank you,' she said gratefully. The rosehip tea was warm and sweet.

Taliesin sat down beside her and eyed her thoughtfully. 'It is time you had some answers.'

'I am not Epona,' she said patiently.

'You don't know that.'

'Yes, I do.'

Taliesin stood up unsteadily. 'Come with me.'

'Where are we going?'

'To the beach.'

'No, you might catch a chill. Let's wait for a better day.'

But the old priest was already fastening his cloak about his shoulders, his swollen fingers struggling with the brooch clasp. 'It must be now. You need answers and today is Samhain Eve. There is no better time to visit the cave of fires.'

Taliesin held on tightly to Anya's arm as they climbed down the winding cliff path. Lately, his medicines were having little effect on his aching limbs and he pursed his lips against the shooting pains in his joints. It was raining heavily now and the path had become a stream of fast flowing water, littered with tumbling pebbles.

'We should go back!' Anya urged, concerned Taliesin might slip and fall. The old priest shook his head, his eyes burning with fierce determination.

The tide was out and the beach was drenched in mist and spray. As they approached the sacred cave, crabs scuttled away from them into shadowy recesses. Inside, the air was cold and damp. Anya looked about her in awe. The dripping walls were carved with symbols she did not recognise.

'What do they mean?' she asked.

'They are so ancient, I can only guess at their meaning.' Taliesin replied. His voice echoed around the dark cave and instinctively, Anya bowed.

'What are you doing?' Taliesin asked curiously.

Anya smiled apologetically. 'I am acknowledging the dwarves. They dwell in the dark places of the earth, and they reply in their dwarf tongue whenever anyone shouts to them.'

Bemused, Taliesin shook his head. He leant against a rock and caught his breath whilst Anya gathered driftwood, and then they sprinkled their fire with crushed dried rhizome and root of valerian until the flames were blue, and the air was bitter on their tongues. Taliesin raised his hands towards the black arch of the cave roof and called upon the gods of the sky, the earth, and the underworld, the sacred power of three.

Anya knelt in the wet sand, unaware of the cold sea water soaking into her cloak. The blue flames were licking at her fingers, stripping her skin and melting her bones until she was no longer solid flesh but spirit and air. She was floating above the flames, soaring far beyond the dark cave, flying over flat plains of stubble fields, majestic, slow moving rivers and high mountains growing towards the sun.

She saw Horsa, the blood-lust of battle upon him, and death, a grey ghoul, stood close by. She saw Vortigern marching on Dumnonia, slaughter and famine following in his wake, but Lucan and Mairi rode at his side, and their son bore the crown of Dumnonia. She saw Silvanus and felt a sudden flare of longing. She pushed his image away, and slipped further into her dream paths.

She saw the village in the shadow of the mountains. She heard the stream as it raced over its rocky bed, and the bleating of sheep as dusk fell. It was peaceful, safe, and the pull was stronger than ever before, a siren call that reached out and touched her soul.

Her mother's home. Her kin.

The dream path darkened.

The land was steeped in blood. It stained the dark mountains and soured the fast-flowing rivers. It dripped from the mouldy thatch of the deserted round-houses, and it ran in deep rivulets through silent villages. Britannia was drowning in blood.

The dream twisted, as if the wind had changed direction.

The sword was ancient. Its blade had seen much slaughter, for its sharp edges bore marks of violent use. The land was drowning, but the surging blood slipped harmlessly off the blade, and left the sword unscathed.

As the smoke cleared, and the world of the gods receded, Taliesin looked keenly at her.

'What did you see?' he asked. His face was haggard with the intense effort required to walk with the gods.

Anya's head was throbbing painfully and she did not reply.

'Anya!' Taliesin urged. 'Did you see the sword?'

She looked at him then. 'Yes, I saw the sword.'

Taliesin stood up. He was swaying and she hurried to his side.

'Rest a while,' she said, settling him on a low rock. She sat down beside him, rubbed her stinging eyes and looked about the dark, damp cave. Outside, the rain was still beating down. The sacred cave had raised more questions than it had answered, but for the first time in many months, she had felt close to her gods.

'Thank you, Taliesin,' she said softly.

He smiled. 'All will be well.'

Anya laughed helplessly. She had fallen in love with the heir to the throne of Dumnonia, and yet she was promised to another. Her heart yearned to stay in Dumnonia, yet her dream paths were drawing her towards a village in the far mountains of Britannia.

She glanced sadly at Taliesin. She knew how much he

wanted her to stay in Dumnonia and fulfil an ancient prophecy, yet she also knew she had no choice but to sail away with Lucius to the far corners of the known world, and the thought filled her with a profound sense of loss.

'Silvanus needs you,' Taliesin said suddenly. 'In more ways than you can begin to imagine.'

Anya felt tears prick her eyes. 'I have known him forever,' she whispered. 'Through all the ages of men.'

'I know,' Taliesin replied.

'Our paths have crossed a hundred times, but there has never been a happy ending.'

'The gods sent you to Britannia for a purpose,' Taliesin repeated firmly. 'You must have faith.'

That night, the hall was crowded for no-one had grown tired of Lucius's marvellous tales. People were crammed shoulder to shoulder at the long oak table and those who could find no space there, had squeezed onto the benches around the walls, with food platters balanced on their knees, and cups at their feet. The atmosphere, fuelled by good food and even better wine, was loud and exuberant.

Anya was seated beside Silvanus. Their companionship had become commonplace, no longer attracting whispered comments and furtive glances. She turned to face him, breathing in his familiar, intoxicating scent and fought an almost overwhelming urge to lean forward and put her lips to his.

'When do you suppose Lucan will return?' she asked unevenly, her breath catching in her throat.

'I expect him any day now. He doesn't enjoy the company of Mairi's parents.'

'They live in the north?'

Silvanus nodded. 'In the borderlands between Dumnonia and the Durotriges. If we are invaded by land, Marcellus and his warband will be our first defence.' He grimaced. 'Perhaps our only defence.'

'Would the Durotriges fight for you?' Anya asked, thinking of her dream paths - Vortigern marching over the land of the Dumnonii beneath the black boar banner, scorching a trail of slaughter.

'My grandfather made an alliance with the Durotriges many years ago. Officially it has never been broken but nor has it ever been tested.'

Anya took a sip of wine, remembering the cave of fires. She had seen a sword, its blade full of nicks, made blunt by much killing. It was ancient and sacred, a treasure beyond imagining. Where was it? Did it rest in a scabbard at a great man's belt, or was it lost, waiting patiently through the turning years to be found again? And why had she dreamed of it?

She stared at Silvanus, lost in thought.

'What is it?' he asked.

She did not reply but beneath the table, his hand reached for hers and their fingers intertwined.

Further along the table, Jago and Boult were listening to one of Evric's jokes. Jago was holding his hands playfully over Eloise's ears, shielding her from Evric's crude humour. She was laughing as she batted her husband away.

Lucius sat close by. He was surrounded by a crowd of giggling girls who were hanging on his every word. A rainbow of silks and sashes, he was a flamboyantly exotic figure beside Silvanus's plainly dressed kin. When Anya had turned down his marriage proposal, he had gone straight to the great hall and drowned his sorrows. He had collapsed in a drunken stupor and Anya had found him the following morning with his head on the table in a pool of wine. He had apologised repeatedly for daring to hope she would ever marry such an old, sea-soused fool, and promised once again to leave Tintagel before the first winter storms.

In the meantime, while the leaves still clung to the trees, Lucius was clinging to the warmth and comfort of Etar's great hall. Raising his wine glass, he saluted Silvanus.

'Lord Silvanus,' he said loudly. 'Would I be permitted to offer you a tale of love and war, of treachery and of triumph?'

Silvanus tore his eyes from Anya and raised his own glass.

We would be delighted to hear your tale, my friend!'

Lucius cleared his throat, and began:

'Some of you may already have heard the story I will tell you tonight. It comes from the eastern lands around the Black Sea. It tells of Paris, a prince of Troy who stole the beautiful Helen, the wife of Menelaus, king of Sparta. He carried her away, over the wine-dark sea to Troy, the fortress of high walls. But Menelaus launched a thousand ships, and this is the story of how Troy was razed to the ground as punishment for Paris's arrogant wrongdoing.'

Lucius was a skilled storyteller. He held Etar's men in thrall, so few noticed Anya's discomfort. She stared fixedly at the table, guilt and shame bringing a flush of colour to her cheeks. She felt Silvanus's questioning eyes upon her, felt his hand clasp hers more tightly than before, but she could not return his gaze.

THIRTY FIVE

Tintagel's great hall was stiflingly hot, suffused with the aroma of wood smoke, wet hounds, sweet-scented rushes and roasting meat. Silvanus was sitting at the long table, his head bowed over an unfurled parchment scroll. He was finding it increasingly difficult to concentrate on the summary of the moot court's hearings, his thoughts returning again and again to Anya.

Why, after all this time, did her eyes still hold secrets he could not begin to fathom? And why had she been so distracted of late, so infuriatingly distant, even when she was so close he could smell the scent of chamomile in her hair?

'Does our father still live?'

The sound of Lucan's voice pulled Silvanus from his thoughts. He looked up from the parchment and smiled at his brother.

'He lives. Did you have a good journey?'

'It's rained for days. The roads have become rivers,' Lucan replied grimly.

Silvanus nodded sympathetically. 'How fares Marcellus?'

Lucan walked slowly across the hall. 'My father-in-law is as deaf as a post and a grumpy old bastard.'

Silvanus grinned. 'Sit down, have a drink.'

Lucan removed his cloak and sat down. He downed a cup of wine, then began to twirl the empty cup round and round as if it were a child's spinning top.

Silvanus raised an eyebrow. His brother seemed tense, and in a worse mood than usual. 'Aren't you glad your parents in law live so far away, and you see them but rarely?' he asked lightly.

Lucan ignored Silvanus's attempt at humour. He dragged the pitcher of wine across the table and refilled his cup. 'Has Anya ever told you anything about her past life?' he asked casually.

'You know that she has not,' Silvanus replied cautiously. 'Why do you ask?'

Lucan's eyes glinted. 'She is the daughter of Athelwald, high king of Saxony.'

Silvanus's mouth fell open. 'Anya is a princess?'

Lucan nodded. 'Her brothers fight for Vortigern of the Dobunni.' He paused, as if relishing the moment. 'To seal their treaty, Anya was betrothed to Vortigern.'

'Anya is betrothed?' Silvanus repeated incredulously. 'To Vortigern? No, you are mistaken!'

Lucan smiled triumphantly. 'Trust me, there is no mistake.'

Silvanus stared at Lucan, his mind spiralling in shock and disbelief.

'Nothing to say?' Lucan taunted.

'I don't believe it,' Silvanus said faintly. 'It can't be true. How did you hear of this?'

For the briefest heartbeat, Silvanus thought he sensed his brother hesitate. 'Vortigern's betrothal to a red haired, green-eyed Saxon girl is common knowledge in the north,' Lucan said airily. 'She ran away from him. He has been looking for her ever since, sending out search parties far and wide.'

Despite the heat of the hall, Silvanus felt suddenly deathly cold. 'Why didn't she tell me?' he asked, his voice little more than a whisper.

'That's hardly important. The fact is, you must send her back to Vortigern as quickly as possible.'

'No!' Silvanus gasped before he could stop himself.

Lucan shook his head sadly, as if he were addressing a naughty child. 'I told you months ago that you should let her go, but you wouldn't listen.'

Silvanus stood up unsteadily. 'I'm going to speak to Anya.'

'She won't deny it,' Lucan called after him gleefully. 'I think she will be relieved the truth is out. It must have been a heavy secret to keep.'

Anya walked briskly towards Taliesin's round house. There was a chill wind from the sea, and the sky was a cold blue, dotted with high, fast moving, clouds. Autumn had come, and the leaves were tinged with russet and gold, as rich as the fabrics of the Byzantine world. Tintagel was quiet today, its sounds muffled as life went on behind closed doors.

'Anya!'

She spun around. It was Silvanus. His eyes were full of anguish.

'Is it your father?' she asked, fearing the worst.

'No,' he replied bluntly.

Anya looked up at his handsome face. She thought of Paris, who had carried Helen away over the wine-dark sea to Troy, and Menelaus who launched a thousand ships to bring her home.

'Then what is it?' she asked anxiously.

'Is it true that you are betrothed to Vortigern of the Dobunni?'

Anya felt as if she was falling from a great height. As the weeks had passed, she had almost begun to hope Vortigern was a mere figment of her imagination, a monster from a nightmare rather than living flesh and blood, but Silvanus's words were a brutal affirmation.

'Not here,' she said quietly.

She led him away from Taliesin's house towards the low dry-stone wall overlooking the sea. She looked down at Lucius's ship, still moored on the quayside, and then she looked into his eyes. In truth, she had always known this day would come, but that did not make it any easier to bear.

'I have wanted to tell you for a long time.'

'So it's true?' Silvanus's voice sounded hollow.

'It is true,' Anya replied.

Silvanus recoiled as if he had been stabbed in the gut.

Anya swallowed hard, struggling to control the lump in her throat.

'I'm so sorry, Silvanus.'

He stared at her, his expression a storm of conflicting emotions: shock, betrayal and grief. 'Do you love him?' he asked hesitantly.

'No! The marriage was arranged against my wishes to seal my brothers' treaty with Vortigern.' There were tears in her eyes and she wiped them away angrily. She looked up at him, drowning in the sight of him. 'How did you find out?' Her voice was little more than a whisper.

'When Lucan and Mairi were in the north, they heard talk of Vortigern's search for a Saxon girl with red hair and green eyes.'

Anya froze, remembering her dream paths. Lucan and Mairi at Vortigern's side, riding to Dumnonia, bringing suffering and death in their wake.

'Are you happy here?' Silvanus asked urgently, startling Anya from her dark thoughts.

'You know that I am. I have come to love this place.'

'Then you must stay. The laws of my country do not permit a marriage if either party is unwilling.'

'Vortigern has no interest in the laws of the Dumnonii,' Anya said sadly. 'Sooner or later he will find me and when he does, he will send his army against you, for daring to take what belongs to him. I'm so sorry. I have put you all in terrible danger.'

Silvanus shook his head fervently. 'You are one of us now, Anya. We will protect you. We won't let anyone hurt you.'

Anya clasped his hands in hers. 'You can't protect me, Silvanus and it would be wrong of you to try. I have to go with Lucius. I have to go far away from Britannia.'

'No, that's insane! You are not going with Lucius. I might never see you again.'

'It's all arranged,' Anya said gently. 'It has been arranged for many months.'

'Why didn't you tell me?'

His eyes were so full of hurt that Anya's resolve wavered. She loved this man so much. She had loved him forever, through all the ages of men, and she felt as if her heart would break in two. She yearned to fling her arms around him, hold him close and never let him go.

'Dumnonia is so pure, so untouched,' she whispered. 'All I have ever wanted was to keep you safe.'

Silvanus's face was racked with emotion. 'I will make this right. I will protect you - I will make my father understand how much you mean to me.'

'You can't. You have to let me go.'

'But Taliesin needs you. He's too old, too fragile, to cope

with the burdens of priesthood, and healing the sick alone.'

'He will find another assistant.'

'It will break his heart to watch you sail away with Lucius, knowing he might never see you again,' Silvanus said gruffly. 'I swear to you, I will find a way to make this right.'

Anya looked into his eyes. 'Please, Silvanus, I would give anything to stay here with you but you have to let me go, or Vortigern will destroy you all.'

Silvanus sat down gently on the bed and clasped his father's thin hand in his. Etar's influence had once stretched the length and breadth of Dumnonia, encompassing fields, forests, moors and sea but was now reduced to this warm, smoky room. Silvanus looked at his father as he slept and his heart tightened with grief. Etar was not long for this world. Soon he would join his ancestors in the feasting halls of the afterlife, and they would surely welcome him, for he had been a great and wise king.

Silvanus felt a stab of fear. Soon the throne of Dumnonia would be his; a lifetime of responsibility, duty and sacrifice. It was a truly daunting prospect but it would be a thousand times easier to bear if Anya were by his side.

Etar slowly opened his eyes. For a moment he looked confused.

'Is Branwen with you?'

Silvanus took a deep breath. 'No, Father, Branwen is dead. She has been dead these five years.'

He watched his father's face crumple in remembered grief. Etar nodded, tears filling his opaque eyes. 'I loved her so much.'

Silvanus had accepted long ago that Etar's love for his second wife ran very deep. He hesitated. Over the last few days he had spent many hours on the beach, staring out at the waves. His thoughts had run wild, tumbling over themselves like butter in a churn, but they had returned doggedly to the same fixed point. He loved Anya and he needed her to stay in Dumnonia.

'What is it, my son?' Etar said softly.

Silvanus smiled weakly. His father's body was failing him, but, at times, his mind was still as sharp as a sword blade.

'Anya is betrothed to Vortigern of the Dobunni. Isn't that what you were about to tell our father?'

Silvanus turned abruptly. Lucan was standing in the doorway of the darkened room.

Etar's chest rattled as he took a laboured breath. 'Is this true?'

Silvanus stared at his father. He could find no words.

'Yes, father,' Lucan replied. 'It is true. She ran away from him.'

Etar's face contorted in pain as he struggled for breath.

'How long have you known of this?'

'I discovered the truth during my visit to Marcellus.' Lucan walked over to the bed with an ebullient air.

Etar was attempting to sit up, his frail hands fluttering fretfully over his bed rugs. 'Anya has put us all in great danger. We must send word to Vortigern immediately.'

Silvanus jolted. 'No! Father, listen to me. Anya did not agree to the betrothal. She does not wish to marry Vortigern.'

'Then I feel pity for her, but it is no concern of ours.'

'How can you say such a thing? Taliesin is convinced she is Epona, come to save us all,' Silvanus said urgently.

'She looked me in the eye and she told me she was not Epona,' Etar said, sinking back onto the cushions.

'And you believed her, over and above your high priest?'

Etar looked at his son and his eyes were cold. 'Yes, I believed her. I am a pragmatist, Silvanus. I cannot risk open war on the strength of dreams and prophesies. Taliesin is old and we all know that his dream paths are confused of late.'

'But she is one of us now,' Silvanus went on desperately. 'We cannot turn our back on her.'

Etar patted Silvanus's arm with a trembling hand. 'Anya is a skilled healer and there are many here who hold her close to their hearts. Indeed, her medicines have been a great comfort to me, but these things change nothing. I am sorry, my son. It is clear that you have feelings for Anya, but she does not belong to you. I cannot risk my kingdom for one girl.'

Silvanus stared at his father. It seemed Etar would die adhering to the same principles he had lived by. His primary concern was his duty to his people, to Dumnonia.

But that did not change the way Silvanus felt about Anya. Nothing made sense without her.

'My son,' Etar said softly. 'I think you have fallen in love with this girl.'

Silvanus did not reply.

Etar's eyes narrowed. 'Is she pure? Have you defiled her?'

'Father!' Silvanus looked away, embarrassed.

'Well, have you?'

'I have not, I swear.'

'Good.' Etar sighed. 'You must let her go. The longer she remains in Dumnonia, the greater the risk she poses to our kingdom. If we continue to offer her sanctuary, Vortigern will see it as an act of blatant aggression, of war. I thought you would understand this? I thought you cared for Dumnonia, for our people?'

'You know I do, father.' Silvanus felt as if he was drowning. 'But if she cannot remain in Dumnonia, then she must leave with Lucius, as she originally planned. She must sail far away so that Vortigern will never find her.'

Etar shook his head. 'That will not be possible. I have given you my answer. She belongs to Vortigern, and she must go back to him. Lucan – you will send a messenger to Aquae Sulis informing Vortigern that we have his betrothed in our safe keeping and we await his instruction.'

From the corner of his eye Silvanus saw Lucan's barely suppressed smirk of delight.

Etar's hand reached out and grasped Silvanus's arm. His grip was surprisingly strong. 'No-one must know about my decision. Not Anya, not Taliesin, not Mairi. No-one, do you understand?'

Silvanus's eyes widened in alarm. 'But -' he began.

Etar's grip tightened on his arm. 'I am old and I am sick, but you will not disobey me. Never forget, I am still your king.'

'*I* will not disobey you, father,' Lucan said without hesitation.

Silvanus stared helplessly at his father. The burden of duty had never felt so heavy. 'Nor I,' he replied.

THIRTY SIX

The colder weather brought sickness to Tintagel and the surrounding villages. A long line of bedraggled humanity waited patiently outside Taliesin's round-house, their shoulders hunched against the drizzle, whilst inside every available patch of floor was crammed with makeshift beds. Taliesin's supplies were running low and Anya had resorted to asking the local children to search for marsh-mallow roots in the ditches and the last of the rose hips in the hedgerows.

Anya wrung out the cloth and gently bathed the woman's feverish skin. She could not remember when she had last slept for more than a few hours at a time. Her evenings spent beside Silvanus in the great hall seemed a distant memory.

She glanced anxiously at Taliesin. She had pleaded with him to rest, but he had steadfastly refused. How much longer could the old priest withstand such a punishing routine? Taliesin looked up and their eyes met. He smiled, but his face was gaunt with exhaustion.

Anya moved on to the next bed. The little girl was sitting up, drinking a cup of water.

'I believe your fever has broken, thanks be to Nerthus,' Anya said, relieved.

The girl tipped her head to one side. 'Who is Nerthus?'

Anya smiled. 'Nerthus protects my people, just as Epona protects the Dumnonii.'

'You are Epona,' the little girl replied. 'And you have healed me.'

'I am not Epona,' Anya said gently.

'My mother says you are.'

In recent days, Anya had given little thought to the world beyond the walls of Taliesin's house of healing. She had been too exhausted to worry about goddesses rising from the sea, or Vortigern, or the fact that Lucius's ship would soon carry her many oceans away from Tintagel.

Her gaze focussed. Through the open door she could see Silvanus striding through the drizzle. The line of men, women and children parted to let him through, and bowed their heads in respect for their future king.

'I must speak with you,' Silvanus mouthed over the din of crying babies and whining children.

Anya stood up and followed Silvanus outside. After the warmth of Taliesin's round-house, the wind was biting and she shivered, wrapping her cloak tightly about herself.

'It's good to see you,' she began, but her smile quickly faded.

She had not seen Silvanus for many days and she was shocked by his appearance. He looked pale and drawn and dark smudges of tiredness were etched beneath his eyes.

'Are you sick?' she asked anxiously.

'My father wishes to see you,' Silvanus said dully.

'Why?'

Silvanus stared into her eyes but he did not reply.

'Silvanus? What's wrong? What's happened?'

She reached out to touch his forearm, but Silvanus turned and walked away. He did not look back, and she followed him, a cold sense of dread growing in the pit of her stomach.

They had carried Etar from his sick bed, and enveloped him in fine, crimson robes. They had cut his finger nails and combed his long hair but nothing could hide his frailty. He looked somehow diminished, an insubstantial presence on the high seat of Dumnonia. Lucan stood at his father's right hand. His expression was curiously animated and expectant.

Anya guessed a council meeting had recently taken place. Beneath the dais stood twelve men, including Evric, Jago, Boult, and Gorran. Unlike Lucan, their faces were sombre.

Anya and Silvanus came to a halt before the dais. Anya bowed her head respectfully. She did not look up, but Etar looked long and hard at her.

'I am sorry that you must leave us, Anya,' Etar said, his voice as brittle as dead leaves.

Anya kept her eyes fixed firmly on the floor, confused and alarmed. If Lucius had announced his imminent departure, why had he not told her of his plans?

'I wish to thank you for all you have done during your time at Tintagel,' Etar went on. 'In particular, I wish to thank you for all you have done for me. Your medicines have been a great comfort.'

Anya looked up into his ravaged, fragile face. 'Although I am far from home, I have felt a sense of belonging here,' she replied. 'And I thank you for that.'

Etar shifted in his seat, trying to relieve the agony of the bed sores that covered his skin. When he spoke again, there was a sudden chill in his voice. 'But we all know that you do not belong to us, Anya, much as some of us would wish it.'

Anya's heart began to pound alarmingly.

'An outrider has reached us from Aquae Sulis,' Etar continued. 'He has brought news that Rufus Aufidius

Maximus will arrive tomorrow to escort you to Vortigern of the Dobunni - your betrothed.'

'No!' Anya gasped, horror-struck. She glanced at the group of councillors. Only Evric was brave enough to return her gaze. The others lowered their eyes.

She rounded on Silvanus incredulously. 'You sent word to Vortigern? How could you do this to me?'

But Silvanus stared straight ahead, as if he had not heard her. Only the muscles twitching at his jaw line hinted at his torment.

Anya walked towards Etar and from the corner of her eye, she saw his guards edge forward protectively. 'I have no desire to lay eyes upon Vortigern of the Dobunni ever again, but neither do I wish to bring war to Dumnonia. I will sail with Lucius,' she said calmly. 'It has been arranged for some time.'

'Lucius has gone. It will be at least a year before we see him again. I am sorry, Anya, but my loyalty is to my people,' Etar replied.

Anya stared in stunned disbelief at the king. Her skin felt ice cold despite the stifling warmth of the great hall.

'Lucan!' Etar commanded. 'Keep watch upon Anya. I do not wish her to come to any harm before we hand her over to Rufus's safe-keeping.'

Lucan stepped forward. He did not attempt to hide the grin upon his face, and Anya watched him exchange hostile glances with Silvanus. She realised Lucan was taking pleasure in her suffering, and in his brother's also.

Lucan took her roughly by the arm. 'By the gods, you look sickly today,' he said under his breath.

'Get your hands off me,' she whispered back, for she did not wish to cause further distress to the ailing king.

'I have ears. I can still hear.' Etar's voice was unexpectedly forceful. 'Treat Anya with respect, Lucan.'

Lucan bowed in an over-exaggerated manner. 'If you will follow me, Lady Anya.'

Anya followed Lucan from the great hall. She did not look back or she would have seen the shame, regret, and torment clearly etched upon Silvanus's stricken face.

THIRTY SEVEN

Silvanus tossed and turned, his thoughts a maelstrom of frustration and anguish, and it was only as dawn broke that a disturbed sleep finally came to him. He awoke several hours later, his head heavy with exhaustion. Stumbling wearily from his bed, he dressed as if in a dream. Evric was waiting for him in the ante-room to the great hall.

'Rufus is here - Vortigern's man,' he said urgently. 'You look terrible. Can I bring you something? A comb perhaps?'

Silvanus ignored his sarcasm.

'Where is Anya?' he asked urgently.

'Lucan is bringing her to Rufus.'

'If Lucan lays one finger,' Silvanus began, but Evric interrupted him.

'Rufus has been waiting for several hours.'

Silvanus took a deep breath and opened the doors to the great hall. Rufus, who was seated at the long table, hastily stood up.

'Please accept my apologies for not being here to welcome you but there was an urgent matter to attend to,' Silvanus lied smoothly.

'There is no need to apologise, Sir. Evric has been extremely attentive. Your hospitality is to be commended.'

'Please, sit.' Silvanus gestured to the bench, eyeing Rufus curiously. He was slight of bearing, an emissary rather than a warrior, presumably chosen for his brain rather than his skill with a blade. A knot of anguish tightened in Silvanus's gut. This man had come to take Anya away from him. Come to take her to Vortigern, a man he had never met but who was widely regarded as being one of the most powerful, most feared men in Britannia.

As if sensing his master's distress, Breg the hound stirred from beside the fire and put his head on Silvanus's lap. He stroked the animal's snout, and felt its warm breath against his fingers.

'I am sorry to hear your father is unwell,' Rufus said formally.

'We have high hopes for his recovery,' Silvanus lied.

'Vortigern is grateful that you have attended to his betrothed,' Rufus went on smoothly.

'Of course.' The muscles at Silvanus's jawline clenched. He had heard it said that Vortigern was a cold and brutish man, and he could not bear to think of Anya in his bed.

'Where is Anya?' Rufus asked, as if reading his thoughts.

'She will be here momentarily.'

Rufus nodded. 'And how fares the kingdom of the Dumnonii, Sir?'

'It fares well,' Silvanus replied. 'The gods continue to bless us.'

Rufus smiled and an awkward silence fell.

Silvanus began to twist his sun stone signet round his finger. 'And how fare the Dobunni?' he asked, when the silence became blatantly discourteous.

'We fare well.' Rufus's smile did not waver. 'As we speak, Vortigern is marching to face the Coritani. When the battle is won, he will be overlord of all lands north of the Severn.'

'Ah yes, how tragic that an unfortunate misunderstanding at a betrothal ceremony should lead to war,' Silvanus said mildly, and enjoyed watching Rufus's discomfort.

'Please assure Vortigern of our continuing friendship,' Silvanus went on formally. The words choked in his throat, but they needed to be said. Although he loved and respected his father, he thought Etar was misguided to place so little importance on alliances.

'I will convey your message,' Rufus replied.

The doors opened and Anya entered the hall. They both stood to greet her. Silvanus noticed that Rufus's eyes wandered greedily over Anya's tall, slender frame and the knot tightened still further in his gut.

'Anya,' Rufus inclined his head in greeting. 'According to the dispatch you alone survived the storm. Truly a miracle.'

'The gods took it upon themselves to save Vortigern's betrothed, yet send her captors to their watery graves. I thought you Romans believed in divine vengeance?' Silvanus cut in sharply.

A look of undisguised scorn crossed Rufus's face. 'I leave that kind of philosophy to the priests.'

'I am glad to see you survived the Irish attack, Rufus,' Anya said. 'The gods are merciful.'

'I was fortunate indeed,' Rufus replied. He looked suddenly uncomfortable, his eyes swerving to the floor.

Silvanus glanced at Anya. He wondered if she was mocking Rufus in some way, but he had sensed no sarcasm in her voice.

Anya took a step forward. 'Tell me, do you have news of my brothers? I am anxious for their safety.'

Rufus looked up again. 'They are still serving on the

northern wall. Their warband is holding the Picts at bay.'

'You are certain they are unharmed?' Anya persisted.

Rufus shrugged. 'Last I heard.'

Anya smiled and her eyes filled with tears of relief. Silvanus gritted his teeth, fighting against an almost overwhelming desire to take her in his arms.

'So, you are strong enough for the journey to Aquae Sulis?' Rufus enquired.

Anya nodded wordlessly.

'Then we will leave at sunrise tomorrow. I would not wish to outstay our welcome.'

'No! I -' Silvanus checked himself abruptly. 'You must accept a little more of our hospitality,' he finished lamely.

'Forgive me, I would not wish to give offence, but Vortigern is eager to see his betrothed,' Rufus replied, his gaze lingering insolently over Anya's body.

Anya was glaring furiously at Rufus, her cheeks flushed with humiliation. Silvanus's mind flashed back to the day she had first stepped into the great hall, all those months ago. She had looked so brave and yet so vulnerable, and now she was about to be taken from him, by a man who leered at her as if she were a common whore.

Rufus continued to stare, unabashed, at Anya. Silvanus's right hand strayed to the grip of his sword. The atmosphere in the room was charged with palpable tension, like the moments before a thunder storm.

If you will excuse me, I must…' Anya began, sensing the situation was reaching breaking point. She nodded curtly at Silvanus and hurried from the room.

Silvanus took a step forward as if to follow her. With both hands clenched into fists at his sides, he forced himself to a halt. He felt as trapped and helpless as a bear in a cage. His blood was pounding in his ears, his entire body taut with rage.

Rufus picked up his wine glass. He held it up to the light, squinted at it, then carefully removed an invisible speck of dirt from the rim. Swirling the wine around the glass, he glanced slyly at Silvanus. 'Vortigern is in your debt. In honour of this, he wishes you to rule in peace, as an ally.'

Silvanus laughed humourlessly. 'Am I to take it that as a reward for rescuing his betrothed, Vortigern will not send his army against me - at least not for the foreseeable future?'

Rufus's face set hard. 'They are not the words I would choose.'

Silvanus raised his cup. 'No, but I see that we understand one another. A toast then, to our future alliance.'

'I have another toast,' Rufus replied. 'To Vortigern and Anya. May they have a long life together, and be blessed with many children.'

Silvanus's flesh turned cold. The two men looked at each other, and a heavy silence fell. Rufus raised his glass, a slow smile spreading across his pinched face.

Lucan's guards opened the door to the watch-tower room and stood back to allow Silvanus inside. Anya shot to her feet. It was bitterly cold in the small, bare room and her breath misted the air.

'Close the door,' Silvanus ordered.

For several moments, Silvanus and Anya stared at each other in silence. The tension in the air was as taut as a hangman's rope.

'My father ordered Lucius to sail away in the dead of night,' Silvanus said at last. 'He told no-one. I will never forgive him.'

'Your father is dying. You have to forgive him, before it's

too late. He was only doing his duty, as any good king should.'

'Is there no hatred in you, Anya? Perhaps you are the goddess, after all.'

Anya smiled bleakly. 'Believe me, I feel hate, like everyone else.'

'Is that so?' Silvanus asked dubiously.

'I hate my brother for giving me to Vortigern against my wishes,' she said quietly.

Silvanus nodded. 'Your brother betrayed you, and I sometimes wonder if mine wishes to be king in my place.'

'You should keep a close eye on Lucan,' Anya said solemnly.

'Why? What have you seen?'

Anya glanced away. Her dream paths were never clear, but Lucan's dark shadow loomed over Silvanus, a growing threat.

'Nothing to speak of,' she said truthfully, but a shiver ran rapidly down her spine.

'You are cold.' Silvanus unfastened his cloak and put it around her shoulders.

'Thank you.' Anya sat down on the edge of the bed.

Silvanus sat beside her, angrily twisting the sun-stone signet ring round and round his finger. He stared at the floorboards, his body rigid with rage. A heavy silence fell.

'You can't leave,' Silvanus said at last. 'Nothing makes any sense without you.'

Anya placed her hand lightly over his fingers. Her touch seemed to calm him, and he stopped his restless fidgeting.

'Everything in life happens for a reason, and what is done, cannot be undone, no matter how hard we may try,' she said.

'Did your priests teach you that?'

'Yes, they did.'

'I've never been very good at accepting things I don't like. I'm much better at railing against them,' Silvanus replied.

Anya looked into his eyes and smiled.

'I have noticed that,' she said lightly.

Silvanus shook his head miserably. 'You can't leave me,' he repeated, like a lost child. 'I don't know what to do. I don't even know where to start.'

'Yes, you do. You start at the beginning, and the rest will follow. Trust your instincts.'

Footsteps sounded on the spiral staircase, and then they heard Evric's voice. The door swung open, and a blast of even colder air surged into the room.

Silvanus tore his eyes from Anya, and glared at his oldest friend. 'Evric! What gives you the right to enter, uninvited?'

'Lord Silvanus,' Evric bowed. 'Forgive me, but is this wise?' He glanced at Anya.

'Close the door!' Silvanus roared at the guards. And then he rounded on Evric furiously. 'We are talking to one another. Nothing more. And, by the gods, this is no business of yours!'

'Forgive me,' Evric repeated. 'But you must know I have your best interests at heart.'

'My best interests?' Silvanus asked bitterly. 'Don't you mean Dumnonia's best interests?'

'They are one and the same. At least, they should be,' Anya said softly.

Silvanus grunted something unintelligible.

'You shouldn't be here,' Evric said firmly.

Silvanus ran a hand through his short hair, looked up at the rafters, and let out a roar of frustration.

Anya stood up slowly. She was trembling, as if the blood was slowly draining from her veins. With the smallest nod of her head towards Evric, an unspoken agreement passed between them.

'Evric is right. You shouldn't be here. I want you to leave now,' she said quietly.

Silvanus looked at her incredulously. 'You don't mean that?'

'Yes, I do. As impossible as it seems at this moment, I have no doubt that our lives are unfolding as they should.'

Silvanus stared at Anya for a long, long time. Finally, he stood up. Without preamble, he pulled her into his arms, and briefly held her close.

'May the gods keep you safe,' he said, as he released her.

Evric opened the door but Silvanus turned to face her again and, with his back to the guards, he silently mouthed two words. 'Thank you.'

The door closed. Anya sat down heavily on the bed. She put her head in her hands, and gave in to the tears she had been holding back for so long.

Anya did not sleep, her thoughts a storm of grief and anger and regret, interspersed with visions so vivid they made her head pound. She saw the village in the shadow of the mountains, drowning in blood. Horsa upon a nameless battlefield with death, a black ghoul, close by. She saw the sword, its blade nicked and scarred by countless ages of warfare. And Silvanus was holding the sword, holding it aloft, riding into battle. She saw Tristan plunging to his death. There was a man on the clifftop, watching him fall…

Anya opened her eyes, her heart beating fiercely. She stumbled from her bed, reaching blindly for her clothes in the darkness. Pulling on her boots, and tugging her gown over her head, she felt her way towards the door.

Banging on it loudly, she shouted: 'I know you're out there. I demand to be taken to Silvanus.'

She heard men's voices, speaking urgently to one another, then silence. Anya thumped her fist against the door again.

'Listen to me! I am the daughter of a king, and a priestess of the sacred grove. I must speak to Silvanus. It's a matter of life or death!'

She heard more voices, some kind of heated debate, and then the sound of the key turning in the lock. The door opened and Anya took a step back, blinded by the fierce glow of a burning torch. Without a word, the guard took her by the arm and led her down the narrow spiral staircase.

Silvanus was in the great hall, pacing up and down beside the hearth. He looked as if he had dressed in a hurry. Over a pair of breeches, he wore a loose linen shirt and his feet were bare. The hall was in semi darkness, lit only by the glowing embers of the fire, but Anya could see the tension on his face. She made to run to him, but the guard held her back.

'Let her go!' Silvanus said sharply.

The guard released her arm.

'What's wrong?' Silvanus ran towards her, looking her up and down, as if searching for signs of injury. 'Did someone hurt you? Are you sick?'

'No, I'm quite well. But I need to talk to you – alone.'

Silvanus glanced over her shoulder at the guard.

'You can go.'

The man nodded, turned on his heel and walked away.

Anya and Silvanus began to move at the exact same moment, closing the distance between them in a heartbeat. Silvanus enveloped her in his arms and held her close. She shut her eyes and felt his heartbeat against her cheek, and marvelled at how exquisite it felt to be held in his embrace.

'I was so worried…' he began.

Reluctantly, Anya pulled away from him. 'Let's sit.'

Silvanus nodded. Clasping her hand in his, he led her to the table. They sat down together, fingers intertwined.

'What did you want to talk to me about?' he asked.

Anya took a deep breath and tried to concentrate, but it wasn't easy in such close proximity to him. His thigh was brushing against her leg; she could feel the heat of his skin through her gown. Her hands were cold, but his were distractingly warm and his thumb was gently circling her palm, over and over again. She felt her breath catch in her throat and her cheeks began to flush.

'I believe Lucan killed Tristan, the little kitchen boy,' she said hurriedly.

Silvanus's eyes widened. He ran a hand through his hair, a sure sign he was thinking hard. When he finally spoke, he did not laugh or call her foolish. 'Do you have proof?' he asked calmly.

Anya shook her head. 'Not yet. But, with your help, I believe I might.'

Silvanus stared into her eyes for a long time. She knew he was trying to make up his mind, trying to decide if he should believe her. She didn't blame him. Blood was always thicker than water. The runes above the lintel of her father's great hall read: 'Kin above all else.'

Finally, Silvanus exhaled loudly then nodded.

'What is it you would have me do?'

Silvanus stood at Lucan and Mairi's bedside, his hand on the hilt of his sword. He looked down at their sleeping forms and felt a pang of guilt. This was wrong. He was a trespasser here. But then he remembered the look in Anya's eyes, the certainty he had seen there. 'Wake up, brother!' he said loudly.

Lucan turned over, bleary eyed and confused. His gaze focussed on Silvanus and he shot upright, instantly awake.

'How dare you enter my bed chamber in the middle of the night? Has Anya bewitched you into madness?'

At his side, Mairi sat up and looked about, bewildered.

'Get dressed - both of you,' Silvanus said bluntly. 'My guards will escort you to the council chamber. You will wait for me there.'

'We will do no such thing!' Lucan retorted.

'I order you - by command of our father the king.'

'This is outrageous! Of what are we accused?'

Silvanus did not reply.

'If you have nothing to say for yourself, I demand you leave my bedchamber!' Lucan bellowed.

Silvanus turned to the guards waiting outside in the corridor. Raising his right hand, he snapped his fingers and pointed at the bed. Mairi, still half asleep, went without a struggle but Lucan fought like an enraged bull, his flailing arms sending pewter cups crashing to the floor, his wildly kicking feet tearing a tapestry from the wall.

Anya waited until Lucan's blood-curdling curses had faded into the distance then stepped out from the shadows to join Silvanus. She could see the barely controlled emotion in his eyes and she sensed how much this was costing him. She could only pray it would be worth it.

'What are we looking for?' he asked, his voice hollow.

'We'll know it when we find it.'

Anya knew it was an unsatisfactory reply, but she could offer nothing more.

Silvanus nodded. 'Then let's get started.'

But neither of them moved. They just stood, side by side, looking about the bedchamber. Lit only by the embers of the fire, it smelled of musty sleep and wood smoke and clean linen, with undercurrents of expensive, exotic perfume. Anya glanced nervously at Silvanus. There was something so personal, so intimate about a bed chamber. May the goddess forgive her; this felt like a terrible invasion of privacy.

Silvanus took a deep breath. 'You start with her jewellery – I imagine it's in that box over there. I'll start on the bed.'

The jewellery box was inlaid with ivory, a work of art in itself. Anya opened the lid and tipped its contents onto the table. Rings of jade and amber, necklaces of creamy pearls, clasps and brooches of gold and silver tumbled out. Scooping everything back into the box, she shook her head, frustrated.

She turned next to the leather bound chest at the end of the bed. It was crammed with Mairi's gowns and underskirts and linens. Feeling like a thief in the night, Anya carefully removed them, one by one. At the very bottom of the chest, she found a rag doll. It had been much loved; its embroidered face was worn away with kisses.

Anya felt a sudden stab of pity for Mairi. She had been little more than a child when Lucan had taken her to their marriage bed. Anya glanced at Silvanus. He was stripping that very same bed, throwing pillows and sheets and blankets into the corner of the room. He flipped the mattress, sending it thudding to the floor. There was nothing underneath it apart from two dead spiders and a sprinkling of stray feathers. He got down on his hands and knees and peered under the slatted base.

As he rose to his feet, their eyes met and she saw his unease as clearly as if he had spoken it. There was nowhere else to look. Anya felt a surge of guilt, so fierce it took her breath away. She had been wrong. And Lucan would never forgive Silvanus for this. She had succeeded only in stirring up a great deal of trouble.

'We should re-make the bed,' she said softly.

Silvanus nodded mutely.

As she bent down to lift the mattress, her boot caught on the curling edge of a rug. It was a complicated design of geometric patterns that reminded her painfully of Emma's embroidery. The colours were those of autumn; golds and russets, the rich colours of Byzantium.

Anya took a step forward then back again. A floorboard was creaking beneath her feet. She knelt down and pulled the rug back. One of the dark oak boards had been neatly sawn in two. Squeezing her fingers into the gap, she prized it up. Her breath caught in her throat. The hidden compartment was lined with ancient, fraying linen. It was packed with keepsakes; locks of hair, shiny pebbles, portraits on small wooden plaques, another doll. And there at the bottom, was the ruby ring. She held it out to Silvanus.

'This belonged to Tristan. He wore it around his neck.'

Silvanus took it from her, his face betraying his anguish.

'Yes, I remember. It was his father's ring.'

'I'm so sorry -' Anya began, but Silvanus waved her words away, the muscles of his jaw clenched tight.

To give him a moment to compose himself, she began to slowly empty the compartment. She unfastened a small linen bag and peered inside. Laburnum seeds. She unstopped a vial and sniffed cautiously. The unmistakeable bitter tang of belladonna.

She turned to face Silvanus again and took a deep breath, gathering her courage. 'These are laburnum seeds. They're poisonous when crushed into food. And this is belladonna.

It's equally poisonous when dropped into drinking cups. I couldn't understand what ailed your father, but it makes sense now. Mairi insists of taking Etar his midday meal - they've been slowly poisoning him, day by day.'

Silvanus looked as if his legs were about to give way beneath him, his face ghostly white.

'Why would Lucan want to poison his own flesh and blood?' he asked incredulously.

'They visited a wise woman,' Anya replied. 'She told them their son will be king. And it seems they believe her. So, Etar must die. And so must you, Silvanus.'

Silvanus ran a hand through his hair. 'But why did they kill Tristan?'

Anya shook her head. 'I don't know.'

Silvanus's breathing was fast and shallow, and Anya wondered if he was sinking into shock.

'You should go to them,' she said quietly. 'You need to hear it from their own lips.'

'Yes,' he said vaguely, looking blankly about the chamber, then more firmly, 'Yes.'

At the door of the council chamber, Anya put her hand lightly on his arm.

'You should talk to Mairi first – without Lucan.'

Silvanus raised an eyebrow. 'Why?'

'Because she will do anything to protect her unborn child, even betray her own husband.'

Mairi had been crying. Her eyes were red rimmed and her face was very pale, but she held her head high as the guard led her into the great hall.

'It's the middle of the night! Why are you doing this? And why is *she* here?' She pointed defiantly at Anya.

'Sit down, Mairi,' Silvanus said coolly.

Mairi sat.

Silvanus looked long and hard at her, his expression impenetrable. 'Why was Tristan's ring hidden in your bedchamber?' he asked at last.

'I have no idea what you're talking about,' Mairi replied sharply.

Silvanus slowly unfurled the fingers of his right hand. Tristan's ring lay in his palm.

She eyed it scornfully. '*You* put it in our room, to incriminate us. You've always hated Lucan, you've always been jealous of him. Etar never loved *your* mother, but he adored Branwen, and you just couldn't bear it, could you?'

Silvanus exhaled loudly. 'Tell me, why did Lucan throw Tristan off the cliffs?'

'You're talking nonsense. The Saxon witch has made you moon mad.'

Anya pushed the vial of belladonna and the linen bag of laburnum seeds down the table towards Mairi.

'These are poisons. Why were they hidden in your bedchamber?'

'I've never seen them before in my life.'

'Mairi, look at me!' Silvanus said harshly. 'You and Lucan have committed murder – infanticide to be precise. And you have committed treason by attempting to poison your king. You will be tried and when you are found guilty, you will be put to death in a manner of your high king's choosing. Do you understand?'

Mairi's eyes darted from Silvanus to Anya then back again. Tears were welling in her eyes.

'Etar adores me. I am carrying his first grandchild. He trusts me. He will not see me harmed.'

Silvanus's expression darkened. 'Yes, my father trusted you and you repaid him with treachery. How could you sit at his bedside every day and watch him take your poison? Do you have no heart, no pity?'

'You're mistaken,' Mairi stammered. 'You're both mistaken. Etar loves me. He won't forgive you for this.'

Anya and Silvanus's eyes met. He was suffering; she could see the torment in his eyes. She nodded, hoping to offer some silent, heartfelt encouragement.

Silvanus's fist came down on the table with such force that Mairi jumped violently.

'I don't think you're listening to me, Mairi. Etar will choose the manner of your death – it is the way it has always been. He prefers the punishment to fit the crime, so he will either throw you off the cliffs or he will poison you.'

Tears began to fall from Mairi's eyes, her courage visibly crumbling.

Silvanus let his words sink in for a moment. 'Even if Etar shows mercy and spares your life, you will be exiled, without husband or kin. Winter is coming. You and your unborn babe will starve to death in a hedgerow. Is that what you truly want for your son?'

Mairi put her head in her hands and began to sob.

'But if you tell me the truth, I swear you and your child will be spared,' Silvanus added.

Mairi looked up at him. There was a glimmer of hope in her tear-filled eyes. 'You swear?'

'I swear on my father's life.'

The irony appeared to be lost on Mairi. 'The wise woman told us our child would be king,' she began falteringly. 'It was Lucan's idea to poison Etar, not mine.'

But you were the one who dropped the belladonna into his

blackcurrant juice, day after day,' Anya thought angrily.

'And you planned to poison me too.' Silvanus sounded strangely calm, but Anya could see barely contained anguish and fury in his eyes.

'It was Lucan's idea, not mine,' Mairi repeated faintly.

'So why did Lucan murder Tristan?' Silvanus asked.

'The boy overheard us talking about Etar. We were in the wine cellars.' Mairi's voice was shaking now. 'We thought we were alone, but the boy was down there, looking for his stupid puppy. I begged Lucan not to do it, but he said the boy had heard too much. So he told the boy he would help him find his dog. He took him to the cliffs…'

Tears were running unchecked down Mairi's cheeks as she went on. 'I felt Adain's grief, truly I did. But what's the life of one kitchen boy compared to the life of a future king? I can feel my son growing inside me. I love him so much, even though I've never seen his face, never held him in my arms. Everything I do, I do for him. He's so strong, sometimes I feel as if I no longer exist, as if I am nothing. I swear to you, I did it for my son. I had no choice.'

Anya felt a wave of revulsion wash over her. She leant forward and forced herself to look into Mairi's eyes.

'You didn't visit your parents, did you? You went to Aquae Sulis and you met with Vortigern.'

Mairi was silent.

'If you don't tell us the truth,' Silvanus warned, 'our deal is off and you and your son will die.'

A sob escaped Mairi's throat. Her hands fluttered to her belly and settled there protectively.

'Lucan asked Vortigern for an alliance,' she began, her voice little more than a whisper. 'He wanted his army. In exchange for half the wealth of Dumnonia Lucan wanted

Vortigern to march on Tintagel, kill Etar and put him on the throne.'

Anya's heart was thudding violently against her ribs. 'But the poison was killing Etar, and it would have killed Silvanus too. I don't understand why Lucan felt he needed Vortigern's help.'

'I didn't either,' Mairi said miserably. 'I told Lucan he was mad. I told him Vortigern would make him a puppet king at best. At worst, he would kill us all. But he didn't listen to me.'

The muscle was flickering in Silvanus's jaw again. His voice was ominously quiet. 'And what was Vortigern's response to Lucan's proposition?'

'He laughed in Lucan's face. He said he didn't make alliances with turncoats. And then he spoke of a Saxon girl called Anya with red hair and green eyes.' Mairi focussed her gaze on Anya and her voice grew louder, more confident. 'He said he would never stop searching for you. Well, thanks to Lucan and me, he's found you. And tomorrow you're going back to him, to share his bed and bear his children, for the rest of your pitiful life. So there'll be no more talk of Epona coming from the sea.' Mairi's voice was loaded with spite. 'And there'll be no happy ending for you two either.'

Her venom seemed to curdle the air. Silvanus stared grimly at her for a long time. Finally, he stood up and nodded to the guard.

'Take Lucan's wife back to her chamber. And keep her under guard.'

'No!' Mairi pleaded desperately, her eyes darting from Silvanus to Anya and back again. 'I'm not to blame. You have to believe me. Lucan doesn't love me, he isn't kind.' She looked beseechingly at Anya and lowered her voice. 'He's brutish in the marriage bed. He hurts me, even now, when I am carrying his child.' The guard took Mairi by the arm but she fought against him, twisting in his arms. 'You have to believe me! None of this is my fault…'

Silvanus and Anya stood side by side as Mairi was manhandled from the great hall.

'Do you believe her?' Silvanus asked at last. 'Do you believe this was all my brother's doing?'

'No, I don't,' Anya replied honestly. 'She was willing to poison both you and your father for the sake of her unborn child. I finally understand why she hated me so much. She was terrified you and I would marry and have children, and push her own precious son further from the throne.'

'She never once asked what was going to happen to Lucan. I think she truly hated him,' Silvanus said softly.

'What *is* going to happen to your brother?'

'There will be a trial. And then my father must decide what is to be done. I fear he will not have the strength to bear it.' Silvanus shook his head. 'Enough! I will think no more of it tonight.' Without warning, he took her face in his hands and looked searchingly into her eyes 'This is your last night here. You have no idea how much I want to take you to my bed and make love to you. But I can't because you belong to Vortigern. And it makes me feel so angry and so helpless I can scarcely breathe.'

Tears welled in Anya's eyes. Silvanus was a good man, an honourable man. She loved him so much and she yearned to lie in his arms tonight. But throwing caution to the wind would break the terms of Hengist's already fragile treaty. How could she risk Horsa's life for one night of selfish pleasure?

She stared into his eyes, drowning in the sight of him.

One kiss. Where was the harm in that?

'You have never kissed me,' she whispered.

'Until now,' Silvanus said softly, pulling her closer.

'Until now,' she agreed.

Anya wrapped her arms about him. His lips felt soft and warm and utterly intoxicating. The great hall faded away until there was only Silvanus and the heady, exhilarating scent and feel and taste of him. His kiss lasted a very long time and when they finally drew apart, Anya was breathless and light headed.

'I *will* come back to you,' she said softly, 'because I can't bear to think we will never do that again.'

Silvanus laughed out loud, but there were tears in his eyes as he began to kiss her all over again.

Jago came for her at dawn. A surge of bitterly cold air rushed inside the small watchtower room and she shivered violently. After their embrace in the great hall, Silvanus had escorted her back to her chamber and left her there, alone. Her entire body ached for him, and she had not slept. Now, her eyes were red rimmed and sore and her body weary with exhaustion. She climbed down the spiral stairs in numb silence, trailing her fingers against the cold stone; her last, lingering contact with the stronghold of Etar, high king of Dumnonia. Rufus was waiting for them at the gates.

'Where is Silvanus?' he asked.

'He and Lucan rode south an hour ago,' Jago lied brightly. 'An unexpected problem at one of our mines. They send their apologies, and wish you a safe journey.'

Taliesin stepped forward and gestured to the chest Rufus's men were loading into the covered wagon. 'I have a gift for you, Anya. It contains all the essential herbs. It will tide you over until you can create your own garden.'

'Thank you, Taliesin.'

'Thank *you*.' Taliesin's voice was choked with emotion and he cleared his throat. 'I want you to have this.' He thrust a musty scroll into her hands.

'What is it?' Anya asked curiously.

'A map of Britannia. So you may find your way back to us, one day.'

Anya was about to thank him again, but he shook his head.

'You must also take these.' He drew a handful of coins from his cloak pocket and carefully placed them in her palm. 'They are solid gold, Anya. Truly precious.'

'No, Taliesin. I cannot!'

'I want you to have them,' the old man said firmly.

'Thank you.' She placed both the coins and the map into the wax-lined pocket inside her cloak then she wrapped her arms around the old priest and held him close. A sob constricted her throat.

'I don't want to leave you. How will you cope on your own?'

'The house of healing is quiet today. The fevers have broken. The worst has passed,' Taliesin assured her.

Anya wiped away a tear. 'I will miss you so much.'

'I will miss you too, child.'

'Look after Silvanus,' she whispered in his ear. 'He will need you more than ever, now that Lucan...' Her voice trailed away.

'Of course,' he replied under his breath. 'You *will* come back to us, Anya. Have faith.'

Reluctantly, Anya released the old priest and mounted up, grasping the reins with unsteady hands.

'May the gods keep you safe,' Taliesin called as Rufus, Anya and their guards made their way slowly down the track beneath the banner of the black boar.

Anya turned in her saddle and looked back at the imposing fortress. She did not believe Silvanus had ridden south; she sensed he was close by and it was a comforting thought. She remembered Epona's Circle, how the life blood of Dumnonia had pulsed through the stones, and she remembered the people of Dumnonia, who had showered her with gifts despite having so little to give. This land and its people were pure and untainted. She would go to Vortigern in the fervent hope that they would remain so.

Silvanus watched Anya and Rufus from the top of the tower, until they were no more than specks on the horizon. In the turning of a season, his priorities had shifted irrevocably. Anya was the focus of his life now, as fixed and as fundamental as the altar at the centre of a circle of stones.

'What have I done, Evric?' he asked plaintively.

'Your duty,' Evric replied grimly.

'Vortigern will forget his debt,' Silvanus said. 'And then he will turn his gaze towards us. I have a warband of fifty warriors, no more. Yes, I can defeat the Irish raiders, but Vortigern's massed cavalry? Impossible.'

'Then we will create our own army.'

'From fishermen and farmers?' Silvanus asked angrily.

'Any man can be taught to hurl a spear, or wield a sword. It just takes time.'

'Then let us pray to the gods that we have time,' Silvanus replied.

THIRTY EIGHT

Rufus and Anya travelled on the old Roman road that ran north-east, from Isca in Dumnonia as far as Lindum in Parisi territory. Rufus said very little but she often caught him staring intently at her, as if he wanted to say a great deal. They spent the first night in an old *mansio* hostelry. It had once been a staging post, offering food and warm baths to travellers. It was now home to several families, refugees from the countryside, who had refortified its walls and surrounded it with a deep ditch. They would not take Rufus's old, debased Roman coins, for they rightly feared the silver content was minimal, but they accepted a small bag of fine silver tableware, hacked into small pieces, as payment for the night.

Rufus demanded a hot bath, but they looked at him as if he was mad. After several minutes of awkward silence, he removed a folded linen cloth from his cloak, swept the crumbs from the table, wiped the chair seat and sat down with a pained look on his face. During their meal of bean stew and stale bread, Anya asked him about her brothers again.

'As I've told you, they're alive. For some inexplicable reason, Vortigern continues to believe that if he pays them enough they will remain faithful to him - despite the fact it is the banner of the white wolf that flies over the fort of Andereida. If I had my way, I'd execute Hengist and his entire warband for treason.'

Anya put down her spoon, her appetite gone.

The roof leaked and the wind howled, and Anya lay awake for a long time that night. She wondered if Etar would find it in his heart to sentence his own son to death. But if he chose clemency, what would become of Lucan and Mairi? Surely Etar couldn't risk allowing them to go into exile?

She yearned for Silvanus. She felt adrift without him, as empty as a fallow field. Was this to be her fate - an exile, forever searching for a hearth and home? When sleep found her at last, her dreams turned to blood. It stained the high mountains and it surged down her throat, but it ran harmlessly off the sword and the polished steel blazed like a fire beacon on a dark night.

The next morning the weather worsened. Winter had come to Britannia, bringing with it strong winds and heavy rain. The Roman road had not been repaired for many years. Successive winters had washed away much of its metalled surface and the wagon and horses struggled through quagmires of deep mud.

They passed many deserted villas and villages cowering behind shallow ditches. Anya wondered if the people of Britannia were afraid not only of Irish and Saxon warbands but also of Vortigern and the terrible retribution he meted out to those who dared oppose him.

They crossed the river Avon at dusk on the third day. To the east, the river curled around in a great three quarter circle and in that protective cradle, stood the Roman city of Aquae Sulis. The old cemeteries stretched out on either side of the road, the grand mausoleums and the smaller tombs crowding together in the growing darkness. Anya listened to the groaning thud as the heavy gates of the city closed behind them and felt suddenly trapped, like a bird in a cage. Even in the growing darkness, the long, straight streets of Aquae Sulis were crowded with refugees, just as Calleva's had been.

'We have half the surrounding countryside in Aquae Sulis,' Rufus said grimly. 'They feel safer behind our walls.'

Feral dogs roamed in packs. Beggars raised thin arms beseechingly to Anya as she rode by. She reined in and opened her saddle bag for her few remaining bread cakes. Her heart twisted as she watched gaunt women hurriedly tearing the cakes into equal portions for their children, but taking none for themselves.

'You are wasting your time,' Rufus sniffed. 'It's but a drop in the ocean.'

They rode on through the crowded streets. A group of soldiers hurried past, shouting to one another, their shields jostling against her horse. Gradually the rowdy voices of the soldiers faded and the streets grew quieter. Up ahead, loomed the vast forum; it was silent and deserted.

'We are here, at last.' Rufus offered her his hand, but Anya ignored it and dismounted.

She gripped the saddle momentarily, dizzy with exhaustion then followed Rufus up the marble steps to the basilica. He opened the bronze doors and Anya looked about her in awestruck amazement. The nave of the basilica hall towered more than seventy feet high. Slender Corinthian columns soared towards brightly coloured frescoes around the upper reaches of the walls and marble statues watched them silently from dark recesses. Torches along the walls sent long shadows sliding across the gleaming marble floor. Their footsteps echoed as Rufus hurried her towards the doorway at the far end of the hall.

In contrast, the council chamber was stiflingly hot, a suffocating mix of burning wood and stale air. A fire was burning in the centre of the mosaic floor and Anya's eyes narrowed against the stinging haze of smoke. Vortigern was standing beside the fire, his hands outstretched to the flames.

Anya's throat dried with fear. She had made an oath in Calleva that she would never marry this man and yet fate had brought her full circle. She could not believe this was what the goddess wanted of her. She *would* not believe it.

Rufus walked towards Vortigern.

'The battle is won, Lord?' he asked.

'It was never in doubt. The Coritani mustered a rabble of farmers brandishing pitch forks. Pascent is dead – Ronan killed him, but his son fled the battlefield, so I've no doubt he will give us trouble in years to come. What is the purpose of sons if not to avenge their fathers?' Vortigern broke off abruptly. He had noticed Anya. He hurried towards her, looking her up and down appraisingly, like a farmer might examine a heifer at market.

'Did they harm you? Are you untouched?'

Anya hesitated. Perhaps if she told him she was no longer a virgin, he might choose to cast her aside. Could a simple lie put an end to this marriage? And yet, she knew enough of Vortigern to realise he was unpredictable and quickly provoked to anger. He might easily choose to believe it was Silvanus, not the Irish, who had dishonoured his betrothed.

'I am a virgin,' she replied honestly.

'Yes, I believe you are. I know when someone is lying to me.'

His calloused fingers grazed against her lips and she

recoiled from his touch. From the corner of her eye she saw Rufus's expression falter. He looked deeply uncomfortable, as if he had eaten something that did not agree with him.

'I think Anya is tired and would like to rest,' Rufus said loudly.

'I'm not interested in what you think, Rufus. You're good for nothing but taxing my people until they bleed. You told me Pascent's daughter was fair, but she was as ugly as a mongrel bitch. You tricked me into that betrothal. Good men died as a result, and their deaths are on your head.'

Vortigern turned back to Anya. 'Did you know my cowardly little scribe hid in the undergrowth whilst my men died around him, and whilst you were carried off by the Irish?'

From the corner of her eye, Anya watched strong emotions race across Rufus's face: resentment, anger, hatred. He fixed his gaze on the middle distance but a muscle twitched in his tightly clenched jaw.

'I was unarmed, Lord,' he said, his voice strained.

'You are a coward, Rufus. A worthless coward.'

The atmosphere in the smoky chamber curdled.

'This marriage is a mistake,' Anya said hurriedly. 'We will not bring each other happiness.'

Vortigern leant closer. 'I *will* marry you because I want you in my bed. In fact, I've waited far too long already. The ceremony will take place tomorrow.'

Anya felt as if the air had been knocked from her lungs. She stared, open mouthed at Vortigern.

'Tomorrow? So soon?' she thought, horrified.

'You still intend to marry her?' Rufus erupted, like a statue come to life.

'Yes, I do. If I defile his sister and then cast her aside,

Hengist won't dither like the old king of the Coritani. I need his loyalty, not his wrath.'

Anya stared at Vortigern in astonishment. He was speaking about her kin as if she was invisible.

'Men of Germania are terrorising the south coast. Hengist's banner flies from the fort of Andereida. And yet you still believe he is loyal to you?' Rufus asked incredulously.

'Hengist has no power. He is merely a mercenary, and like all mercenaries, he is driven by his greed for wealth. And don't you dare question me, scribe! Your last foray into politics led my people to war.'

'You raped Pascent's daughter,' Rufus muttered under his breath.

'What did you say?' Vortigern asked sharply.

Rufus shook his head and turned away wordlessly.

'Wait!' Vortigern called after him.

Rufus turned back.

'You've seen Dumnonia for yourself, so tell me, is it as unprotected as Lucan would have us believe?'

'They have no army whatsoever. Save for some stakes at the bottom of a ditch, they are utterly defenceless,' Rufus said carelessly.

'Are they now…' Vortigern replied and a tremor of alarm raced across Anya's skin.

She realised Vortigern was staring at her again. She took a deep breath. 'We are not suited to one another. You should release me from this betrothal.'

'Your brother sealed the treaty. I own you, Anya.'

'In Saxony, a marriage contract can only be ratified if both marriage partners are in agreement. I am *not* in agreement.'

'I don't give a wolf's arse whether you're in agreement or not.'

Anya could feel her anger rising. 'I warn you – it would be unwise to cross me.'

'Are you threatening me?' Vortigern laughed.

He stepped closer still, and instinctively she held out her left hand like a barrier against him.

'What are you trying to do?' Vortigern was still laughing.

He grabbed her wrist hard, and she gasped with pain. Anger boiled in her veins, rippling to the surface of her skin; it felt burning hot, as if she were on fire. Vortigern flinched and a look of panic darted across his face.

'By Christ!' He took a sharp intake of breath, and abruptly released her wrist. Clasping his right hand with his left, he nursed it loosely against his chest.

'Lord? Are you unwell?' Rufus asked curiously.

Vortigern's dumbfounded expression hardened.

'I *will* marry you,' he said quietly, 'but if you ever hurt me again I will kill you more painfully than you could ever imagine.'

Anya forced herself to meet his eyes, but the council chamber was revolving dizzily and she felt painfully light headed. What had just happened? She had not intended to hurt Vortigern and yet he had recoiled from her as if she had struck him.

Vortigern nodded to a slave girl. 'Show my betrothed to her chambers.'

Anya took a series of deep breaths as she followed the girl across the vast mosaic floor. She held her head high, but her entire body was trembling with shock and disbelief.

The slave girl led Anya up a broad marble staircase and along a wide, echoing corridor. Anya's chamber was plainly furnished. A simple fresco ran around the walls at waist height, a thin band of intertwining geometric design. A narrow bed stood against one wall, a table and chair against the other. The table was empty save for three small lamps that gave off very little light, their wicks guttering in the pungent oil.

There was just one small window, its green glass cracked and its frame rotten. Anya lifted the rusting latch and a gust of cold air surged into the room. She looked down in amazement at the rain-swept forum, for she had never been so high above the ground. The flock of pigeons drinking from the puddles were as minute as bread crumbs. A wave of dizziness swept over her and she hurriedly closed the window again.

The slave girl was standing patiently in the doorway. 'Would you like me to help you with your belongings?' she asked cautiously.

'I have no belongings.'

The slave girl's eyes widened with surprise. 'Then may I fetch you some food?'

'No, thank you,' Anya replied. 'You may go.'

The slave girl bowed her head and closed the door behind her.

Anya sat down on the edge of the bed. When her father's soldiers had dragged her from the forest in Saxony, she had spent a long and lonely night waiting for dawn, waiting for death at the high priest's hands. Tonight, she was far away from Saxony and far away from Silvanus, waiting for another dawn to come. She did not expect the morning would bring death, but her marriage to Vortigern felt like a kind of execution none the less. It was an ending, rather than a beginning. A denial, rather than a promise. A denial of everything and everyone she had ever cared about.

Anya looked down at her mother's ring. Eown had been torn from her homeland, bought and sold like a beast. And yet the gods had taken pity on her, for she had ended her days a queen, a beloved wife of a high king. Anya twisted the copper band round her finger. Her mother had always appeared so serene and so content but had her heart secretly grieved for her homeland, for the ones she had left behind?

Anya stood up and walked to the door. She lifted the latch and two soldiers moved in unison, instantly blocking her way.

'Move aside,' she said firmly.

'We are here for your protection.'

'Protection from whom?'

'You are not to leave your chamber. If there is anything you require then it will be brought to you.'

'There is nothing I require.'

Anya slammed the door and sat down on the edge of the bed again.

Fear was beginning to creep through her veins. She was as trapped as a salmon in a net. If she refused to marry Vortigern, the terms of the treaty would be broken, and she had no doubt Hengist and Horsa would pay a heavy price for her cowardice.

She put her hand tentatively to her mouth, remembering how Vortigern's calloused fingers had grazed against her lips in the smoky council chamber. There had been such naked lust in his eyes. Vortigern was such a coarse man, in appearance, word and deed. She did not believe he would be gentle or loving in the marriage bed.

Silvanus, on the other hand, had a kind heart beneath all the brooding, bluster and complaint. She remembered that kiss; that intoxicating, heart stopping kiss. Silvanus made her feel safe and vividly alive and exquisitely happy, all at the same time. A tug of longing tightened deep inside her and she closed her eyes. Taliesin had assured her she would return to Dumnonia one day. She prayed he was right, for it was unbearable to think she would never see Silvanus again, never find comfort in his arms.

Anya leant back against the cold, hard wall and sought her goddess. She cleared her mind, losing herself in the silence. She saw the village of her mother's kin, the huddle of slate and stone and the bleating of sheep as dusk fell. The vision shifted violently, like the flames of a fire caught by a fierce wind:

The fire was hot. It caught the mouldy thatch of the round houses and its flames lit up the night sky. Silvanus was holding the sword aloft and the flames veered away from it, as if afraid of its ancient blade.

Anya opened her eyes abruptly and the vision faded. She stood up shakily and opened the window, taking a deep breath of the cold night air. The rain had ceased and the sky was full of stars. She fixed her gaze on Nerthus, the brightest star in the sky.

'Why am I here,' she whispered into the darkness. 'What do you want from me?'

THIRTY NINE

The slave girl returned at dawn. She was carrying a tray bearing a platter of bread and cheese, a cup of watered wine and an assortment of toiletries, including a highly polished silver mirror. A striking gown of madder-root-red silk was draped over the girl's right arm. Anya stepped into the gown without protest and then sat down at the table, scarcely aware of the tug of the hair brush, or the slave girl's gentle fingers as she skilfully wove strings of creamy pearls into her hair.

Her mind felt numb, as if Loki, the god of mischief, had crept inside her ear as she slept and stolen away her thoughts. She sat motionless, staring at her own blurred image in the mirror. Suddenly, she shivered. Her life had veered from the path she had always believed she would take, and now her future seemed as distorted as the face that stared sullenly back at her.

It had rained heavily again in the night, and as Anya rode out of the forum at Vortigern's side, a light drizzle still fell from a heavy, grey sky. The Christian church was a small, square structure built of stone, surrounded by a low, moss covered wall. Anya dismounted before the gateway and ran a hand over the bright green moss. It was soft and springy to the touch, a splash of colour in a grey world. In a city of cold, dead stone, it felt full of life beneath her finger tips, a vibrant and comforting presence. She turned to Vortigern.

'Tell them you have changed your mind.'

Vortigern laughed. 'I haven't changed my mind. Just the thought of you in my bed makes me hard.'

Anya's cheeks flushed with humiliation. 'I will marry you,' she said unsteadily, 'but I will never share your bed.'

Vortigern leant closer. 'Our marriage won't be sealed until I fuck you, so you *will* share my bed, whether you like it or not.'

His hand closed around her forearm and he pulled her inside the church. Anya stumbled over the worn stone threshold, her mind heavy with fear. The church was a plain building, unadorned by ornament or decoration. She had worshipped her goddess in the sacred grove, surrounded by the natural elements of earth, air, fire and water. But these Christians stood in ordered rows, surrounded by cold, hard, white-washed stone. What, for the love of the goddess, was she doing here?

She noticed a young man with such a strong resemblance to Vortigern that he could only be his son. Rufus had called Ronan a wastrel, but Anya sensed intelligence in his pale brown eyes. Like his father, he had the bearing of a warrior. His stance was sturdy, strong and vaguely menacing. But whereas Vortigern was rapidly turning to fat, his son's body was muscular and honed. Sensing Anya's gaze upon him, Ronan turned to face her appraisingly.

'Today, in the sight of God, you are here to witness the joining of this man and this woman.'

Anya tore her gaze from Vortigern's son and looked up at the bishop, resplendent in his ornate red and gold vestments, his arms stretched heavenwards in prayer. His bald head reminded her of a boiled egg, solitary wisps of grey hair rising from his pallid scalp like steam. As she watched, a bead of perspiration ran from his forehead and down the bridge of his nose. It lingered at the pointed tip until it fell to the black and white chequered floor tiles. Anya fixed her eyes upon the tiles and the bishop's words became a mindless blur.

'And do you, Anya, take Vortigern to be your lawful husband?'

The silence in the church was stifling, as if the entire congregation was holding its breath. The bishop's pallid face peered down at Anya, his eyes full of suspicion and mistrust. She continued to stare at the floor, unable to match his gaze. Vortigern's hand tightened its grip, crushing her cold fingers until she winced with pain. She thought of Dumnonia, the kingdom at the edge of the world. She had returned to Vortigern to keep Silvanus and his people safe.

'I do,' she breathed.

It was done. Numb with shock and disbelief, Anya did not move. The walls of the church were receding, racing away from her like a moon-crazed tide. A thousand images poured into the void, clamouring to be heard. So many unions blessed within these walls, so many births celebrated, so many deaths, so much joy and so much grief.

'Anya!' Vortigern's voice tore across her mind like a dagger. She tried to focus but the mists of vision were still swimming before her eyes. She was only vaguely aware of the brush of Vortigern's hand as the plain gold wedding band was slipped around her finger, only vaguely aware of pressure at the small of her back as he manhandled her away from the bishop. Faces floated before her and moved on.

As the doors of the church opened, she turned to look at Vortigern, struggling to comprehend the enormity of what had come to pass. How had her life sunk to this?

The wedding feast took place in the council chamber of the basilica. It was a hurried affair, with few guests other than Vortigern's warriors and his council. Nevertheless, Rufus had ordered slaves into the fields to gather winter foliage and the chamber was bedecked with holly and ivy, lit with the warm glow of a hundred oil lamps and embellished with the finest silverware.

Vortigern had not chosen to reward his tax collector for his thoughtfulness. Instead, Rufus had been placed at the far end of the table, where the poorest cuts of meat were served.

Anya sat beside her new husband, her mind darting alarmingly from numbness, to anger, to an overwhelming sense of grief. She neither ate nor drank nor spoke, but she sensed a great deal. There were strong undercurrents of tension and resentment in the air. She knew enough of politics to understand that her marriage had sealed a treaty that few thought was wise, binding Vortigern's great house to that of a motley band of Saxon mercenaries.

She glanced at her husband. His nose and cheeks were mottled with red veins, his eyes were rheumy, and his straggling beard was wet with ale. He had been eating and drinking all afternoon, but he had not spoken a single word to her since the marriage ceremony.

Rufus on the other hand, had been staring at her intently for some time. She was no longer so naïve not to realise when a man desired her, but she could see frustration as well as lust in Rufus's eyes. He reminded her of an over-filled cauldron suspended over a blazing fire. At any moment, his resentment might boil over in an uncontrollable outpouring of rage. She wondered why he continued to serve a man who treated him with such blatant contempt but in truth, she already knew the answer. Vortigern was the most powerful man in Britannia. He was feared and hated in equal measure and yet men were drawn to him like flies to a dung heap, eager for a share of his gold and glory.

Anya bowed her head, staring unseeingly at the untouched food on her plate. She felt breathless with fear, as if the serpent of Mitgard, Loki's foul offspring, had coiled itself tightly around her lungs.

Vortigern was exceedingly drunk now. He rounded on his son, not caring who heard him. 'You came late to my marriage ceremony. You have not attended a single council meeting this week. You were a disaster in Venta. I swear your mother was a whore, because you cannot be of my blood. I pray this Saxon girl gives me sons, for you'll not inherit an inch of my kingdom.'

Vortigern noticed Rufus eyeing him from the bottom of the table.

'And you look as if you've got a wasp up your arse,' he shouted. 'Something you wish to say, scribe?'

'No, Lord.' Rufus looked down at his plate.

Vortigern turned back to his son. Anya noticed Ronan had adopted a curiously blank expression, as if to shield himself from his father's harsh words. She wondered if Vortigern regularly meted out such public humiliation to his son.

'God's teeth! Listen to me, boy!' Vortigern slurred.

'No father, *you* listen to me,' Ronan replied quietly, so only those closest to him could hear. 'It was I who killed Pascent of the Coritani, on the field of battle, not three weeks since. And it was I who kept order in Venta. And one more thing - you are making a grave mistake.' Ronan leant closer to his father. 'You should be killing every Saxon in Britannia, not make alliances with them. They cannot be trusted.'

'How dare you question my decisions, you insolent puppy!'

But Ronan was paying no attention to his father's rebuke. Instead, he was staring at Anya, with cold, sly eyes.

The image was abrupt and vivid:

A small boy, cowering, whimpering, his hands raised defensively against Vortigern's vicious blows, the stick breaking the child's pale skin until his blood ran freely. But the boy's pain and hurt went much deeper than the visible wounds upon his flesh. The wounds were with him still, buried deep.

Anya put a hand to her head, forcing the vision away, and looked afresh at Vortigern's son. He had learnt to hide his scars well. His outward demeanour was one of brash arrogance; there were no outward signs of the vulnerability she had sensed. On the journey from Dumnonia, Rufus had told her how Ronan had chosen the terrible punishment of decimation for the townspeople of Venta in the kingdom of the Atrebates.

She wondered why he had acted so cruelly. What drove a man to such barbarism? Perhaps, as the only son of the most powerful warlord in Britannia, Ronan had believed he had no choice but to prove himself, not only to his father, but also to the rest of the world. She could never condone such a choice, but at that moment she pitied Ronan that he should have been born to such a father, and in such turbulent days as these.

'A toast to Vortigern and his new bride!' someone shouted.

Anya jolted back into the council chamber. The assembled guests stood up in a scraping of chairs and clinking of wine cups. 'To Vortigern and his new bride!' they cried.

Without warning, Vortigern hauled Anya to her feet. He swept an arm around her waist and kissed her full on the mouth, a slathering assault of warm spittle and stale ale. He released her to an enthusiastic round of applause from his warriors and pushed her unceremoniously back into her chair.

Anya wiped her mouth and clasped her trembling hands together in her lap. She had ridden away from Dumnonia, consoling herself with the thought that her marriage to Vortigern would keep Silvanus and his kingdom safe from harm. The idea had seemed so noble, so just, but the reality was much harder to bear. Soon, too soon, she would be expected to offer her body to her husband and to be an obedient wife.

Absently, her fingers reached for her dagger and then she remembered it was in her chamber. Vortigern had not deemed it to be a fitting bridal accessory. One half of her brain was urging her to pick up the knife Vortigern had used to skewer his beef and ram it through his heart. The other half was telling her to run, and keep running. She glanced towards the ornate brass doors and then back at Vortigern.

'My wife is ready for bed!' Vortigern announced, as if he had read her thoughts. The council chamber erupted in a cacophony of lewd cheers and chants.

Vortigern grasped her elbow discreetly but held her fast as he led her from the wedding feast. Away from the heat of the council chamber the air felt bitterly cold. Whistling drafts raced like furies down long, empty corridors and tugged at the flaming torches that lined the walls.

Vortigern's bedchamber was small in comparison to the rooms he chose to spend his days. There was little in the way of ornament. Skins covered the wooden floor boards. A fresco of a coursing scene ran along one wall; a pack of hounds was at full stretch, their tongues lolling, their muscles tense from the chase. Just ahead, a hare was running for its life, the fear clearly visible in its little black eyes. Further along the wall, the hounds had reached their prey and were ripping it limb from limb.

'By God, you look beautiful.' Vortigern's words were slurred, his eyes hooded and heavy. He moved towards her, and Anya instinctively stepped back a pace. Her heart was hammering with fear.

'Don't touch me,' she whispered.

'You're my wife. You belong to me now.'

'I belong to Nerthus, the earth goddess of Saxony.'

Vortigern snorted dismissively. He strolled to the table and poured himself a cup of wine.

'Please, I am a priestess. My body belongs to the goddess,' Anya stammered.

Vortigern downed the wine. 'She doesn't want your body as much as I do. There's no need to be afraid. You're my wife now and you'll want for nothing - fine gowns, jewels, perfume.'

'I don't want jewels or fine gowns. I am a priestess. I heal the sick and I care for the dying. I cannot be the wife you want, or need.'

Vortigern's eyes hardened. 'You are no longer a priestess. That life is over and you must accept it. Besides, I have excellent physicians. The Dobunni don't want to be healed by a pagan witch.'

'You think I'm a witch?' Anya asked, taken aback.

'No, of course not,' Vortigern said quickly. 'But my people are deeply superstitious. They are wary of heathen magic.'

'You would be surprised how many cling to the old religion,' Anya replied carefully.

Vortigern waved his right hand dismissively. 'Come and sit with me.'

Anya did not move. Vortigern shook his head in

amusement. He clasped her forearm and dragged her towards the bed.

'You must forget all this pagan nonsense, Anya. I warn you now - we burn witches. We burn them slowly, so they live long enough to watch their own flesh melt from their bones.'

Anya shuddered. Had she offended the goddess so terribly? Was this her punishment for speaking out in the sacred grove? Vortigern sat down on the edge of bed and pulled her down beside him. He put his hand on her knee but she pushed it away. She rose to her feet but Vortigern simply pulled her back down again.

'You have spirit, Anya. It was one of the first things I noticed about you.'

He was not looking at her face; his gaze was firmly fixed on the outline of her breasts, visible through the fine silk of her red gown. His hand began to slide up her thigh and Anya clamped her legs tightly together.

'Feisty to the end!' Vortigern laughed, his gaze still fixed upon her breasts.

A wave of panic washed over her. Vortigern was no longer in his youth, but he was still a strong, powerful man. Her dagger was still attached to her belt, back in her chamber. She had no way to stop this. Unless…

Vortigern had recoiled from her touch in the council chamber. Had she hurt him in some way? She wished she knew what had caused the fear in his eyes. She glanced despairingly over his shoulder. The far wall was in shadow but she could dimly see the outline of another doorway. Perhaps it was an adjoining door to another room? Perhaps it was unlocked?

Infinitely slowly, she began to part her knees. Vortigern's eyes registered both surprise and delight and he released his iron like grip on her thigh. She leapt to her feet, bouncing off the bed post in her haste to be away from him. She heard Vortigern roar a curse, heard his weighty footsteps thudding across the floor. The rug skidded across the polished floor boards as if she was skating on ice, and she almost lost her footing. She glanced over her shoulder. Vortigern was barely an arm's length away from her.

She lifted the heavy latch, wrenched the door open and ran into the next room. It was in darkness save for a faint glimmer of moonlight filtering through the green window glass. Anya did not wait for her eyes to adjust to the gloom. She ran headlong into the blackness and crashed blindly into the huge table that occupied the centre of the floor. She barely felt the pain, her eyes darting wildly as she searched for a way out of the room. There was another door to her right, and she guessed it lead back onto the corridor.

From the corner of her eye, she saw Vortigern lunge towards her. He was strong but she was faster. Ducking to her right, she launched herself away from the table. She raced towards the door, her heart thudding against her ribs. She was running so fast that she stumbled, her shoulder ramming hard against the door frame. She did not need to turn around to know that Vortigern was almost upon her. His heavy breathing sounded like an enraged bull in the semi darkness. Desperately, she reached out for the door latch. Vortigern's fist closed around a handful of her hair and her fingers froze in mid-air. He jerked her viciously backwards and she screamed, her body contorting as sharp pains tore across her scalp.

'By God, you are divine!' Vortigern laughed.

He wrenched her away from the door, rotating his closed fist like a weaver winding wool, until her hair was tightly entwined around his wrist. He dragged her to the long table and she felt its hard edge pressing against her thighs.

'I like this game,' Vortigern said, his breathing ragged. 'I like it very much.'

There was feverish anticipation in his eyes and Anya realised to her horror that her defiance was only inflaming his desire. But what choice did she have? She could not give herself willingly to this man.

'You are mine,' Vortigern whispered. 'All mine.'

Without warning, he released her hair and pushed her backwards onto the table. Her skull cracked against the solid oak and her head swam. Vortigern climbed onto the table. He knelt over her and began to untie the delicate laces of her gown. The fine silk fell open to her waist and she heard Vortigern's breath catch in his throat.

'My God, you were worth the wait,' he breathed. He bent down and clamped his mouth around her exposed nipple. His teeth sank into sensitive flesh and Anya let out a loud scream of pain. The door to the corridor burst open. A soldier stepped inside, his sword drawn, his eyes darting about the room. Vortigern looked up.

'Get out!' he roared.

The soldier retreated, a look of mortified bewilderment upon his face.

Tears were welling in Anya's eyes. She placed both hands on Vortigern's chest, holding him at bay. 'Have pity, I beg you. You know that I am a virgin. If it must be done, let it be on our marriage bed.'

Vortigern stared down at her thoughtfully. 'Yes,' he said at last. 'It should be so.'

Anya tried to sit up but Vortigern pushed her back down onto the table. Holding her fast, he suckled hard on the blood that was trickling from her bleeding nipple. A brief gasp of shock escaped from her throat.

Vortigern sat back and licked his lips. 'You have strong blood. You'll give me fine sons.'

Anya stared up at him, horror-struck. He smiled back at her, his eyes burning with triumph and she realised that he was revelling in her humiliation and taking pleasure in her pain.

'My beautiful, feisty wife!' Vortigern manhandled her down from the table. Overwhelmed by fear and revulsion, Anya's entire body was trembling as she tried to cover her breasts. She had won a temporary reprieve, but for how long? What should she do now? She had tried persuasion and she had tried to run, and both had failed.

She glanced hesitantly towards the window. She remembered how tiny the pigeons had appeared in the forum far below her. If she climbed onto the narrow window ledge and leapt into the blackness, she would be falling to her death. Was that what the goddess wanted?

Vortigern dragged her back into his bedchamber and left her standing barefoot upon the itchy rug. With trembling fingers, she tried to retie the laces of her gown but Vortigern shook his head.

'Don't hide your body from me. I am your husband now. Take your gown off. I want to see you.'

Anya did not move.

'Take it off.'

Anya retreated a pace. She was barely a yard away from the bedchamber door and she could not remember seeing Vortigern lock it. There would be a guard outside, but if she moved fast…

Vortigern pulled her away from the door. 'I will enjoy

teaching you obedience but in the meantime, I will undress you myself.'

Taking his dagger from his belt, he cut the remaining ties of her gown, one at a time. He tugged eagerly at the fine silk, but his clumsy fingers failed to lift the gown over her shoulders. Impatiently, he took his dagger again and slit the gown open as if he was gutting a deer. The blade narrowly missed her flesh, skimming between her breasts, across her belly, her naval, her thighs, her knees. The gown fell from her shoulders and floated to the floor.

A trickle of blood ran from her breast and dropped onto the fallen gown. Utterly mortified, Anya's hands moved to cover her naked body, but Vortigern slapped them away with the flat edge of his dagger.

'Let me look at you,' he breathed, his gaze wandering greedily over her body.

Anya stared fixedly at the patch of blood soaking into her discarded gown until it faded into a meaningless blur before her eyes. She felt completely exposed, as bloodied and raw as a skinned carcass. Perhaps she should have opened the window. Perhaps she should have jumped and felt the cold winter air washing over her naked flesh, cleansing her as she fell.

Suddenly, Vortigern pulled her towards him, put a hand behind her head and kissed her full on the mouth. His breath stank of ale and of the rotting meat trapped in the crevices between his teeth. It was not a gentle kiss. He bit her lips hungrily until Anya tasted the metallic tang of her own blood. Revulsion rose in her throat. Gripping his arms for support, she brought her knee sharply into his groin.

'You bitch!' Vortigern hissed.

His hands slipped from her body and he doubled up, his

face contorted with pain. Anya scrambled towards the door. She tried desperately to lift the latch but it held fast. She glanced over her shoulder. Vortigern was vertical again, storming towards her, his eyes full of fury. She wrenched at the latch again, but it did not move.

'Enough, Anya!'

Vortigern grabbed hold of her shoulder, dragging her backwards. She looked about wildly. There was an oil lamp, curiously fashioned to resemble a sandal clad foot, on the small table by the door. She twisted in his grasp, snatched the lamp and hurled it in his face. Hampered by his vice-like hold, her aim was poor and the lamp bounced harmlessly off his chest, splattering hot oil as it fell to the floor.

'No more games!' Vortigern spun her around to face him and swiped her cheek viciously with the back of his hand. She tried to wrench herself from his arms, but he hit her again. This time, her knees buckled, and he caught her as she fell. He dragged her to the bed, and pushed her down onto the rugs. Anya's head was throbbing with waves of nausea. Vortigern heaved his huge frame onto the bed and rolled on top of her. His heavy weight was crushing the air from her lungs and she was struggling to breathe. She writhed beneath him, kicking and twisting.

'I told you, no more games. This is your last chance. Will you behave?'

Anya shook her head defiantly. 'I swore an oath to the goddess. I belong to her, and her alone.'

'As you wish.' His words sounded final, resigned.

Anya stopped struggling, filled with a sudden sense of foreboding. Vortigern heaved himself upright again, unfastened his ornate belt buckle and pulled his belt from his waist. She wondered if he meant to beat her. His face was a mask of studied concentration, as if he had moved beyond lust and desire to another, much darker place.

She began to struggle again and he struck her hard across the cheek. The pain in her head pulsed violently. She tried to focus, but her vision swam and the bedchamber revolved sickeningly. Vortigern wrenched her left arm above her head, fastened one end of the belt around her wrist and the other to the bed post. Panic stricken, Anya tried to sit up, her fingers fumbling ineffectually at the knotted leather. From the corner of her eye she saw Vortigern grab another belt from the table beside the bed. With her one remaining free hand, she reached desperately for his face, her fingers clawing at his eyes.

'Lay still!'

Vortigern brought the belt down hard. Anya moved fast to protect her face and the belt buckle tore a deep gash in her forearm. Ignoring her scream of pain, Vortigern quickly tied her free wrist to the opposite bed post. Anya wrenched desperately at her bonds but they held fast. Fear and shame engulfed her. Fear that she was destined to live out her days with such a cruel and brutish man, and shame that she had not found a way to stop the terrible indignity of this wedding night.

'I warn you, the goddess will curse you for this,' she screamed.

'I don't believe in the curses of your pagan gods.'

Quite suddenly, Anya froze, as the vision ripped viciously through her tormented brain:

The battle was over; the field was strewn with the dead and the dying. Vortigern's bloodied and cleaved body lay in the moonlight, un-mourned and without honour, mere carrion for the crows.

'Anya? Look at me!'

Her gaze slowly focussed upon his face.

'What's wrong with you, damn you?' he snarled.

'I saw your death day,' she whispered truthfully.

Vortigern was silent for a moment. 'You're lying.'

'You know that I am not.'

Fear flickered behind Vortigern's eyes and without warning his right hand shot to her neck.

'You. Are. A. Barbarian. Heathen. Witch.' With each word, his fingers increased their grip around her throat.

Anya tried and failed to take a breath. Her body began to heave violently, her lungs burning for air. A part of her brain was overwhelmed with panic and terror, but another part was strangely, serenely calm. She would die as Emma had died. It seemed fate had come full circle; two sisters, meeting their gods, as one.

She stopped struggling. There was some comfort in the knowledge that she would not have to endure marriage to a man she despised. Very soon, she would see her sister and her mother again.

Vortigern released his grip on her throat.

'Breathe, damn you!' He began to shake her roughly by the shoulders.

Anya took a deep, rasping breath and air surged into her aching lungs. She began to cough and splutter, her eyes full of confusion. She was still alive. She looked about, bewildered. She was still held fast upon Vortigern's bed.

'You can't die yet. Not until I have had my fill of you.' Vortigern was straddling her now, crushing her into the bed rugs as he pulled off his tunic. She closed her eyes, and turned her head away from his stale breath. She felt him struggling to remove his breeches, felt his knees force her legs apart.

'*You will not have me*,' she thought.

She focussed her mind on those five simple words. They span around and around inside her head, faster and faster, until she could barely feel Vortigern's weight pressing the air from her lungs, nor the itchy rugs beneath her naked skin. The bed chamber was receding, fading as if twilight had fallen. She was far, far away, where he could not reach her.

Grunting like a beast, Vortigern rammed his heavy frame against her, again and again and again, until his heart pounded, his cheeks turned scarlet and beads of sweat formed on his deeply lined forehead. And yet no matter how brutally he thrust against her, his body would not respond to his aching lust. Finally, when his body was slick with glistening sweat, he rolled off her, looking down at her with a mixture of suspicion, loathing and disgust.

'This has never happened before,' he hissed. 'Did you unman me, you witch?'

'No witchcraft,' she stammered. 'Most likely an excess of ale.'

Vortigern grunted an obscenity. 'If you speak of this to anyone, I will kill you. Do you understand?'

Anya nodded wordlessly.

Vortigern heaved himself off the bed.

'Untie me,' she pleaded, utterly mortified.

But he ignored her. He picked up his tunic and breeches from the floor, dressed quickly and stormed from the room without looking back.

Anya inched her way up the bed and used her teeth to untie first one wrist then, with trembling fingers, the other. The gash on her arm from Vortigern's belt buckle had stopped bleeding, but it still felt painfully raw. Shaking from head to toe, Anya tugged a blanket around her shoulders, pulled her knees to her chest and stared into the middle distance. Vortigern had not consummated the marriage. She remained a virgin, and yet she felt abused, bloodied and defiled.

A long time passed before she climbed off the bed. Stepping over the discarded red gown, she drew the blanket more tightly about herself like a shield and walked unsteadily to the door. She lifted the latch and the guard turned, instantly alert. Anya willed herself to sound more composed that she felt.

'I am going back to my own chamber.'

The soldier nodded curtly, following her down the corridor like an obedient hound. When they reached her chamber, he opened the door and she stepped inside. Anya heard the metallic, grating sound as the key turned in the lock behind her and then a deep silence descended.

She stood, utterly still, in the centre of the cold, dark room. She longed for a hot bath, steeped in the purifying balms of oak, burnet saxifrage and parsley root, but in truth, she doubted she would ever feel clean again. Tears welled and she wiped them away. Self-pity would not help her now. She had returned to Aquae Sulis and married Vortigern as Hengist had decreed and as Etar had commanded. She had kept Dumnonia safe. Her debt was paid. So, what should she do now?

She closed her eyes and let the silence envelop her. She felt it calm her tortured mind and soothe her bruised and bleeding body.

The answer darted out of the darkness. Anya took a sharp intake of breath and opened her eyes. Slowly, her hands balled into fists at her sides. If this truly was the will of the goddess, she had no choice but to see it done.

FORTY

Anya dressed slowly. She found comfort in the familiarity of her old, much worn, gown and the reassuring weight of her dagger at her belt again. Bruises were beginning to rise on her pale skin and she moved about the chamber slowly, as if in a trance. Her life in Saxony had not called for courage, merely obedience. When she had spoken out against Emma's sacrifice, it had not been a conscious act of bravery, but rather a desperate cry from the heart. So was she brave enough to do this? But the alternative – a life of abuse as Vortigern's wife – was far, far worse.

With trembling fingers, she took her dagger from her belt and stared at the blue veins that ran beneath the pale skin of her wrist. She knew from her lessons at the priests' school that they carried arterial blood and that if the wound was deep enough, no amount of balms or bandages could heal it.

She had always known her life might be short, over before it had truly begun. From the moment of her birth, the signs had been there for all to see. Eown had brought her into the world under a waning moon and the life line in the palm of her left hand petered out half way across her palm, like a path lost in a dense forest.

Anya knelt down on the bare floorboards. The dagger felt

heavy in her left hand, weighed down by her reluctance and her cowardice. A wave of self-pity washed over her, as bitter as juniper. One half of her brain was screaming: '*I don't want to die. I want to be with Silvanus.*' The other half was reasoned and reassuring: '*You have known Silvanus forever, through all the ages of men. Your paths have crossed a thousand times. One day, many centuries from now, perhaps they will cross again.*'

Her gaze focussed on her wrist.

'Now.

Do it now.'

Slowly, Anya rotated her wrist. Drawing back her sleeve, she noted dispassionately that her bare arms were tanned the colour of honey from the long summer in Dumnonia. Taking a deep breath, she drew the dagger's blade lightly along the gash Vortigern's belt had made on her forearm. The wound re-opened and the sharp pain that followed made her gasp. She quickly dropped the dagger, reached for the empty beaker on the supper tray and placed it on the floor beside her. Supporting her right hand firmly with her left, she watched her blood begin to drip steadily into the beaker.

Her mind drifted to Silvanus. She wanted to ride to Dumnonia. She wanted to fall into his arms and never leave him. She loved him, irrevocably and unconditionally and yet she could not go back to him. As long as she lived, she would do everything in her power to keep Dumnonia safe.

Wincing with pain, she used her forefinger and thumb to close the wound again and carefully pressed the jagged edges together. Tugging the linen cloth from the tray, she wrapped it tightly around her forearm, tied it off and then pulled down her sleeve to hide the make-shift bandage.

Anya looked fearfully at the closed door. But she had no choice. She had to do this. With the beaker in her hand, she turned towards the door and shouted at the top of her voice.

'Help! Help me!'

She heard the sound of the key beginning to turn in the lock. Tilting her head back, Anya tipped the blood into her mouth. It tasted thick and warm and metallic. Resisting a natural instinct to swallow, she held the blood in her mouth and pushed the beaker and the dagger out of sight beneath the bed. A heartbeat later, the door burst open. The soldier ran into the room and crouched at her side.

'What's wrong? Are you unwell?'

Anya turned slightly. She convulsed as if she was about to retch, and a spray of blood spurted from her mouth and splattered across the floorboards. The guard recoiled in shock.

'I need a physician,' she gasped.

The guard was already on his feet, backing away from her. She could see the fear in his eyes. Fear that this girl from a distant kingdom had unwittingly brought the plague to Aquae Sulis.

'I need a physician,' she repeated faintly, staring as if horror struck at her blood splattered hands.

'Yes, yes, right away.' The guard retreated, his footsteps pounding down the corridor and gradually fading to silence.

Anya retrieved her dagger from beneath the bed and leapt to her feet, dazed and bewildered. She knew from her work in the place of healing that even the smallest amount of spilled blood could look horrific, but she had not dared to believe her plan might work. She had not thought further than getting rid of the guard.

What was she supposed to do now?

Grabbing her cloak from behind the door, she flung it around her shoulders. She had to find a way out of the basilica before the guard returned. Pulling the hood of her cloak about her face, she hurried down the dark corridor. Taliesin's coins were jingling in her pocket and they sounded agonisingly loud in the silence. She reached inside her cloak, clamping her hand over them.

At the top of the sweeping staircase, she hesitated for a moment. The basilica hall was deserted. The double doors to the council chamber were slightly ajar and she could see firelight flickering within. Was Vortigern in the council chamber, drowning his humiliation in ale? She listened intently but she could hear no voices, only silence.

With her heart pounding against her ribs, she crept down the staircase. Keeping to the shadows, she walked on tip toe to the bronze doors that led out to the forum. The door handle was fashioned to resemble the snarling face of a monstrous beast, its features worn and smooth with age. Anya pulled hard, but the door did not open. Seized with panic, she tried the handle again, wrenching at it with all her strength. The door moved fractionally before it crashed back onto its hinges, reverberating like thunder around the hall. Anya willed her tired brain to think. There had to be another way out of the basilica.

Somewhere in the distance she heard the sounds of a door opening, rapid footfall and raised voices. Determination drove away her exhaustion and she ran back the way she had come. From the corner of her eye, she noticed a partially open door. She could vaguely remember seeing slaves coming and going through it, bearing platters of food. Anya slid to a halt and squeezed around the door.

The kitchen was deserted and in darkness, save for a shaft of moonlight from a high window. A long wooden table stood in the centre of the room, its ancient oak deeply scarred by centuries of use. The walls were lined with high shelves, stacked with utensils, storage jars, platters, and bowls. Above her head a brace of hares swung idly, caught in an icy draft. Anya glanced over her shoulder. The basilica hall was no longer in darkness. Torchlight illuminated its marble floor and voices echoed. She looked around the silent kitchen. There had to be another way out.

She took a step forward then stopped in her tracks. Someone was coming. Darting behind the door, she pressed her back against the wall. A heartbeat later, someone nudged the door open. It bounced gently off the tip of her boot and then came to rest, shielding her from sight. Anya closed her eyes in a silent prayer of thanks. A torch hissed and long shadows danced across the ceiling. The sound of heavy, deliberate footfall reverberated across the kitchen floor tiles.

A man's step.

A guard.

She heard a door open at the far end of the room. There was a rush of cold air, a brief silence and the door closed again. The footsteps were coming back. Without warning, a hand grabbed the edge of the door and Anya felt a rush of pure terror. The door began to swing away from the wall. Time seemed to slow, but her mind was racing. Her fingers tightened around the grip of the dagger. Could she kill this man? A man who had done her no harm?

Shouts rang out in the hall. She thought she heard Vortigern's name, but her heart was pounding too loudly in her ears to be certain. The hand let go of the door. She felt the heat of a flaming torch, heard boots scraping against the tiles, and then the guard was gone. Anya stared into the darkness, her mind engulfed by conflicting emotions: fear, relief, shock and elation.

Finally, a persistent voice began to nag inside her head. '*Keep moving. You have to keep moving.*'

There was a large basket on the kitchen table with three flat bread cakes in the bottom. They were no longer fresh, but she put them into the pocket of her cloak. In the far corner, obscured by shadows, she could just make out the outline of another door.

Tentatively, she lifted the latch and peered out. Dilapidated lean-to buildings clung to the towering walls of the basilica: stables, workshops, storerooms, a laundry. A grey dawn was beginning to creep across the city and the courtyard was coming to life. Stable boys, pale faced and yawning, trundled barrows of horse manure towards the kitchen garden; laundry girls, their hands chapped red raw, carried buckets of water from the well; a cook, knife in hand, was prizing open a barrel of salted eels.

Slaves were coming and going through an iron gate in the high wall that surrounded the forum. Anya's eyes widened. The gate led onto the street. Could she simply walk out of the basilica unnoticed? Perhaps the goddess was watching over her after all.

Anya glanced around the courtyard again. Two guards were approaching from the direction of the forum. They idled to a halt and slumped wearily against the stable wall. One blew on his hands and then yawned. The other took a long draft from a leather water bottle and closed his eyes. Anya shrank back into the shadows of the kitchen. She had come so close. What should she do now?

Should she try to brazen it out, walk straight past the guards and out into the street? Admittedly, they looked half-asleep after a long, cold night watch, but it was more than twenty yards to the gate. Since arriving in Aquae Sulis, she had been a virtual prisoner in her room. Everyone knew Vortigern had taken a Saxon bride, but very few had seen her face. And yet, there was always a chance one of them might recognise her.

She bit her lip, torn with indecision. She knew it was only a matter of moments before someone told the guards she had disappeared. Every moment she hesitated was reducing her chances of escape. She glanced anxiously around the courtyard again and her gaze fell on the slave girls. Could she pass as one of them?

They all looked painfully thin and shivering with cold, thin gowns and meagre shawls their only protection against the elements. Anya looked down at her own thick, woollen cloak. Made in Dumnonia, its fine weave and detailed stitching marked her apart from the scantily dressed slaves. She had no choice but to remove it.

Anya hurried to the table and grabbed the empty bread basket. Unfastening her cartwheel brooch, she neatly folded her cloak, put it in the bottom of the basket and placed the bread cakes on top. Next, she needed a shawl. Someone had hung a row of kitchen cloths to dry on the iron spit over the hearth. She took the largest cloth and flung it around her shoulders. Then she put the basket over her arm and walked back to the door again. The guards were still slumped against the wall.

Gathering every ounce of her courage, Anya stepped out onto the cobbles. Without her cloak, the air felt cold and she had to grit her teeth to stop them from chattering. The gate suddenly seemed very far away. She desperately wanted to break into a run, but a voice inside her head was urging her to walk slowly, urging her not to draw attention to herself.

Each step felt like an eternity. She had never felt more

conspicuous, as if a bright light from the heavens was focussed on her alone and she fought an almost overwhelming urge to throw a quick glance over her shoulder at the guards. She felt certain they must be watching her, for the back of her neck was tingling, every nerve gratingly raw. Light headed now, she realised she had forgotten to breathe. The gate was very close, just a few more steps. Panic and reason were fighting a vicious tug of war inside her head:

'There's no time. Run!'

'No, walk! One more step and you'll be at the gate.'

Taking a deep, ragged breath, Anya stepped through the gate and out into a muddy street lined with small shops. Even at this early hour, the street was crowded with families, slaves, merchants, water carriers, mule wagons, mangy dogs and scratching chickens.

Anya felt as if her legs had turned to marrow jelly and her entire body was trembling. Without warning, her head filled with images of her brutal wedding night, a tidal wave of pain she had no strength to hold back. Tears welled in her eyes and it took all of her will-power not to sink into the mud, curl into a ball and weep.

Suddenly, three piercing blasts from an ancient Roman trumpet rang out from the direction of the forum, quickly followed by three more. Vortigern was sounding the alarm. Anya stumbled on, keeping her head down, avoiding eye contact with passers-by. The drizzle turned to rain and the temperature plummeted.

She shivered violently, struggling to control a mounting sense of panic. She was still barely a stone's throw away from the basilica and now every guard in the city was looking for her. How, for the love of the goddess, was she supposed to leave the city undetected? Aquae Sulis was ringed by high stone walls. She had entered the city by the south gate, but she doubted she could remember the way back to it. She looked up at the heavy, grey sky. It was almost impossible to find her bearings without the sun for guidance. And it was hard to think straight when her fingers and toes were numb with cold.

There was nothing for it. Unless she wanted to freeze to death, she needed her cloak. Turning into a side alley, she swung it around her shoulders again, revelling in its comforting, luxurious warmth. Tugging her hood tightly about her face, she turned and walked back to the main street. The street was awash with filthy puddles and the hem of her cloak was soon caked in mud. A stray strand of her hair escaped from the hood of her cloak and she pushed it hurriedly behind her ear. It was far too distinctive, a flash of fire against the grey of Aquae Sulis.

To her left, above the rooftops of the city, she could see the domes and soaring pediments of the great temple and baths complex. The baths of Aquae Sulis were famous throughout Germania. Many a merchant had earned a night at her father's fireside with stories of their wealth and treasures. Three nights since, she and Rufus had ridden past their imposing entrance. If she could retrace her steps from there, perhaps she could find her way to the south gate.

Anya looked up. She could sense fear in the air. Something was wrong. A heartbeat later, the crowds up ahead began to part. A merchant hurriedly manoeuvred his hard-cart to the side of the street. A woman shouted to her children, rounding them up and snatching their hands. Anya frowned. A man's voice was barking orders. At that moment, a group of at least twenty soldiers rounded the corner and immediately split up.

Half turned towards the baths, but the remaining soldiers

began to walk towards Anya. She slowed her pace, looking about frantically. There were no side alleys to hide in, just a seemingly endless row of shops. If she turned back the way she had come, she would only draw attention to herself. She had no choice but to continue to walk into the guards' path. Tugging her hood more tightly about her face, she continued to wade slowly through the filthy puddles.

The soldiers spread out across the street, shoulder to shoulder, moving inexorably forward. Their eyes were roving back and forth, systematically scanning the crowd. Anya had no doubt they were looking for Vortigern's Saxon bride, a woman with hair the colour of fire, a woman travelling alone.

They were only yards away from her now. Anya glanced about desperately. The mouth-watering aroma of freshly baked bread was drifting from a nearby shop. The window board was laden with loaves of all shapes and sizes, and two men were struggling to erect a leather canopy to protect it from the rain. A wooden pole slipped from one of the men's grasp and tore a gaping hole in the hide. An accumulation of rain water cascaded through. Drenched, and cursing loudly, both men retreated into the shop.

Anya had no time to think. Stepping in front of the baker's shop, she took a bread cake from her basket and held it out beseechingly to the soldiers. She opened her mouth to speak, but then thought better of it. Her Saxony accent would only draw attention.

The soldiers did not slacken their pace as they marched by, splashing through the puddles, an impermeable wall of muscle and brawn. One gave her a cursory, dismissive glance. The rest simply ignored her. Anya stared at their retreating backs in astonishment. In Saxony, she had never noticed the slaves who pulled water from the well or baked bread by moonlight so Athelwald's kin could eat fresh, warm loaves at dawn. Slaves had been invisible in Saxony. And it seemed they were invisible in Britannia too.

The rain turned to snow and a flake landed on her nose. There were voices inside the shop. The bakers were coming back. She returned the bread-cake to her basket and quickly walked away. She needed a quieter, less conspicuous route to the baths. At the crossroads she turned right, then immediately left into a parallel street. To her right, a row of abandoned shops, their ancient wooden shutters closed, stared blindly onto the street. To her left, fine town houses were slowly falling into ruin.

The snow was falling more heavily now, beginning to settle on the rooftops. Directly ahead, another trumpet blared. It sounded very close and Anya came to an abrupt halt. She turned around tentatively. There were men's voices, loud and urgent, not far behind. Her heart began to pound with fear. She could not go forward, and she could not go back. She had no choice but to try and hide.

The door of the house to her right was ajar. Anya ran up the worn marble steps and into the dilapidated house. The roof of the atrium had collapsed and rainwater was bleaching the frescoes from the walls. The place reeked of damp and mould, its marble floor awash with mud and windblown leaves. She shivered. Britannia had never seemed more forsaken, a land of fallen towers, shedding their red tiles like leaves in autumn.

She looked over her shoulder. There were soldiers in the street. She could hear the sound of their heavy boots splashing through puddles. Turning back to the atrium, she peered into the adjoining rooms. They were stripped bare of furniture; there was nowhere to hide. With a mounting sense of alarm, she began to pick her way around the heaps of fallen roof tiles. In the open courtyard beyond, the garden statues and straggling box hedges were choked with dead grasses, nettles and thistles. There was nowhere to hide here either.

She hurried on, following a narrow, gravel path that led away from the overgrown garden. She glanced over her shoulder again and her heart sank. She could hear men's voices in the atrium and fallen roof tiles breaking beneath their boots. On tip toes now, she quickened her pace. The path led to an orchard of ancient, misshapen apple trees, a small, dilapidated building and beyond, a high, ivy clad wall.

She was trapped.

Anya's mind raced. There were no leaves on the apple trees, even if she climbed one, it would not shield her from sight. Her gaze fell on the old building. In desperation she opened the door and crept inside. A table, littered with mouse droppings, occupied the centre of the room. A stone washing trough, a bread oven and a large cupboard stood against the far wall. Rain was dripping through a hole in the roof and splashing into a dirty puddle on the floor.

Could she hide inside the cupboard?

But wouldn't that be the first place they would look?

Heavy footsteps were crunching down the gravel path.

She had to do something. She couldn't just stand there.

Anya glanced frantically around the kitchen. There was a door to her left, leading to a small, gloomy store-room. A dead, maggot-ridden rat lay on the floor and the air was foul. Anya hesitated for a moment then clamped a hand over her nose and mouth and edged inside. The empty shelves were festooned with cobwebs, their contents long since looted. A back door led outside. Small animals had gnawed away the bottom panel, allowing a sliver of daylight and a stream of rainwater and detritus to flood across the floor.

The kitchen door opened with such force that it banged against the rough stone wall, rattling a pile of broken pottery on the floor. Anya peered through the crack between the frame and the door jamb. Two soldiers were moving through the kitchen at speed. One wrenched at the cupboard with such force that the door came off in his hand. He swore under his breath and let it fall to the floor. Anya watched his eyes roam around the kitchen before they settled on the storeroom door.

Terror knotted her stomach. She could not go back to Vortigern. She could not live out the rest of her days in fear of such a man. In her heart, she did not believe she could outrun Vortigern's men. They were battle- hardened warriors who would not tire easily.

And yet, she could not give in.

She took a bread cake from the basket and slipped it into the wax-lined pocket of her cloak. Leaving the basket on the floor, she took a deep breath and charged towards the back door. Twisting her torso at the last moment, she rammed her left shoulder against the rotten timbers. The door flew open and her momentum carried her out into a snow storm.

Huge snow-flakes splattered against her cheeks, so icy cold they took her breath away. Perhaps fifty strides away, a section of the boundary wall had collapsed. Bricks were tumbling into the street beyond like a child's building blocks. Anya sprinted towards the gap. The bare branches of the trees snared her cloak, reaching out like malevolent fingers. More than once she almost lost her footing, her boots sliding across slippery, decaying apples.

She glanced over her shoulder. The soldiers were close

now, running flat out, hands on the hilts of their swords, catching up. Blood was pounding in her ears and her mind whirred as fast as a dragonfly's wings.

What were Vortigern's orders?

If they caught up with her, would they show respect, or would they treat her like a common criminal and drag her, hands bound, through the streets?

She began to scramble over the pile of bricks. They wobbled precariously beneath her feet, and an avalanche of tumbling masonry propelled her into the muddy street. Anya landed awkwardly, wincing with pain. Gritting her teeth, she looked up and down the snow-swept street. To her right, she could see the distinctive domed roofs of the baths. Behind her, the soldiers were clambering over the fallen wall.

'Vortigern commands…'

Anya did not wait to hear the rest. As a child, she had often raced against her brothers. Over the straight, Hengist and Horsa had beaten her every time. But sometimes she had managed to outrun them by dodging and weaving through the narrow lanes of her father's stronghold.

Spinning on her heel, she raced down a side street and ran straight into a noisy market. The jostling crowd swallowed her up in a crush of crated chickens, caged pigeons, penned pigs and crying children. Over the heads of the crowd, she could see another alleyway, just up ahead. She began to push her way through the densely packed throng.

The soldiers were gaining on her; physically stronger, they were simply manhandling people out of their path. Anya gritted her teeth and continued to shove and elbow her way through the melee. With one last effort, she changed direction. No longer in the grip of the crowd, she stumbled and almost fell into the narrow alley. It was a dark gorge of tall, dilapidated buildings with a river of foul water running down the middle. The stench made Anya want to wretch. She lifted the hem of her cloak and sprinted down it, splashing noisily through the river of filth.

It led to a broad, cobbled street and after the darkness of the alley, the daylight made her squint. On the other side of the street the high walls of the city sat atop a steep bank of grassy earth. The filthy water was cascading across the cobbled street and disappearing into a culvert in the bank. In the distance to her right, she could see the domed roofs of the baths.

Anya frowned, struggling to muster her tired brain. It looked a long way to the baths. A race over the straight, of five hundred strides, maybe more. The odds were not in her favour. She had to think of something, and quickly. Her gaze settled on the culvert. They had such things in Saxony, dug into the banks of her father's stronghold to drain away excess rainwater.

Anya ran across the road, squatted on her haunches and peered into the culvert. It was a narrow tunnel of running water and stinking sludge, but it was stone built. She thought it unlikely to collapse and bury her alive. Through a heavy metal grille at the far end of the tunnel, she could see daylight. Crouching down, she crawled inside on all fours.

The water surged around her. It was icy cold and made her gasp with shock. As she crawled deeper into the fetid tunnel, she could feel her lungs beginning to close with terror. She had been eight years old when Hengist had thrown her into a storage pit and sealed the lid, and she had been morbidly afraid of enclosed spaces ever since.

The soldiers must be close now. She tried to look over her shoulder, but the tunnel was so narrow she cracked her head against the side wall. The sound echoed ominously around the tunnel walls and Anya came to an abrupt halt. She was making far too much noise. Shivering violently, she sat down in the freezing water and pulled her knees to her chin. She saw the men appear from the alleyway, watched them fan out across the broad street.

'She can't have gone far. Search every house!'

Anya did not know how long she waited, but gradually she became aware that her fingers and her toes were aching with cold. The temperature had dropped and a chill was beginning to seep into her bones. With difficulty, she shifted herself onto all fours again and crawled to the grille.

The river of filthy water was surging out between the corroded metal bars and into a steep, waterlogged ditch below. Beyond, a bleak, snowy landscape stretched to the far horizon. Grabbing hold of the slimy grille, Anya pulled hard but the metal held fast. She shuffled into a better position and tried again, wrenching with all her strength. The sharp, corroded metal tore into her palms and blood began to trickle down her wrist but still the grille did not move.

Anya swore under her breath. She gazed out across the land of the Dobunni. Crows' nests perched in the bare trees and in the distance, a kestrel hovered high above a hedge-line. She was so close now she could almost smell the clean air. Manoeuvring herself onto her back, she used her feet to push against the grille but the heavy metal bars refused to budge. Anya kicked the grille again and again but to no avail, tears of frustration beginning to well in her eyes.

At last, when every muscle in her body was screaming in protest, she heaved herself into a sitting position again. Her cloak was saturated with foul water; it felt cold and heavy on her shoulders. She slumped against the tunnel wall, overwhelmed by disappointment and despair. She could no longer feel her fingers or her toes, and she thought it strange that she was no longer shivering. She felt very tired, her eyelids heavy. She longed to sleep, just for a little while, but she knew she must not give up. What if Horsa was right? What if the goddess had sent her to Britannia for a reason? And what if Taliesin was right? What if, one day, she was meant to find her way back to Silvanus?

Sluggish with fatigue, she fell onto all fours and began to crawl slowly back up the tunnel. At the entrance, she peered cautiously up and down the street. The soldiers had gone but she felt too weary for either elation or relief. Clambering to her feet, she began to walk towards the baths. Aquae Sulis was eerily quiet, the rapidly falling snow muffling the sounds of the city. She knew she should make haste, but her drenched cloak weighed her down and each step felt like a monumental effort.

At the crossroads, Anya paused. The streets were quiet, just a handful of people hurrying through the snow, heads down, shoulders' hunched. There was still no sign of the soldiers. Through the monumental archway ahead, she could see the baths and the temple precinct, a vast grey sea of puddles reflecting a vast grey sky. Sul's temple dwarfed the surrounding buildings. A long flight of steps led up to a portico fronted by four soaring pillars. Above them, the pediment bore an enormous carving of a man's head. His moustache was as long and lustrous as any Saxon warrior, and his hair was as wild as Medusa's snakes.

Anya's mind was beginning to drift and it was becoming harder and harder to concentrate. No paint remained on Sul's face but even so, she felt certain she could see the whites of his eyes, for he looked as if he was in the grip of battle frenzy, possessed by the gods of war. She found herself wondering why the Romans had depicted Sul, a peaceful water god, in such a fearsome way.

She rubbed her eyes, willing her tired brain to focus. She had passed this way with Rufus, just three nights since, but the memory of their route from the south gate to the basilica was infuriatingly hazy. She had been exhausted then, and she was even more exhausted now.

Very slowly, she began to turn on the spot, stopping before she had come full circle. She opened her eyes. She was facing east, facing Germania. She could sense its pull, like a man is drawn to a roaring fire on a cold winter's night.

Anya pivoted on her heels, a quarter of a turn. Now she was facing south, facing Dumnonia, facing Silvanus. And the pull was even fiercer than before, as powerful as a full moon tugging the oceans across the face of the earth. She felt certain the south gate was close. A surge of hope flowed through her then quickly faded. Vortigern had sounded the alarm. The gate was sure to be barred, bolted and heavily guarded.

She had no idea what to do next.

A sense of despair enveloped her. Even if, by some miracle, she did manage to find a way through the south gate, she could not return to Dumnonia, for she had sworn to do everything in her power to keep Silvanus's kingdom at the edge of the world safe from harm. If she went north, Hengist would most likely throw her in the back of a cart and send her back to Aquae Sulis. And she could not return to Germania, for she was an exile, with no hope of reprieve.

She stared through the rapidly falling snow and sensed rather than saw the approaching guards, a surge of energy in the air up ahead. Anya looked about anxiously. The street was quiet, the citizens of Aquae Sulis driven inside by the snow. She was far too conspicuous. She could not simply brazen it out and walk into their path. She had no choice but to try and hide again.

Turning back the way she had come, she broke into a run, uncomfortably aware that her boots were leaving tell-tale prints in the settling snow. She passed beneath the monumental arch, raced across the precinct, up a flight of wide steps and into the imposing atrium of the great baths of Sul. The entrance doors had been taken for fire wood long ago and snow flurries followed her inside, quickly melting on the cracked marble floor.

Anya hurried on through a series of small chambers. She guessed they were once changing rooms, for small, storage alcoves lined the walls. Mould clung to frescos of naked weight-lifters, gymnasts and dancing girls, and the air smelled damp, like badly aired linen. Each room was as empty as the last. There was nowhere to hide here.

She came at last to a high-vaulted hall. The air was as hot as a summer's day. Steam rose from the swirling water of the great bath and the air smelled foul, like rotten eggs. Anya's eyes widened with amazement. The merchants who traded across Germania had told how the rich and fashionable citizens of Britannia travelled great distances to take the hot, healing waters that surged from the depths of the earth. But now, the fine frescos were crumbling in the steamy air, green algae floated upon Sul's sacred water and the bath was overflowing. Puddles lapped gently against a row of water-marked pillars.

At one time, men had taken refuge here. A heap of abandoned rags lay in one corner, and in another, traces of a fire and a scatter of broken storage jars. Anya looked about desperately. There was nowhere to hide here either.

Through an archway on the other side of the hall she could hear the sound of cascading water, like a waterfall in full spate. Curious now, she splashed through the warm puddles and peered inside. Sul's mighty spring waters were tumbling furiously into a deep, stone tank and the noise was deafening. Green tendrils of ivy were exploring the crumbling walls of the tiny chamber and dull, grey light slanted through a high window. It reflected the churning waters onto the vaulted ceiling, transforming the flaking stucco into a transparent lake of gently undulating waves.

Anya smiled to herself. This was a sacred place. She imagined the tribe of the Dobunni had left offerings for Sul at the spring head since time began. Then the Romans had arrived and encased the spring in lead and stone but despite all their brutal engineering, she could still feel Sul's spirit here.

Without warning, Anya's stomach rumbled loudly. She could not remember the last time she had had anything to eat or drink. Sinking down onto the tiled floor, she rested her back against the tank and stretched out her aching legs. She took the bread cake from the pocket of her cloak. The wax lining had served its purpose; the bread was still bone-dry.

She felt almost too tired to eat, but she forced herself to swallow a few mouthfuls, all the while staring watchfully across the swirling waters of the great bath. What if the soldiers had already spotted her footprints in the snow? She was taking a huge risk, sitting here in plain sight, but every bone in her body was crying out for a moment's rest.

Her saturated cloak began to steam and her mind began to drift. She was back in Vortigern's bed chamber, held fast, wrenching at her bonds. And Vortigern's heavy frame was crushing the air from her lungs. She was powerless beneath him…Tears welled up in her eyes and a flush of anger and shame surged across her cheeks. She stood up shakily, pushing the painful memories away.

Her throat felt parched so she cupped her hands and took a gulp of the steaming water. It was startlingly hot and tasted foul, and Anya's tired stomach rejected it instantly. Gagging and retching, she clung to the stone tank, engulfed with self-pity.

The voice inside her head was stern: '*You are the daughter of a king, descended from the gods themselves. Stop feeling sorry for yourself and find a way out of this city.*'

Anya wiped away her tears. She pushed the remainder of the bread cake back into her pocket, took a series of deep breaths, and walked back to the great bath. The high-vaulted hall was too open, too exposed; she knew she should not linger here. She was about to turn away when she saw movement from the corner of her eye. The heap of rags in the corner was rising up from the ground, like a wraith on Samhain's eve.

She had heard the bards speak of evil spirits who dragged men to their deaths in the watery marshes. Cold fear slid across her skin. Was this such a spirit? The priests had taught her that an enchantment of basil, angelica, fennel and garlic would repel any evil, but she had none of those things to hand.

The wraith was upright now, and very slowly it began to take human form. Anya frowned. It no longer looked like a malevolent spirit of the underworld but a frail old man, his limbs as knobbly and crooked as the roots of an ancient willow. His clothes were rags and his filthy feet were bare. In his right hand, he held a dagger.

Anya held out both hands in a gesture of surrender.

‘I mean you no harm,’ she stammered, in Latin.

The man snarled something in a language she did not understand. He took a step toward her and she retreated a pace.

‘Please,’ she said urgently. ‘I am not your enemy.’

The old man continued to move forward, the dagger wavering in his shaky grasp. Anya’s eyes darted rapidly around the hall. She could see another archway in the shadows behind the old man. Should she try and make a dash for it? Or should she run back the way she had come?

Suddenly, men’s voices sounded in the distance, booming like thunder as they echoed around the bare walls of the changing rooms. Anya and the old man turned in unison. The old man’s face registered his fear and the dagger fell from his wavering hand. He turned on his heel, hobbling on unsteady legs towards the archway behind him. The voices were louder now and Anya’s eyes widened with alarm.

What should she do?

There was no time to follow the raggedy old man. She crouched down, picked up his fallen dagger then darted behind the nearest column. She watched the old man pause for a moment beneath the archway. He caught his breath and then plunged into the darkness beyond.

‘Over there, Sir!’

Anya felt a surge of fear. What had they seen - a glimpse of the old man as he disappeared through the archway, or a glimpse of her cloak as she darted behind the pillar?

The soldiers were close now; she could hear them splashing through the puddles as they charged across the hall. She took a deep breath and, with her back pressed firmly against the stone pillar, shuffled slowly to her right. If she moved too quickly, or too slowly, she knew she ran the risk of edging into their line of sight. Every nerve in her body was taut with a terrible anticipation. Time seemed to slow then stop altogether. And in those suspended moments, her mind raced.

Had they seen her? She would know soon enough. Any moment now. If they found her, if they dragged her back to Vortigern, what sadistic punishment would he force her to endure? Perhaps Sul would protect her? She had sensed his presence here, a primal force, but did he care about the fate of a lowly priestess from a distant kingdom?

The soldiers were almost upon her. She could hear the sound of their heavy breathing, the creak of leather, the splash of displaced water. Time was speeding up again, much too fast now. They passed close by, a blur of black cloaks disappearing through the archway beyond, and on into the darkness.

Anya let out a ragged exhale of breath. She knew she did not have long. The soldiers would quickly catch up with the old man and realise their mistake. With a whisper of thanks to Sul, she raced back the way she had come, through the suite of changing rooms, across the atrium, down the steps and out into the temple precinct.

It was still snowing and the world had turned to white. After the stifling heat of the baths, the cold air hit her like a wall. Light headed with hunger and exhaustion, her legs felt like lead as she ran across the precinct, her boots leaving a trail of prints through the freshly fallen snow.

At the monumental arch she turned right, scanning the road ahead as she ran. She had ridden this way with Rufus. She recognised the dolphin atop the water fountain and the graffiti on the opposite wall: '*Tavern of Marcellus - best girls and best beer.*'

As she approached the next crossroads, Anya slowed her pace to a walk. At one time, this must have been a poor part of the city for the buildings were not made of stone, but of wood and thatch. Many were derelict now, but occasionally she saw glimmers of firelight creeping around the edge of a closed shutter.

She peered cautiously around the corner. In the distance, through a haze of rapidly falling snow, she could see the dark silhouette of the south gate. Hope flared, then died. The double gates were closed and barred. She counted five guards. Anya sank back against the wall.

What should she do now?

FORTY ONE

A group of merchants were moving slowly along the street. They were making a lot of noise. Cart wheels stuck in the mud, donkeys brayed and men shouted. Anya watched them as they drew nearer, and listened to their heated debate.

'But the snow's getting worse. It's madness to leave now.'

'Well, we can't stay here. Those bastards stole everything from us. We haven't a denarius to our name.'

Another man joined in the debate. 'Milo's right. This is a lawless place. No-one's going to offer us a bed for the night out of the kindness of their hearts.'

Inside a covered wagon, a baby began to cry; a thin wail of a sick and hungry child.

'You hear that? My daughter's sick. I won't take her out into this storm.'

A girl of perhaps eight summers old stepped down from the wagon. She was dressed in a thin, knee length gown, her legs were bare and the boots on her feet were several sizes too big. She held a writhing baby in her arms.

'Pa?' The little girl said plaintively. 'She won't stop crying but there's no goat's milk left.'

Her father turned to the other merchants. 'You see?'

'Sego, you've got to be realistic.' The man's voice was

resigned. 'Without a mother's milk, the baby's going to die.'

Another voice now: 'Camerton's not far. We could make it before nightfall. My sister would take us in.'

The young girl was rocking the baby back and forth but the infant continued to wail piteously. An idea was forming in Anya's mind. Pushing herself away from the wall, she walked up to the merchants.

'I couldn't help but overhear you. Will you take me with you, to Camerton?'

The merchants, noticing her for the first time, turned in unison. 'Who in hell are you?' Milo asked.

Anya thought fast. 'I'm no-one of importance, but I need to get away from here.' She dropped the hood of her cloak, revealing the dark bruise Vortigern had etched across her cheekbone. 'My husband did this. He drinks too much. Next time, he'll kill me.'

'That's no concern of ours,' Milo said bluntly.

'What happened to you, Milo?' Sego sounded appalled. 'Since when did you become so heartless?'

Anya hesitated, torn with indecision. Should she bribe them with one of Taliesin's coins? But, with gold in their palm, there was every chance they would decide to stay in Aquae Sulis. A pang of guilt seized her. Perhaps they *should* stay in the city, for the baby's sake. The infant's screams were ear-splitting now and the young girl was looking increasingly distressed. Anya stepped forward and held out her arms.

'Let me?' she asked softly.

A flash of suspicion darted across the young girl's face. She hesitated, but only for a moment.

'Alright,' she said gratefully and thrust the screaming baby into Anya's arms.

Drawing back her cloak, Anya placed the tiny baby against

her heart. The child was painfully thin, and she could hear her tiny lungs rasping for air. Anya closed her eyes and took a series of deep, steady breaths. It was harder than usual to clear her mind, but gradually her fear faded until she was no longer aware of the falling snow, or the braying donkeys, or the guards at the south gate. She held the baby close and, little by little, her wails turned to snuffles, her tiny body relaxed and she fell soundly asleep.

Someone was tugging at Anya's cloak, dragging her back.

'How did you do that?' the little girl asked in awe.

'It's easy. I'll teach you. But first, I need your father's help.' Anya turned to face the merchants. 'So, are we going to Camerton, or not?'

Sego looked expectantly at Milo.

'You're a soft bastard,' Milo said gruffly. He began to walk away, glancing over his shoulder at Anya. 'Get in the wagon - quickly now, before I change my mind.'

'Thank you. If the guards ask, will you say I am Sego's wife?'

Milo turned to face her again, his expression hostile.

'Get in.'

The wagon was dark and stank of soiled baby linens. It was empty, save for a makeshift cradle fashioned from a wooden crate lined with a blanket. Anya sat down on the dirty floor, taking care not to wake the baby. The young girl dragged a threadbare woollen blanket from the corner of the wagon, tugged it about her shoulders and sat down next to her.

'I'm hungry,' she said matter of factly.

Cradling the baby with one hand, Anya took the remains of the bread cake from her pocket. The little girl snatched it from her hand and devoured it instantly.

'Do you have any more?' she asked, wide eyed.

Anya shook her head. 'No, I'm sorry, I don't.'

The little girl seemed to accept this. She moved closer to Anya and launched into a stream of endless chatter: 'I'm Nemetona – but everyone calls me Nemmy…'

Anya smiled vaguely at her, but she was only half listening. The wagons were moving off again, jolting through the pot holes towards the south gate. A whip cracked, a donkey brayed and she heard Milo curse loudly. Panic was beginning to creep through Anya's veins again. What if one of the gate guards recognised her?

She took a deep breath and attempted to reassure herself. Only a handful of Vortigern's guards knew what she looked like. The rest were simply looking out for a woman with red hair, travelling alone – not for a merchant's wife with a baby at her breast. But if the soldiers at the gate started asking questions, Milo could easily give her up, for he had made no promises. And if the guards mentioned they were looking for Vortigern's runaway wife, Milo would *certainly* give her up. Anya's heart missed a beat and the baby began to stir.

The wagon rolled into another pot hole, pitched violently then moved forward again. Anya's entire body felt taut with fear. They must be close to the gate now.

'Stop!' an authoritative voice commanded.

The wagon came to an abrupt halt. Anya and Nemetona shot forward in unison then crashed back onto the floor again. Nemetona stopped talking and began to pick nervously at the loose threads of her blanket. The baby opened her eyes and began to cry.

'No corn to leave the city.'

'We know the rules.' Milo's voice, surly, hostile.

'So, what's in the wagon?'

'It's empty.'

'Still need to search it.'

Anya's heart was pounding violently now. She heard the guard step onto the running board, and felt the wagon give under his weight. He pulled back the hide and peered into the darkness. Anya kept her gaze fixed upon the baby screaming pitifully in her arms.

'Christ! It stinks in here!'

She forced herself to look up at the soldier. There was an expression of appalled disgust on his face. Their eyes met for a heartbeat before he hurriedly backed out of the wagon, leaving Anya and Nemetona in darkness once again. A donkey began to bray loudly, then another joined in, and another.

'For the love of God, get you gone!' a guard shouted irritably and the wagon lurched forward again.

'Will they have bread in Camerton?' Nemetona asked suddenly.

'Yes,' Anya smiled, but her mind was revolving like a spindle whorl. Cautiously, she lifted the edge of the hide and peered out into the snow storm. She could see guards standing around a brazier, hands outstretched to the flames, and beyond, the towering silhouette of the gate house. Anya felt a glimmer of hope. Just a few more yards, and she would be through the gates of Aquae Sulis. A few more yards and she would be free of Vortigern. A few more yards and this nightmare would be over. She wished the merchants would move faster. Struggling through the mire, their progress was painfully, agonisingly slow.

'Stop!'

The wagon came to a halt again. A man had stepped out from the guard room. He was as huge and as solid as an ox and his head was shaved in the brutally short style that

Vortigern and his men favoured. He walked slowly along the merchants' column, pausing every now and then to throw back a waxed-linen covering of a cart.

'I'll need an exit tax.'

'We were robbed while we slept.' Sego sounded afraid. 'We have nothing left to give you.'

Anya's fragile spark of hope died. She began to tremble, a maelstrom of emotions crashing around her exhausted brain, and the baby, sensing her despair, wailed louder still.

'I can't even buy bread for my family,' Sego went on, shouting above the screams of the baby.

The guard's eyes turned towards the wagon. Anya hurriedly let go of the hide. She tried to take a breath but it was as if a leather belt was tightening around her lungs. She heard the guard clamber onto the running board, and felt a surge of cold air as he drew back the hide and stepped down into the wagon. Nemetona's fingers stopped playing with the frayed blanket. She shuffled closer to Anya and nestled against her shoulder. The guard made no comment about the stench but his nose wrinkled in distaste. He glanced around the wagon, his gaze finally settling on Anya and Nemetona.

'That baby's hungry. Aren't you going to feed it?'

'Not in front of you, Sir,' Anya replied, attempting to sound both respectful and embarrassed at the same time.

The guard laughed. 'I've seen paps before.'

She dropped her gaze and did not reply. The guard stepped closer and, beside her, Anya felt Nemetona stiffen with fear.

'Where are you from?' the man asked suddenly. 'I don't recognise your accent.'

'Siluria,' Anya replied, surreptitiously slipping her little finger into the baby's mouth. The infant began to suckle hard and her heart twisted with pity.

A shaft of light fell across the floor as Sego entered the wagon. 'Is there a problem here?' he asked coldly.

'No.' The guard quickly stepped back, bumping into Sego's shoulder in his haste to leave the wagon.

Sego winked at Anya and Nemetona, then turned and followed the guard outside. Some sort of heated debate ensued but the baby was screaming so loudly, Anya found it impossible to follow. Suddenly, the wagon set off again, men began to shout and recalcitrant donkeys began to bray. Nemetona shuffled to the front of the wagon and lifted the hide. Over the heads of the merchants, Anya she could see the road that led south, perfectly framed by the black silhouette of the towering archway.

The gates were open.

She was close now. So close she could almost smell the clean, earthy tang of the countryside beyond the gates. The world slowed as they passed the guards, until even the smallest thing seemed strangely significant; the Roman numerals roughly etched on the side of the brazier, a tiny snail clinging to the gatehouse wall.

There was a brief respite from the elements beneath the arch and then, suddenly, the wagon was out into the storm once again. Anya stared fixedly at the road ahead, as straight as a spear through the snow covered fields of the Dobunni.

'Is it far to Camerton?' Nemetona asked.

'No,' Anya replied, although in truth, she did not know.

The wagon rumbled on but Anya remained transfixed, hardly daring to breathe, hardly daring to hope, her ears straining for any sound. Her imagination worked feverishly. She felt certain she could hear the sound of a hunting horn, the muffled beat of horses' hooves on the road, Vortigern's commanding voice ordering the merchants to halt.

But every turn of the wagon's wheels was taking her further away from Aquae Sulis and further away from Vortigern. Little by little, she felt herself start to relax, felt the terrible tension begin to leave her body. The baby yawned and fell asleep again, lulled by the rolling motion of the wagon and the steady pulse of Anya's heart.

Anya continued to stare at the open road. She was free at last. Free from Hengist, the brother who had sought to destroy her, and free from Vortigern, the man who had sought to possess her. But she had paid a high price for her freedom. She was alone. An exile, doomed to sail the lonely paths of the ice-cold sea, dreaming in vain of a hall where she would find a welcome from loving kin.

What should she do now? Where should she go? She could not go to Dumnonia, for death would surely follow her there. She could not go home, for death awaited her there also. Nor could she go to Horsa in the northern lands, for Hengist would simply throw her in a cart and send her back to Vortigern.

Anya laid the sleeping baby down in her makeshift cradle. Then she took the ancient map of Britannia from the pocket of her cloak and carefully unfurled the fragile parchment. She traced her finger along the southern coastline, remembering Cato's ship, the terrifying power of the storm, and the moment she had first spotted Britannia on the horizon, all those months ago. Further inland, Calleva was marked in neat Latin script. Here she had met Vortigern, and here she had said good-bye to Horsa. She prayed he was safe, and that she might see him again one day. Anya's finger brushed the long, straight Roman road that led from Calleva to Aquae Sulis. She remembered the moment the Irish had poured from the silent forest, how Vortigern's men had died protecting her. Anya's gaze fell upon Dumnonia. There she had met Silvanus, her soul-mate through all the ages of men.

'Are you alright?'

Anya jumped. She had been so lost in her thoughts she had not heard Sego step into the wagon. Nemetona ran to her father, and he put his arms around her and held her close.

'Thank you,' Anya said, looking up at them both. 'Thank you so much.'

'You mustn't worry. Nerius's sister won't turn you away,' Sego said gently. 'You can stay in Camerton as long as you wish.'

'I truly am grateful. But I can't go with you to Camerton.'

'Oh? Why not?' Sego sounded surprised.

Anya looked down at the parchment map. The kingdom of Siluria bore just one annotation upon the parchment - a perfectly outlined, steep sided, snow-capped mountain range. She glanced at her mother's simple ring and her eyes filled with tears as she remembered Eown's kindness and the comfort of her embrace. In her heart, she had always known what she must do. She must go to Siluria, to her mother's home, to the village she had been dreaming about for so long. A huddle of stone and slate, the bleating of sheep as dusk fell. Perhaps, if the gods were kind, she would find what she was looking for in the land of her mother's kin.

A place to belong beneath the heavens.

A home, a hearth, a welcome.

Author's Note

Until recently, the period after the end of Roman rule in Britain was called the Dark Ages, because historians had little idea what happened after 410AD, when the Emperor Honorius famously told Britain to 'look to your own defences'. In all likelihood, it wasn't so much a case of 'last one to leave, turn off the light'; rather a gradual withdrawal to defend the eastern borders of an Empire fatally over-stretched and weakened by internal strife and corruption.

There is some debate about how 'Romanised' Britain actually became during the occupation. However, there is no doubt that in lowland regions, large towns were superimposed upon previously existing tribal settlements and the inhabitants were quick to adopt Roman ways. And in the countryside, many Britons grew rich supplying grain to feed the Roman army. They built sumptuous villas in the Roman style, with fine mosaics and bath houses.

But farm labourers couldn't afford to buy in to the 'Romanised' way of life, and so they continued to live in their wattle and daub round houses, just as they had done for centuries. And whilst Christianity had become the official religion of the Roman Empire in 315AD, many rural Britons probably still clung to the old gods. After all, the word 'pagan' means 'of the countryside'.

Similarly, whilst the Roman authorities successfully exploited Cornwall and Wales for their gold, silver and tin, their influence over the people of these remote regions remained ephemeral. Scotland retained its independence entirely - despite repeated attempts, the Romans never conquered the tribes beyond Hadrian's wall.

Anya's character is fictitious, but her religion is not. In the early days of the Roman Empire, the Druids were a powerful force in Europe, as both religious and political leaders. They did not leave any written records, but Roman sources claim they carried out human sacrifice. It has been suggested this was merely propaganda, designed to discredit them, but human sacrifice was central to many ancient religions, so it's likely there was some truth in it.

Threatened by its powerful associations with nationalism, the Romans brutally crushed Druidism in Britain. But Anya's homeland of Saxony (the northern plains of modern Westphalia, Germany) was never conquered by the Roman Empire, thus enabling the Druid religion to survive well into the seventh century.

So what was the situation in post-Roman Britain in 455AD? Archaeological evidence hints that tribal identities remained strong throughout the occupation, and quickly reasserted themselves to form warring, political units after the withdrawal. Archaeology also shows us that whilst life continued in the cities for some time, a lack of infrastructure and central government made for a hand to mouth existence at best. There is a wonderfully evocative Anglo Saxon poem called 'The Ruin' which describes decaying cities of tumbled roofs, ruined towers and crumbling ramparts.

There are few written records from this time, but Gildas, writing in the sixth century, tells us that a 'proud tyrant' foolishly invited 'the ferocious Saxons into the island like wolves into the fold, to beat back the peoples of the North.' A century later, the Venerable Bede in his 'History of Britain', names the tyrant as Vortigern, and the two first Saxon commanders as Hengist and Horsa.

Many of the places mentioned in this novel still exist. Anya lands at the fort of Andereida on the south coast of Britannia. Its impressive 'D' shaped towers and walls are now integrated into the later medieval castle at Portchester, Hampshire.

Calleva Atrebatum (Silchester, Hampshire) is one of the few Roman towns which didn't develop into a medieval town. It was gradually abandoned, probably because it was miles from a navigable river - the motorways of their day. Although Calleva now lies under farmland, its town walls are some of the best preserved in Britain, and it also has an excellent amphitheatre.

Vortigern's stronghold at Aquae Sulis is still famous for its hot spring and Roman baths, just as it was in Anya's time. The startling sculpture of the gorgon's head (which adorned the pediment of the temple) is on display in the museum.

Tintagel, a spectacular promontory in Cornwall, has long been associated with the legend of King Arthur. The visible castle ruins on the cliff top are medieval, (built by Richard Earl of Cornwall in the thirteenth century), but archaeological excavations have proved there was a thriving, high status settlement there in the fifth century. A great hall, with associated smaller structures, stood on the cliff top, and finds have included luxury goods from the Mediterranean world and beyond. Etar and Silvanus may be fictional, but their stronghold is not.

At the end of 'The Saxon Wolves', Anya sets out on a journey to Siluria (Wales), but that is another story…

Look out for 'The Saxon Plague', to be published in 2018.